PENGUIN BOOKS
CHOWRINGHEE

SANKAR (Mani Sankar Mukherji) is one of Bengal's most widely read novelists in recent times. He also has several non-fiction best-sellers, including a biography of Swami Vivekananda, to his credit. Two of his novels, *Seemabaddha* (Company Limited) and *Jana Aranya* (The Middleman), were turned into films by Satyajit Ray. He lives and works in Kolkata.

ARUNAVA SINHA is an Internet product specialist and former journalist. Born in Kolkata, he graduated in English Literature from Jadavpur University and went on to join the team that set up *Calcutta Skyline*, a city magazine, for which he translated short stories by several modern and contemporary Bengali writers. Arunava blogs at blogs.ibibo.com/readonly. He lives in New Delhi with his wife and son.

D1028123

Chowringhee

SANKAR

Translated from the Bengali by
Arunava Sinha

June 2009

Happy birthday,
baby.

PENGUIN BOOKS

PENGUIN BOOKS

Published by the Penguin Group

Penguin Books India Pvt. Ltd, 11 Community Centre, Panchsheel Park, New Delhi 110 017, India

Penguin Group (USA) Inc., 375 Hudson Street, New York, New York 10014, USA

Penguin Group (Canada), 90 Eglinton Avenue East, Suite 700, Toronto, Ontario, M4P 2Y3, Canada (a division of Pearson Penguin Canada Inc.)

Penguin Books Ltd, 80 Strand, London WC2R 0RL, England

Penguin Ireland, 25 St Stephen's Green, Dublin 2, Ireland (a division of Penguin Books Ltd)

Penguin Group (Australia), 250 Camberwell Road, Camberwell, Victoria 3124, Australia (a division of Pearson Australia Group Pty Ltd)

Penguin Group (NZ), 67 Apollo Drive, Rosedale, North Shore 0632, New Zealand (a division of Pearson New Zealand Ltd)

Penguin Group (South Africa) (Pty) Ltd, 24 Sturdee Avenue, Rosebank, Johannesburg 2196, South Africa

Penguin Books Ltd, Registered Offices: 80 Strand, London WC2R 0RL, England

First published in Bengali as *Chowringhee* by Dey's Publishing, Kolkata, 1962
First published in English by Penguin Books India 2007

Copyright © Mani Shankar Mukherji 1962, 2007
Translation copyright © Dey's Publishing 2007

All rights reserved

10 9

ISBN-13: 978-0-14310-103-1   ISBN-10: 0-14310-103-X

Typeset in Bembo by SŪRYA, New Delhi
Printed at Pauls Press, New Delhi

This book is sold subject to the condition that it shall not, by way of trade or otherwise, be lent, resold, hired out, or otherwise circulated without the publisher's prior written consent in any form of binding or cover other than that in which it is published and without a similar condition including this condition being imposed on the subsequent purchaser and without limiting the rights under copyright reserved above, no part of this publication may be reproduced, stored in or introduced into a retrieval system, or transmitted in any form or by any means (electronic, mechanical, photocopying, recording or otherwise), without the prior written permission of both the copyright owner and the above-mentioned publisher of this book.

To Sri Shankariprasad Basu,
the producer, director and composer of my literary life

Acknowledgements

The revered foreigner who inspired me to write *Chowringhee* is no more. Many people—living and dead, Indians and foreigners, known and unknown—have helped me in various ways, some publicly and others from behind the scenes. I respectfully acknowledge each one of them.

—Sankar

My biggest champion for this translation is, of course, the author of *Chowringhee*, Sankar—Mani Sankar Mukherji—who has been a veritable elixir of encouragement all through, and whose trust in me I am truly grateful for. My special thanks go to the first editor of my career as a journalist, Sara Adhikari, who introduced me to Sankar and was instrumental in getting me my first translation assignment of the writer's works, back in 1988.

The first draft of the translation was completed in 1992. That it is being published now is thanks in no small measure to Diya Kar Hazra at Penguin India, who chased down the translator of an English version of *Chowringhee* that she unearthed when she wanted the novel published in English—thirteen years later! A heartfelt 'thank you' goes out to my editor for this translation from Penguin, Shantanu Ray Chaudhuri, whose sensitivity is a joy to work with.

And finally, thank you, Calcutta—the once and future city...

I dedicate this translation to my wife Sanghamitra and son Srijon.

—Arunava Sinha

Our life is but a winter's day:
Some only breakfast and away
Others to dinner stay and are full fed;
The oldest man but sups and goes to bed:
He that goes soonest has the least to pay.

—A.C. Maffen

1

They call it Esplanade; we call it Chowringhee. And Curzon Park in Chowringhee is where I stopped to rest when my body, weary of the day's toils, refused to take another step. Bengal has heaped many curses upon Lord Curzon—it seems that the history of our misfortunes began the day the idea of dividing this green, fertile land of ours into two occurred to him. But that was a long time ago, and now, standing in the heart of Calcutta on a sun-battered May afternoon in the twentieth century, I saluted the English lord, much maligned by history. May his soul rest in peace. I also saluted Rai Hariram Goenka Bahadur, KT, CIE, at whose feet were inscribed the words 'Born June 3, 1862. Died February 28, 1935'.

You might remember me as the wide-eyed adolescent from the small neighbourhood of Kashundia who had, years ago, crossed the Ganga on the steamer *Amba* from Ramkeshtopur Ghat to gape at the high court. That teenager had not only secured a job with a British barrister, but had also gained the affection of older colleagues like Chhoka-da. Basking in the love showered upon him by judge, barrister and client alike, he had revelled in the role of the babu, the lawyer's clerk, soaking up with wonderstruck eyes the beauty of a new world.

In the midst of the desert of poverty and penury that had

been my lot till then, the kindness and benevolence of my English employer was like an oasis, helping me to forget the past, leading me to believe that this would last forever. However, with the ever-alert auditor of this world always on the prowl for mistakes, mine, too, were discovered. The Englishman died. For the wretched of the world like us, the slightest storm is enough to destroy the oasis. 'Move again, onward march!' was the order from the cruel commander of victorious Providence to the vanquished prisoner. Reluctantly, I hitched my battered and bruised mind to the exhausted wagon of the body and started my journey afresh.

Onward, onward! Don't look back.

I had only the road behind and in front. It was as if my tired and weary soul had found an unknown inn on Old Post Office Street for the night. With the first light of dawn, it was time to hit the road again. My fellow clerks at the high court shed tears for me. 'To lose one's job at such a young and tender age!' Chhoka-da said. I hadn't cried, though—not one drop. The bolt from the blue had dried my tears.

Chhoka-da made me sit next to him and treated me to a cup of tea. 'I understand,' he said. 'I understand everything, but this cursed stomach doesn't. You'd better eat something.'

That was my last cup of tea on Old Post Office Street. Of course, Chhoka-da tried to comfort me, 'Don't worry, you'll get another job, here among us. Which barrister wouldn't want a babu like you? It's just that when you already have a wife, getting another one...they all have babus already.'

It isn't like me to force my way into a conversation, but that day I butted in, 'I can't, Chhoka-da. Even if I get a job I can't stay in this neighbourhood.'

Chhoka-da, Arjun-da, Haru-da—all of them were overwhelmed by my grief. A despondent Chhoka-da said, 'We couldn't do it but if anyone can, it's you. Get out while you can—we'll have the satisfaction of knowing that at least one of us has managed to escape from this wretched maze.'

Bidding them farewell, I slung my bag, complete with lunch box, over my shoulder and set out. The melancholy sun in the western sky set before my eyes that day.

But then...what next? Did I have the slightest notion that life could be so ruthless, the world such a difficult place to live in, its people so cruel?

A job. I needed a job to live like a human being. But where were the jobs?

Matriculation certificate in hand, I looked up people I knew. They were sympathetic, even told me how devastated they were at the news of the sudden disaster, but they blanched at the mention of a job. Times were bad, the company's financial situation wasn't very bright. Of course, they'd let me know if there was a vacancy.

I went to another office. Mr Dutta from that company had once turned to me for help when he was in trouble. It was at my request that our firm had taken up his case gratis. But now he refused to see me—the bearer returned with a slip of paper. Mr Dutta was very busy and had scribbled his regret at not being able to see me, adding that, much as he would have liked to, he would be too busy over the next few weeks to enjoy the pleasure of my company. The bearer asked me to write a note. Swallowing my pride, I did. Needless to say, there was no reply.

I sent applications by the dozen. I wrote with details of my qualifications to people known and unknown, even to box numbers. They served no purpose other than increasing the revenue of the post office.

I was exhausted. I'd never saved for a rainy day, and whatever I had was nearly spent. Starvation stared me in the face. O God! Is this what was ordained for the last babu of the last English barrister of Calcutta High Court?

Eventually, I got a job—as a peddler. Or, to put it more elegantly, a salesman's job. I would have to go from office to

office selling wastepaper baskets. The company's name, Magpil
& Clerk, had echoes of Burmah Shell, Jardin Henderson or
Andrew Yule. But the man at the helm of it all, Mr M.G.
Pillai, a young fellow from Madras, had nothing besides two
pairs of trousers and a tie—a grubby one at that. One dingy
room in Chhatawala Lane served as his factory, office,
showroom, kitchen and bedroom. M.G. Pillai had
metamorphosed into Magpil. And Mr Clerk? None other than
Magpil's clerk!

The baskets were to be sold to various companies and I
would get four annas as commission for each one sold. It
sounded like heaven!

But I couldn't sell even those. Baskets in hand, I did the
rounds of various offices, peering beneath the babus' tables.
Many of them asked suspiciously, 'What are you looking at?'

'Your wastepaper basket, sir,' I'd reply.

How elated I was if it looked shabby. I'd say, 'Your
basket's in a bad way, sir, why don't you get a new one? Look,
excellent product—guaranteed to last ten years.'

One day, the head clerk in an office glanced at the basket
under his table and said, 'Seems fine to me. It'll last another
year easily.'

I looked at him mournfully, but he couldn't read my
thoughts. I felt like screaming, 'Maybe the basket will last
another year but what about me? I won't last another day!' But
in this strange city of Job Charnock, you can't say something
just because you want to. So I left silently.

I even met Westernized Bengalis in suits and ties. Tapping
his elegantly shod foot, one of them said, 'Very good. It's very
heartening that young Bengalis are going into business.'

'Shall I give you a few, sir?' I asked.

Pat came the reply, 'Six, but don't forget my share.'

Selling six baskets meant a commission of one-and-a-half
rupees. Clutching the sales proceeds in my hand, I said, 'This
is what I make from six baskets, take whatever you think fit.'

Puffing at his cigarette, he said, 'I could have easily got thirty per cent from someone else, but since you're a Bengali, I'll settle for twenty-five,' and then proceeded to take the entire amount, after which he mourned the fact that our race possessed no semblance of honesty. 'You've become quite a pro, claiming you don't make more than one-and-a-half rupees from six baskets. Think we're wet behind the ears?'

Too nonplussed to say anything, I left silently, wondering again at this strange world.

Amazing! Wasn't it the same world where I had once discovered beauty, respected people, even believed that God is to be found in man? Now I felt like an ass. Not even life's blows had bestowed wisdom upon me—would I never learn? This wouldn't do. I had to become cannier. And I did. I raised the price of a basket from one rupee to one-and-a-quarter, and unhesitatingly gave away one anna to any buyer who demanded his cut. I would even keep a straight face as I said, 'I make nothing out of it, sir, it's a very competitive market. I'm selling without a margin to survive.'

I felt no qualms about the fact that I lied. All I knew was that I was alone in this self-seeking world and the only way I could make my way here was through ingenuity and cunning. I knew I would never be an honoured guest in any of life's joyous festivals. So I had to gatecrash. It was then that I visited this office in Dalhousie Square.

It was the month of May. Even the asphalt on the streets seemed to be melting. The afternoon thoroughfares, as deserted as at midnight, shimmered in the light of a raging sun. Only a few unfortunate souls like me were on the move. They couldn't afford to stop—they had to keep moving, hoping to run into luck somewhere.

My shirt was drenched with perspiration, as though I'd just taken a dip at Laldighi, and I was parched. There were arrangements by the roadside for even horses to drink water, but not for us. Oh well, the Society for Prevention of Cruelty to Animals was not responsible for preventing cruelty to the unemployed, so they could hardly be blamed.

Spotting a large building, I walked in. There was a lift inside. I stepped in, panting. No sooner had the liftman shut the gates than he noticed two wastepaper baskets in my hand. One look at my face told the experienced fellow who I was. He threw the shutters open and contemptuously pointed to the stairs, informing me for good measure, 'This lift is only for officers and clerks. The company doesn't pay me to service nawab-bahadurs like you.'

Indeed, why should there be lifts for humble hawkers like us? For us there was the spiral staircase. So climb my way up I did, without complaining—not even to fate. This was the way the world worked. Not everyone gets a lift to move up.

It had been a bad day. I hadn't sold a thing, but had spent three annas already: one on tram fare, another on a plate of alu-kabli, and then, no longer able to resist the temptation, in utter recklessness, one on phuchka. I knew I had done something grievously wrong, squandering one anna on a moment's weakness.

Entering the office, I peered beneath the tables and spotted baskets under each of them. A middle-aged lady seated at a desk near the door asked in an irritated tone, 'What is it?'

'Wastepaper baskets,' I said in English. 'Very good madam, very strong, and very, very durable.'

But the sales pitch didn't help. She waved me away and I stumbled out of the room on my tired feet.

On a bench near the entrance sat a doorman with a huge moustache and an enormous turban, chewing tobacco. He was dressed in a white uniform, the company's name glittering on a breastplate.

He stopped me and asked how much I made from every basket I sold.

I realized he was interested. 'Four annas,' I replied.

He asked how much a basket cost. I wasn't a fool any more. I answered without batting an eyelid, 'A rupee and a quarter.'

As he examined the basket closely, I spotted an opening and said, 'Very good stuff, buy one and you can relax for ten years.'

Basket in hand, he walked into the office. The lady looked up, 'I said we don't want any.' But the doorman wouldn't take no for an answer. 'Mr Ghosh doesn't have one,' he told her, 'and Mr Mitra's is broken, and the manager's basket too is coming apart. We need to keep a few in stock.'

Eventually, the lady relented. I got an order for six baskets at one go.

I practically flew back to Chhatawala Lane. Tying six baskets together, I returned to the office. The doorman smiled at me.

Sending the baskets to the storeroom, the lady said, 'Can't pay you today. Have to draw up a bill.'

On my way out, the doorman grabbed me. 'Got paid?'

He probably thought I was about to make off without giving him his cut. 'Not today,' I said.

'Why?' Rising again, he went straight to the lady's table. His words revealed years of experience. 'He's a poor man, madam, has to do the rounds of many offices.'

A little later I was summoned. 'Your payment's been cleared,' he told me triumphantly and, pushing a voucher across, asked if I could sign—if not, a thumb impression would do.

Seeing my signature, he laughed, 'My god, you actually signed in English!'

Money in hand, I came out. I knew enough of such doormen—I would now have to share the commission, but this time I had already taken that into account.

When he looked at me, I was ready, and held out one-and-a-half rupees. 'This is my commission. Whatever you want...'

I hadn't bargained for his reaction. He paled visibly, as if all the blood had drained from his face. I still remember how his tall upright figure shook, and the genial expression was wiped off his face. I thought perhaps he was not satisfied with the share. I was about to add, 'I swear I don't make more than one-and-a-half rupees on six baskets.' But I was wrong. I had misunderstood him completely.

Before I could respond he thundered, 'How dare you? I felt bad for you...you think I got them to buy your baskets so I could make something out of it! Ram Ram!'

I could not control my tears that day. All was not lost yet. The world was not devoid of all goodness, after all. Men like him still existed.

He made me sit down for a cup of tea. As we sipped our tea, he put his hand on my shoulder and said, 'Don't be disheartened, son. Have you heard of Sir Hariram Goenka, whose bronze statue stands before the governor's house? He too had to struggle to survive. I can see the same fire in your eyes. One day you'll be as great as he is.'

I looked at him, unable to hold back my tears.

Before I left, he said, 'Remember that the one above always watches over us—stay honest and keep Him happy, don't cheat Him.'

The memory of that day overwhelms me even now. On this long road of life I've seen much wealth and an endless parade of splendour. Fame, status, influence, happiness, property, affluence—these are no longer beyond my reach. I've even had the opportunity of coming in close contact with those who are revered by society, those who create history, those who strive to better humanity through education, science, art, literature. But the unknown doorman in that unknown office in Clive

Building is still the guiding star in my firmament, an indelible part of my memory.

Bidding him goodbye, it occurred to me that though he had trusted me, I was nothing better than a liar and a thief. I had charged four annas extra for each basket. I had betrayed his trust. From Dalhousie I walked straight to Curzon Park in Chowringhee. Whether it is people without offices to go to but anxious to get there, or people without a refuge but most in need of it, everyone stops for a few moments' rest at Curzon Park. Time seems to stop there—no hustle-bustle, no hurrying around, no anxiety; just a sense of calm. On the verdant grass, many vagrants slept peacefully under the shade of trees, while a pair of crows perched silently on Sir Hariram Goenka's shoulder.

I silently thanked all those people whose generous donations had made Curzon Park possible, including Lord Curzon. And Sir Hariram Goenka? It seemed he was unhappy with me and had turned his face away. As I sat at his feet, my lips trembled. With folded hands I said respectfully, 'Sir Hariram, forgive me, I am innocent. That foolish doorman saw shades of you in me, but believe me, I have no intention of insulting you.'

I have no idea how long I sat there. Suddenly, I realized that like a young clerk playing truant, even the sun had taken a look at the clock, shut his files, and gone home. I was the only soul sitting there.

What else could I do? I had nowhere to go.

'Hello, sir!' A voice startled me out of my reverie.

A man in trousers and a jacket, briefcase in hand, stood before me. The briefcase was unmistakable—it was Byron. If his sudden appearance had surprised me, he was just as astonished to see me dozing in the park. After all, he had always seen me in Old Post Office Street. 'Babu!' he exclaimed.

I haven't yet forgotten our first meeting. I had been sitting in my chamber, typing away, when a man with a briefcase entered. His skin was the colour of mahogany, but it had a sheen—just like shoes after they have received the four-anna treatment from the shoeshine boys at Dharmatala.

'Good morning,' he had said, and promptly sat down without waiting for my permission, as though we were old friends. The first thing he did was to draw out of his pocket a pack of cigarettes, a brand which, even in those hard times, sold for seven paise a packet.

'Try one,' he said.

When I refused, he had laughed loudly. 'Don't like this brand, eh? Very faithful, can't leave someone you've loved once!'

At first I had thought he was a salesman for that cigarette company, but just as I was about to tell him it was no use offering such pleasures to an ascetic, he spoke again. 'Got a case?'

Case? It was we who accepted cases. Before I could reply, he said, 'I'm available for any investigation, family or personal.' After a pause, he added, 'Any case, however complicated and mysterious, will be made as clear as daylight, as transparent as water.'

I shook my head. 'I'm afraid we don't have anything right now.'

He put on his hat and got up. 'That's all right, that's all right. But no one can say when or where I might be needed. If not by you, perhaps by people you know.'

He handed me a card. It said: B. BYRON, YOUR FRIEND IN NEED. TELEPHONE:

There was no number. Just a blank space after the word TELEPHONE. 'I don't have a telephone as yet,' he said. 'But I'm bound to in the future, so I've left space for the number. I'll get it. Eventually, I'll get it all. Not just a telephone, but also a car and a house and a large office. You have no idea what a private detective can do if he puts his mind to it. He can earn more than the chief justice.'

Private detective! I'd only read about them. I must have devoured a thousand detective stories ever since I laid my eyes on the printed word. Had I applied the same sincerity and devotion to Jadab Chakraborty, K.P. Bose and Nesfield's textbooks as I had to Byomkesh, Jayanta–Manik, Subrata–Kiriti, Blake–Smith and other famous detectives, I wouldn't have been in such dire straits. But these detectives existed only in my fantasies. Never for a moment had I imagined that they could be physically present, roaming around in this mortal world—that too in this city of Calcutta.

With great awe and reverence I had requested Byron to sit, and enquired whether he would like some tea. He agreed readily, and drained his cup in a minute. As he stood up to leave, he said, 'Don't forget me.'

I felt rather depressed. Surely detectives didn't have to go from door-to-door looking for cases! As far as I knew, it happened differently: The detective chats with his assistant over toast, omelette and a cup of tea in his south Calcutta residence, when the telephone starts ringing. A trifle irritated, he rises from his sofa to take the call. A voice, perhaps the daughter or widow of the slain raja-bahadur pleads with him, 'You must take up the Shibgarh murder case. Don't worry about fees, we'll pay whatever you want.'

Or, on a rain-soaked June evening, when a deluge descends on Calcutta, when trams and buses stop plying, when there's no way of stepping out, a stranger clad in a dripping black raincoat bursts into the detective's drawing room. Placing a fat cheque on the table, he starts recounting the thrilling tale of his mysterious past. Unruffled, the detective emits a cloud of smoke from his Burma cigar and says, 'You should have gone to the police.' Whereupon the stranger jumps up, grabs the sleuth's hand and begs him, 'Don't disappoint me, please.'

And look at Byron here. He was out himself, case-hunting!

With many unusual people frequenting the legal offices of Old Post Office Street, I had thought I'd be able to help him—and taking up a case on my request, Byron would solve the mystery and earn nationwide fame. 'Keep in touch,' I had said to him.

Byron did present his varnished countenance again at Temple Chambers. This time he was carrying some life insurance papers. I was worried at first, for, despite the short time I had been here, I'd been accosted by at least two dozen agents already. Looking at those papers out of the corner of my eye, I began planning a way out. He seemed to read my mind, though, for he sat down and said, 'Don't worry, I won't try to sell you a policy.'

My face reddened in embarrassment. Without giving me a chance to answer, he said, 'A detective has to be a chameleon. One of my disguises is of an insurance agent.'

I had ordered a cup of tea for him, which he'd drained, and left.

I'd felt rather sorry for him—I really would have loved to be of use. If only wishes were horses... But I couldn't get hold of anything for him. I told Chhoka-da, 'If you have an enquiry to be conducted, why don't you give it to Byron?'

Chhoka-da said, 'You don't seem to be up to any good, young lad. Why are you rooting for that Anglo? Be very careful. Many a young man has gone to ruin under the influence of these Eliot Road types.'

I did not heed his advice. To Byron I'd said, 'I feel bad. You take the trouble to visit me but I can't find an assignment for you.'

He was an optimist, though, and had said, laughing, 'You never can tell who can help whom—at least, not in our line of work.'

It was on the strength of this brief acquaintance that Byron stared at my tired form in Curzon Park. 'Babu, what's the matter?'

I kept looking at Sir Hariram's statue without replying, but he didn't give up. He took my hands instead, probably guessing what the problem was, and muttered, 'This is very bad, very bad,' he said.

'What do you mean?'

'Be a soldier. Everyone has to fight to survive in this unfriendly world. Fight to the finish.'

Finally, I looked at him closely. His fortunes seemed to have changed for the better. He was wearing a clean shirt and a pair of brightly polished shoes. He went on with a homily on the value of life. Maybe he thought I was contemplating suicide.

Now, unsolicited advice is something I have never been able to stomach. I retorted somewhat bitterly, 'I am aware, Mr Byron, that on the branches of that tree overhanging the stone-hearted Hariram Goenka, KT, CIE, many a troubled soul has attained eternal peace. You must have seen it in the papers. But don't worry, I'm not going to do anything like that.'

Paying no attention to my philosophical reply, he carried on, 'Cheer up, it could have been much worse. We could have been much worse off.'

A hawker came by selling tea. Cutting short my protests, Byron asked for two cups, then pulling out his diary, he said, 'That's one cup repaid. Forty-two to go.'

Sipping his tea, he asked, 'Do you have a clean suit?'

'At home,' I said.

He jumped with joy. 'Then there's nothing to worry about. It's all God's will—why else would I have run into you today?'

I had no idea what he was talking about. 'You will,' he said. 'All in good time. Do you suppose that I had that woman

from Shahjahan Hotel figured out right away?' He stopped
talking and looked at his watch. 'How long will it take—for
you to go home, put on your suit and come back here?'

'Where do I have to go?'

'All in good time. For now, just come back here, below
Sir Hariram Goenka's statue, in an hour. Ask questions later,
hurry up now. Quick!'

Even now I marvel at how I got back from Chowringhee
to Chowdhury Bagan that day. In my hurry I stepped on
several toes in the bus. The passengers protested, but I was
oblivious—I was even prepared to put up with a few blows
and kicks.

By the time I had shaved, donned my one and only suit
and returned to Curzon Park, it was 7.30. Night in Chowringhee
had taken on the form of a temptress. In the blinding glare of
neon lights, Curzon Park looked an altogether different place—
unrecognizable from the Curzon Park of mid-afternoon. It was
as though a perennially unemployed young man had suddenly
got a thousand-rupee job and had taken his girlfriend out on
a date.

I am not particularly fond of poetry, but some lines I'd
read long ago came rushing back. It was the same Curzon Park
that had inspired Samar Sen to write:

> After ages of snowbound silence
> The mountain desires to be May's missing clouds.
> So at spring in Curzon Park,
> Silent like rain-drenched animals sit
> Groups of arch-bodied heroes
> Razor-sharp dreams in melting melancholy are dreamed
> By groups of men in the Maidan from wasted homes
> At the invitation of French cinema, at the hint of a
>   phaeton
> Clouds bloodied in a mining fire, sunset comes

I could feel that in my fresh suit I no longer looked like an unemployed wretch. As if to prove me right, a masseur came up to me and asked, 'Massage, sir?'

When I said no and moved on, he sidled up even closer and muttered, 'Girlfriend, sir? College girl, Punjabi, Bengali, Anglo-Indian…' The list might have become longer, but by now I was running hastily to meet Byron. Maybe he had got tired of waiting and left, maybe I had lost a golden opportunity forever.

But no, he hadn't gone away. He was sitting quietly at Sir Hariram's feet, his dark frame merging into the night so that his white trousers and shirt seemed to be draped over a phantom.

Spotting me, he rose and said, 'I must have smoked at least ten cigarettes since you left. And with each puff I couldn't help thinking that all of this has turned out for the best—for you as well as for me.'

Leaving Curzon Park, we passed the statue of Sir Ashutosh to our left and walked along Central Avenue towards Shahjahan Hotel.

I was filled with gratitude for Byron. I hadn't been able to help him at all during my days at Old Post Office Street; it suddenly struck me that I hadn't even tried hard enough. I knew so many attorneys, after all—they would have found it difficult to turn down a request from the English barrister's babu. But to keep my self-respect intact, I hadn't asked anyone for a favour. And today Byron had become my benefactor.

'That's Shahjahan Hotel,' he pointed out from a distance. 'Your job's guaranteed. Their manager can't refuse me.'

I looked at the most famous of Calcutta's hotels. Around twenty-five cars were parked in front of the gate, and there were more coming. Flaunting nine or ten decorations on his chest, the doorman stood proudly, occasionally advancing to the portico to open a car door. A lady in an evening dress stepped out daintily, a gentleman in a bow tie behind her. Contorting her painted lips like she was about to burp, she said, 'Thank you.' Her companion had materialized in front of her by now. He held out his hand and, taking it, she walked in. The doorman took the opportunity to click his boots and salute in military fashion. The couple's heads also moved a little, like clockwork dolls, in response. Then the doorman spotted Byron and, with utmost humility, offered a double-sized salute.

Even to this day, I never cease to be amazed at the thoughts that went through my mind as I crossed the hallowed portals of that awe-inspiring hotel. Thanks to my previous employer, I had had the opportunity of seeing many a pleasure garden, a few hotels too. But Shahjahan Hotel—it was a class apart. It was incomparable. It wasn't so much a building as a mini township. The width of the corridors would put many roads, streets and even avenues to shame.

I followed Byron into the lift, and then out of it, with not a little trepidation. The May evening seemed to have a touch of December about it. I no longer remember how many corners we turned, but I am certain I would never have found my way out of the labyrinth alone. Eventually, he stopped before a door.

The liveried bearer standing outside said, 'Sir got back a short while ago from kitchen inspection, he's had his bath and is resting now.'

Byron wasn't put off. Running his fingers through his curly hair he smiled at me and told the bearer, 'Tell him it's Mr Byron.'

It worked like a charm. The bearer came out in no time and said, bowing low, 'Come in, please.'

I wasn't at all prepared to see the all-in-all of Shahjahan Hotel, Marco Polo, in the state he was in: a sleeveless vest and tiny red briefs tried in vain to cover the essentials of his manly body. Not that he was bothered by the lack of clothing—he looked as though he was lounging by the poolside.

Spotting me, though, he jumped out of the bed in alarm and, muttering 'Excuse me, excuse me', ran towards the wardrobe. He quickly took out a pair of shorts, put them on, slipped on a pair of sandals and turned towards me. There was a thick gold chain round his neck. It had a black locket with something inscribed on it. His left arm sported a huge tattoo and so did his hairy chest, part of it peering out from behind the vest.

I'd expected Byron to open the conversation, but it was the manager who spoke first. Pushing a tin of cigarettes towards us, he asked, 'Any luck?'

Byron shook his head. 'Not yet.' He paused and added, 'Calcutta's a mysterious city, Mr Macro Polo. Much bigger than we think.'

The light in Marco Polo's eyes died out. He said, 'Not yet? Then when? When?'

Some other time, I'd have smelt something fishy in this exchange and become curious. But now I wasn't interested. Even if all of Calcutta went to hell, I wouldn't care—as long as it meant a job for me.

Byron read my mind and broached the subject. Introducing me, he said to Marco Polo, 'You have to give him a job in your hotel, he'll be very useful.'

Marco Polo gestured helplessly. 'Impossible. I have rooms to let in my hotel but not one job—we're overstaffed.'

I was prepared for this answer—I'd heard it many times before, and would have been surprised not to hear it once more.

But Byron didn't give up. Twirling his keys around his finger, he said, 'But I know you have a vacancy.'

'Impossible,' shouted the manager.

'Nothing is impossible—there is an opening, you'll hear about it tomorrow.'

'What do you mean?'

'I mean advance news—we get a lot of information beforehand. Your secretary Rosie...'

The manager was startled. 'Rosie? But she's upstairs.'

With the solemnity of all the detectives I had read about, Byron said, 'Why don't you find out? Check with your bearer whether the lady was in her room last night or not.'

Marco Polo still refused to believe Byron. 'Impossible,' he said, and shouted for bearer number 73.

Number 73 had been on duty the previous night, and was on again that evening. He had barely perched himself on his stool when the manager's summons came. Certain that he had committed some blunder he came in, quaking in terror.

The manager asked in Hindi whether he had stayed up all of the previous night.

Number 73 said, 'God is my witness, sahib, I was awake all night, didn't shut my eyes even once.'

In reply to Marco Polo's query, he admitted that room number 362 had been locked from the outside all night—he had seen the key on the board.

With a faint smile Byron said, 'At precisely the same time last night, room number seventy-two of another hotel in Chowringhee was locked on the inside.'

'What do you mean?' asked Marco Polo apprehensively.

'I mean that it wasn't just Rosie who was in the room but someone else as well. And I know him rather well—a client's husband. Of course, I am not supposed to know all this, but Mrs Banerjee hired me for a fee. I submitted my report today on how far he has gone. No hope, I told her. This evening your assistant and Banerjee have made off by train. The bird has flown. So you might just as well instal this young man into that empty cage.'

The manager and I were both thunderstruck. Byron laughed loudly. 'I was on my way to you with the news,' he said, addressing Marco Polo, 'when I met my friend here.'

After this Marco Polo couldn't say no. But all the same he warned, 'Rosie hasn't quit; if she returns in a couple of days…'

'Get rid of him then if you like,' said Byron on my behalf.

The manager of Shahjahan Hotel agreed. And I got the job. It must have been written thus by the gods in the ledger of my fate.

2

I was reborn. The last clerk of the last English barrister of the Calcutta High Court was lost forever. He would no longer spend time chatting with other babus on Old Post Office Street, no longer listen to the tales of his clients' joys and sorrows in his chamber. His relationship with the law had ended for good. And yet it gave him a sense of great relief. The cyclone-battered ship was returning from the violent seas to the safety of the harbour.

Early next morning, I bathed, put on my last pair of clean trousers and shirt, and left home. I could see the majestic yellow building of Shahjahan Hotel from afar. 'Building' isn't the right word, 'palace' is more like it. And that too not one for small-time rulers. The Nizam or the Maharaja of Baroda could unhesitatingly take up residence here—their glory and grandeur would not be compromised in any way.

Even at that early hour, several cars were parked outside the hotel. Their number plates made it clear that their owners weren't permanent residents of Calcutta. Many a car of many a make, built in various factories in England, Germany, Italy and America, represented cities as distant as Madras, Bombay and Delhi and also the states of Mayurbhanj and Dhenkanal. One could spend hours watching these cars. A close observation would reveal that the caste system operated even in the automobile society, with the doorman tailoring his salute to the lineage of the car. Resplendent in his well-starched military uniform with its array of medals glittering on his chest; his impressive moustache and the way he occasionally bowed to usher in a guest, the gatekeeper uncannily resembled the world-famous Maharaja of Air India. I wouldn't be surprised if someone told me that this man was the inspiration for the artist who designed the logo.

From the gatekeeper's salute as I approached the entrance I realized that he had mistaken me for a patron. My first sensation on setting foot inside the hotel was of walking on butter. It felt like I was sinking under my weight on a soft satin bed and was then being gently raised aloft by a loving, kind-hearted fairy. With the next step I sank again, and the fairy, without the slightest show of irritation, lifted me up again. It was as though two invisible but beautiful fairies were playing ping-pong with my body on a carpeted table. Unaware that the best carpets in the world had this quality, I was disconcerted for a moment or two.

I literally waltzed my way across to the other side of the carpet—to the area marked 'Reception'. The gentleman standing behind the counter showed all the signs of fatigue resulting from a sleepless night. But as I approached, he snapped alert and, conjuring up a smile, wished me good morning.

I was a little flustered. Without returning the greeting, I introduced myself. 'I've got a job here, I met the manager Mr Marco Polo last night. He asked me to report today. Can I meet him now?'

His expression changed in a trice. The formal politeness gave way to a warm, friendly smile. 'Welcome! Welcome!' he said. 'The Orient's oldest hotel welcomes its youngest staff member.'

I was tongue-tied with nervousness. He extended his right hand and said, 'My name is Satyasundar Bose—at least, that's what my father christened me. As luck would have it, I have now become Sata Bose.'

I must have been staring blankly at him for some time, for with an affectionate nudge he said, 'You will tire of this accursed face soon. In the long run it may even nauseate you. You may even throw up every time you see it. Come round behind the counter, so that I can complete the coronation formalities of Shahjahan Hotel's young prince.'

I said, 'I should meet Mr Marco Polo and...'

'No need,' said Bose, 'he briefed me last night. It's time to rev up.'

'Meaning?'

'You know how cars refuel and rev up their engines, don't you? You must do the same.' I smiled at his manner of speech. He continued, 'Have you heard of the AAB?

'Automobile Association of Bengal?'

'That's right. They have two competitions—a speed test to see how fast one can drive and an endurance test to see how long one can drive. We have a combination of the two here— a speed-cum-endurance test. The management of Shahjahan wants to find out how quickly you can do how much work.'

The telephone next to him rang. He picked up the receiver and in an artificial Anglo-Indian accent said, 'Good morning, Shahjahan Hotel reception. Just a minute, Mr and Mrs Satarawalla, yes, room number two thirty-two, you're welcome...'

I couldn't comprehend a word. Bose smiled at me and said, 'For now, concentrate on listening, you'll get the hang of it eventually. Just don't let your memory rust...electroplate it and keep it shining. The rest will come to you automatically. Take room numbers, for example...it helps a lot to know every guest's room number.'

I looked at the reception counter carefully. There were three chairs behind it, but it was the done thing to keep standing. The table behind it had a typewriter and, next to it, a few thick ledgers: the hotel registers. The pendulum of an old, large clock oscillated lazily on the wall, as though it had just woken up from a long slumber and was ruminating.

'Come around inside,' said Bose again.

My thoughts must have shown on my face, which was probably why he asked, 'Unnerved already?'

Embarrassed, I shook my head. 'No, of course not.'

He laughed, looked around warily and said in a conspiratorial whisper, 'Wait till the hotel wakes up—you'll be amazed.'

I went behind the counter. As the telephone rang again, Bose picked up the receiver with practiced ease and spoke in a soft and stylish voice, 'Shahjahan reception.' Hearing the speaker at the other end he laughed and said, 'Yes, Sata here.' The two perhaps exchanged some joke, as Bose guffawed loudly. He put the receiver down and said, 'The steward will be here any minute. Try to "butter" him up a little and keep him in good humour.'

In a few minutes, I saw a huge figure approaching the reception, a veritable Mount Vesuvius. But despite his girth, the man's gait reminded me of a feather drifting in the breeze. His complexion was a dark shade of burnt copper, his eyes a pair of flaming wicks. He charged at me like a bull. 'So, you're the chap who got rid of Rosie!'

Without giving me a chance to reply, he thrust his left wrist under my nose. Drawing my attention to his watch he said that breakfast would be ready in fifteen minutes, and since the breakfast cards hadn't been prepared the previous night they had to be done immediately. It was obvious from the way he spoke that he wasn't an Englishman. In halting, European English he said, 'Take down, take down quickly.'

Bose pushed a shorthand pad across and said softly, 'Write it down.'

Without further ado the steward barked out a list of items. Strange words, some of which I had never heard before, assailed my ears: chilled pineapple juice, rice crisps, eggs—boiled, fried, poached, scrambled. The man stopped a while, gulped, and then continued yelling in the manner of reciting a multiplication table: omelette—prawn, cheese, tomato...and so on. Words came tumbling out of his mouth like gunfire as he came to a halt with 'coffee'.

'Jaldi, jaldi mangta,' he said, without even looking at me, and disappeared without giving me a chance to ask anything.

I was nearly in tears, never having heard the names of all those strange dishes before. I hadn't been able to take down even half of what he'd said.

'Fifty breakfast cards have to be prepared immediately,' said Bose.

Seeing my face, he tried to console me. 'Never mind Jimmy—the fellow always behaves that way—grunts like an old boar all the time.'

'I haven't been able to write down the breakfast list,' I told him piteously.

'Don't worry about that. I know Jimmy's list by heart. I'll call out the names and you can type them out slowly. Ever since I came to this hotel I've been seeing the same menu, and he still wants new cards every day. At first I used to feel scared too, but now it makes me laugh—so many exotic names and pronunciations. In a couple of days you'll be able to tell from the steward's face what the menu will be—the moment he says Salad Italienne, you will know that our Italian steward wants consommé froid en tasse and potage albion.'

A novice, I made a lot of spelling errors in typing out the menu that day. Eventually, Bose took over the task himself, while I walked out from behind the counter and looked around the building. Things were very quiet at this hour of the morning—Shahjahan Hotel was not fully awake yet. The kitchen and pantry, however, hummed with a suppressed excitement. The bearers were pouring milk into pots, arranging cups and saucers, polishing the cutlery.

Returning to the reception counter I found Bose typing furiously. Had we waited for me to type the cards, breakfast would not have been served before lunch. But Bose's practised fingers waltzed through the French words with speed and dexterity. How old was he? I wondered. Not more than thirty-two, thirty-three surely. He had an athletic build—not an ounce of excess fat anywhere on his body. His well-ironed jacket and trousers and matching tie set off his figure very well.

'You know French?' I asked.

'French!' He made a face. 'You couldn't get a word of French out of me at gunpoint. Of course, I know the names of the dishes—but then, even our head cook, who can't sign his name, knows those names by heart.' Arranging the cards, he continued, 'The English, so clever in so many ways, don't know to cook—you won't find the name of a single decent preparation in John Bull's dictionary.'

My knowledge of occidental cooking was limited to 'Keshto Café', situated next to Ripon College. The chop and the cutlet—gastronomic delights in my student days—were almost synonymous with British civilization. I was also acquainted with another rare English dish—the mamlette. I now discovered that the English had no hand in the invention of the chop or the cutlet, and that the mamlette was really an omelette, for which there were so many recipes in continental cuisine that a thick tome titled *The Dictionary of Omelettes* had been published in English.

Earlier, every time I ate out with my old employer, I always attacked the food without worrying about its name. It was he who had told me about the honest and inquisitive gentleman who had vowed never to eat anything without knowing its 'background story', and had added in a grave tone that, as a result, the poor man had eventually died of starvation.

Dispatching the cards to the dining room, Bose said, 'You must have heard of Henry the eighth. His fat bearded face in the history textbook made me so angry that I cut out his picture with a blade and threw it away. Had I known then that he had dug our graves for us, I wouldn't have stopped there. I'd have burnt it as well.'

'Why?' I asked, astonished.

'Henry the eighth was as fond of eating as he was of getting married,' said Bose. 'He once went to a duke's house for dinner. The other guests at the table noticed that he kept glancing at a piece of paper on the table every now and then before going back to the food. The assembled lords and counts, earls and dukes were at a loss—it must be a very important document, they thought, for His Majesty to have to read it even during dinner. After the meal, though, the king left the piece of paper on the table and retired to the drawing room. The attendants crowded around the table—but alas, it carried no state secret, only the names of a few dishes—the ones they had just had. The host had put them down on a piece of paper and given it to the king. Everyone said, "What a wonderful idea! This way you don't have to stuff yourself with the boring items and then regret it when something lip-smacking turns up. If you know in advance you can decide what to eat and what to avoid, which ones to take more of and which ones less."'

Bose smiled and continued, 'That was the beginning of the menu card. What was intended as a convenience for a king has become a source of endless trouble for us hotel employees. Type the breakfast, lunch and dinner menu cards every day, arrange for them to be displayed at every table, and after the meals send the cards back to the storeroom where they gather dust for about a year. Then, one day, the Salvation Army is sent for, and they lift all the old papers and carry them off in a lorry.'

Glancing at the clock, he said, 'Here, at Shahjahan, we have divided time in a different way. We start our day here with bed tea. Then comes breakfast time. What the world calls noon is lunchtime for us. Afternoon teatime and dinnertime follow—and no, it doesn't end there. The date on the calendar might change; we don't, as you will see.'

The workload at the hotel counter increases right from breakfast. It leaves one with no time for idle chitchat. Some of the guests leave the comfort of their cosy rooms around this time and come down to relax in the lounge. As they file past the counter in ones and twos, there is a mechanical exchange of good mornings—a guest serves a perfunctory 'good morning' which Bose volleys back with the expertise of a professional tennis player: 'Good morning, Mr Claybar!' 'Good Morning, madam, hope you slept well.'

'Madam' was an elderly American lady. Bose had obviously touched upon a raw nerve.

'Sleep? My dear boy, I haven't known sleep for eight years. At first I took pills, then injections—but nothing works now. That's why I've come to the Orient. One has heard so much about miracle healing in this country.'

Bose was appropriately sympathetic. 'That's sad! With so many rogues and scoundrels in the world, why does God have to be so cruel to someone as good as you? But don't worry, this illness is easily cured.'

The lady sighed. 'I don't believe I'll be able to sleep again in this lifetime.'

'God forbid! My aunt had the same problem, but she recovered.'

'Really! What medicine did she take?' The lady practically threw herself over the counter.

'No medicines...simply prayers. My aunt used to say: There is no power greater than prayer. Prayer can move even mountains.'

The lady was impressed. Putting down her vanity bag and

camera on the counter and adjusting the scarf on her head, she asked, 'Does she have supernatural powers?'

Before Bose could reply, another gentleman came along and stood across the counter—a foreigner, good-looking, six feet tall, impressively built as if moulded in Dorman Long steel. Bose leaned towards him and said, 'Good morning, doctor.'

Looking sharply from behind his glasses, the doctor returned the greeting and said gravely, 'May I have ten rupees?'

'Of course.' Bose opened the cash box to his right, took out ten one-rupee notes and gave them to the doctor, who scribbled his signature with his left hand on a printed voucher form and left.

'Who is he?' whispered the lady.

'Dr Sutherland,' replied Bose. 'He's here representing the World Health Organization.'

The lady seemed upset. She said disapprovingly, 'You people are mad, you make no effort whatsoever to rediscover your ancient medical sciences. These foreign doctors whom you worship like demigods and spend millions of dollars on can't even make an ordinary American sleep. While the naked fakirs of this country can stay asleep a couple of hundred years if they want to.'

Caught in a bind, Bose opted for silence.

The lady continued, 'I'm not interested in your Sutherland, I'm interested in your aunt. I want to meet the great lady; if necessary I'll arrange for her to go on television. You have no idea how much the United States needs your aunt.'

Bose's eyes misted over. He pulled out a handkerchief and wiped them.

The lady asked in consternation, 'What is it? Have I said something to upset you?'

Still wiping his eyes, Bose answered, 'No, no, it's not your fault. How could you have known that I lost my aunt just two months ago?'

'Please forgive me, Mr Bose, I'm awfully sorry—may your aunt's soul rest in peace,' said the mortified lady and left hurriedly in search of a taxi.

Bose's sudden outburst had caught me unawares, too. I tried to console him, 'No one lives forever, Mr Bose. My father used to say that all of us have to learn to live alone in this world.'

Bose began laughing, leaving me utterly bewildered. 'I have no aunt,' he said. 'I made it all up. If I hadn't killed my aunt quickly, that woman would have wasted another hour of my time, and there's a lot of work piled up.'

I was speechless for a while. 'You know the high court on Old Post Office Street, near St John's Church? That's the right place for you,' I told him when I had recovered. 'With this sort of presence of mind you would have owned a car and a house by now.'

Bose seemed lost in thought. 'House? Car?' he mused almost to himself. 'Never mind, you're new, so we'll leave you out if it.' He might have said more, but a bearer came and informed him that the manager was downstairs on kitchen inspection.

Bose turned towards me. 'Go and have a darshan of Mr Marco Polo's beautiful face. You'll have to set up home with him.'

'What's he like?' I asked apprehensively.

'What do you think?'

'It's a romantic name. I had no idea such names were still in vogue.'

'Romantic indeed,' said Bose. 'His more famous namesake spent his last days in jail, let's see where this one goes.'

'Is that a possibility?' I asked.

'Oh no, I merely said that in passing. He's very efficient, a perfect manager. You know what Omar Khayyam said, don't you? "It's difficult for a country to get a good prime minister, but it's even more difficult to get a good hotel manager." They are born, not made. Countries have been known to survive bad ministers but no hotel can survive a bad manager,' Bose said, laughing.

'He was the manager of the biggest hotel in Rangoon,' he continued. 'Used to earn twice as much as here. But some whim brought him to Calcutta. At first we thought he may have been running away from some trouble he had got into, but the steward of that hotel, who stayed with us for two days on his way back to France, said that the Rangoon hotel was still sending requests to Marco Polo to go back.'

'Why hasn't the floor been cleaned? Even a pigsty is cleaner than this,' screamed the manager, standing in the middle of the kitchen.

The head cook and an assistant were scurrying about the room, while Marco Polo scoured the corners for grime. He raised his head on hearing my footsteps. 'Hello, so you're here.'

I bade him good morning.

'Learning the ropes, I hope?' he asked.

The inquisition of the head cook was called to a halt, as the manager set off with me towards his office.

It was a small room, sparsely furnished. Three chairs were arranged around a table. On one side of the table was a pile of files, on another a typewriter. Two steel cupboards stood in a corner. There was a door in the wall to the right, which probably connected the office to Marco Polo's bedroom.

He sat down and lit a cigar—a tall, manly figure, a trifle overweight for his age. He was balding a little as well, but because his hair was close-cropped, the bald patch didn't show too much. The cigar made the grave face look even more so— he could have easily played Churchill onstage.

Preparing to dictate letters, he looked at me and said sadly, 'Such a good girl—I'll never find another Rosie. I had nothing to worry about in the office thanks to her. She typed my letters whenever I asked her to—even at midnight. There are some letters we get that can't be left unanswered, they have to be replied to immediately.'

He went on to dictate a couple of letters. The language wasn't very polished, but humility dripped from every line. It was obvious he kept detailed tabs on what wines were available. Having imported some liquor recently, he proudly dictated a circular: 'We're the only ones in India to import this world-famous liquor.'

Dictation over, Marco Polo left. Evidently he had a lot of other work pending. It is easier to rule over a small kingdom than manage a large hotel. Two hundred guests could give rise to two hundred problems a minute. The manager has to solve them all personally.

Typing letters was not something I was unused to, so it didn't take much time. Sending them to the manager's room for him to sign, I started sorting the papers. Though I owed my job to her departure, Rosie had left me in the lurch by running away suddenly—I had no idea where things were. I couldn't even find a list. Trusting only my eyes and hands I started rearranging the mountains of files.

Opening the left-hand drawer of the table, I discovered some of Rosie's personal effects—a bottle of nail polish, new blades and a small mirror. I felt depressed. Why was I even bothering to set things in order here? The much-loved young lady might reappear tomorrow, and then I would have to go back to Curzon Park. What was the use of putting down roots for just a couple of days?

Immersed in my work, I did not realize how the day wore away—I didn't even realize that the hands of the clock had crossed the breakfast and lunch hours and were approaching teatime.

'You've been working all day, sir, don't you want a cup of tea?'

I raised my head and saw the manager's bearer. He smiled pleasantly at me. He was getting on in years, his hair had turned grey, but he looked in good shape. 'My name is Mathura Singh,' he said.

'Pleased to make your acquaintance, Mathura Singh.'

'Shall I get some tea for you, sir?' he asked.

'Tea? Where will you get it from?'

'Leave that to me, sir. They haven't issued a slip for you yet, but once they do, you'll have no problems about your meals.'

He brought the tea to the office, poured it, handed me the cup and said, 'So this is where you've ended up, sir.'

'You know who I am, Mathura?' I asked, surprised.

'You were the barrister's clerk, weren't you?' he said. 'Everyone knew the barrister. His bearer Mohan is from our village.'

'So you're from Kumaon?'

'Yes, sir. I've been to your old office several times to meet Mohan, and I saw you there.'

I felt very happy at finally coming across a familiar face in a crowd of strangers. If Bengal was my motherland, Kumaon was my foster mother. It's a beautiful place and recently it had been made famous by some well-known visitors. It had no dearth of admirers, but even if it had been the worst place on earth, home to malaria, dysentery and dengue, I would still have loved it. It's amazing that there are still such places in this accursed country where people do not put up walls around their homes or in their minds.

Mathura said, 'It's good to have you here. A word of advice though. You will see many a thing here which you may not even have imagined in your life. But don't let it affect you. I've seen a lot over forty years, but I've survived with pride. By God's grace even my son has got a job.'

'In this hotel?'

'Forgive me, sir, but who would willingly send his son here?'

I said, 'Most people are contemptuous of their own workplaces, Mathura. Everybody says the same thing: I have suffered myself but won't like my son to suffer likewise.'

'Sir, you have seen a lot at the barrister's place. Now just keep your eyes open here. You will see...by God's grace your eyesight isn't failing.'

I set down my cup and said, 'Mathura, what time is closing hour?'

'The sun does set occasionally on the British Empire, sir, but the lights never go out in a hotel. Nothing closes down here—but haven't they told you how long you have to work?'

'No,' I said.

'Then you might as well go—it's your first day.'

'I'd better meet the manager before that,' I said.

'You can't see him now.'

'Why not?' I asked.

Mathura was taken aback. It was obvious that he had not expected this question. He seemed acutely embarrassed and mumbled in a hushed tone, 'No one's allowed to enter his room now. You go on, I'll tell him if he asks.'

I went out and stepped across the corridor to the stairs. Walking down, I saw the name of the hotel on the carpet on every step. The wooden banisters were so smooth my hand slipped on them. Right at the bottom of the stairs an ancient grandfather clock ticked away, announcing the aristocratic lineage of the place. Guests usually take the lift, but I found a rare one or two almost playfully dancing down the stairs, hand in hand with their female companions. I nearly collided with one of them.

The reception counter was quite crowded, with Bose still stationed there. The telephone rang frequently, and all the chairs and sofas in the lounge were occupied.

When I reached the counter, Bose said in lowered tones, 'Stuck in the manager's office all day?'

'First day,' I said. 'Lots to do.'

Bose was about to say something, but a fresh set of guests appeared at the counter, with porters in tow carrying their luggage.

'See you later,' I said, and left.

At the main entrance, the doorman was busy dispensing salutes at a furious pace.

A splendid bus stood in the porch. I'd seen such buses only in English films—I had no idea that the old hag Calcutta possessed such things. If there were ever a beauty contest among the city's buses, I could swear this one would be crowned Miss Calcutta. Porters were unloading luggage from the rear of the bus. Men and women, obviously airline employees, emerged from the bus and disappeared into the hotel. Skirting them, I started walking along Central Avenue.

Chowringhee lay ahead. Here, day and night were interchangeable. The immaculately dressed Chowringhee, radiant in her youth, had just stepped on to the floor at the nightclub. On the other side, the great leader Surendranath Banerjee appeared to be held captive, motionless, seemingly numbed by the sight of the naked form of his beloved daughter. In utter contempt, this great father of Indian nationalism had turned his eyes towards the darkness to the south.

I walked down to the western end of Curzon Park, to Sir Hariram. He was still staring fixedly at Raj Bhavan, as though asking: Are the merchant's scales really weaker than the ruler's sceptre? Over the centuries, thousands of people have set foot on this city cursed by history. Many arrived penniless but went on to amass wealth and glory. They were of varying descents, spoke different languages, followed diverse customs and cultures—but all of them had the same end in view. And Time assiduously swept the known and unknown, the rich and the poor, the native and the foreigner alike into the dustbin of oblivion. Only a few succeeded in escaping that purge and surviving the death-dealing banks of the Ganga, albeit as statues.

I addressed Sir Hariram, one of the most illustrious among the dead citizens of this dead city, 'My situation has changed since you last saw me. I'm working now, at Shahjahan Hotel. When you were alive, when you ruled over the business empire of this city, the nights in Shahjahan must have been as bright as the days—you must have been there many times...'

I stopped, and began laughing—why was I babbling like a madman? What did I know about Sir Hariram? For all I knew, he might have been an extremely conservative man who never went anywhere near a hotel. The more I thought about it the more I was surprised at my childishness. I remembered the doorman in Clive Building who had chosen to bind me in a kinship with, of all people, Sir Hariram.

I caught a glimpse of the clock on the building of Whiteway Laidlow afar. It was quite late—time to go home. I had no qualms about going home now. I had a home, I had my near and dear ones and, above all, I had a job.

3

'Our life is but a winter's day. Some only breakfast and away, others to dinner stay and are full fed, the oldest man but sups and goes to bed, he who goes soonest has the least to pay,' said Mr Bose.

'That's very philosophical.'

'Yes, but I didn't make that up. It's an English poem. There was an old man here who used to quote the lines quite often. I even jotted them down somewhere, if I can find them I'll show them to you.'

'A nice idea,' I said. 'The longer you stay in this world, the bigger the bill you have to pay.'

'But the poet couldn't have worked in a hotel—if he had,

he would definitely have written about people who have ploughed their way through breakfast, lunch and dinner and then passed the bill on to somebody else before disappearing from the world. And he would have written about us too—we who put away breakfast, lunch and dinner every day but don't pay the bill, rather, work off our debt instead.'

He paused and added, 'To tell you the truth, I feel weary at times. Of course, that only adds to our woes—nobody dies that easily of weariness. A soul-destroying opium of illusion hangs about this place. It's like a fatal addiction, with no escape route. Once you come in, you can't get out, not even if the door is opened for you.'

I was listening to him as I typed.

Looking at me, he asked, 'Why are you looking so low? Can't sleep at night for fear of Rosie coming back?'

I had to confess. 'There's no sign of her now, but suppose she returned suddenly?'

'True,' he said. 'But keep your garden well watered. The boss must be kept happy.'

That was what I was trying to do. It was the manager himself who taught me how to keep him happy. As they say: seeing is believing. Omar Khayyam hit the nail right on the head when he said, 'There's no dearth of learned men to write thick books in this world, no dearth even of intrepid people to lead armies to war; there are a lot of political talents who can run kingdoms—but alas, there's a great shortage of people to run hotels.'

The number and variety of problems that can arise every minute in the running of a hotel is truly mind-boggling, and the poor manager has to solve all of them. He is blamed for everything—if the bathwater is too hot, guests usually summon him instead of telling the bearer. They seem to believe in summit meetings. Rather than settle matters at the lower levels, they prefer to involve the manager himself.

If a guest discovers that the colour of the bed sheet doesn't match the colour of the curtains, he or she hysterically sends for the manager at once. It's happened before my own eyes. Receiving an SOS over the telephone one day, Marco Polo practically ran out of the room, with me following, to find out what was up. He knocked at the door and a female voice said, 'Come in.'

A middle-aged Englishwoman stood there looking as though the sky had fallen on her. With bloodshot eyes she told the manager, 'You are *dangerous*—you can kill people. No one but a murderer could choose such colours. I've never seen such hideous shades in a hotel room in my life, it was enough to make me faint!'

I was furious, but Marco Polo displayed no such emotion. I believe they squeeze out the hormones responsible for anger when a person enters a hotel management school. Marco Polo started by apologizing profusely, 'I sincerely hope you haven't suffered any physical or psychological damage, madam. I'll have three sets of bedclothes sent to you immediately—please choose the shade you want. I've have never understood why American tourists like this colour—I was forced to have these made specially. I had no idea you were going to be staying in this room.'

The lady's stand having been vindicated and her ruffled feathers soothed, she now definitely preened as she said, 'Wherever I go, I find *them* corrupting good taste—chewing on their gum, bulldozing through beauty everywhere. My dear friend, they might have money, but it'll take them another five hundred years to learn refinement.'

Marco Polo agreed wholeheartedly with her and left the room. Mr Bose told me later that if the lady had been American, the manager would have said, 'I just can't understand why the English prefer this old-fashioned colour. Trouble is, we're helpless—till the other day, Calcutta was the second city of the Empire. We're trying, though...gradually the signs of British imperialism are being wiped out.'

Of course, the manager makes up for his politeness with

guests in his conduct with employees. Bearers, sweepers, bartenders and chefs all have their hearts in their mouths under his reign of terror.

He is even more fearsome in another respect—one is never sure about his mood swings, and his temperamental nature keeps everybody on their toes.

When giving me instructions, he often looks distracted. Some evenings he goes out in white shorts and a white half-sleeved shirt, cane in hand, though nobody knows where. Even at dinner, when the dining hall is chock-a-block with people, he's missing, so the poor steward and Mr Bose have to cope all by themselves.

'How much longer, Sata?' the steward asks.

'Don't worry,' Mr Bose replies. 'A system that's been running for a hundred and fifty years will keep running on its own steam—no point wearing out our brains over it.'

When the manager returns, it is in a completely different mood—as though a dormant volcano had become active. He starts by taking off his clothes, one by one, and flinging them across his room while poor Mathura Singh stands helplessly outside. It isn't any use going in, for in a drunken fit the man might well throw a shoe at him. A short while later, he summons Mathura and orders in a slurred voice, 'Call the head barman.'

As soon as he receives the summons, the head barman Ram Singh realizes what's happening. In his red cummerbund, armband and turban, he would at the time be pouring out drinks, but now he asks someone else to take over while he pays court to the manager's wishes.

Snorting like a bull, the manager asks, 'How's business, Ram Singh, my darling Ram Singh?'

Wiping his hands on the duster hanging at his waist, Ram Singh replies, 'The bar's packed, sir. Two Dimple Haigs and three White Horses emptied already—it was race day.' More customers are coming, he adds, and it is essential for him to be at the bar.

'Let those vermin go to hell,' the manager grunts. 'I want to talk to you.'

Ram Singh stands there nonplussed, glancing at Mathura Singh for help. Mathura remains silent, though secretly pleased. 'Serves you right. You've made a lot from sucking those drunkards dry every day—for once you can go without and give the others a chance.'

Meanwhile, the manager bursts into drunken song. He has had his fill elsewhere; finding his own cellar unable to quench his thirst, the all-in-all of Shahjahan Hotel had opted for hooch at a disgusting Anglo-Indian slum. Used as he is to foreign liquor, Ram Singh finds his stomach churning at the smell, but he has to keep standing there.

The manager hasn't satisfied his soul yet, which is why he starts singing. It is a very old ditty—Calcutta's ancient, poisoned blood had mingled with this song written by the humorist Davy Carson. It had rent the silence of many a midnight at the Shahjahan Bar. In the nineteenth century, when the neighbourhoods of Madan Datta Lane, Bankim Chatterjee Street and Shyamacharan Dey Street lay fast asleep, hundreds of foreign voices used to welcome the new day with this song breaking through the still night, scaring the bearers out of their wits.

The long-lost, wanton, dissolute soul of Calcutta takes possession of Marco Polo's drunken body as he sings:

> To Wilson's or Spence's Hall
> On holiday I stay;
> With freedom call for the mutton chops
> And billiards play all day;
> The servant catches from after the hukum: 'Jaldi jao
> Hey Khitmatgar, brandy sharab, bilati pani lao.'

The manager's thirst hasn't been quenched yet—like a madman he screams, 'Bring it on, bring the whiskey and soda!'

Soon after, he goes into a drunken frenzy—not even two servants can keep that enormous body, dressed in nothing but underclothes, under control. He breaks glasses, smashes bottles on the ground, embraces Ram Singh and dances, singing all the while. He hugs Ram Singh and continues singing, 'Darling, my sweet darling,' and tries to kiss the poor man. It is then that realization dawns on him. He throws Ram Singh out of the room and collapses on the bed.

Then one has to cautiously switch the lights off and stealthily spread a sheet over his body and move out. About an hour later, Mathura Singh returns to clean the floor. Because when the master gets up at dawn he will remember nothing. He might hurt himself if the pieces of broken glass lay scattered on the floor.

It happened once. Nobody had dared enter the room at night after a particularly bad session of drunkenness. And in the morning, Marco Polo had stepped on a piece of broken glass and cut his foot. He'd called Mathura Singh and complained like a small child, 'Just because I was drunk you punish me like this! Do none of you care for me?'

From then on, Mathura never sleeps on such nights. He sits on a stool outside the room, occasionally looking at the clock, waiting for the dreadful night to end, for the sun to rise, and for the defiled, demented planet to recover its sanity by daylight.

It was Mathura who told me about these nocturnal dramas, though I could never discern it from the manager's appearance at breakfast the next morning. He had an unlimited source of energy. Even after such excesses he could slave like a beast.

He was beginning to be a little favourably disposed towards me. Though he was stern with others, he would actually smile a little when talking to me, even telling me one day after work, 'Why are you still here? Have you turned into a monk?'

'Of course not,' I said.

'Then why are you stuck in this coop? So many temptations floating about in this city—grab a couple of them and have some fun.'

One day, he asked me about Byron. I hadn't seen him since that night when he got me the job at the hotel. It was as though he had materialized from nowhere before Sir Hariram's statue and vanished again into thin air.

'Do you run into Byron at all?' Marco Polo asked.

'No,' I admitted.

He looked rather worried and glanced at his wristwatch before turning to look at the sky through the window. The sun hadn't set yet, but evening was nigh.

I wasn't at all prepared for what he said next. Shaking his head and narrowing his eyes, he said, 'You're a clever young fellow—you pretend to look innocent though you know a lot.'

I was taken aback at first. Then I realized that for some reason he thought I had some information which I was hiding from him. 'I don't quite know what you're talking about, sir,' I said.

Marco Polo waved his hands, a little abashed. 'No…never mind,' he said, 'I was joking.'

Suddenly he stopped talking and looked at me. Disconcerted at his gaze I stared at the floor instead. When I glanced at him a little later, I found him still looking at me, a mournful expression on his face.

He spoke slowly. 'Will you do me a favour? Will you go and meet Byron? Please?'

How could I refuse? 'What should I tell him?' I asked.

'There's nothing to tell him. If you meet him, just let him know that I'm getting impatient.'

I was about to set out immediately, but he stopped me.

'It's teatime, young man,' he said. 'Tea will be served immediately, have a cup before you leave.'

He thumped the bell. The hands of the clock showed 'teatime', which meant that 250-odd rooms would now have to be served tea simultaneously. The bearers must have gathered at the pantry muttering, 'Quick, quick!'

The bearer didn't respond to the bell. He must have been waiting at the pantry, where two men would be swiftly pouring hot water into kettles while another one mechanically poured tea into them. The bearers had already taken the milk out of the fridge and the sugar from the shelves. Unless you saw it with your own eyes, you wouldn't believe how efficient they were.

It didn't take long for the tea to be brought to the manager's room. Lifting the tea cosy, Mathura Singh saluted and stepped aside, which meant: 'Will sir pour, or would he like Mathura to do the needful?'

Marco Polo nodded and said, 'All right.' Mathura Singh saluted once more and departed.

No sooner had he stirred the tea in the pot than the manager jumped up in horror. 'Poor quality!' he exclaimed.

Mathura was summoned. Quaking with fear, he said, 'No, sir, it's the same tea as you had this morning.'

The manager sent for the steward. He was the man in charge of the stores, which meant he was the first target in case anything went wrong. A little later there was a knock on the door, and Jimmy came in. Forcing him into a chair, Marco Polo said, 'I was dying to have a cup of tea with you, hence the summons.'

Jimmy read between the lines and realized that there was trouble brewing. 'Something wrong?' he asked apprehensively.

The manager exploded. 'My dear fellow, I wouldn't be surprised if a guest set fire to the hotel after a cup of your tea. If that tea gets to the stomach one might even feel like murdering someone.'

Taken aback, the steward said, 'Perhaps there's something the matter with your teapot?'

The manager made a face and said, 'That question can be answered by the horses in the nearest stable.'

Dripping obsequiousness, the steward said, 'I'll open a new packet and have some fresh tea sent to you right away.'

Marco Polo guffawed. 'You will, Jimmy, you will,' he said. 'You'll be able to take my chair very soon.' Turning to me he said, 'You're looking at your future boss.'

Mathura Singh brought fresh tea. Pouring it out, Marco Polo handed me a cup saying, 'This business of running a hotel—you can talk your way through it. There was this hotelier named Stephen in your very own Calcutta, who reigned simply on the gift of the gab.'

'Who was he?' asked the steward.

'The founder of Calcutta's biggest hotel. For that matter, also of one of the best-known hotels outside Calcutta. And don't forget Stephen House in Dalhousie Square. The story goes that he found himself in a worse spot than you. One of his boarders found not only tea leaves in the kettle but a cockroach in the hot water.'

'And then?' Jimmy asked eagerly.

'The guest marched straight to Stephen's room, teapot in hand, quivering with rage. But Stephen wasn't the kind of person to lose his nerve. Very cordially he asked his bearer to fetch another pot of tea. Then he poured a cup himself and gave it to the guest. The guest saw Stephen muttering something to himself, trying to work something out mentally.

'"What are you thinking?" he asked.

'Stephen replied, "We have five hundred rooms, which means five hundred pots of tea. One cockroach works out to one out of five hundred."'

The steward burst out laughing. 'Wonderful! What presence of mind!'

'Hmm. But times are changing fast, Jimmy. Mere words no longer make a difference,' the manager said with a serious expression. 'Unless we tread carefully we'll be in for a lot of trouble.'

Jimmy rose; so I had to, as well.

After Jimmy left, Marco Polo said to me, 'I could have given you a hotel car, but I don't want this to get out.'

That was no problem. I was used to riding a tramcar.

I have never understood how it is that when a particular class of people live in the same neighbourhood, even the air in the locality acquires a distinctive smell. It's difficult to say how this happens but it does. I could distinguish between Chhatawala Lane and Dacre's Lane blindfolded. Even as the Esplanade–Park Circus tram crossed Wellesley Street and entered Eliot Road I sensed a distinct smell, a particularly unpleasant one at that. It wasn't as though this area led Calcutta Corporation's list of dirty neighbourhoods—in fact, I have spent a lot of time in lanes far dirtier—but I had never felt so uncomfortable.

Getting off the tram, I tried to figure out the way to Byron's home. A few half-naked Anglo-Indian children were playing marbles. It's reassuring, somehow, to be in a place where small boys mill about playing games. There was a liquor store just a few yards away, but only its signboard was visible from the road. A dim light shining on the signboard tried to stimulate a little forbidden curiosity among innocent passers-by.

The boys stopped their game and turned their attention towards me. When I took out a piece of paper from my pocket and asked them where the road mentioned in it was, they showed me the way in a strange cocktail of English and our national language. I was about to thank them and move away, when one of the senior lads told me that they expected something in return for their service.

I knew one had to pay the lads to catch a taxi in

Chowringhee, but this was the first time I had to pay four annas to locate an address in Calcutta. By the time I stood before Byron's house, darkness had set in.

The name had probably been marked in plastic letters on the front door, but some of the letters had, over time, forsaken their attachment and bid farewell, leaving only the letters R, O and N, which apparently could not give up on their love for the owner and were somehow managing to keep the show going.

There was a doorbell, but when several attempts at ringing it elicited no response, I realized it wasn't in the soundest of health, and started banging on the door in good old Indian fashion. It worked. I could hear a shackled dog raising cries of freedom from inside. There was a sound of a door being unlatched, and the person who emerged was Byron himself.

Rubbing his eyes, he said, 'What a surprise!'

He ushered me inside with great affection. Had he been sleeping at this time of the evening?

Offering me a battered cane chair, he went into the bathroom to splash water on his face. I spotted a pile of old American detective magazines on the table, and cobwebs and dust in the corners.

Wiping his hands on a dirty towel as he came out of the bathroom, he said, 'Surprised, eh? You must be wondering why I'm sleeping at this hour. I'll tell you, but first things first—let me make some tea.'

'I had a cup of tea a little while ago with Marco Polo himself,' I said.

'I have no objection to your drinking one hundred per cent pure nectar with the Agmark stamp on it. But how can you not have some tea with me? I still owe you forty-two cups.'

He busied himself with the arrangements, saying, 'My wife won't be returning tonight, she's going to her friend's place in Batanagar straight from work.'

Putting the kettle on the stove, he continued, 'As I was saying, you must have been very surprised to find me asleep. But remember: whatever we detectives do, it is with a purpose.'

'Of course,' I agreed.

'Yes,' he said. 'I try to explain that to my wife all the time, but she refuses to accept it as easily as you do. Instead, she asks a thousand questions, not all of which I can answer. We make a living out of secrecy, after all. There are many things in our profession we can't tell even our wives. After all, we live in India. If walls have ears anywhere, it's in this country, particularly here, in Calcutta.'

'So you have quite a lot of trouble?' I asked.

He nodded. 'That's why there's a school of thought in our detective world which says that detectives shouldn't get married.'

'What!' This was an astonishing theory.

'Don't be surprised,' he said. 'There's an age-old controversy in the Church over whether priests should marry—it's the same here. The members of the bachelor school of detectives say that wives are a positive nuisance to this profession.'

'Many of the top barristers in the high court secretly believe the same thing,' I said.

'They're bound to. Every ambitious and intelligent man will say as much.' Taking the kettle off the stove, he went on, 'But to be honest, I can't blame my wife. Suspicion is not only the last word in our profession—it's also the first. Since I posses that virtue in abundance, it is not fair to expect my wife not to have it.'

Handing me a hot cup of tea, he continued, 'As I was telling you, do you know why I was asleep at this unearthly hour? I probably won't get a wink of sleep tonight—I'll have to search for someone. The name of the person might interest you, but we will come to that later. This secret's like the government's budget—until it's announced in parliament, it's top secret, but after that it's public property.'

Now he asked after me. 'How are things? Is the job treating you well?'

'Yes,' I said. 'That woman isn't back yet.'

'Mmm, I haven't checked on Rosie, I've been very busy for some time. I must find out now whether she's coming back at all. Mrs Banerjee's getting very restless, too, she sent her daughter to see me twice.'

Eventually, Byron asked about the manager, and I had to tell him that it was because of him that I had come all this way.

'Did he say anything?' Byron asked.

'He told me to tell you that he's getting very impatient.'

Byron looked grave. Pushing his cup aside, he took out a cheap cigarette from his pocket, lit it and said, 'Do you know what comes in the way of becoming a great doctor? You must not feel too much for the patient. It's the same with us—you come to me in trouble, I try to help you; if I can, that's wonderful, if not, better luck next time. But I can't do it; I try to, but I can't. Poor Marco Polo, I really feel sorry for him.'

I looked on at the poor, half-clownish Anglo-Indian. He stubbed out his cigarette and lit another. I felt a trifle uncomfortable in the smoke-filled, cloistered room.

'I see you are feeling uneasy,' Byron said, 'but opening the windows will only make matters worse, with all the smoke of burning coal fire from the neighbouring houses.' He paused. 'Life's like that. Overcome by the smoke of my own sorrows, I rushed outside only to discover that it's even worse there. It has overwhelmed my own suffering and often made life that much more difficult to endure. You have spent many years at the court, you've never seen life through the coloured prism of Shahjahan Hotel. You'll enjoy poor Marco Polo's tale.'

And he proceeded to tell me.

It is as fascinating a story as that of the boy from the aristocratic family in Venice who, in the second half of the thirteenth century, responding to the call of the unknown, presented himself in the court of Kublai Khan.

'He appears quite a contented man, doesn't he?' asked Byron. 'A two-thousand-rupee job.'

'Two thousand rupees!'

'Yes sir. One outcome of the war in Europe is that there aren't too many competent people left—and those who are don't come cheap. If you want to run a big hotel well, you can't get a manager at that salary these days. In Rangoon, he earned not only the same amount but also commissions on sales.

'But Marco Polo didn't have things easy all his life. His father was a Greek innkeeper in the Middle East who had set off with his meagre savings, his wife and newborn son on a voyage. Many a heartbreak awaited them. Arriving at an Arab town, they put up for the night at a hotel, but they did not have to pay the bill—in fact, they didn't even manage to come out of that hotel room, because a devastating earthquake flattened the entire town that day. People from all over the world came forward to help the ill-fated town where several thousand people were supposed to have been trapped in the debris and died.

'At that time a group of Italian priests was working about thirty miles away. It was their mission to travel around the world, bringing sight to the blind. Their equipment loaded on two ambulances with red crosses on them, they would go from village to village like a circus party. Tents would be pitched, their flag would be hoisted, portable iron cots joined together to create fifteen-odd beds, and a small tent used as the operation theatre.

'Local charitable organizations would be informed beforehand, and word would be sent far and wide that the priests had arrived. They would camp for a fortnight in each village, treat a variety of serious eye diseases and perform operations if necessary. Then, they would move on to the next destination.

'Hearing about the earthquake, they rushed to the site. Sifting through the debris, they discovered a European baby, alive, while the bodies of its parents lay a few feet away. The priests took the orphaned child back with them to Italy and brought him up at their orphanage.

'What would they call him? The head priest must have been partial to travelling—as well as to history. He said, "He seems to be ruled by a wandering star—look at where he was born, where we found him, and where we have brought him. The only apt name for him is Marco Polo."

'No one objected, and, as a result, Marco Polo was reborn in Italy in the twentieth century. The priests left no stone unturned to ensure that the orphans under their care became self-sufficient as soon as they grew up. They sent Marco Polo to an institute of hotel management. In our country, those who can't do anything else become homoeopaths, learn shorthand or open roadside restaurants. It isn't like that abroad— people on the Continent, especially the Swiss and the Italians, don't take the hotel business lightly. Students from all over the world visit those countries to specialize in hotel management— and degree and diploma holders from there work in big hotels all around the world.

'This is one business where the English hadn't been able to make much headway. Even in their own kingdom of Calcutta, barring one or two places, all the hotels and confectionery shops were run by people from the Continent. And even the few establishments owned by the English had people from Switzerland, France or Italy as senior staff members.

'After graduating from the institute the lonely Marco Polo set out job hunting. A mere degree didn't mean one would get a senior post. One had to start from the ranks. And it took time to learn, too. Experts say it takes five years to get to know the kitchen, two years to memorize the names and vintages of various wines and spirits, two more to learn accounts. And the rest of the time is spent unravelling the mysteries of human nature.

'Marco Polo was extremely diligent. He worked hard and gradually moved up through the ranks, till he arrived in Calcutta. The hotel he joined as under-manager still glitters in a blaze of neon and is one of the most popular hotels in the city.

'The god-fearing and grateful Marco Polo never forgot the Roman Catholic priests who had given him a new lease of life. In spite of many constraints, he went to church every Sunday, giving a hundred thousands thanks to the Almighty for sparing his life. Whenever he found time, he took a train to Bandel Church to light candles before the Virgin and to pray. He consciously kept himself away from the kind of life he could have easily slipped into by virtue of living at the hotel and looking after the bar.

'That was when he met Miss Munro. Looking for respite from the din and bustle of his own hotel, he had entered a small restaurant on Park Street for dinner one evening. And Susan Munro happened to be singing there.'

Byron paused. Opening his briefcase, he pulled out an old newspaper, extended it lovingly towards me and said, 'You move around a lot—ever seen this lady?'

I tried to match the face in the picture with the faces of all the strange people I had known—but I couldn't recall anybody like that.

Byron said, 'I got hold of the picture with great difficulty from the *Statesman* office. The restaurant owner had put in an ad. I had to buy that issue of the newspaper.'

It wasn't possible to fathom Susan Munro's beauty from the old newspaper photograph. 'She wasn't particularly pretty,' said Byron.

But Marco Polo was convinced a nymph was dancing before him. Abandoning his dinner, he concentrated on her singing, inviting her afterwards to his table.

'How did you like it?' asked Miss Munro as she seated herself.

'Marvellous. It was as though you were putting up an exhibition of paintings at the Academy of Fine Arts before a distinguished audience of blind men.'

The lady smiled and said softly, 'What can I do? Where can I find discerning listeners?'

'Is everybody in this city deaf?' smiled Marco Polo.

'Deaf, but not blind! Their eyes are very alert, their sight very keen. Restaurant owners here know that, which is why they pay more attention to the visual aspects of the singer than to the aural ones.'

Marco Polo laughed as he ordered two bottles of beer and told her, 'But believe me, you sing beautifully. You'd be appreciated even in Europe.'

'Any chance of a break in your hotel?' Miss Munro asked.

Marco Polo was surprised. 'You know who I am?'

With a wan smile she said, 'I may sing at a small establishment, but does that mean I don't keep track of big ones.'

Marco Polo looked dejected. Woefully he said, 'I'm really sorry, but those who run our hotel and those who visit it for pleasure don't patronize anything made in Calcutta. Those who sing or dance at our hotel are all made in Europe or made in the USA. Even made in Turkey or Egypt will do, but never made in Calcutta.'

Pushing the beer bottles aside, the lady got up to resume her act. As she left, she said, 'Please forgive me if I disturbed your dinner.'

Marco Polo pawned his middle-class heart with the infamous Susan Munro of Park Street that day.

The two of them met again at the restaurant.

Marco Polo tried to make his way into Susan Munro's heart. 'Really?' he said to her in surprise one day. 'You never formally learnt to sing? You mean nature has created a musical voice like this of its own accord?'

'Where would I learn? Going to music school costs money,' she replied.

Gradually he learnt the whole story. First in the restaurant, then in her room, he heard how her fate had run parallel to his. With both parents dead, she had been brought up by the SPCI, who had made every effort to equip her to cope. And as an adult she had tried to be independent—first selling cakes at a Swiss confectionery near New Market. But her passion was music, her fascination was with fame—she was even prepared to sing for free in restaurants.

She had got into this one with great difficulty. It was very hard at first, standing in the shop all day selling cakes then going straight to the restaurant, where she got dressed—there was no time to go back home. Yet it was the sort of place that didn't believe in luxuries like ladies' toilets. Asking a waiter to keep guard, she had to use the common toilet, the smell almost making her throw up.

'Don't they pay you anything?' asked Marco Polo.

'Dinner, and ten rupees a month.'

'Just ten rupees? Disgraceful! Breed of leeches,' he said indignantly.

'And that, too, who knows for how long?' she said glumly.

'What do you mean?' he asked.

'There's another girl who used to sing here—Lisa. She's broken her leg and is lying in bed, which is why they've let me sing. As soon as the doctor removes her plaster my singing days will be over.'

Marco Polo felt bad for Susan. The thought that she had no parents either attracted him greatly towards her. She wasn't particularly pretty, she may have had youth on her side, but surely just the fragile cord of youth would not have been enough for her to tether a seafaring ship like Marco. But he gave himself up and allowed himself to be anchored. Of his own accord, he brought Susan to the hotel as his bride.

It was because of her that he eventually had to leave Calcutta. Everyone knew her, which meant that she'd never make it big in the city. Someone who had hawked her music on Park Street could never aspire to the heights of Chowringhee.

Marco Polo got himself a hotel manager's job in Rangoon. They would have no worries now—nobody there knew of Susan's past. The hotel owners in Calcutta said to him, 'What's the hurry? You will be the manager here someday.'

Marco Polo laughed. 'Calcutta may be my wife's home, but it isn't mine. Rangoon and Calcutta are all the same to me.'

They didn't have a bad time in Rangoon. For a while, at least. Susan's dream and Marco Polo's work kept them both busy. He made quite a job of the hotel, so that foreign guests were mesmerized by it—they couldn't believe there was a hotel like that in Burma.

But one day the skies of Rangoon filled with bomber planes—the Japanese were coming. Burma would have to be evacuated. No one had known something like that would happen. No one had expected it—not even Marco Polo. They returned to Calcutta. But circumstances had changed. Those who had once pleaded with Marco Polo to stay on now turned away, some even wrinkling their noses because of his Italian connection. They might even have sent him to jail for being an Italian, if it hadn't been for the Greek passport in his pocket. The priests had displayed that one bit of foresight— they had changed his name but not his nationality.

Though Marco Polo's stock had dipped, the demand for Susan's services had risen. Thousands of English and American soldiers filled the city. They wanted to eat at restaurants and listen to music as they ate.

Marco Polo objected. 'If you keep singing this way you'll never make it big. You have to aspire to greater heights. One day people all over the world will want to listen to you, your records will be played everywhere.'

'But until then?' said Susan. 'Should we starve until then? Those who wouldn't pay ten rupees once are now begging me with five hundred. Lisa's run away. Without a musical show the soldiers will go wild.'

Marco Polo had to agree. A husband who couldn't feed his wife couldn't afford to enforce his wishes.

He started looking around for a job. And Susan sang.

'I've bought a watch,' she said one day.

'Where did you get the money?'

'There's plenty of money,' she said. 'Some American soldiers were so pleased with my singing they pooled in to buy me the watch.'

Marco Polo nodded.

Another day he said, 'You return home so late these days. I get worried.'

'Earlier the licence was till ten, but there's no time limit now. I have to sing till one in the morning.'

'Don't you find it tough, Susan? Do you like singing like this?' Marco Polo asked.

'But they pay. They pay so much, you know,' a tired Susan replied.

'I've got a job for you,' she said one day. 'Will you take it? It's the manager's post at the army canteen at Liluah. On hearing it's for my husband they were very keen. Major Shannon will come tomorrow to talk to you about it.'

Marco Polo's wild, primordial Greek blood seemed to boil. 'A job thanks to your singing? Out of pity?'

'Why such aversion to pity? It's pity that brought you up,' Susan shot back immediately.

He didn't react, preferring to leave home before it was time for Major Shannon to arrive. The major waited for him with a bottle of beer and then left in disgust.

A few days later Susan said, 'The management is pleading with me to sing at lunchtime also—they'll pay three hundred more.'

He didn't reply. Later he asked, 'Is this what your passion for music was all about, Susan?'

'What do those who sing dream of?' she asked in reply. Without waiting for an answer, she continued, 'They want popularity—and I've got it. I'm popular.'

Marco Polo went to Patna in search of a job. He found one, but didn't find satisfaction. From Patna he went to Karachi—and finally got a job with a big hotel there. He wrote to Susan from Karachi.

She wrote back, 'I have no idea how time flies. I'm singing all the time—people love music so much.'

Marco Polo wrote, 'It's a nice place, you're bound to like it here. The city's much more organized than Calcutta, too, and there's no risk of Japanese bombs.'

'I'm in love with Calcutta,' she wrote back. 'Those who wouldn't pay ten rupees once are now paying thousands. Another restaurant's promising even more.'

'I miss you,' he wrote.

'Take a few days off and come over,' she replied. 'At worst they won't pay you when you're away.'

His letter from Karachi said, 'This is a new job. I can't take leave whenever I want to. The hotel's packed, but there are very few responsible people. Why don't you come—even musicians need rest.'

Her letter from Calcutta said, 'Received your letter. I'm off on a six-week tour to sing at American bases on special invitation. Sorry.'

Marco Polo tried to take a few days off, but couldn't. When he did succeed eventually, an entire year had passed.

He was amazed when he came to Calcutta. His wife's home was unrecognizable. At a time when even tyres were hard to come by, Susan had bought a car.

'You never told me,' he said.

'Oh, sorry, I forgot. Got it very cheap—Major Shannon arranged it for me.'

Marco Polo could not have dreamt of what he was seeing. Money…a cheap career…were these more important to Susan? Didn't she spare a thought for her art, her passion? But what was the use of showering advice on her? The tigress had tasted blood. Military officers' cars were parked practically round the clock at her house.

He took her aside and asked, 'Have you seen yourself in the mirror lately?'

'Of course I have, every day. I've put on some weight, that's all,' she replied.

'Your eyes?'

'They look a little tired. Even the Madonna's eyes would have looked this way if she worked as hard as I do.'

'I have to know your future plans, Susan,' he said seriously.

'They're very bright,' said Susan. 'I'm quitting the restaurant job, it's a dead loss. Instead, I'll sing here, at this Theatre Road house, with a few snacks thrown in. Major Shannon has promised to get me a bar licence. I won't let every Tom, Dick and Harry in—only select guests will be entertained. And if you take on the responsibility for the arrangements, I can concentrate on my music.'

'What? With a degree from the Swiss College of Caterers you want me to become a call girl's manager? God help me!' His entire body revolted in disgust.

That night Marco Polo realized that it was all over.

Standing on the terrace of the Theatre Road house, he asked the Almighty, 'Why did this have to happen? What have I done to deserve such punishment?'

At the breakfast table the next morning, he said to Susan, 'Enough—it's time we separated.'

'Divorce!' Susan didn't agree at first. 'It's because I'm married that all these undesirable elements don't dare to bother me. Even the American military police don't prevent officers from coming to my flat. You won't give up till you ruin my respectable profession, will you?'

'We're already separated. What's required is only a legal acknowledgement,' he said.

'Which means you'll accuse me of adultery in court? You'll say I'm attracted to other men?'

Though he'd been married in an Indian church, Marco Polo had had neither the time nor the opportunity to learn the country's laws. And his leave was running out. He intended to do something somehow and get out of this sinful city forever.

He sought legal advice. Getting a divorce wasn't that simple. He'd have to spend not only effort but also time and money. The plaintiff for the divorce would have to be present in court, and witnesses would have to be produced.

'How long will it take?' he asked.

'Nobody can say—it might take up to two years,' the attorney replied.

It was eventually decided that, to make things easier, it would be Susan who would file for divorce. She would accuse her husband of philandering, which would not only leave her reputation intact, but would also give Marco Polo what he wanted. From his distant workplace he would be unable to take part in the case, and a decree would be issued quite easily.

Before leaving he talked it over with Susan. She wasn't keen at all, since the stamp of marriage was an advantage in her profession. Taking her hands in his, he said, 'If I've ever loved you do me this favour in return.'

'But what kind of debauchery will I accuse you of?' she asked. 'Whose name will I link with yours?'

He was at his wits' end. Was there any woman who would agree to be a co-respondent in a divorce case?

Eventually she said, 'I could ask Lisa. She doesn't have a reputation to lose, and besides, I've done her some favours.'

A few days later she said, 'I spoke to Lisa. She says she wants to take a look at the person I'm accusing her of having a secret affair with.'

Early one morning, he appeared with Susan at Lisa's house. Having been up all night, she had barely gone to bed, and woke up when they arrived.

Seeing them, she burst into peals of laughter. 'My god, it's the dutiful wife and the adulterous husband!'

Marco Polo explained it all to Lisa. 'You don't have to explain,' she said. 'I've passed one test already—my own divorce proceedings came up in the same court.'

'Susan will say in court that it was she who introduced me to you,' he told her.

Lisa laughed in her high-pitched voice. 'That's not a lie. It is she who introduced you to me.'

He continued, 'On a few specific occasions, say, four or five nights—Susan, put down the dates in your notebook—I was spotted here...'

He felt too embarrassed to continue.

'Spending the night, right?' Lisa flopped onto her bed, laughing.

'And I'm going to write a few letters to you, after consulting the lawyer. Please excuse the language—just send them in their envelopes to Susan, they'll serve as proof. And if you could write a couple to me, nothing like it—we'd be home and dry,' Marco Polo forced the words out.

'Anything else?' asked Lisa, lighting a cigarette.

'It wouldn't be a bad idea if we could be spotted together in a restaurant a couple of times,' he said with a grimace.

Lisa's laughter now became grotesque. Rolling on the bed

in mirth, she tried to stifle her guffaws in the pillows. Coughing, she said, 'Acting, all of it. Very interesting.'

He stared at the floor without replying.

'Fine,' said Lisa, 'we can spend some time together this evening.'

'Many thanks,' he said. 'Both my wife and I will forever be indebted to you.'

Lisa sat up and thought about something. Then, in theatrical style, said, 'O grateful prince among men, would you deign to wait outside this unworthy woman's chamber for a minute? Your wife, the paragon of virtue, will follow you in a moment.'

He stood outside the room for some time. Ten minutes passed instead of one, after which Susan emerged.

Back home, she said, 'How much will you be able to spend?'

'You know about my finances,' he said.

'Lisa wants money. Why should she go to all this trouble, she wants to know,' said Susan.

Marco Polo was silent for a while. Then, very hesitantly, he asked, 'Could you help...?'

She was furious. 'You know my views. With you in Karachi and me here, we're separated anyway. If you want to enjoy the luxury of a divorce in spite of that, it's you who'll have to spend the money.'

'How much does she want?'

'Two thousand.'

He had never imagined he'd be in such a situation. Sitting in a restaurant in the afternoon, he wrote a few fake letters to Lisa. His stomach turned at the thought of what one had to do for the sake of the law. In the evening he went to Lisa's place and knocked on the door.

'Ah, you're here, darling,' said Lisa. 'Just a minute, I'm almost ready.'

For that one long minute, he stood outside the barred door in that dirty lane in Wellesley and cursed himself.

The door opened and Lisa emerged. Marco Polo couldn't recognize her with all that garish make-up on. She must have used an entire tin of powder—and rouge on top of that. And the cheap perfume made him sick. It really looked like she was going on a group date.

Out on the road, he hailed a taxi. 'Where would you like to go?' he asked. 'Chung Wah?'

'No, somewhere well known,' she replied.

'How about the Grand or Great Eastern?' he asked.

She shook her head—today her heart craved Shahjahan. The dining hall was probably packed with soldiers, but even so they might be able to squeeze into a table somewhere.

Shahjahan Hotel. Lisa had visited the place once many years ago. It hadn't seemed real—it looked more like dreamland. They had charged seven or eight rupees for dinner all right, but the ambience was magical. Lisa had stolen a menu card, which she used to read in her bed at night: Pamplemous au Shahjahan, Consommé Ajoblanco, Beckti Allemby, Baron d'vos Roti, Gateau Citron, Cafe Noir and much more!

The blue lights of Shahjahan Hotel transformed night to day. Marco Polo felt funny being a guest—when actors became the audience and watched a play, they probably felt the same way. Lisa wanted a drink, and Marco Polo ordered a Bronx cocktail—gin, French vermouth, Italian vermouth and orange juice. Five-and-a-half rupees a drink.

After the cocktail it was straight to whiskey. As she drank, Lisa said, 'I'm sorry I couldn't help you like a friend, but I need the money—I'm not as well-off as Susan is. And besides, when she has the money, why shouldn't she give it? You can be sure I'll do exactly as you want me to.'

She looked at him and smiled sadly. It was her smile that seemed to give her age away—she was much younger than the dark circles under her eyes suggested.

'I haven't yet recovered from the time I broke my leg,' she continued. 'It hurts at times—I can't stand too long at the mike and sing. Do you know what a customer screamed out the other day?'

'What?' he had to ask though he was not in the least interested.

'Lame old dame! These Bengali customers—the dustbin of hell.'

She poured a little more whisky down her throat and said, 'I've decided to carry my birth certificate inside my bodice from now on—if anyone says anything I'll fling it in his face.'

Marco Polo did not reply. After some time he said, 'Perhaps you don't know that I'm not taking a single rupee from Susan for this case.'

'Silly old fool, you're still behaving like an idiot. You haven't learned at all,' she said, clutching her glass.

That very night he gave her one thousand rupees and said, 'Whatever little I have left I have to give the attorney. When I get back I'll send you some more.'

The attorney was paid and Susan's plea for a divorce from Marco Polo on grounds of adultery was also made in court.

On the day of signing the petition, the attorney said, 'I must warn you about something. In the petition you have to say that there's no conspiracy between the two parties for getting a divorce—what we call collusion. If the court suspects something's been prearranged, that will be dangerous. No one must know that you've paid the expenses for the suit on behalf of Susan. From today it's only Susan who's our client—we haven't seen you, we don't know you. Don't write to us even by mistake.'

Byron paused again in his storytelling. I had quite forgotten I was sitting in a dingy lane off Eliot Road—it was more like watching a film at Metro cinema.

Byron said, 'What happened after that really makes one feel bad. If only Marco Polo had gone to your ex-boss instead.'

'It wouldn't have been of any use,' I said. 'He wouldn't have taken a case of collusion between husband and wife.'

'Perhaps not, but he could have suggested some other route,' Byron said.

'Perhaps,' I said.

'Anyway, what's the use of crying over spilt milk? Let me tell you what happened...'

Having more or less finalized things in Calcutta, Marco Polo went back to his job. He scraped together five hundred rupees somehow and sent it to Lisa, promising to send her the rest in the near future. There was no way of writing and finding out what was happening; there wasn't even a friend who could keep him informed.

Susan did write once, informing him that she had bought another car. And that what he was anxious about was also progressing, but the attorney had asked for more money. He borrowed the money and sent it to Susan's address.

That was when disaster struck. The police arrested him. His Italian connection had suddenly alerted the authorities once again, and everyone knew what the relationship between Italy and the Allies was at that time.

Till the last day of the war, Marco Polo remained a prisoner, going straight back to Italy in disgust afterwards. In no shape to worry about anything else, he somehow kept body and soul together doing odd jobs on the Riviera.

One day it occurred to him that there was a major discrepancy in the balance sheet of his life—a large sum in the ledger was lying in a suspense account in an accursed city of the east. His desolate soul was afire with deep resentment.

He started looking for a job—first in a hotel in Rangoon, where he was taken on with a handsome salary, thanks to the lack of suitable candidates. But he hadn't left the Italian Riviera to live in Rangoon. After working there for some time, he started looking for another job.

This time it was Calcutta. The manager's post in Shahjahan Hotel was vacant. Finding someone with his qualifications and credentials, the owners took him on with due respect.

But where was Susan? And what about the divorce?

The woman who had set wartime Calcutta on fire had disappeared somewhere in the jungle of humanity. He enquired at the attorney's office, but they refused to divulge anything. The old attorney had, in the meantime, sold his share to his partner and departed for the other world. He enquired at the court. No divorce order had been issued in his name.

Byron stopped.

'And then?' I asked.

'Then I was summoned—and I'm still trying,' he said.

I looked at the clock—it was late, time to go.

'Ask him not to be impatient,' said Byron. 'Something is bound to turn up soon. Now that you've got to know him quite well I might call upon you for help.'

'Considering it was you who got me my job, you don't have to hesitate to ask.'

He embraced me affectionately and said, 'Don't bring all that up.'

Many thoughts milled about in my head that night. Try as I might, I couldn't sleep—though I had never set eyes on Susan or Lisa, whenever I shut my eyes their figures rose before me.

Where was Susan now? Was she passing her days in hardship in a dingy room in an unknown alley of the city, or had she bid adieu to restaurants and music forever to enjoy the fruits of retirement? Surely she no longer lived at that Theatre Road house—if she did, Byron would have tracked her down ages ago and solved Marco Polo's problems. Where was she today, her marital tangle unresolved? Did she ever think of the man who had sacrificed so much for her, who had been prepared to sacrifice so much more?

I felt genuinely sad thinking about Marco Polo's personal

life, so full of pain, but I also looked at it from the other point of view. How strange the world is, I mused. So many people had a tough time simply staying alive, and those who didn't have to worry about their next meal cooked up fashionable problems, tired of their boring pleasures. But then it occurred to me that I had no right to be judgemental—if it hadn't been for the problems of life, half the joys of staying alive might have been lost. It was because there was sorrow, because there were worries, because there was poverty, that life hadn't become shallow and monotonous. None of us is interested in the history of happiness in this world. The great souls of the world whom we revere were all baptized in sorrow—none of them was nurtured in comfort or was a slave of Mammon.

When I arrived at the hotel early next morning, the previous night's thoughts hadn't quite disappeared, which was why the contrast seemed amazing. Even a few moments ago I was surrounded by slums, open drains and dustbins. But here? Garbage was generated here too, only I could never figure out where it disappeared. Here they had perfected the art of sweeping away from view whatever was unseemly and offensive. The enormous effort involved in this process of staying perpetually beautiful could be understood only if one visited Shahjahan Hotel early in the morning.

At an hour when most people in this city were still in bed, the carpets at Shahjahan were being cleaned with vacuum cleaners. The tired cleaners having finished scrubbing the floors squatted on it, resting briefly. They can do nothing till one in the morning, since people sit in the lounge and the bar late into the night. The hotel is named Shahjahan, but the bar-and-restaurant is christened Mumtaz. I don't know what the historical Mumtaz was like, but I am sure our Mumtaz is lovelier, much more mysterious. She sleeps all day, reserving her sport for the night. But Calcutta Police is not amused. Nor is the excise department a connoisseur. They keep a watch over Calcuttans like children, under the impression that staying up late will make them ill. Normally, curfew is at ten, but it has been extended to midnight after much pleading. A little before the appointed hour, the head barman hangs up the small notice normally kept in the corner: BAR CLOSES AT TWELVE TONIGHT.

The guests suddenly seem to wake up from their slumber: time to start winding up. Of course, the canny ones never worry—they simply gesture to the barman.

The waiters know the sign. 'How many pegs, sir?' they ask.

The customer calculates—if one could swallow half-an-hour with each peg, eight pegs would see the night metamorphose into the light of dawn. The bar had to close down at twelve, but there was no problem in staying on and consuming drinks ordered before the deadline. Tobarak Ali, who serves the eight pegs, puts up the 'BAR CLOSED' notice and disappears rubbing his eyes, only to reappear at the bar after his night's sleep, rewrapping the red badge on his right arm. There he finds his customer, having exhausted his supplies long ago, glancing at his watch in anticipation, waiting for the bar to reopen.

I walked through the main gate and entered the lobby. Mr Bose was on duty at the counter, cradling the telephone in his left hand and probably taking down a message with his right. He jerked his head at me as if to say, 'Go straight to the kitchen, there's something you have to do there.' What did I have to do? Who would tell me what I had to do? By then Mr Bose was hunched over the piece of paper, saying, 'Yes, yes, this is Sata Bose from the Shahjahan reception. You can't get Karabi Guha on the phone right now—if there's something you want to tell her, leave a message with me, I'll make sure she gets it as soon as she wakes up.'

Mr Bose's expression made it clear that the person at the

other end of the phone wasn't happy with the reply. 'I understand perfectly,' he said, 'but unless there are special instructions we don't disturb guests while they're asleep. ABC...what kind of name is that? You mean Miss Guha will know who it is? But our custom is to take down the full name, address and telephone number—no, no, please don't be angry, it's up to you how much you want to tell us. I'll let her know Mr ABC had telephoned.'

Without waiting for the telephone saga to be completed, I set off towards the kitchen.

'Sack them, sack them!' Even from a distance, I could hear Marco Polo bellowing. Inside, I found the sweepers lined up, their heads bowed, quaking with fright. They looked as though they had been lined up before a firing squad at a military camp—and were waiting for the general to give the command to fire.

'Is there a dirtier hotel anywhere in the universe?' Marco Polo asked at the top of his voice.

All of them stood silent, their eyes on the floor. Goaded by their silence, Marco Polo roared, 'Have all the ex-students of the deaf-and-dumb school taken jobs in this hotel? Why don't you speak?'

His probing eyes started sweeping the place like a searchlight, coming to a halt at the point where the steward stood. He fired another cannonball: 'Jimmy, have you joined the Gandhi party? Have you taken a vow of silence?'

The steward, whose own authority I had some experience of, seemed to have turned into a worm. 'Quite true, it really is very dirty, as you said...' he stuttered.

'And you're the steward of a hotel through whose kitchen rats as big as crocodiles run about in the daylight.'

At last I understood what the matter was. Two rats had been scurrying about on the kitchen floor under the manager's gaze, and hence the present scene. He would not spare anybody.

Marco Polo emitted a cloud of smoke from his pipe, turned around and said, 'My dear fellows, the way you're going, the way you keep the stores and kitchen in a mess, I wouldn't be surprised if next week I saw elephants instead of rats in here.'

The sweepers had started mopping the floor carefully by then. The steward called the head cook and told him, 'I'll be here immediately after lunch—I want to see everything spick and span. Nobody should leave today, I want to see everyone here.'

As he was about to turn away, pipe in hand, Marco Polo spotted me. A pleasant smile flitted across the face of the same person who had hit the roof only a moment ago. The steward obviously didn't care for such unexpected good fortune being showered on me, as his dirty look and expression indicated. But I had no time to waste on that, as Marco Polo clapped me on the shoulder and said, 'Come along.'

Now I saw him in a different light—he was no longer only my lord and master, the manager of Shahjahan Hotel. I had discovered him the night before. Inside the man hardened by the blows of life I had unearthed that little child who had lost everything in an earthquake in that Arab town, who had been given everything by the Italian priests, and whom Calcutta had once again robbed of everything. I could now see all of him, up close. And like a magician, he, too, transformed himself— who'd have believed that the same man was taking his employees to task after spotting a couple of rats?

Why was he looking at me like that? Perhaps he was under the impression I knew everything, and yet couldn't be entirely sure—who knows how much Byron had told this chap and how much he had held back. I was feeling uncomfortable, too. To overcome the sense of unease, I said, 'I went to Mr Byron's house last night, sir.'

'I hope the place wasn't hard to locate?'

'Oh no...I didn't know the neighbourhood, but I did have the address.'

'I hope that neighbourhood remains unfamiliar all your life. My dear young man, always try to stay away from sinful temptations. I don't want to preach to you, but believe me, we usually create our own sorrows.'

I kept quiet and he continued to look probingly at me. I gulped and said, 'I met Mr Byron last night, he asked me to tell you not to lose patience.'

'Patience! Was a more patient human ever brought up on earth?' I couldn't make out whom the question was addressed to, but for the first time it seemed to me that the man whom I'd thought was made of stone was actually a big slab of ice which was beginning to melt. The man with whom I was supposed to have an employer-employee relationship, forgot for a moment who I was and said, 'I hardly know you to speak of, but you look as though you don't know this world. Be very careful.'

I did not say anything, but I could only thank my stars. I have found undeserved, unwarranted love from people on so many occasions—and having received it, my craving for it has increased even more. That day, too, there was no lack of such affection.

'I have to admit you're not a bad typist,' said Marco Polo, fingering the chain around his neck.

I accepted his praise with bowed head—what could be better than having pleased him in such a short time? I had had a taste of what life without a job could be like, especially for someone who had once been employed. Mr Bose had once laughed and said, 'The fellow who's never had a job and the fellow who's lost his job are like the virgin and the widow; neither has a husband, but only the widow knows the difference.'

As Mr Bose would have put it, I had lost one husband and found another. Even without my trying, the words emerged, 'Nice of you to say so, sir.'

Marco Polo's round eyes danced with merry mischief as he said, 'Your years at the high court haven't taught you to size people up—I'm not nice at all.'

Seeing me look uncomfortable, he changed the subject. 'I'm sorry,' he said. 'I'm quite scared of that neighbourhood of yours—I've been there a few times, but to tell you the truth, if a bull were to chase me, I would rather jump into the river to save my life than run into a building on Old Post Office Street.'

I smiled.

'Where do you live?' he asked.

'Howrah,' I said.

'Where on earth is that?'

'It's to the west of the Ganga,' I explained, 'beyond the station.'

It looked as though he didn't know there was solid ground beyond Howrah Station—as though that was where land ended and the sea began.

Mr Bose had already hinted to me the proposal that Marco Polo now made. 'This is not your ordinary office,' Mr Bose had said, 'with a ten-to-five life, half-day on Saturdays and full holiday on Sundays. If there's any chance of getting a permanent position here, someday the boss will order you to renounce your relationship with the world and take shelter in Shahjahan Hotel.'

To save my job I was prepared to live in any building in the world.

Divining my feelings, Mr Bose had said, 'As far as I can tell you're going to be eating off Shahjahan Hotel for a long time yet. I can guess from Jimmy's behaviour—he's quite soft on you now, and he tailors his behaviour to the boss's attitude.'

Mr Bose's prophecy came true as Marco Polo lit a Burma cigar and said, 'You'll have to take an important decision. Your predecessor, Rosie, used to live here—it suited the management. I wouldn't have to hurry and finish off everything by five—and all important letters could be attended to immediately. I have to admit I've never seen a secretary as wonderful as Rosie—not only did her fingers race over the typewriter keyboard like the Delhi Mail, the smile never left her face. She was completely ungrudging, and she never felt unhappy about working.

'One time the poor girl had to take dictation at midnight—not from me, but from a guest. He was leaving early in the morning for London, and a letter simply had to be delivered on the way to Karachi. He neither had a typewriter, nor could he type. He came to me at eleven that night. "Where will I find a stenographer at this hour?" I asked. He was insistent—Calcutta's such a big city, nothing is impossible here if you try.

'So I thought of Rosie. Believe you me, that night she typed till nearly three o'clock. I didn't know that, I'd simply put her to work and gone off to sleep. She didn't tell me anything either the next morning—but later I received a letter from England from the guest, in which he wrote, "Your secretary rescued me that night like an angel. I have no idea how to thank her—or you. She typed till three in the morning, and then, without the slightest show of irritation, said good morning to me after completing her work and went to her room,"' Marco Polo proudly completed his secretary's tale.

'You'd better move in, too,' he added.

Without waiting for my assent, he left the room, saying, 'I've told Jimmy already, he must have made all the arrangements. Tell him to see me if there's any problem.'

He proceeded towards the counter to examine the billing register. First uncomprehendingly, and then with gradually dawning realization, I flopped down on a chair. Who knew what the stars were conspiring—depriving me of my home or providing me a new one?

I used to have a name of my own, which I lost at the High

Court. I had an address, which I'd managed to preserve against all odds, even saving enough money to get a letterhead printed. In the European style, it carried only the address on the right hand side and, in a daze of self-importance, I'd even spent twelve annas on a rubber stamp with my name and address. I'd used that stamp unstintingly all over the place, proudly broadcasting my lineage! Now both had become redundant on the same day. Anyone who was sucked into the enormous black hole of Shahjahan Hotel could have neither name nor address—he could only be a nameless, kinless, unknown traveller at the inn.

Writing names in the register, Mr Bose raised his head and said, 'I've heard already.' There was a foreigner standing before him. As soon as the bearer ran up from a distance, Mr Bose instructed, 'Suite number one.'

The bearer picked up one of the countless keys hanging on the board and saluted. The foreigner arranged his blond hair and, twirling the key in his right hand, went upstairs.

Bose whispered, 'He's come alone, but he's taken a double room; our best suite, which costs two hundred and fifty rupees a day—and that, too, bed and breakfast only.'

I didn't know yet what the term bed-and-breakfast meant—now I learnt that it implied that only breakfast would be served along with board; other meals were extra. Tourists who travelled around all day preferred the bread-and-breakfast rate, and the hotel wasn't unhappy either, since it meant less trouble.

'He isn't very old,' I said. 'Must be very rich...'

'My foot!' Mr Bose laughed. 'He does have a job, but you can't book suite number one at Shahjahan on that salary.'

'Maybe he's here on behalf of his company,' I said.

'Oh, his office is right here in Calcutta. He stays with an Englishman in Ballygunge as a paying guest, but comes to the hotel occasionally—alone, but he takes a double room. In fact, he comes at least four or five times a month. It's just as well that he belongs to the Commonwealth, or else we'd have to give a report to the security police each time, and they'd wonder why someone from Ballygunge comes to Shahjahan so often.'

I hadn't become familiar with this kind of lifestyle yet. Mr Bose said, 'Even someone spending no more than a few hours here in the evening will know what's going on. She'll come at night in dark glasses—her husband owns seven or eight cars, but she'll take a taxi. One thing I can vouch for, though—that Mr So-and-so is not in Calcutta tonight. He must have gone to Bombay, or Delhi, or even to England, on business.'

'Who is this gentleman? And who's the lady?' I couldn't contain my curiosity.

'Even walls have ears in this godforsaken country,' said Mr Bose.

I grabbed his hand and said, 'I may have ears, but I'm dumb. Whatever makes its way in through these ears stays in there—it never comes out.'

Mr Bose said, 'Mrs Pakrashi. In Madhab Pakrashi's account books she's already been written off. Pakrashi has lots of things in life—lots of cars, companies, houses, and money, but what he had just one of is precisely what he has lost. He has Mrs Pakrashi without having her. By day she's a social worker—she gives speeches and worries for the country. And by night she comes over to the Shahjahan. During the day she's a Bengali to the hilt, but here she's completely international—I've never seen an Indian with her. The last regular visitor to suite number one was a twenty-three-year-old Frenchman, but we have to report anyone from outside the Commonwealth who visits the hotel, which is probably why she's chosen this Englishman. Poor Pakrashi.'

'You needn't feel too much sympathy for either of them,' I said.

'That's what Mrs Pakrashi feels, too. Who knows whether Pakrashi books single rooms or double rooms at the Taj in Bombay or the Maidens in Delhi? But she hasn't succeeded in catching her husband off guard yet. I have a feeling he's a decent chap—I've seen him drop in occasionally for lunch, he doesn't even order a beer. Mrs Pakrashi had put your friend Byron on his tail; he chased him to Bombay a couple of times, but as far as I know, nothing came of it.'

'How did you get to know all this?' I asked in surprise.

'I just picked it up—you will, too. In a few days you will also get to know Mrs Pakrashi, and you'll hear a lot about her boyfriend. You'll not only be surprised, you probably won't believe your own eyes.'

'Why not?'

'Not now—all in good time, if you're still interested, that is. Meanwhile, give me a few minutes, let me finish these chores. One fifty-two, one fifty-five and one fifty-eight will be vacated any moment—the bills are ready, but I have to check whether they've signed for anything at the last minute. If anything's left out it'll be deducted from my salary.'

Having checked the bills, Mr Bose called the bearer. The poor chap was seated on a stool—he hurried over on being summoned.

There was a particular way people talked here—one's voice had to be pitched so low that nobody but the person being addressed could hear, and yet it wasn't whispering. It was in this style that Mr Bose told the porter, 'The gentlemen are in their room, their packing is almost done, so don't waste any more time.'

'How did you perfect this tone?' I asked.

'Just as you have what is known as BBC pronunciation—this is what is known as the hotel voice. Mastering it is a very difficult art—you'll have to do it, too, Mr Mukherjee.'

'Isn't it time you dispensed with the formality?' I asked.

'I'd like to think there's at least one person in Shahjahan Hotel who uses my first name.'

'And what will you call me instead of Mr Bose?' he asked.

'I've decided that already,' I said. 'I'll call you Bose-da.'

'I don't mind,' he said, 'but I'd like you to use Sata-da sometimes. Don't let the pet name lovingly given by Sahibganj Colony turn rusty with disuse.'

'Why?' I said in surprise. 'Everyone here uses that name anyway.'

'Their using it and a dear one using it is hardly the same thing, is it?'

He came back to the subject of my change of residence. 'I heard from Jimmy that you're moving here permanently. Good news.'

I still had my misgivings. 'You think so?' I said. 'I'm feeling a little nervous.'

'Don't be silly,' he said with smile. 'As for feeling nervous—who isn't intimidated by Shahjahan Hotel from a distance? Seasoned wood from Sahibganj Colony as I was, even I came close to developing a crack or two.'

There was no way one could spend too much time chatting at the reception counter. The telephone rang again, and Bose-da took the call. 'Shahjahan reception. Beg your pardon? Mr Mitsubishi, oh yes, he's arrived here from Tokyo, room number two hundred and ten.'

The caller probably asked whether Mr Mitsubishi was in.

'Just a minute,' said Bose-da and glanced at the board on which the keys hung. The key to 210 was visible, so he said into the phone, 'No, I'm sorry, he's gone out.'

Bose-da put the phone down and said, 'Why waste time, go and call it off with Kashundia.'

Now I had to explain the reason for my anxiety—I could have sunk through the floor in embarrassment, but somehow I forced the words out. 'I don't have any of the things you need to live in such a big hotel. My mattress is in bad shape, and I can't even borrow a holdall at such short notice to hide it in. Isn't there another door one could use?'

Bose-da bailed me out. Chiding me for my foolishness, he said, 'Why should anyone move in here if they have a stylish mattress? The better the hotel you put up in, the fewer the things you need to bring. In fact, there's this French hotel whose advertisement says, "You need bring nothing except your appetite"—and this appetite refers not only to hunger but to many other things as well.'

Pulling out the pencil he had tucked behind his right ear, he started writing on a slip of paper. After he had finished, he said, 'You have to bring nothing but what you need to preserve your modesty—everything else will be taken care of.'

He thought a little and added, 'Sorry, you'll have to bring something else—a very essential item. I hope yours is in good shape.'

'What's that?' I asked.

'Your toothbrush. Nothing else. Hurry up, say a prayer to the thousand-handed Kali at Kashundia, cut off connections with the Howrah Municipality and make a beeline for Chittaranjan Avenue. And meanwhile we'll prepare a civic reception for you.'

When I came back to Shahjahan with my luggage, it was with a strange sensation. The neon light was still glowing, and in its dreamy glow, I discovered the hotel anew.

It wasn't so much a hotel as a framed picture. In the alluring curves was not the arrogance of modern skyscrapers but the stamp of ancient aristocracy. Like a beautiful bride's bracelet, the neon lights glinted in the darkness. It had three bands—green at the extremities and red in the middle; the flirtatious winking was limited to the green, while the red was like the unblinking eye of an angry monster.

The enormous portico sheltered not only the entrance to

the hotel but also several glittering shops. They all seemed part of the hotel—bookshops, magazine stands, medicine stores, government stores with the best samples of Indian handicrafts, curio shops selling Nataraj statuettes, ivory and woodwork, a counter selling Shahjahan-brand cakes and bread, an automobile showroom, a post office, a bank, a tailoring shop to get suits made, dyers and cleaners to get those suits drycleaned. And somehow, amidst this motley crowd, a taxidermist had survived. Whoever hunted tigers and lions these days—and even if they did, who lavished money and attention on stuffing straw into the dead tiger's stomach and wood into its shoulders and practically bring it back to life?

But there was a story behind the taxidermist's presence here. The founder of this hotel was extremely fond of hunting as was one of his friends. If you entered the shop you'd spot an oil painting of the two of them standing triumphantly with their feet on the carcass of a Royal Bengal tiger. But the Englishman couldn't plant his foot on it forever—some intrepid member of the Royal Bengal clan wreaked vengeance during a subsequent expedition. Simpson, the owner of Shahjahan, and his friend Skinner had set off on their hunt with four legs, but they came back with three. Skinner's job had involved travelling, and now with the loss of a leg he lost the job as well. Simpson couldn't stop worrying for his friend. Since Skinner had once learnt taxidermy, his friend told him, 'Why don't you set up shop in my hotel arcade—it won't cost you anything, and I'll try to send the hunters among our guests to your shop.'

We all know how many Indian tigers, lions, deer and elephants have lost their lives in the hundred and twenty-five years since. And we can also guess how many of the carcasses of these children of the forest who suffered untimely deaths are still being displayed in English homes across the ocean. It probably isn't difficult to understand how the lame Mr Skinner managed to buy a castle in Scotland, and how he converted, even in that day and age, a few hundred thousand rupees into pounds and set sail for England.

I wouldn't have got to know the story of the killing Skinner made. Leave alone me, it's doubtful whether even the present owner of Skinner and Co., Muktaram Saha, would have known, had it not been for a cutting from an old issue of the *Englishman* lovingly framed and hung behind the counter. The editor of the paper had published that special piece on the day of Skinner's departure.

A major portion of the framed piece was occupied by a sketch of Shahjahan Hotel done by the *Englishman*'s own artist. I'd examined that sketch carefully for a long time. Even the hotel lounge had a few sketches by some unknown artist of the time. These pictures greeted the stranger, informing him that this inn was not a Johnny-come-lately Yankee hotel, that behind it lay the weight of history, of tradition—an ancient inn to the east of Suez welcoming you.

There was nobody in the lounge when I entered with my small bag. Bose-da emerged from behind the counter and welcomed me dramatically. Noticing my embarrassment, he laughed and said, 'As you know, shyness, hatred and fear are no good for a job out here.' Glancing at the clock, he added, 'Give me five minutes, my shift will end and William Ghosh will be here to take over.'

'Does William stay at the hotel?' I asked.

'No, he lives at Madan Dutta Lane in Bowbazar. You haven't met him yet, have you? Very interesting chap,' said Bose-da.

By then my eyes had settled on the old sketches in the lounge. Bose-da was through as well, and the two of us examined them together. 'Amazing, isn't it?' he said. 'These go back so many decades, but Simpson's Shahjahan Hotel has withstood the ebb and flow of time and stands firm where it was.'

'Who could look at this building and guess its age!' I marvelled.

'William knows nice little rhymes, and has even stocked up on many Bengali proverbs. Houses don't age, he says. Ageing depends entirely on the owner. His diary has these lines:

Maintenance for a building
A landowner's revenues
Signing the register

'What does it mean?' I asked.

Bose said, 'If William had been here, he'd have been able to tell you. Simply put, I think it means that repairing buildings, paying taxes and attending office all have to be done on time.'

'I don't think the owners of this building have ever skimped on repairs,' I said.

'It's because the old lady puts on her cosmetics of plaster and lime at the right time that she's managed to preserve her looks,' Bose-da said, laughing. 'But then, this is only the façade—you might regret it if you make any comments without looking around inside!' He winked.

I saw a picture of a pond, the governor's house visible in the background. I wondered how this pond had suddenly disappeared from the heart of Calcutta.

Bose-da said, 'That is the famous tank of Esplanade, where trams move around now. If you want to know all the stories connected with that tank, I'll introduce you to a very interesting man, an imperial library of old anecdotes. You wouldn't believe so many things have actually happened, or that one man can remember so much, until you meet him. An old Englishman, he's been in Calcutta for a long time.'

He continued, 'It was from him that I heard that people in the olden days believed that this Esplanade tank had no bottom—however deep you went, you found only water. There were lots of fish in the tank; when they decided to pump all the water out, Finberg, the owner of Hotel de Europe, agreed to buy all the fish in it for six hundred and fifty rupees. The draining began, and Chowringhee was chock-a-block with people, crowds coming from enormous distances to find out whether the lake was indeed bottomless. Meanwhile, Finberg couldn't sleep nights for worrying over whether all that money would go down the drain for who knew how much fish there would be.

'The water began to be pumped up into drains and porters carried baskets of mud to the maidan. It was on that mud that the grounds of the Dalhousie Club were built. It seems Finberg made lots of money on his investment. Many varieties of fish were found—giant ones, each at least a stone or so in weight. A few of them were thrashing around in the mud. Finberg's people swooped down on them and brought them back.'

The story might have continued much longer, but somebody came and stood behind us. Startling us, he asked, 'When the fish of Chowringhee was being auctioned off dirt cheap what was the owner of Shahjahan Hotel doing?'

'William!' said Bose, turning around. 'You're late.'

'Sorry, Sata, but this is Calcutta, after all. These trams aren't always in the best of moods—like today, for instance,' William smiled and replied.

I stood gaping open-mouthed at Ghosh—you seldom set eyes on someone so dark and yet so handsome. If he'd been a little fairer, and had been wearing Indian attire instead of Western, he'd have looked like a god. Only Putu-di from my childhood had such lovely dark eyes—but then, she used a lot of mascara. From a distance, you suspected the same thing about Ghosh, but up close, you realized he had been born with the mascara. He had on a black bow tie with his white shirt. His pointed moustache seemed to have been clipped in tune with the butterfly at his neck. The trousers were light blue, and so was the jacket. The breast pocket of the white shirt was visible through the undone buttons of the jacket, and it had a coloured silk monogram on it: S. Obviously it stood for Shahjahan.

Handing over charge, Bose-da said, 'William, you're a lucky man, you're on duty on an auspicious night.'

Ghosh didn't have to be told anything more; he seemed to have understood. 'Has suite number one been booked? Has Mrs— arrived?'

'Mrs Pakrashi isn't here yet. She booked the room on the phone herself today, probably didn't have advance information; her husband must have left suddenly.'

'Is Thomson here yet?' asked Ghosh.

'Yes, he is. You're sure to get your two ten-rupee notes!'

'My misfortune, brother. With fairer skin I'd have been able to earn much more than two tenners.'

'Don't be ungrateful, William. I've never known anybody but Mrs Pakrashi to pay anything to the receptionist—she's very generous.'

Ghosh was about to respond, but Bose-da butted in, 'Now my friend, off to your abode.' I was about to pick up my leather case, but he called out, 'Porter!'

The porter, who was seated on a stool in the distance, rose and saluted us, but Bose flew into a rage. 'Why isn't your cap on straight? If the manager saw you, you'd get the sack immediately.'

The porter looked just like a circus clown—it was as though the uniform for porters at Shahjahan Hotel had been designed keeping circus clowns in mind. A violet, high-necked jacket with half-sleeves, and long green piping running down the sides of the trousers. The round velvet cap on the head had the same green piping—it was as though, after a porter had put on his trousers, jacket and cap, someone had taken a long ruler and a brush and drawn a straight green line from top to bottom. The line on the cap was bound to bend at times, because frequently it had to be tucked into the shoulder strap to make it easier to carry luggage.

The porter quickly straightened his cap and said, 'I am sorry, sir.'

'What are all those mirrors in the lounge for? Can't you check?'

The porter picked up my case, and the two of us followed Bose-da. 'Lift or stairs?' he asked, and then said on an impulse, 'No, let's take the lift.' It started moving. After a brief halt on the first floor, it continued upwards.

All the rooms on the first floor were for guests—Marco Polo's being the only exception. The lift stopped on the second floor, and a waft of cold air danced across our faces. The second floor was only for guests. As the lift moved further up, the very atmosphere seemed to change. The liftman, who had been standing ramrod straight all this while, leaned against the wall and scratched his leg with one hand. The cold air also seized the opportunity and started turning warm. 'That's the end of the air-conditioned area,' said Bose-da, 'and the beginning of ours.'

The spot where we stepped out of the lift was pitch dark. As the collapsible gates closed and the lift went back downstairs, it felt as though someone had pushed us into a dark prison, clanged the gates shut and run away. I'd have felt scared if we'd remained in that darkness for long, but the porter reached out and opened a door before us. Light flooded through the door—in it I saw red letters on the door: PULL. As we crossed the door it slammed shut by itself—on the other side were letters written in the same style: PUSH.

I couldn't quite make out what it was all about. Bose-da smiled and said, 'Don't you see? It's the old adage—push from this side, pull from that. The lucky ones find the door to fortune opening like this. And with the luckless it's just the opposite—they push when they should be pulling, and vice versa, which is why the doors of their fate never seem to open. We've put the instructions there to warn those of us who are likely to make that mistake.'

The terrace was dotted with countless cubicles, with tile or asbestos roofs over them. 'This is where we hole up; our free inn, and the concealed interiors of Shahjahan Hotel,' said Bose-da. A hazy glow filtered through the curtained windows. I hadn't quite realized in the dark—a practically nude woman was sitting on an easy chair. Spotting us, the female figure disappeared in a trice.

As though he had forgotten I was with him, Bose-da started whistling and stood before the door to his room, which was dark as well. A bearer in a white uniform rushed up. Seeing him, Bose-da lowered his head and said softly, 'O spectre of the night, to see who you are I need some light!'

The light came on in Bose-da's room. The room offered precious little privacy—the walls weren't even brick ones. In fact, it was a wooden cabin, with two small windows to the west and north. There was also a door to the south, looking out on the road.

Exhausted after being on his feet all day, the first thing Bose-da did on entering his room was to dive on to the bed. After spending a couple of minutes sprawled like a corpse, he moved. Still lying on the bed, he summoned the bearer. Now I got a sampling of Bose-da's authority among the bearers—the one who came in straightway proceeded to unlace his shoes and take them off, without saying a word. Carefully tucking the shoes under the bed, the bearer also removed the socks with a practised hand. Opening a cheap, worn cupboard next to the bed, he took out a pair of rubber slippers and placed them on the floor.

'The two of you should get acquainted,' said Bose-da. Pointing towards the bearer, he said, 'This is my guardian—Gurberia.' And pointing at me, he added, 'My dear Gurberia, this son of Bengal has joined recently—think of him as the junior governor of Shahjahan Hotel. He'll be put up in Rosie's room for the moment.'

Poor Gurberia bent his turbaned head and saluted me.

'Get the key to three sixty-two, Gurberia,' said Bose-da. 'The gentleman will retire to his room now for a rest.'

Gurberia immediately did an about-turn and almost raced off in search of the key.

'Nice fellow,' I said to Bose-da.

'He has no choice but to be nice now.' Bose-da smiled. 'Master Gurberia is living in exile at the moment.'

'What do you mean?'

'He used to be on duty on the second floor—but after he broke half-a-dozen cups one day, the boss dispatched him here. Being transferred from serving hotel guests to devoting oneself to the staff is like giving up a job with Burmah Shell to write the books at the provision shop round the corner. The manager hasn't killed him, but he's taken away his chances of making a killing by banishing him from the fountain of tips to the desert of the terrace. What's more, the head bearer, Parabashia, had arranged a match with Gurberia for his daughter, but this sudden setback in the fortunes of his prospective son-in-law has compelled him to back out. The poor fellow's now trying to extricate himself by lavishing his attention on me—he seems to think I have a lot of influence with both Parabashia and Marco Polo, and that neither of them can refuse my request.'

Bose-da might have told me more, but with Gurberia's arrival, key in hand, he stopped. Gurberia said, 'This way, sir.'

Bose-da asked, 'Do you need me to come along?'

'Of course not, Gurberia will show me the way,' I said and took my leave.

The dust accumulated at the door made it clear that number 362 hadn't been opened for some time. Gurberia opened the door, switched on the light and immediately departed on some private errand.

I felt rather uncomfortable from the moment I entered the room. The cosmetics carefully arranged on the dressing table made it clear that this was where Rosie used to live. It seemed she hadn't taken anything with her—all her possessions were still lying around. It was as though she'd taken a few hours off to go to the movies, and would return any moment—to find that, taking advantage of her absence, a stranger had quietly occupied her bedroom.

This room was at the eastern end of the terrace. The walls and doors were painted dark green both inside and outside, but the hessian ceiling was white. It was a tiny room, with a bed, a dressing table and a wardrobe occupying most of it. There was a chair, but just the one—the deliberate and artificial short supply seemed aimed at keeping down the number of curious guests.

Rosie's bed was covered with a multicoloured bedspread—I sat on it and took off my shoes. I had barely taken off my shirt and trousers and, in Bengali style, put on a dhoti, when a whistling sound began. I hadn't noticed that the sky had become overcast—it was as though, irked by the way we had ignored nature, the nor'wester was giving vent to its anger.

The force of the wind slammed the door against the wall, forcing me to lock it. By the time I turned my attention to the windows, the spray had already doused parts of the bed. Occasional flashes of lightning entered the room through cracks in the wall and castigated me—they seemed to have realized that I was a trespasser. The torrential rain sounded like a group of neighbourhood hooligans drumming indefatigably on the roof. I didn't feel as though I were sitting in a small room on the terrace—it was more like living in exile on some

uninhabited island, miles and miles from civilization, contact
with the rest of the world lost forever.

When I opened the wardrobe to put my clothes in, I got
a shock. Rosie's gowns were still hanging inside. The wind
barged in and played havoc in the garden of gowns—the silk,
rayon and nylon garments giggling and falling against one
another in feminine coquettishness. Even the order in which
they hung suggested a terrible conspiracy—first the deep black,
then the dark green, then the stark white, and then the flaming
red. The lady probably spent all her money on clothes. On the
left-hand door of the cupboard, a photograph was captured in
a bright steel frame, as though crucified.

It was obvious to me that the woman in the frame was
Rosie. Had I not seen this picture, I would never have
believed that a woman would allow herself to be photographed
in such a provocative pose—or, even if she did, that she would
actually preserve the photograph carefully. Her entire body
wasn't visible in the photo—not even half of it, for that matter.
But whatever there was smiled under a satanic influence. Her
thick lips pouted slightly while the eyes seemed to have turned
away in embarrassment from its own body.

Her hair was curly—those locks, coiled like snakes, hinted
at a story long lost in some dense African jungle. And this
woman was supposed to be a typist! Her teeth peeped out
through the lips—she had been shot in light and shade, but
someone had highlighted her teeth by lighting them up. The
same beam of light had tried to bend the rules a little and reach
her breast, but being alerted in time, Rosie hadn't allowed it,
and had quickly gathered up her loose dress.

I had thought of her as Eurasian, but the photograph
hinted at another continent. All over her eyes, her face, her
body, was written the name of the mass of land which was
once known as the Dark Continent—now, it was known
simply as Africa.

Since there was no other place available, I had to put my clothes in the wardrobe.

Rosie may not have been there in person, but her spirit was all-pervasive. As were the disembodied souls of this ancient hotel who probably took shelter in this empty room in the darkness of night. And now a stripling from across the Ganga had turned up to intrude on their peace, which was why the May thundershowers had asked bitterly, 'Who is it? Who are you?'

Thinking of that night makes me laugh even now—I'm amazed at my own immaturity! But back then, its questions unanswered, it appeared that the rain had joined hands with the storm to go on a rampage. The centuries-old spirit of Shahjahan Hotel kept asking, ever louder, 'Who are you? Why are you here?'

The toilet was attached to the bedroom, but no one seemed to have paid any attention to it in the past few days. Some soap water still remained in the bathtub. I unplugged the mouth of the tub, let the water out and turned on the tap, the jet of water cleaning up the tub. One could feel Rosie's presence here too—her soap case, toiletries, toothpaste and toothbrush still lying there in neglect.

Unused to all this, I would have felt more secure had the rain stopped—I could have gone to Bose-da and asked, 'Where have I ended up?' He would probably have replied in his customary humorous vein, 'Calcutta's most ancient inn, Shahjahan Hotel.'

Most ancient, indeed. It was Bose-da who told me the story.

It went back a long time—to some remote century, on an unsung rain-swept afternoon, a man named Job Charnock anchored his barge by the river Hooghly on the banks of this very Calcutta. His misery knew no bounds that day, but no hotel door opened to provide shelter to the tired guest—the people of Sutanuti and Hooghly hadn't even heard of a hotel. Charnock must have made his own arrangements, as all travellers had done since time immemorial.

Ages passed. Many more strangers stepped on Calcutta's soil, but even so no hotel came up on the city's saline soil for their benefit.

Laughing, Bose-da had said, 'As a child there was this Tagore poem I'd memorized, but I hadn't realized its meaning then: "In all countries I have an abode, yet I have spent my life searching for it." Now I realize what the poet meant—that all countries in the world have hotel rooms, I've seen many of them, but none of them seem up to the mark, which is why I'm still searching. If the poet had been born a hundred years earlier, this beautiful poem wouldn't have been written—after all, there were no hotels in Calcutta then.'

What had sprung up in the city were taverns—or, as William put it, 'Petrol pumps to tank up on liquor.' Anchoring their ships on the Hooghly, the pleasure-seeking, homeless sailors would rush to the city's taverns. Many strange chapters of life would be enacted on that stage.

Even after all these years, the mad cacophony of another century seemed to be ringing in my ears. I could feel the hot, amorous breath of that age—it sent a shiver down my spine. The colossal palace, in whose desolate room on the terrace I lay awake in the middle of the night, and in which I would spend many more nights, was also the custodian of many unread chapters of history languishing in the dirt. The building in which I waited for an encounter with morning, from which I wanted to see off the beautiful night on a golden chariot, was not a contemporary one. It didn't even belong to this century.

'Nothing is permanent in this astounding city,' Bose-da had said, 'not even life. Even the formidable Charnock had to bite the dust of Calcutta within two years. Only after sending him to his grave did Calcutta seem to breathe a sigh of relief.'

The previous day, he had said, 'Fame? That's also as fleeting as a comet rushing across the sky. Yesterday's emperor, who spent the night in Shahjahan Hotel's most expensive room, is today a pauper who finds shelter only on the street. Life, youth and everything else in this city are transitory—nothing can defy eternity and keep standing in Calcutta. But Shahjahan Hotel stands upright with unbelievable arrogance, nurturing the sorrows and joys, the suffering and pleasure, the celebration and desire and the greed, acceptance and sacrifice of many nights in its breast. It survives—and not even Simpson could have imagined that it would have withstood the ravages of time and lasted so long.'

If Simpson could have risen from his grave in St John's churchyard to stand in front of his beloved Shahjahan, he would have been amazed. His creation had far outstripped him. Many years ago people had thought him mad. 'Are you permanently under the influence of the bottle these days?' they had asked.

He had replied angrily, 'I'm a teetotaller, I don't touch alcohol.'

'Are you then dreaming your multicoloured dreams under the divine power of opium from the sensual Orient?'

'Not dreams, but plans—a business scheme.'

'Plans to build Fort William in the air!'

'Not at all, this is down to earth—I'm planning a hotel here, next to Fort William. Calcutta is going to determine the fate of India, which means that lots of people will have to come here—and they won't hesitate to loosen their purse strings for a place to stay the night. For them I'm going to build a hotel that not just you, but also your sons and grandsons, are going to thank me for. No statue will be put up in my memory, but I will live on in every breakfast, lunch and dinner at Shahjahan Hotel.'

That day, Simpson didn't dare look into the future beyond

the next two generations. But tonight, if he could evade the
eyes of the priests at St John's Church and come here, the
people he would see at his hotel would be neither his friends'
grandsons, nor their grandsons' grandsons. Great, great, great—
he could have added as many of those greats as he wanted and
visited this terrace of ours.

Suddenly I heard a thumping on the door—someone was
banging on it repeatedly. I woke up with a start and opened
the door to find Gurberia standing outside. It had stopped
raining.

'You went to sleep with your lights on, sir,' he said.

Indeed I had. I hadn't even realized when the lullaby of
the rain made me drop off. I looked at the clock. It was very
late. I was peeved with Gurberia—what did he have to wake
me up at this hour for?

He seemed scared. 'Don't go to sleep with the lights on
at night, sir,' he said. 'It'll mean trouble for you and for me.'

'Why?' I asked, rubbing my eyes.

'Mr Simpson doesn't like it,' he whispered. 'He can't stand
wastage.'

'Mr Simpson?'

'Yes, sir,' he said. 'All those who are on night duty are
scared of him—he comes on inspection at night, you see. He's
very strict, sir, merciless. All night he roams around from the
ground floor to the terrace.'

'You know Mr Simpson?'

'Yes sir, the number one owner of this hotel. He drags his
right foot a little—all of us know him.'

Gurberia seemed to be choking. Trying to moisten his
throat by swallowing, he said, 'Thanks to him there's no rest
for even a moment on night shift. I can understand human
bosses, sir, but ghost bosses are heartless—they show no
mercy.' After a pause he continued, 'One night soon after I got
my job, at two o' clock, all the guests were asleep, all the doors

were locked from within, there wasn't a sound anywhere, the corridor lights had been dimmed. I hadn't been feeling too well, and was nodding off on my stool—but no sooner had I put my feet up and closed my eyes than I felt someone taking off the belt at my waist. As I clutched it in surprise, I realized it was Mr Simpson. I tried to prostrate myself at his feet, sir, but you can't do that with a ghost. All the while I felt the belt being pulled off, so eventually I started crying and said, "I'm new, sir, I'll never do it again." Without paying the slightest attention, he walked off with the belt, but on some impulse left it behind at the farthest corner of the second floor.'

Half-asleep as I was, I was about to laugh at the story, but Gurberia said, 'Don't laugh, sir, please ask Blackey. Everyone here knows that when he was alive Mr Simpson used to roam around all evening, checking whether everyone was doing his job. If he caught anyone sleeping, he'd take off his belt—the next morning, one had to pay a fine to have the belt released, because reporting for duty without wearing one's belt was not allowed.'

Apologizing for not putting out the light, I was about to retreat, when I heard four or five voices—male and female—laughing near the stairs.

'I'm off,' said Gurberia softly. 'Please don't say another word.'

Not following him, I asked a little angrily, 'Why not?'

'It's very late,' he whispered. 'The naked ladies are on their way back. Put out your light and go to bed.' On that mysterious note, he strode away.

I did both, but I simply couldn't go back to sleep. The sleep I knew at Kashundia didn't seem to have the nerve to enter Shahjahan Hotel.

Meanwhile, some people were going off in peals of laughter on the terrace. It was the voices of the women who had come up the stairs, whom Gurberia had referred to with his unconventional description. A couple of them entered the room next door. Their words filtered clearly through the thin wooden partition—not that they were trying to talk softly. Though my room was dark, the light was still on in theirs— filtering in through the gaps in the partition.

'Butler, butler!' called out a female voice.

Even from my bed, I could make out that poor Gurberia had rushed to the room.

'You the butler?' the lady asked sharply.

'No madam. I Gurberia waiter.'

Just waiter would have been enough, but by putting his name in there, Gurberia for some reason seemed to have upset his 'madam'. With a few obscene oaths she said, 'What kind of waiter are you?' There was probably another lady in the room, for I heard the first one say, 'I tell you, Mummy, this is my last visit to India, I'll never return to this wretched country.' She explained to her mother repeatedly that her trip to India had been a colossal mistake. 'Why on earth did you agree to come to India of all places, Mummy?' she asked.

Who were they? I couldn't tell—but I could tell that they might talk all night.

The lady now asked Gurberia in pure Hindi, 'What's the Hindi for whiskey?'

On being told that the Hindi for whiskey was whiskey, she said, 'I want some, right away.'

'Bar under lock and key,' Gurberia explained in a mixture of pidgin English and his mother tongue. He couldn't serve anything but cold water now.

'O Mummy, what wilderness have you brought me to?' sobbed the daughter.

Her mother tried to comfort her, 'How would I know bars aren't open in Calcutta after one o'clock? Darling, sweetie pie, try to go to sleep, it'll be morning soon.'

The girl started abusing her mother now. 'Get out, get out

of my room. All you care for is my money—you would feed your daughter to the sharks for the sake of money.'

'Pamela, Pamela...' the lady tried piteously to calm down her daughter.

'Get out, go to your own room, I'm going to undress now, no one will stay here,' the daughter screamed through clenched teeth.

'My dear girl, I'm your mother, you don't have to feel embarrassed before me. I had a mother, too—I never disobeyed her,' the lady tried to explain.

'Is that why you left home at eighteen? Ran away with the butler?' the daughter shouted mockingly.

Her mother flew into a rage. 'Pamela, the person I ran away with was your father!'

'Yes, but he was a butler.' The daughter burst into laughter.

I was feeling quite sick by now—where had I landed up? I could comprehend nothing of this world. I felt angry with Bose-da—he had abandoned me here and was sleeping peacefully.

Many familiar faces swam up before my eyes—Chhoka-da from Ramji Lane, Hejo from Umesh Banerjee Lane, Panu from Nabakumar Nandy Lane, Keshto from Kashundia; they were all fast asleep. Only I was awake—I didn't want to be, but I was. I didn't dare close my eyes.

Meanwhile the verbal skirmish continued in full swing next door—I had already learnt half the secrets about the lady's butler-father. The mother eventually said, 'Should I sleep next door then?'

'Yes, yes, how many times do I have to tell you? And if you still don't go, I'll call the boy and have you thrown out.'

Bursting into tears, the mother said, 'Will you be able to sleep by yourself—you won't feel scared?'

Her daughter laughed loudly and said, 'I know you'll be by my side till the day I die.'

The mother probably took her leave now, saying, 'Goodnight, my girl—God bless you.'

At last the light went out next door, and Shahjahan Hotel finally surrendered to the night. And timid sleep from Kashundia eventually summoned up enough courage to tiptoe into my room and hold me in a close embrace.

I have no idea how long I stayed that way, but suddenly I woke up—someone was knocking very lightly at the door. I'd tried to learn the telegraph at the George Telegraph institute once—I'd even bought a telegraph machine—and the sound was identical.

As soon as I got up and unlocked the door in the dark, I heard a soft masculine voice, 'Pamela! So you opened the door. I thought you wouldn't.'

In a sleep-slurred voice I cried in panic, 'What? Who are you?'

The stranger probably realized his mistake. Running away with his head bowed, he said, 'Sorry, wrong number.'

I was trembling by now—I couldn't make out where the figure in the nightgown had disappeared. Turning on the light, I went outside and discovered Gurberia fast asleep on his stool. At his feet was a cat happily enjoying a night's rest, while on the other side of the stool was another one doing exactly the same thing. Only a light was keeping vigil above Gurberia's head—and even that seemed taken aback by the turn of events.

There was no question of going back to sleep. There seemed nothing for me to do but wait for morning. The dirty sky above Shahjahan Hotel was gradually clearing up. Just like a head clerk arriving early and waiting for the junior clerks to arrive, glancing at the clock every now and then, I stared at the eastern horizon. Darkness hadn't quite disappeared yet—but the bride had started throwing coy glances from behind her golden veil. In that near-darkness I spotted a man in briefs and vest at the corner of the terrace, doing freehand exercises, jogging on the spot, just like in slow motion pictures.

A darkish man, not quite young—a tight, lithe figure with, as I could make out even from a distance, grizzled sideburns. I went closer and saw that while he exercised in concentration, water boiled on a stove before him—as he did his routine, he glanced occasionally at the water.

He smiled at me and said in chaste Bengali, 'Good morning. Are you an early riser too?'

'Oh no,' I replied. 'My mother couldn't get me out of bed come what may, but for some reason I'm up early today.'

I realized he knew who I was when he said, 'You're here to replace Rosie, aren't you?'

He introduced himself at last. 'My name is P.C. Gomez, Prabhat Chandra Gomez. I'm the musician here—the bandmaster.'

'Do you live here?' I asked.

'I have no choice,' he said. 'When the cabaret ends at night, buses or trams don't run in the city.'

He went into his room, emerged with a glass of water and poured it into the pan on the stove. 'I'll make a cup for you as well.'

I was about to object, but he paid no attention. 'Our first meeting,' he said. 'I'm an ordinary man, let's celebrate with a little coffee.'

'Coffee? At this hour?'

Gomez smiled. 'Yes. At exactly four in the morning, I normally have a very strong cup, without milk or sugar. You won't be able to stomach it so strong, so I'll give you some sugar. But I have no milk—sorry.'

I felt quite miserable putting the gentleman to all this trouble at that hour of the morning.

Pouring coffee into the cup, he said, 'Brahms, the great composer, used to have coffee like this every morning.'

As I sipped the coffee I heard how Brahms made his coffee—and how, while sipping this bitter, strong and black brew, he had composed four symphonies, two piano concertos, one violin concerto and a double concerto for violin and cello. I couldn't quite follow all that Gomez said, but it was obvious that he was speaking with feeling. I was about to wash my cup, but he wouldn't let me. 'I couldn't possibly,' he smiled and said. 'When Schumann visited Brahms, did he wash his own coffee cup?'

I had no idea who Schumann was. My expression probably indicated to Gomez the depth of my knowledge of music. 'The great Schumann,' he said. 'One article by whom turned the unknown Brahms into an overnight celebrity.'

My relationship with music had never been a very sweet one, but I hid my ignorance and asked Gomez, 'Does that mean I'm Schumann, the king of music connoisseurs?'

'Maybe not, but you're my guest,' he said. Without changing the subject, he continued, 'What I've learnt from Brahms is that no pain on earth is pain, no want is a want, no agony is agony. Glorifying all our thorns, the flower of music blooms.'

Meanwhile, the sun was climbing in the sky. Gomez smiled sweetly and went into his room, saying, 'The boys are still asleep, they have to be woken up.'

And I returned to my room.

I simply couldn't forget the night's experience. I peeped out and discovered that the door to the next room was shut. But Gurberia walked in, tea tray in hand. In a couple of seconds, however, he was back outside, having deposited the tray, and, making a face, started muttering to himself, 'What a problem—this cabaret woman will neither lock her door nor wear any clothes.'

I was sitting quietly in my room when there was a knock at the door. I opened it to find Bose-da. Entering and closing the door behind him, he said, 'You don't have to open the door yourself—just say, come in. And if you're not in a position to open the door, say, just a minute. With that minute you can take up to half-an-hour in a hotel. Got your bed tea?'

'Bed tea?'

'Yes. The tea that the Shahjahans of Shahjahan Hotel drink in their beds, without brushing their teeth, is known as bed tea.'

I said, 'I just had coffee...'

I didn't have to complete my sentence, he seemed to have understood as soon as I opened my mouth. 'Terrace coffee on the first day—you're a very lucky chap. Only two people in the world drink coffee at that hour—our Gomez and Brahma from Germany.'

'Brahms, not Brahma,' I smiled.

'Six of one and half-a-dozen of the other. Besides, hasn't Shakespeare said, what's in a name? If I call Brahms Brahma, will his standing as a composer suffer, or will the Brahmo Samaj stop worshipping their god?'

Glancing at me, he changed his tone. 'Didn't get any sleep last night?' he asked.

'No, I managed,' I muttered.

Bose-da nodded in understanding. 'One feels that way at first—I did, too. But then your eyes will get used to it, you'll start thinking of all this as everyday affairs.'

Getting up off my bed, he said, 'Take a bath quickly, we'll go downstairs together. Mr William Ghosh must have consigned fourteen generations of my forefathers to hell by now.'

Breakfast began with bread and butter and omelettes. I was surprised at the shape of the teacups—Bose-da observed my reaction and said, 'These are known as breakfast cups. One likes having a little more tea at breakfast.'

We might have carried on talking, but the bearer informed us that someone was waiting outside for me.

'For me!' I was astonished, but before I could say anything more, the visitor came in—it was Byron.

'Good morning, sorry for intruding without notice,' he said.

Doing the introductions, I said, 'Bose-da, this is Byron, he's the one who got me my job here.'

Bose-da was about to introduce himself, but Byron smiled and said, 'And you are Shankar's friend, the right hand of the manager of Shahjahan Hotel, Satyasundar Bose. You've been working here for eleven years, before that you tried to use your uncle's connections to get a job at the Grand.'

Both of us were surprised—Bose-da simply couldn't believe it.

'There's nothing to be surprised at,' said Byron. 'We're private detectives, we have to be in the know—knowledge is our capital, and information our business.'

He broached the real subject at last. 'Should I leave?' asked Bose-da.

'No, no, not at all, I need you. I got some bad news this morning, which is why I came immediately.'

'What news?' I asked.

'My dear friend, Rosie is probably coming back.'

'What!' I cried out in anguish.

Byron said, 'Mrs Banerjee has got some news of her husband. Her brother Khoka Chatterjee in Bombay has tracked him down, using the address I'd sent. All the admonitions have brought Banerjee's attention back to family life—and Chatterjee has managed to pacify Rosie. Since Banerjee is on his way back, how can Rosie be left behind, especially in Bombay?'

I wasn't prepared at all for such news early in the morning.

'Don't lose heart yet,' said Byron. 'I'll meet Marco Polo before I leave—but the problem is, what if no other post is available?'

Bose-da thought for a while, and then cheered up and said, 'Not to worry.'

Without wasting any more time, the two of them went off

to meet Marco Polo. Not daring to go in with them, I paced outside the room. Mathura Singh asked, 'Why are you waiting here? Please go in.' I couldn't tell him why. The three dignitaries had, in the meantime, started their conference over my future. I gave thanks to God, who had, unasked, given me friends like Bose-da and Byron, who in times of trouble fought for me without expecting anything in return.

When they emerged after about fifteen minutes, both were smiling. 'If you have any thanks to give,' said Byron, 'reserve them for Mr Bose. It was he who explained in clear terms to Marco Polo how two persons are not enough to man the reception counter, how there's no one to sell tickets for the cabaret, how he has no choice but to take the orders for food and drinks at Mumtaz himself even after ten hours at the reception desk.'

I looked at Bose-da gratefully. He clapped me on the back and said, 'You've been sitting and thumping on the typewriter all these days—now you'll have to stand with us and do some real work. Rosie or no Rosie, you'll be on duty with us at the counter. The gain is mine, Mr Byron. Where's the pleasure of being alive unless you get an obedient wife or a faithful assistant?'

'Counter duty?' I asked.

'Yes, yes, it's not very difficult, anyone can do it,' he said. 'You'll have to get a couple of suits made—but you don't have to foot the bill, the hotel will pay.'

'But you people rattle off so many languages effortlessly— I can't speak any of them properly,' I said apprehensively.

Bose-da laughed loudly and said, 'Let's go to the counter, I'll tell you about my experience.'

William Ghosh was waiting at the counter for Bose-da, his papers all in order. Bidding him goodbye, Bose-da said, 'Since the boss isn't giving you dictation now, you might as well run my errands, and I'll teach you the trade secrets one by one. As

I was saying, when I got the job, the advertisement they had put in the papers implied that they wanted someone who knew English like Shakespeare, Bengali like Tagore, and Hindi like Tulsidas—salary: seventy-five rupees. And in response they got me. I had all the qualifications, but a little mixed up—English like Tulsidas's, Bengali like Shakespeare's and Hindi like Tagore's. But does that mean things have come to a standstill? Not at all. Anyway, forget all this nonsense and come round behind the counter.'

4

Now for the receptionist's tale, also the tale of the reappearance of a woman capable of sending an entire hotel into a flurry of excitement, a woman named Rosie. The story of how, thanks to Bose-da's benevolence, I learnt the different aspects of working in a hotel, how I learnt to please people, and how from my vantage point at the counter I saw the black magic of Calcutta unfold before my eyes.

But before all that, Sutherland's saga. Even after all these years his face still floats up before me.

Sutherland's lovely oval eyes reminded me of Lord Krishna.

Bose-da said, 'You're rather narrow-minded, trying to slap an Indian metaphor on to everything. Even if the metaphor isn't appropriate, you won't relinquish it. You cling to the Ishwar Gupta of old: observe, my countrymen, in how many ways I love my country's dogs, casting aside foreign gods.'

'That's not fair!' I said. 'I'm turning a foreigner into my country's god.'

'However much you publicize him, was our Kishenchand as tall as Sutherland?'

'We don't measure our gods' greatness with a tape measure,' I said.

'Perhaps not, but in describing Radhika's physical beauty

you leave no part from head to toe untouched,' he shot back immediately. 'Our gods were as short as we are,' he continued, 'while if anything can be compared with Sutherland, it's Greek sculpture. You don't have to go to Greece to see samples of it—the few that remain in old aristocratic houses in Calcutta will tell you what I mean. If one of those statues were lost, Sutherland could take its place.'

Even today, when Sutherland's appearance becomes a bit hazy in my memory, I put Bose-da's advice to reverse use and visit an old house I know on Chitpore Road to look at a nude male sculpted in the Grecian style. The exquisite figure has been damaged badly by neglect and vandalism—one arm is broken, a part of the face has disappeared in an accident. But that doesn't pose any problem—in fact, it makes things easier, for I can see all over again the agony on his face at the cemetery in Lower Circular Road.

I had just started my career at the Shahjahan when I first saw Sutherland. I was told he had come to India on behalf of the World Health Organisation. I didn't see him for quite a while after that, and I didn't enquire after him either—after all, so many people came to the hotel every day and left. How many of these daily arrivals and departures could I remember? I'd heard that he had come in connection with work on an important vaccine, and that he had left India with the germs of a few dangerous diseases preserved in an icebox.

The next time I saw him was on the terrace of Shahjahan. The flight from London had landed at Dum Dum well after the scheduled time the previous night, so that by the time Dr Sutherland came back to the hotel, I was fast asleep in my room. I hadn't even dreamt that when I woke up the next morning, it would be to find him in an easy chair on the terrace. In a singlet and trousers, he was gazing at the eastern horizon like a man in a trance. The rumbling of early morning buses and trucks floated in from the road in the distance, and he seemed to be listening intently to these sounds. Taken by surprise, I rushed back into my room. I was wearing nothing but a lungi.

When Gurberia turned up with the bed tea I asked, 'How did that gentleman get to the terrace?'

'I don't know, sir,' he said. 'Bose sahib came upstairs with him at night—number three seventy was empty, we put him in there.'

'Are these rooms given out to guests?' I asked.

'I don't know what Bose sahib's plans are.' I knew Gurberia was a little unhappy with Bose-da, and there was good reason for it—Parabashia was arranging a match for his daughter with a chap from the Coffee House. 'He isn't doing anything for me,' Gurberia continued, 'and yet he brings that gentleman up here late at night. I got scared at first—the naked ladies were sleeping in the three rooms over there. If it hadn't been for Bose sahib, I wouldn't have let the gentleman in— Markapala sahib has issued strict orders.'

I had learnt a lot of new words from Gurberia: he called Marco Polo Markapala. But I still didn't know who had given the sobriquet 'naked ladies' to the foreign cabaret dancers.

Even the origin of Gurberia's own name was shrouded in mystery. Bose-da claimed that a forefather of Gurberia's must have savoured 'gur' or molasses in Uluberia, a small town close to Calcutta, and coined this name. Gurberia denied this stoutly. First, both he and his father were fond of fried stuff, neither was partial to 'gur'. And secondly, no ancestor of theirs had ever been to Uluberia—their field of activity was strictly limited to Calcutta; specifically, they had long been associated with the problems of the distribution of potable water in the city. His uncle used to repair the Corporation's water pipes, and his father was the 'whole-time' plumber of Shahjahan Hotel. But all his life, he had regretted earning less than the waiters despite being a technical hand. Waiters earned much

more through tips than they did through their salaries, which
was why this far-sighted father had got his son to take up a
hotel job instead of becoming a plumber.

'It's all fate, sir, why else should I get terrace duty?' asked
Gurberia.

'But guests have started coming to the terrace, too, so your
luck seems to be changing,' I said.

Gurberia's face lit up with hope—so it was for his benefit,
after all, that Bose sahib had put that gentleman in number
370.

'Has Bose sahib gone to bed?' I asked him.

'Yes, sir, but he won't be in bed till twelve today like on
other days. I believe he has to go somewhere. He's asked me
to bring him his tea and wake him soon.'

'That's fine,' I said, 'I can meet him when he's up.'

Gurberia began to talk about his wretched luck. 'Bose
sahib can't have pleaded my case properly—why else would
Parabashia even think of giving his daughter's hand to that
Coffee House chap Kalindi?'

I sipped my tea quietly. Gurberia wasn't in the least put
out by my silence and asked, 'Sir, do you think there's a better
hotel than the Shahjahan in the whole wide world?'

'The world is very big,' I said.

'How can you compare the Coffee House to Shahjahan
Hotel, sir?' Gurberia sounded offended.

'That's true,' I said. 'But do you know who Shahjahan
was?'

'Do you think I know nothing simply because I'm not
educated? He was a very great man—built two hotels and
made lots of money. One is in Bombay, named after his
family—Taj Mahal—and the other is our Shahjahan.'

This new lesson in history had me in stitches. 'Don't tell
this story to anyone else. The person who built the Taj Hotel
was Jamshedji Tata, and that was just the other day, while we

are an aristocratic house, our hotel was built by one Mr Simpson.'

Without displaying the slightest interest in what I was saying, Gurberia asked, 'Sir, in the Taj, does each bearer get to keep the tips he gets, or is it all shared equally?'

'Good grief, I have no idea,' I said.

Gurberia had heard that in many big hotels the tip was added to the bill, and was then shared equally between all bearers every week. He was certain that the same system would be introduced at the Shahjahan sooner or later. 'And then?' he asked. Kalindi of Coffee House fame might have been making more than he did at the moment, what with the occasional four- or six-paise tip. But when the tips at Shahjahan began to be shared equally, Parabashia would regret his choice, realizing that he could have found a better match for his daughter.

Gurberia's tirade had already tired me out—I had no idea how much longer I would have to listen to his litany of woes. But at that very moment the alarm clock began to ring next door, and he said, 'Have to wake Bose sahib right away.'

Gathering my cup, he made a final appeal—there was still time, if only we could explain to Parabashia what a mistake he was making.

I learnt about the previous night's incident from Bose-da when I met him in his room sometime later.

'A strange man, this Dr Sutherland,' he began.

'Why?' I asked.

'We didn't have a room—even the two black holes on the second floor had been booked by the Oil Association for their Bombay delegates. Dr Sutherland had written to us by airmail, but we had wired our regret. He got in late last night and said, "I didn't get your wire." I know him, so I made a clean breast of things and told him our position. I even telephoned another hotel, and they agreed to give him a room on my special request. But he seemed far too fond of Shahjahan. "This is my last visit to Calcutta," he said. "I've been dreaming of staying at Shahjahan one last time."

'"The hotel where I've arranged for a room for you is one of the best in the country," I told him.

'But he was adamant. He'd probably had a few at the airport—why else would he say, "I'll sleep on the floor of Shahjahan Hotel if necessary, so for heaven's sake do something."

'So I had to tell him there was an empty room on the terrace—not at all up to the mark, with a tin roof, which might leak if it rained. He agreed readily and, thanking me profusely, came upstairs with me. But from the rest of his conversation it didn't sound as though he was inebriated. Putting him in three seventy, I went to my room and lay down. There wasn't much left of the night anyway—William hadn't gone home; someone else was due on the same flight, so he was waiting in the lounge and dozing. I made him sit at the counter.'

What Bose-da said made me feel that either Marco Polo had hypnotized Sutherland, or that he was working as a spy—it was essential for him to be present here to keep an eye on someone at the hotel.

On my way out, I ran into Sutherland. His disarming smile was really infectious—anyone who saw it couldn't help smiling back. I simply couldn't believe that this was a spy's smile. He beckoned to me. I bid him good morning. He returned the salutation and said, 'Lovely morning, isn't it?'

'Indeed it is.'

'I'm a doctor,' he said, 'illness attracts me, and nature can never mislead me. But today even I feel like turning poetic—it feels as though the beautiful morning has thrown aside the veil on her face to stand before me; Mother India has affectionately revealed to her foreign son everything that she's hidden away for so long.'

'Our mother is very generous—wherever you go in this country, this is the affectionate face you'll see.'

'Perhaps,' he said. 'And yet, though I've been all over India, lived wherever there are epidemics, I've never known her. It's only now—after all these years—that coming to Calcutta on a holiday has led me to discover her.'

The sun was getting stronger. Getting out of his chair, Sutherland entered his room, asking me to come in as well.

Leaving the chair for me, he sat on the bed and said, 'I hope I'm not interrupting your work. Maybe it's time for you to report for duty.'

'I'm off duty now,' I said. 'I start later, and I'll probably have to work through the night.'

'Which means you'll have to stay up all night?' he asked.

'Yes—but then, that's not unexpected; didn't you have night shifts when studying medicine?' I replied.

He smiled and said, 'You can't compare the two. We used to stay up to tend to sick people, whereas you stay up to serve a hotel full of healthy, fit people sleeping on soft beds with their heads on even softer pillows—I can't even imagine it, this unnecessary oriental luxury.' He grew quite angry and said, 'To tell you the truth, I'd say it's a shameful system.'

He rang the bell on the table. 'If you have no objection, let's have a cold drink.' He asked with so much feeling that I simply could not refuse.

Gurberia was off duty—I didn't know the name of the bearer who answered the bell instead of him, we usually called him by his number. 'Two pineapple juices, please,' Dr Sutherland told him after he had saluted.

He was about to depart with another salute, but one look at his face, and Dr Sutherland asked him to stop. Now I saw it too—his face was pockmarked. But Sutherland seemed to be gazing open-mouthed at a wonder of the world.

'When did you get the pox?' he asked.

Embarrassed, the bearer answered, 'Long ago, sir.'

'In childhood?'

'Yes sir.'

'Did you get vaccinated?'

'No sir, it arrived before I could.'

'I see,' said Sutherland.

As the bearer left to bring the drinks, Sutherland said, 'God spared him at the last moment—a little more and he'd have lost his eyes.'

Unless I'd seen it myself, I wouldn't have believed that a foreigner could feel so much for an ordinary bearer whom he didn't even know. Unable to conceal my feelings, I said, 'He'll probably remember you all his life—no guest at this hotel could ever have asked after him with so much concern.'

He looked at me in surprise and said, 'My dear young man, you shouldn't say things like that. How much do we know about this hotel's past? Besides, I'm a doctor, an epidemiologist. The only reason that the WHO pays me a salary and my fare and expenses for travelling to different countries is the hope that I will find out about people's illnesses, that I will try to free them of infectious diseases forever—isn't that so?' He was silent for the next few minutes, obviously quite agitated.

After the drinks arrived, he asked, 'How long have you been working at this hotel?'

'Not very long,' I had to confess.

'Have you been to the bar?' he asked.

'I haven't been on bar duty yet, though I've been there.'

I wasn't prepared for what he asked next. 'There's something I'm very keen to know,' he said. 'Could you tell me whether the bar in your hotel has always been at the same spot, or whether it's been at different sites at different times?'

'Why? Our bar isn't badly located, is it?' I said. 'Do you have any suggestions? I can convey them to Mr Marco Polo.'

He shook his head. 'No, no—all I want to know is exactly how long the bar has been this way.'

That was difficult to say, for the hotel had changed many hands since Simpson sold it. Every new owner had made changes according to his whims, with the result that nothing of Shahjahan Hotel except its outer shell had remained unchanged.

'I don't want to go too far back,' said Sutherland. 'Say, the end of the last century—when barmaids used to sell drinks at the counter.'

That was when the bearer informed me that Bose-da was looking for me.

I asked for him to come to Sutherland's room—since he'd been around much longer than I had, he might be able to satisfy Sutherland's curiosity.

'Did you get a good night's sleep?' Bose-da asked Sutherland as soon as he came in. 'If possible, I'll try to get you a room on the second floor today.' But Sutherland wasn't interested, for he was keen on going back to the olden days of Shahjahan. Having heard me out, Bose-da asked me, 'Do you know Mr Hobbs?'

I had met Mr Hobbs briefly when he had come to a dinner party and spent a few minutes with us at the reception counter.

'If you really want to find out something about the hotel, you should go to him,' said Bose-da.

Sutherland asked, 'Do you know whether there were ever barmaids in this hotel?'

'I've seen plenty of them in English films,' Bose-da said. 'Young ladies handing out drinks at the bar. But oddly enough, I've never seen any in the hotels here.'

I said, 'Yes, indeed, there are all these beautiful women at the cabaret, we spend a fortune on these dance and music professionals, but we haven't put a lady at the bar.'

'Not a bad idea,' said Bose-da, 'Worth sounding Marco Polo out.'

Sutherland smiled sadly. 'I'm afraid it won't help even if your manager likes the idea, because it's illegal to employ women at bars in this country. Your excise laws say that bars which are given a licence to sell liquor cannot employ women without the permission of the government.'

His knowledge of our excise laws surprised me. I wondered whether he had got into some trouble with the police somewhere in India, thanks to the prohibition laws, and had acquainted himself on the bar licence laws in different states.

'Have you ever read your bar licence?' he asked.

We'd seen the yellow piece of paper preserved carefully behind the bar, but none of us had ever felt the slightest interest in finding out what it said.

'If you had you'd have known that the government has given instructions not to sell any drinks at prices below five annas,' said Sutherland.

'Five annas! When does this law go back to?' Bose-da exclaimed.

'To those days when a bottle of Scotch cost one rupee and twelve annas. That was the time when Daniel Crawford was the most popular brand—if anybody died of cirrhosis of the liver they'd say that Mr So-and-so had succumbed to Daniel Crawford's disease.'

'Have you written a book on the bars of the world?' I could not help asking.

'Of course not,' Sutherland replied. 'If I do write anything, it will be about smallpox—I don't have time to waste writing about alcohol.'

I fixed an appointment with Hobbs over the telephone. Bose-da said, 'If I had the time I'd have come along as well, but you'd better take the doctor, Hobbs will be expecting you at about two-thirty.'

After we left Sutherland's room, I asked Bose-da, 'I hope no tongues will wag about my taking Sutherland out.'

'What tongues?' said Bose-da angrily. 'After doing my job to the best of my abilities, if I do something of my own sweet will, who has the right to comment? Has anyone been saying anything to you?'

'No, they haven't, but suppose I lost my job for breaking some rule?'

'Losing your job is not unusual here—I've seen many people come and go, I'm the only one who is constant. Like an age-old banyan tree I stay put. Nobody dares displace me. If anyone can let the cat out of the bag, it's Sata Bose—and let me tell you, if that fellow Jimmy tries to harm you, he'll get into trouble as well.' Bose-da was obviously quite worked up. He paused and continued, as though talking to himself, 'We don't count, do we? Those who have the means are letting their money rot. The rich are happy earning a little interest— they wake up at ten in the morning, have their tea, laze around for a while, have their lunch, go back to bed, go for a spin, get up for dinner, go back to bed. They add to nothing but their families. If only he had the opportunity Sata Bose could have shown people whether the made-in-Calcutta types can run a hotel or not. Those who are intelligent and can work hard have pawned everything in return for a few notes. And on the strength of borrowed money and our brawn, people around the world are changing not only their own fortunes but also the fortunes of their nephews and their sons-in-law.' Bose-da smiled ruefully. 'I know there's no point saying all this here. If I could have said it under the monument at Chowringhee, before a crowd of thousands, it might have helped, but will we ever get that opportunity?'

'So you're off to see old Hobbs?' Bose-da asked at lunch.

Officially, lunchtime began at twelve-thirty, but the employees started earlier. After their meal, they opened the

lunchroom door, whereupon the guests started pouring in—
the boxwallahs of Clive Street didn't have time to waste in the
afternoons!

Many of the hotel guests came a little later. Some of them
even spent some time at the bar before entering the lunchroom,
while others sent for Tobarak Ali, the 'wet boy' with the red
armband, as soon as they came in. A guest usually ordered cold
beer, and while he sipped it, the hot soup arrived. In the
distance, the band struck up a tune at Gomez's signal—five
musicians bent over their scores and started playing.

Gomez was the conductor—and Bose-da affectionately
referred to him as the bandmaster. His five musicians in tow,
he was the first to arrive for lunch every day.

'Set it up quickly,' Gomez called out to the chef, who
considered the employees' meals akin to feeding a charity line.

Seeing Gomez getting impatient, the chef said, 'I can't do
it if you're in such a hurry.'

'Then the Shahjahan Band will remain silent at lunch
today,' Gomez replied.

The chef professed great consternation and said, 'Oh, but
that will be a disaster—it's only to listen to the music that
Calcutta's citizens drop everything and come over to the
Shahjahan!'

Gomez wasn't one to give up easily. 'If you had an insight
into music, why would you be rattling pots and pans?' he
taunted Juneau, the chef.

The chef retorted, 'Maybe I don't understand music, but
I do know that even birds cannot sing on a full stomach. Music
on a full stomach is possible only in Shahjahan.'

Gomez turned to his band. 'You may start, boys,' he said,
whereupon, the devoted boys immediately started spooning
the soup into their mouths. Gomez now turned his attention
to the chef. 'That's where we differ from the birds—they don't
sing for their stomachs, but it's only for our livelihood that we
play in the middle of the afternoon.'

The argument might have continued, but Bose-da butted in. 'Mr Juneau, I'm a staunch Hindu and the two of you are hurting my religious feelings—our scriptures forbid us to talk at mealtimes, and at this rate a communal riot might erupt any moment!'

The argument dissolved into laughter, and Juneau gushed, 'Sata, will your stock of funny lines never run out?'

'My dear Juneau, my stock is like your fridge—ten cups of ice cream are always hidden at the bottom.'

Juneau guffawed heartily. 'Greedy! Greedy boys are not nice for hotel.' He clapped Bose-da affectionately on his back and disappeared into the kitchen, saying in Hindi, 'Get married, Bose. We can't do it, but your wife will be able manage you.'

'High hopes!' Bose-da answered, laughing as he ate. 'I won't get married, and you won't stop enjoying the wages of your sins.'

I listened to their conversation in amazement. The waiters seemed to be taking their time and suddenly Gomez looked at his watch, shocked—barely five minutes before the lunchroom doors were opened. He jumped up from his chair and said, 'Get up, boys, no more time.'

The five youngsters rose immediately, not a word on their lips. There was a small mirror in a corner of the room, and a board above it said, in English: 'Am I correctly dressed?' Someone with a strange sense of humour had taken the trouble of trying to scratch out the word 'correctly', so that at first glance the message read 'Am I dressed?' All of them took turns to stand before the mirror and adjust their ties, while Gomez waited for them at the door. As they marched out, he joined the end of the queue, swinging his arms like them.

Bose-da and I were left behind with Juneau.

'My dear departed mother,' Bose-da continued in his trademark light-hearted vein, 'told me before she died, "Satu, never leave a meal unfinished, even if the world's coming to an end."'

Juneau laughed and said, 'No one can match you—only a wife might someday.'

'Someone else will, too,' Bose-da said pointing at me. 'Very good boy—he deserves one of your special ice creams, so that he will never say anything bad about you.'

Juneau was more than happy to comply. Without bothering to call the bearer, he opened the refrigerator himself and brought out two cups. The ice cream was followed by coffee. Sipping it, Bose-da mused to himself, 'Barmaids! The thirsty guest's wine glass being filled by a beautiful woman with a lovely smile—wonderful! We had them here once—and if we had them today, the British and for that matter even the Bengalis, Marwaris, Gujaratis, Chinese, Japanese, Russians, young men, old men from Clive Street...they would all be pleased. The bar at Shahjahan would become even more prosperous—we would need many more bar stools, many more soda bottles would have to be opened, many more receipts would have to be made out, and much more money would be deposited in the bank. If the government increased taxes, we could have added insult to injury by raising liquor prices as well—how beautiful it would have been!'

Still talking to himself, he continued, 'Barmaids—that's too foreign a concept.' Then he turned to me, 'Now that you've had your ice cream, your brain must be cool enough. Give me an Indian version.'

I couldn't think of anything. 'There's the saqi in the Rubaiyat.'

'Rubbish, that's hardly Indian.'

Just as we were getting intoxicated with barmaids, Juneau said, 'There's a well-built man outside looking for both of you.' Rising in irritation from his chair, Bose-da said, 'Go find out who dares intrude into our haven.'

The intruder was none other than Sutherland. 'I'm going out for lunch,' he said, 'I just wanted to remind you before I left.'

'You can rest easy,' I reassured him. 'We'll definitely meet Mr Hobbs today.'

The person who would have been happiest to see this story being published as a book is no longer alive today. It was he who had unearthed the secrets of Chowringhee for me, it was he who had encouraged and inspired me, saying, 'Dig, and you'll strike gold.' But I wasn't been able to do it while he was alive and there was no proof anywhere in the city of the long years he had spent in Calcutta. A shop named after him had survived for some time as an intrinsic part of the history of Chowringhee, but, away from the public eye, even that shop had disappeared.

Many old-timers might remember Hobbs; even a few people from our generation might do so, but one day his memories will disappear from the minds of the busy citizens of this busy city.

Emerging from the hotel, we walked to the Esplanade. Beside me Sutherland said, 'I feel a little uncomfortable walking down this road. I seem to be stepping on some amazing chapter of history at every step. Hardly any witnesses to those times exist any more—there used to be so many mementoes of old Calcutta on these roads, but you people have destroyed them all.'

Turning to him, I said, 'There's still one witness—the lovely Raj Bhavan, behind a veil of thick greenery, which has seen a great deal over the ages.'

'There will come a day when, like a tape recorder, a past recorder will be available—we'll be able to sit before an old house and listen to its autobiography.'

'If only that were possible!'

'Don't give up hope,' he said. 'I'm sure we'll live long enough to see such a machine being invented. It won't be difficult to rescue the past—after all, nothing of what we do, say or even think goes waste, it only leaves one corner of the universe and accumulates in another.'

'Is that why the poet has said, "none of life's treasures can be discarded?"' I asked.

Smiling, he replied, 'The day we can make the mute past talk, the world will be transformed. Only historians will be in trouble; they might even lose their jobs. All that will be needed instead of research scholars and professors is an operator.' He laughed like a child.

Listening to him, who would guess that his subject was actually medicine, that it had nothing to do with history?

We saw a young man sitting on the pavement, with a parrot in a cage in front of him. 'What's this?' Sutherland asked in surprise.

'Future recorder,' I said with a smile. 'All the documents of the future are with him—you can find out everything here.'

Rubbing his hands together, he said, 'I fear the future very much—let's avoid this.'

Hobbs was waiting for us—his arms wide open in welcome.

'Barmaid?' The old man seemed to have gone back to some distant past at our question. 'Those days are lost forever, never to return. There's only one person who could have answered that question—Mrs Brockway, wife of Father Brockway of the Union Chapel,' he said almost to himself.

Sutherland shook his head. 'I tried to meet Frenner Brockway, the British MP and friend of India, because I was very keen on finding out about his mother, but I couldn't dig up anything. All I learnt was that his father had been a priest, and that he was born in Calcutta, which explained his great fondness for India.'

'Mrs Brockway was very concerned about Calcutta's barmaids,' said Hobbs. 'I've heard she used to weep for them. If it hadn't been for her, we might have been sitting at the bar of Shahjahan, or any other hotel, savouring a mug of beer or a round of whiskey being served by a woman even today.'

Sutherland said gravely but with a touch of embarrassment, 'I don't drink, though.'

'You don't!' Hobbs was astonished. 'Better be on your guard! If Gandhi-ji's disciples find out they won't let you go back home. They'll build you a dispensary in a shanty next to the Sabarmati or some other river, and you'll have to spend the rest of your life there.'

Sutherland smiled a little and said, 'That would be wonderful. I may not know much medicine, but from what I know I can tell that India needs lots of doctors now, lots of trained people.'

Hobbs came back to barmaids. 'Ah, those good old days!' Looking at me, he said, 'Let me test your general knowledge— tell me, when did ships start sailing through the Suez Canal?'

All I'd read in my geography textbook at school was that a Frenchman named Ferdinand de Lesseps had built the Suez Canal, but when he had done it, and when the waters of the Red Sea and the Mediterranean Sea had mingled, holding Europe and Asia in a close embrace, were things I had no idea about. Nor, for that matter, could I make out what the Suez Canal had to do with our story.

'Our story is intimately connected with the Suez Canal,' said Hobbs. 'Before it was built, those reckless adventurers went around the Cape of Good Hope to come to Calcutta. In the absence of hotels they spent the nights in barges at Chandpal Ghat. No blue-eyed beauty came running across the ocean to entertain them, so if the craving got really bad, they had to quench their thirst with the strictly Indian variety.

'Then, in 1762, William Parker decided to open a bar for the entertainment of Calcutta's gentlemen. Only alcohol was on the agenda, barmaids were not part of the scheme of things. The board, too, granted a licence, on the condition that the house couldn't be kept open in the daytime, for if it was, the younger lot would start playing truant.

'Many more bars came up after that, but it was barmen, or khidmatgars as they were called, all the way. Even Le Galle, who had taken the contract for wining and dining the barrister and his cronies during the trial of Nanda Kumar, didn't have barmaids in his tavern. He charged two-and-a-quarter rupees for every lunch and dinner. Mohan Prasad ordered that the meals be sent to the court—sixteen lunches and sixteen dinners every day. We know of Nanda Kumar's hanging, but haven't kept track of Le Galle. After the verdict was delivered, Nanda Kumar became immortal by going to the gallows but there was no trace of Mohan Prasad. Eventually, Le Galle had to go to court to recover his dues for the lunches and dinners he had served—he had to sue to get his six hundred and twenty-nine rupees.'

Hobbs handed cups of coffee to us.

We were about to protest, but he said, 'I'm not anti-India, but those who are under the impression you don't get coffee anywhere in the world except at the India Coffee House should pay me a visit.'

Without sparing a glance at our bewildered faces, Hobbs continued, 'It was after the Suez Canal was opened that eighteen-year-old Englishwomen, with nectar in their breasts and wine glasses in their hands, started coming to Calcutta. Which is why restaurants and hotels in Charnock's city began to flourish after the canal was opened in 1869.'

As he spoke, Hobbs slowly went back to the past when barmaids used to stand at the bar and serve drinks—not local women, but authentic Englishwomen. Newspaper advertisements would announce: 'Our new barmaids will be arriving in Calcutta by such-and-such ship from London.' Some would come on six-month contracts and others on two-year ones. The British representatives of Shahjahan and Hotel de Europe would write, 'Have located a beautiful girl, do you want her?' The reply would be sent immediately: 'We have

great faith in your taste—we hope you won't let us down
before Calcutta's customers!' Back would come the answer:
'I've been sending barmaids not just to Calcutta but to major
ports round the world for many years, and I've never heard a
word of criticism. Girls I've chosen have turned around the
fortunes of hotels—they've doubled sales at the bar. To tell
you the truth, my only concern is that hotels in Calcutta can't
hold on to the girls. Before their contracts run out, the girls
ensconce themselves elsewhere. That harms me—they promise
to send me a part of their salaries, but I don't get it if they
change jobs.'

'Have you seen any of these barmaids?' I couldn't resist
asking.

Hobbs laughed. 'Do you think I'm a spring chicken? And
do you suppose I came to Calcutta just the other day? If I'd
come a little earlier I might have even seen a slave or two.'

'Slaves!'

'You youngsters know nothing. Even halfway through the
last century, human beings used to be sold in Calcutta. English
ladies and gentlemen and even the local gentry would buy boys
and girls from Murgihata and bring them home. If they ran
away, they would place advertisements in the papers, promising
rewards.'

'I only hope those who served drinks at the hotel weren't
slaves too,' Sutherland said seriously.

The old man's face lit up. 'No, as far as the law was
concerned they were certainly not slaves—but the hardships
that I've seen and heard of could add a new word to the
dictionary. I can show you an old advertisement for your very
own Shahjahan Hotel.' Hobbs rose from his chair and brought
out an exercise book from his cupboard. It had newspaper
clippings in it going back many decades. Turning the pages, he
stopped at one. 'You may not believe me, but I have proof.'

We read the advertisement. The manager of Shahjahan

Hotel had announced proudly: 'On 22 September, Miss Marian Booth and Miss Jane Grey will be arriving at Kidderpore on the *SS Hawaii*. They will not hesitate to spare any effort for the pleasure and well-being of the guests of Shahjahan Hotel!' Underneath, bold letters informed readers: 'To maintain the hard-earned reputation of Shahjahan Hotel, the two beauties will be kept under lock and key during the day and after duty hours at night!'

I was feeling a little embarrassed knowing that we were probably intruding on Hobbs's time and work, but Sutherland didn't seem bothered—and nor, for that matter, did Hobbs himself. Shutting the exercise book, he said, 'Lucky I kept this clipping. I had never imagined such a trivial beginning would lead to such momentous happenings. I knew Silverton, the manager of Shahjahan, rather well. In fact, he bought the hotel eventually. The Armenian Christian Gregory Apkar had stayed at Shahjahan Hotel once upon a time. Those were dark days for Shahjahan—the owner didn't pay any attention, the building was crumbling, provisions weren't available. Apkar had quarrelled with the staff, and then written a letter to the manager on the hotel letterhead: "If anyone can identify a hotel worse than this one, I'll give him a reward of five hundred rupees."

'Silverton had rushed to see him. "We're very sorry—but we're very hard up," he had apologized. "If we weren't, we could have shown you what a good hotel is like."

'This was probably the first time in history that a guest became so angry with a hotel that he purchased it. Apkar obviously didn't want for money. He wrote a cheque for the entire amount and made Silverton his working partner.'

'"What was the response from the advertisement like?" I asked Silverton.

'"Very good—lots of people are waiting with bated breath for the twenty-second of September, making enquiries to find out if the barmaids will start work the same evening; the connoisseurs are just too impatient."

'Silverton invited me to the bar on the evening of the twenty-second. Hoteliers normally don't invite people, but my relationship with Silverton was a little different, he did invite me occasionally. That night the bar and dining room at Shahjahan couldn't have held one more guest. Young men with the best of manners and the worst of intentions were present—but the new girls didn't take the stage.

"'Hasn't the ship arrived, then?" many of those present started asking.

"'It has, and so have they, but they're very tired today," Silverton said with folded hands.

"'We're not exactly as fresh as roses ourselves," quipped one of them. "After a hard day's work, we've ignored the rain and even got soaked to make it here."

'With a show of great humility, Silverton said, "It's Shahjahan Hotel's privilege that you haven't forgotten it despite the inconvenience caused to you. Keeping in mind the state of your bodies and hearts, Miss Dickson has brought some of our best bottles from the cellar, specially for you."

'The young men started chuckling. "We demand old wine from new hands."

'The middle-aged Miss Dickson stood at a distance, sour-faced. Next to her stood a barman built like a rock, a small brass bucket of ice in his hand—he looked as though his job was to crush the ice, but that was an excuse, for he was actually a bodyguard. Nobody bought drinks from Miss Dickson that night—no one seemed interested in a bargirl who looked like a coiled, shrivelled length of rope.

"'Should we wait?" the customers asked. "The new ladies could have a rest and then come to the bar."

"'I'm sorry, they're so tired that they must have fallen asleep by now," Silverton explained.

'He was quite agitated by then. The young men shouted, "If necessary we can go and request them. And if that's a problem, we're off—Lola is waiting for us at the Adelphi Bar."

'They left in a group, as Silverton stood by with a long face and Miss Dickson stared at the wood on the counter, refusing to take her eyes off it.

'"What's wrong?" I asked Silverton.

'He took me to his room and said, "Let's have dinner by ourselves in my room. I'm in trouble."

'I heard all about it in his room—it was trouble all right. The lady named Marian Booth who had disembarked was at least forty-five years old. Silverton had discovered this at the jetty itself, though he hadn't been able to say anything. Jane Grey hadn't disappointed, though. Now Silverton was up to his ears in trouble—if it got out that he had spent a fortune to bring an old woman over, Shahjahan's future would be doomed.

'The whole thing did get out later—the hotel had been cheated. The girl whom the agent had chosen, spoken to and even seen off at the ship had substituted the old woman for herself in the hold of the ship at some point and made off. When the switch was discovered in Calcutta, it was too late to do anything.

'Shaking with rage, Silverton called for the woman and asked, "You're Marian Booth? Are you telling the truth?"

'She protested in a shrill voice. "What? You dare doubt the name my father gave me?"

'"And you're twenty-five," Silverton said through clenched teeth.

'"More or less," she replied.

'"Less, no doubt," he said, gnashing his teeth. "If you only knew how much damage you've done me. I don't even have the money to send you back and get someone else—and even if I could scrape together the money, there's no time. I've served notice on Miss Dickson, and Miss Grey can't possibly run such a large bar all by herself."

'I asked Silverton, "Since she is here, what can you do? Aren't there any middle-aged women in London bars?"

'I still clearly remember what he said in reply. Despite repeated usage it hasn't become stale, and it's probably the last word on this city: "Calcutta is Calcutta."

'"It might have worked in London," he said, "but it won't work here. Two old women had cheated two hotels on Chowringhee like this in the past. It would have cost a lot if their return fare and compensation, as stated in the contract, had to be paid. But they didn't go back—they set up shop in the shipping neighbourhood of Kidderpore."

'The old Miss Booth pleaded, "Give me a chance—I promise you sales won't go down."

'Silverton wasn't willing. He sent for Miss Grey. Poor Miss Grey had been tired out by the journey and had fallen asleep. Rubbing her eyes, the demure Jane came and stood before us, looking quite scared at first. I could read the hints of tragedy on her face even then.

'"Do you know how Miss Booth managed to pull the wool over everybody's eyes and turn up in Calcutta?" Silverton asked.

'Miss Grey didn't have the answer to that. With downcast eyes she said, "I was preoccupied—I was leaving home, without knowing if I would ever return."

'I simply couldn't fathom how this reticent, soft-spoken eighteen-year-old would work at the bar. Before leaving the room, she said, "I haven't met a kinder lady than Miss Booth—she looked after me throughout the voyage."

'A few days later, I heard that Miss Booth had joined the ranks of the lipsticked and rouged Kidderpore girls. And that hundreds of made-in-England gentlemen and made-in-India Bengali babus were thronging the Shahjahan bar to accept whiskey from Miss Grey's gentle hands. It was about these Bengali babus that Davy Carson had written in his song: "I very good Bengali babu/in Calcutta I long time e'stop".

'A friend of mine named Robbie—Robbie Adam—confirmed that I hadn't been wrong about Jane. He set eyes on her for the first time when he went to Shahjahan for supper, and saw for himself the plight of a girl from his own country in a Calcutta bar. It would have been better if he hadn't. He would have been spared plenty of misery; he wouldn't have had to go through the ordeals that the Creator had planned for him.

'"Have you seen the new girl at Shahjahan?" Robbie asked me. "She may not be a ravishing beauty, but she's very pleasing on the eye. Couldn't the poor girl have got a job in England? How can anyone come to Calcutta without knowing the ropes? Some top brass from Clive Street grabbed her hand last night, the barman shook him off with great difficulty. Someone else said, 'Give me company, come round to my table and drink with me.' If I hadn't prevented him he would probably have forced her out from behind the counter, and there would have been a scandal. Other customers at the bar would have got upset, all of them would have said, come and sit by me, I'm feeling lonely."

'Our Robbie hadn't become a complete Calcuttan as yet. He'd worked for one of the top firms on Clive Street for about a year, but he hadn't managed to get used to the language, manners or mores of Calcutta. I had no idea it was going to turn out this way. Some invisible attraction drew him to the Shahjahan every day. They couldn't have met in the daytime, since Silverton went to bed only after locking Jane up in her room. And she would be fast asleep, too—since her working hours began in the evening. And bars in those days didn't close at ten or eleven like they do now, they'd stay open till five in the morning. Through the drunken laughter, the sound of glasses tinkling and breaking, two hearts had quietly come close.'

Hobbs smiled and continued, 'I'm a businessman. Poetic

excesses don't appeal to me. But I must say there was
something poetic about their relationship. I believe they spoke
in a code: as she served his glass of whiskey, she would use
strong language; there was no way she could smile or say a few
sweet words—other customers would raise a rumpus. The
barman was possibly the only one who knew what was going
on. If there was a secret message to be passed, it was he who
conveyed it to Robbie. The poor barman didn't have a
moment of peace—while guests may have hesitated to make a
proposition to the barmaid directly, when it came to doing it
through the barman, they felt no embarrassment. Those who
frequented the bar would give him a rupee and a letter to hand
over to the lady. I heard from Jane later that on a single night
she got thirty letters, ten of them proposals for marriage. "My
poor barman—if he can earn thirty rupees a day, I don't
mind," she told me.'

Hobbs paused and swallowed. Ruminating over those
distant memories, he said, 'I warned Robbie, though. I told
him, "Don't forget, Calcutta is Calcutta."'

Sutherland seemed to be in a stupor. 'Indeed,' he said
softly. 'Calcutta is indeed Calcutta.'

'Even when Jane and Robbie were planning to get
married, I told Robbie, "Don't forget, Calcutta is Calcutta. Go
to the hotel for your drinks and your fun, nobody will have a
thing to say. But don't marry a barmaid."'

I was amazed—so you actually ran the risk of being
ostracized on account of your marriage even in English society?
And to think that for ages we Indians have been blamed for
being conservative in our outlook.

Hobbs began his story again. 'Robbie brushed aside all my
objections. "I've promised her," he said. "I have to rescue Jane
from the hellhole of Shahjahan Hotel." Jane didn't object
either—she was dying to get out of Shahjahan. It may have
sounded like a fairy tale—the way she had found her lover

while serving at the bar—but it had indeed happened. Now she could only look longingly at the calendar.

'Silverton was taken aback by the rumours. Drawing Jane aside, he said, "I hope the rumours I'm hearing are untrue. We're happy with your work here—you are the envy of all the barmaids of Calcutta. I'm going to raise your salary in the next contract."

'"Do you have any objection to employing married women?" Jane asked.

'"Married women! Jane, are you mad? How can married women work as barmaids?"

'"Why not? What's the problem?" she asked.

'"I don't have a problem, our patrons do. They'll be insulted, they might even boycott the Shahjahan bar," he said.

'Jane's immediate response was, "I won't sign the contract, then—I'll have to give up my job."

'Silverton tried to tempt her, he asked her to think it over. He was willing to give her a commission on sales. Jane still didn't agree—she hadn't come to Calcutta to make money. Reduced to abject poverty back home, she had come here only to earn a decent livelihood, but now she had seen for herself how things were.

'"I won't interfere in your private life," Silverton said. "That business about keeping you locked up was only for publicity—I'll give you the key if you like, you can do whatever you want."

'Jane said, "There's no need to stay behind locked doors any more, you can give that opportunity to the new barmaid."

'Silverton tried to scare her. "You're inviting disaster, Jane, you have no idea how dangerous this city is. Those who beg and plead with you for a glimpse of your sweet smile at the Shahjahan bar are transformed once they're out on the road. They have their own society, with rules even stricter than those of the Hindus. Women who stay up all night selling liquor have no place there."

'Jane smiled and said, "I'm not asking them to make room for me! As long as the person in my heart also has me in his, I have nothing more to ask.'

'Silverton met Robbie as well. He told him, "Once a barmaid, always a barmaid. We pay a fortune to bring in women from England, and then the Adelphi and Hotel de Europe lure them away with more money—only to throw them out when their youth is on the wane, when their eyes lose their lustre. These women then get their tailors to tighten their clothes and queue up at Kidderpore. At the docks, Africa, Asia and Europe mingle and become one; the British and the African stand shoulder to shoulder."

'Robbie said, "Since I have no intention of writing a book on the subject, I'd rather not know anything about it."

'As a last resort, Silverton called on Robbie's boss. "I see," said the manager, "that girl with a naughty smile. How many duplicates of the keys to her door do you have?"

'To Robbie he said, "Hindus don't bring into their bedrooms the shoes they go out in. If you need to, use a separate pair of bathroom slippers in your room."

'Robbie said, "When setting sail from London, I was told that wherever he goes an Englishman always respects other people's privacy."

'His manager didn't say anything more, except to remind him that as we sow, so we reap. Robbie thanked him for the advice and left. And then, on an auspicious day, having served out her contract at Shahjahan, Jane went to church to link her lifeline to Robert Adam's.

'There wasn't much of a crowd at the Dharmatala Church that day. Jane had no friends, except Miss Dickson, who was under lock and key on the top floor of Shahjahan Hotel. And thanks to the social scandal perpetrated by Robbie's wedding, none of the boxwallahs of Clive Street could make it. I wasn't very familiar with that set yet, which was perhaps why I went to the wedding, and practically forced Silverton to come along with me. "After all, one of your employees is getting married," I told him.

'After they set up home after marriage, I visited them one morning. They welcomed me effusively—Robbie brought out a bottle of brandy. Watching her husband pour our drinks, Jane burst out laughing, and I joined in. "You served me hundreds of times at the Shahjahan counter, now let me try to pay back the debt bit by bit."

'Jane looked as though she had been freed from prison after all this time—her happiness knew no bounds. As we sipped the brandy, I drank to the newly wed couple's health. As she knitted, Jane told me, "Since you've travelled a long way, why don't you have lunch with us? Of course, I should have given you proper notice."

'"That's the problem with you—you didn't give Silverton much notice, either!" said Robbie.

'Jane pretended to be angry saying, "Incompetent people have no problem getting released on short notice. No owner would hesitate a moment to get rid of useless people like me."

'Robbie said, "If everyone were a jeweller, Hamilton and Company of Old Court House Street wouldn't have become so famous."

'"I can't see why you have a weakness for Hamilton," said Jane. Turning to me, she said, "Please make him understand— he's deposited an entire month's salary in their hands to get me a diamond brooch. Isn't that a bit too much?"

'"It's only my fault, is it?" Robbie answered immediately. "If you're so unhappy with Hamilton, why did you have to get the silver teapot for me from them?"

'Taken aback, Jane said, "That's different—I was trying to cure like with like, trying to use tea to drive out liquor."

'I can't forget the attention they lavished upon me that day. When the conversation veered round to music, Robbie said, "She used to play the piano, you know—I want to buy her one if I can."

'A few days later, I heard of a good piano for sale. I was thinking of informing them, but before I could, they turned up at my house. As soon as I saw them I said, "I've tracked down a wonderful piano."

'Jane's face darkened, while Robbie looked like he hadn't slept all night. "We probably cannot afford one now," he said.

"What's the matter?"

"I've lost my job."

"Why? Have you quarrelled with the manager?"

"No—but by marrying a woman who used to serve liquor to strangers all night at a bar, I'm supposed to have lowered the prestige of the company. Having an employee like me would adversely affect sales and business."

'I couldn't believe that an Englishman could lose his job in this manner in Calcutta. But Robbie held out the letter written in the manager's own hand.

'Jane said anxiously, "What do we do now?"

"Look for another job," I comforted them. "There's no shortage of firms in Calcutta, surely."

'But even if there were many employers, it wasn't easy getting a job, as we discovered within a few days. Robbie did the rounds of many companies, but the senior officers jumped out of their skins when they set eyes on him—as though he had been convicted for murder and was looking for a job after being released from jail. They would offer him a seat and say, "Oh yes, we've heard of you—you're the person who ran away with the barmaid at Shahjahan."

"I didn't run away with her—I married her," Robert would protest in a stricken voice.

"Oh, I see, not kidnapping, not an elopement, just plain and simple marriage."

'There wasn't a single job to be had. Gradually Robbie

realized that he wouldn't get a job—no company in Calcutta would employ him. Whatever savings he had were running out, so they had to give up their beautifully decorated home and move to a smaller place.

'"I'll try to get a job," said Jane.

'At that time women had very few opportunities to work. There were no typists or telephone operators. They could become ladies' dressmakers or hairdressers, and set up shop on Park Street. But all that had to be learnt, how else did one dare make dresses or cut hair? Still, I sent Jane to one or two people for a job, but Robbie wasn't willing at all. People in those days weren't as modern as you lot are—the very thought of their wives working made their heads reel. "Don't be so impatient," he said, "I still have some money in the bank."

'Now Jane discovered that even if she did get a job she wouldn't be able to take it—she was pregnant. Robbie came to see me quite often, which was how I kept track of them. "I had no idea that the lords and masters of Calcutta had so many punishments in store for us," he said. "But the two of us will see this to the end, and we'll live happily and comfortably right under their noses. I didn't know marrying a barmaid was a crime—hasn't anyone in Calcutta ever married a hotel girl before?"

'"They have," I said. "You have Sergeant Oakley, who married Peggy. Calcutta's policemen used to do the rounds of the bars every night, and one night Sergeant Oakley arrested Peggy to maintain law and order, but later the same sergeant became a prisoner at the hands of Peggy. There's nothing in the government's laws to prevent marriage, so they're living quite happily. Both their sons are going to school, and not only did he not lose his job, he had the good fortune to be promoted."

'Eventually I managed to get Robbie an agency for textiles. Mr Street from Manchester had come to Calcutta on business and put up at Shahjahan. I had a nodding acquaintance with him, on the strength of which I told him, "Take Robbie on—you needn't give him a salary, he'll work on commission."

'Even those terms were a boon to Robbie. He'd be on his feet all day long with samples of the textiles, going to Barabazar in the morning, returning home for whatever frugal lunch Jane had cooked, and then setting off in a different direction. The company's cloth material for umbrellas was very famous—Robbie even gifted me an umbrella—but how many umbrellas could one sell in a year?

'Not too many, which meant that the commission wasn't much either—so low, in fact, that you couldn't employ a bearer and a cook on it. Jane had to do everything herself. By the time Jane's delivery day drew near, they had fallen on even harder days, living in a ramshackle flat on Williams Lane. There was a priest next door, whom Mrs Brockway knew quite well, Father um...well I can't remember the name now. Both Mrs Brockway and her priest husband used to visit them regularly during their hardship.

'When I went to see Jane, I found her in rags—a woman who had spent her nights in a palace like Shahjahan, who was used to walking only on soft carpets. The flat had two rooms, the plaster was peeling off, exposing the bricks underneath. The same woman whom waiters used to escort carefully to the dining room and whose every comfort was attended to had to cook for herself today, dragging her sickly body around to keep things in order. Shahjahan Hotel had retreated a long way into the distance, and the woman who used to serve at the bar, dispensing her smile like pearls, along with the whiskey, brandy, dry gin, rum and vermouth, was lost. Jane probably read my mind, for she said, "I'll never be able to forgive Shahjahan, even though I found my husband there."

'"Why?" I asked.

'She began sobbing as she said, "Without informing you,

I went to them for a job, telling them that I was prepared to work at the bar again—only, they shouldn't lock me up in the afternoon. I wouldn't eat at the hotel either, and I'd come back home as soon as I was through. I asked them to let me work at least till a new girl arrived from England—they too are having trouble without someone to help out. Silverton made a face and said, 'If you want to stay unlocked go to Kidderpore. Having a married woman as a barmaid is a folly not just I but no hotel in Calcutta would commit. Once you leave Shahjahan, you have no choice but to end up in Kidderpore.''

'Jane was still in tears, but she dried her eyes on hearing Robbie's footsteps. Having scoured Barabazar, Dharmatala and Shyambazar all day, he was exhausted, his clothes soaked with perspiration. He hadn't been able to sell anything, or even get payment for what he had sold earlier. And now the month was drawing to a close, which meant that accounts would have to be sent to England.

'Drawing him aside, I said to him, "Run away—you'll get a job in Madras or Bombay."

'He didn't agree. Jane probably guessed what I was saying, and told me, "Never—we have to stay in Calcutta. We're going to give them a fitting reply. We're not going to be down and out all our lives—we'll take a flat on Russell Street again, and then we'll host a banquet at Shahjahan. We'll invite all of them—we won't leave Calcutta until we've celebrated our silver wedding anniversary at Shahjahan Hotel.'

'Robbie put his arms around Jane. "Right you are, Jane," he said.

'Their optimism, despite their extreme hardship, brought tears to my eyes. I prayed fervently for their wishes to come true. If only I'd known that the tears had just begun, that the deluge was yet to come. I didn't see it for myself though, I heard about it from their neighbour, the priest.

'"Something terrible has happened," he said. "Your friend Robbie Adams has smallpox."

"'Where are they?" I asked.

"'At their home on Williams Lane. He can't be allowed to stay there, he should be sent to the infectious diseases hospital. Who will look after him? Who will take care of him? And most important, where will they get the money? Jane refuses to listen, even in her condition she's by him all day. The poor thing fainted last night."

'Friends warned me, "Smallpox! Don't go within half-a-mile of it, if you want to help send some money through the priest." But I simply couldn't stay away, and walked down Bowbazar Street to their place. I could smell phenol and medicine from a distance, but didn't dare enter. The priest must have been inside, looking after Robbie, applying olive oil with a brush on the scabs—it seemed as though someone had set Robbie's body on fire, twisting it like a lamb on a spit.

'And Jane! In her maternity coat, shopping bag in hand, she was probably on her way to the market when she saw me and stopped. I could barely recognize her. Was this the same person for whom the city's well-heeled gentry had once crowded the bar at Shahjahan? For whom the applause rang out, for whom inebriated young men burst into song, because of whom the sale of liquor at Shahjahan went up?

"'Mr Hobbs! What a surprise," she forced the words out.

"'I came to see how Robbie is," I said with bowed head.

"'I'm sure he'll get better, Father prayed for him in church last night. The local Hindu boys are very nice—they may not go to Shahjahan or Wilson's Hotel, but they're gentlemen. They've all gone to pray to the Firinghee Kali today—I tried to give them some money, but they wouldn't take it. They raised it themselves, and told me, 'After Robbie gets better and gets a job, you can bake us a cake—just like the English cakes which the gentlemen have with their tea, which the ladies bite into and giggle.'"

"'If you don't mind," I said, "some money..."

'She shook her head, saying, "I still have the diamond brooch from Hamilton. And I'd saved some money from my year's work at Shahjahan—Robbie never touched that, I still have it."

'The local boys appeared from nowhere, saying, "Why do you need to go to the market, Mem-boudi, what are we here for?" They grabbed the shopping bag from her hands. "We'll do the shopping—but no fish, strictly vegetarian, or else the goddess will be displeased," they said. "And tonight you must sleep tight, we're going to look after him all night—you needn't worry, we'll wake you if we have the slightest problem."

'Jane said, "Impossible, my boys. You're angels, but you mustn't come anywhere near this dangerous disease—you have people at home, and it isn't a friendly disease at all."

'One of the boys laughed. "Do you think we're fools? We've got the goddess in our grip, we won't fall ill. We have our Indian medicine," they said, rolling up their sleeves to show her some herb tied to their arms with a thread. "We've brought some for you as well—have a bath and tie these on your arm."

'Not another word did I get with her—the boys practically dragged her away. Later, I heard Robbie was worse. Despite the local boys' reluctance, he had to be taken to the hospital, where he now lay practically unconscious. The boys hadn't given up their tug-of-war with the god of death though—outsiders weren't allowed into the ward, but they handed over flowers from the temple to the ward boy every day. There was no knowing who would win the tug-of-war, but the local boys had at least managed to postpone the outcome. Every day, after they returned from the hospital, they went to Jane and gave her as much news about Robbie as they had been able to get. She could no longer go out—she lay on the bed and listened to their accounts. They said, "We know how you feel, Mem-boudi, but there's nothing to worry about."

'She wept inconsolably, saying, "Who are you people? Why are you doing all this for us?"'

'The boys were nonplussed by her question. "Why are we doing this? Oh, only because Saheb-dada is ill—or else we wouldn't have been doing anything, we'd have stolen guavas from the priest's trees."'

'It was from them that I got more news. I was on my way to see Jane, when I saw them standing at the head of the road with glum faces. They moved aside as soon as they saw me, whispering fearfully among themselves. I couldn't meet Jane at home—there was no one there.'

'"Go and see Father," the boys said. One of them took me to the priest. He seemed to be busy so I waited for a while. "Oh, Mr Hobbs! Have you heard?" the priest asked me when he came out. I said I hadn't heard anything so far.'

'"My wife is trying to get the baby to have some milk," he said. "I've got hold of a wet nurse with great difficulty."'

'"What do you mean?" I was stunned.'

'"It's not their fault, it really isn't. They're afraid to come to me. I know that in the eyes of the Almighty they have done no wrong. But they could have asked me, I talk to the doctors every day, I could have told them."'

'I heard the whole story from him.'

Sutherland and I listened to Hobbs's narrative, spellbound. 'That day, too, the neighbourhood boys went to see Robbie with flowers from the temple—that is, they went up to the ward, where it said: NO ADMISSION. As on other days, they gave the ward boy a few coins they had saved, asking him to put the flowers under Robbie's bed.

'"Is he a relative?" the ward boy asked.

'"No, he's not—he lives in our neighbourhood. He's as poor as we are, Mem-boudi eats the same food as we do—what can they do, they have no money."

'"I can tell you then," the ward boy shook his head and

said, "since he isn't related to you. Number thirty-two has lost his eyes—the doctor checked on him this morning."

"'Blind! You mean he'll never see again?" The boys' eyes filled with tears. "Suppose we collected enough money and brought the specialist who charges eight rupees a visit?"

'The ward boy had disappeared by then. They didn't want to tell Jane at first.

"'How was he today?" she asked.

'They tried to lie, but they weren't used to lying. Without speaking, they wiped their eyes, one of them actually started weeping. An unconscious Jane was brought to the priest's home. And that very night she gave birth to a son, a premature baby. In the early hours of the morning, the priests knelt and prayed to the Almighty for the dying Jane. When she died, before the night was out, leaving the boys of Williams Lane in tears, the bar at Shahjahan hadn't closed yet, the patrons must still have been shouting, "Hey miss, bring the whiskey and soda."

'The priest was annoyed. "Who told you he's gone blind?" he'd asked the boys. "Rubbish! One eye, only one, has been damaged, the other's been spared miraculously, it's all right."

'But it was too late—Jane's lifeless body had already been covered with a white sheet.

"'If there's no objection, we'd like to be the pallbearers, we'd like to do everything," the boys said.

'The priest said, "You must be present, but there's a lot more to a Christian funeral—we'll be in trouble unless we ask Llewellyn and Company, they've been doing it for years."

'The local boys walked down to Llewellyn, undertakers, on Chowringhee the same night. Meanwhile, Robbie was recovering. His fever was subsiding, and so was the unbearable agony, as the sores dried. He seemed to have forgotten everything during his illness, but now it was all coming back, including the fact that he had left Jane in a broken-down flat on Williams Lane.

"'Where's my wife?" he asked.

"'Who?" the ward boy enquired.

"'The lady—my wife," Robbie said.

"'No one's allowed in here," the doctor tried to explain to Robbie.

'But his heart refused to take no for an answer, and he started crying.

'At other times he went nearly mad and said, "I understand, she doesn't want to come. The lovely barmaid of Shahjahan made a big mistake marrying me—she must have gone away, Silverton must have taken her back."

'The doctors said, "You're being unfair to your wife—she comes to the hospital gates every day."

'In the afternoon, Robbie asked the ward boy, "Do you see a lady standing at the gates every day?"

"'No sir, no lady comes this way," the ward boy replied.

'Deeply hurt, Robbie broke down. Hearing this, the doctors were afraid. Completely untrue, they said, she comes to see us frequently.

"'I don't understand," Robbie said in confusion. "Even if you won't allow her to come near me, why can't she write to me? Will you ask her to write to me?"

'Peeping in through the window, the local boys could see him crying, waiting for a letter day after day, asking whoever came his way, "Is there a letter for me? Has my wife Jane Adam of Williams Lane written to me?"

'The priest heard the story from the boys and talked things over with the doctors. "Only you can do it, Father," the doctors said. "Only you can explain everything to him—the ward is open to you."

'The priest was used to such responsibilities. He had brought succour and comfort to many a suffering soul, but not this time. Though he broke the news of Jane's death very gently, Robbie collapsed the moment he heard. The same night his fever went up. He dashed the glass of milk to the floor, refusing to eat anything. The doctors spared no effort, but to no avail.

'In the darkness of the night, the local boys went once more to Llewellyn. From the hospital the cortege made its way directly to the cemetery on Lower Circular Road. The boys had no money—they had bought a large wreath for their mem-boudi; they borrowed money to buy a cheaper one for Robbie and put it on the hearse. I don't know what happened after that. The priest went back home soon afterwards, taking the newborn baby with him.'

Hobbs finished his story. I wasn't able to fight back my tears. But Sutherland didn't cry—in fact, he showed no signs of being perturbed. Doctors are probably like that—encountering death on an everyday basis, they don't consider it unusual. Rising, he held out his hand and said, 'Thank you, Mr Hobbs. Thank you, indeed, sir.'

Outside, he didn't say a word. I was in no state of mind to talk, either. The offices had closed for the day—the trams and buses were packed, people were on their way back home.

Sutherland looked at his watch and said, 'I hope you don't have anything special to do.'

I was a little put out at his manner of speaking—as if it was part of my job to escort him around.

'I'll be on counter duty soon,' I said, 'Sata Bose has been manning the counter for hours.'

Paying no attention, he only asked, 'Do you know Williams Lane?'

'I do.'

'What about the Lower Circular Road cemetery?'

'That, too.'

We returned to the hotel, but Sutherland asked me to wait at the gate. He buttonholed Bose-da at the counter and said something to him.

I was on my way to the counter when Sutherland turned back. Bose-da waved, holding a pencil in his hand, and signalled to me to accompany Sutherland—he would stand in for me.

I couldn't quite make Sutherland out. He had asked me to accompany him, but he seemed to have forgotten all about me—as though he had booked a professional guide from the tourist office for sixteen rupees. He seemed to be in a daze, all his senses seemed to have been numbed by the mysteries of the enigmatic Orient.

We got off our taxi at the head of Williams Lane. At the Bowbazar Street crossing, there were a few urchins playing on the road. 'Who are they?' Sutherland asked me with a gesture.

'Local boys,' I said.

It seemed to me for some reason that the local boys from the distant past, who went to Llewellyn to inform them about the funerals, were still standing at the head of the road. But where had those old landmarks disappeared? We couldn't even spot the house where such a poignant drama had been played out.

'Perhaps the house has disappeared from Williams Lane,' said Sutherland. 'Perhaps a new building has come up in its place.'

The locals too did not seem to know. A little beggar boy was filling a tin at a roadside hydrant when he suddenly fell down and burst into tears. I hadn't expected what followed—Sutherland ran to the boy and picked him up; not content with that, he clasped the child to his breast.

'What on earth are you doing? Your clothes will get soiled, and besides, he has a bad sore on his leg.'

Seeing the foreigner pick up a little beggar boy, some people came running. Sutherland paid no attention to them. Wiping the boy's running nose with his own handkerchief, he asked in halting Hindi, 'Where's your daddy? Your mummy?'

The boy pointed towards Sealdah Station and then, suddenly feeling scared, he struggled out of the doctor's arms and ran away, probably afraid that he was about to be taken away. Sutherland stood like a rock. In the near-darkness of the evening, I saw him wipe his eyes with a corner of the handkerchief he had used to wipe the boy's nose.

From Williams Lane we went directly to the Lower Circular Road cemetery. By then darkness had gained ground, as though it had graduated from a temporary job to a quasi-permanent one. A few gardeners were selling flowers at the entrance. One of them came forward and said, 'Flowers?'

I had no money, but Sutherland bought some.

Flowers in hand, we entered that silent city of the dead. We couldn't see a thing—there could well have been snakes or scorpions. Sutherland had a torch in his pocket, but how much light could a mere torch provide? In this quiet gathering of so many souls it was no longer possible to locate the former bargirl of Shahjahan—who knew in which corner of this enormous expanse the boys of Williams Lane had laid her to sleep forever? None of them was probably alive any more, but Shahjahan Hotel lived on, eternally young, beckoning the hungry, the thirsty and the lustful with its bewitching charm.

There was a tree before us. Placing the flowers beside it, Sutherland stood silently. And it seemed to me as though Hobbs were standing behind us, murmuring to himself:

Gone away are the Kidderpore girls,
With their powered faces and their curls,
Gone away are those sirens dark,
Fertile kisses, but barren of heart
Blowing alternately hot and cold
Steadfastly sticking to all they got
Filling a bevy of sailor boys
With maddening hopes of synthetic joys.

Given a choice, Sutherland would probably have stood there all night. But I had to get back to the hotel—Marco Polo may well have started screaming because he didn't know where I was.

'Dr Sutherland, perhaps we could go back now,' I said softly.

I hadn't expected him to respond with such a complete lack of courtesy. Through clenched teeth, he said, 'For heaven's sake, leave me in peace.'

I felt tears springing to my eyes—your whims are about to cost me my hard-earned job. And yet, I didn't have the nerve to complain. Suppose he told the manager, or wrote a letter of complaint? That would be the end of me. 'The customer is always right, the fault, if any, is yours,' as Bose-da had repeatedly reminded me.

I didn't say a word in the taxi on the way back. Sutherland didn't either. Without waiting for his thanks, I got out of the car and went to meet Bose-da at the counter.

Sutherland left for London early the next morning—I didn't meet him before he left. I never met him again. But if it had all ended there, perhaps I would never have been able to forgive him for his rudeness. A few days later, though, I got a letter from him:

My dear Shankar,
I cannot be at peace with myself until I write to you. When I recall how badly I behaved with you before leaving Shahjahan, I feel very sorry. Besides, by keeping the truth from Hobbs and you, I have also sinned in God's eyes. I had meant to apologize to you personally the next time I saw you, but my connections with India are over—the place I'm off to now on behalf of WHO is Tahiti; I hope to spend the few days left to me there.

I apologize for my conduct that evening. I've read and heard a lot of terrible things about Calcutta, but it's different with all of you. I should have told you that very day, but I couldn't. I was born in Williams Lane—my father's name was Robert Adam, my mother's, Jane Grey. The child whose life was saved thanks to the kindness of the local boys of Williams Lane, whom Father Sutherland took back to England with him, was also given the right to use the priest's name. That's why I had wanted to spend my last night in Calcutta in Shahjahan Hotel—thanks to your kindness, the dream was fulfilled.

I breathe a real sigh of relief to think that your bar no longer has barmaids. In my heart, I thank the wife of Father Brockway of Union Chapel—she spared many barmaids a lifetime of misery. She isn't alive any more, or else I would have met her. Unable to do anything else, I've written a letter to her worthy son, Frenner Brockway. The blessings of many unknown women are being showered on her.

I hope you understand now why I lost my composure that evening. Forgive me.

I remain

Yours sincerely

J.P. Sutherland

5

Sutherland's extraordinary story is just one of the many that still overwhelms me at times. I thank my stars—I've had my share of blows; I've frequently sent up silent complaints, impatient with the cruel tests set me by the Creator, but today I feel that my good fortune knows no bounds either. The storms I have encountered have repeatedly demolished the

walls of pettiness that surrounded me, bringing me out under
the open sky. Amidst extreme distress I have discovered the
world's hidden treasures in a small room of Shahjahan Hotel.
I wish I could share more of those riches with my readers—
alas, most of it is not suitable for publication. I've been privy
to the secrets of many a private soul in the quiet corners of
Shahjahan and though the writer in me wants to tell it all, the
human being in me refuses to let me. I am afraid I shall have
to limit my narrative of this world to what I was witness to
from the visitors' gallery, leaving out what was told to me in
confidence.

It's a world where sentiments have no value. The world in
which I moved about thanks to Byron, Marco Polo and Bose-
da was one where people were familiar with just two objects:
the wallet and the chequebook.

I still remember clearly the day Rosie returned to Shahjahan,
a leather case in her hand. Breakfast was over, and so was the
supervision of the lunch arrangements. Menu cards and wine
cards had been typed, cyclostyled and set out on the tables. In
other hotels, only the lunch card was typed afresh every day—
the same wine card was used over and over again. But at
Shahjahan even the red wine card was typed every day, with
the date mentioned in one corner. Next to the dining room,
we had a banquet hall where Rai Bahadur Sadasukhlal Goenka
was throwing a party later that day, to felicitate a top leader
from the capital.

The seating arrangement at this luncheon party was a
matter of complex calculations—in official circles, the hierarchy
of guests, known as the 'list of precedence', was scrupulously
maintained. In addition, there was an unwritten list of
precedence among Calcutta's private citizens, which hotel
owners and many housewives knew by heart. Since the
slightest of deviations from that list could lead to a hotel's sky-
high reputation biting the dust, we used to be quite nervous

of taking upon ourselves the responsibility for laying the places. Let the host seat his guests the way he wanted. As Bose-da put it, 'It's your turkey, carve it anyway you like—why should I put my life and job on the line!' Accordingly, the Rai Bahadur's secretary had arrived with the place cards and the RSVP file.

In Kashundia, I had never understood the mystery of RSVP. 'I couldn't either,' said Bose-da. 'In school we used to say it stood for rashogolla-sandesh-very-pleasing. If those letters appeared at the bottom of the invitation, it meant a major feast was in the offing.'

For the luncheon party, special menu cards had been designed on the instructions of the Rai Bahadur—or rather, of his company, Livingstone, Bottomley and Goenka Ltd. The beautiful menu card had been designed by an internationally renowned advertising agency and printed at Calcutta's best press in seven colours. The Rai Bahadur had insisted on a photograph of himself and the eminent guest on the last page. But the precious card couldn't be used eventually. After the party had been fixed, the eminent guest informed him at the eleventh hour that he wouldn't be able to arrive in time from Patna, thanks to an important committee meeting there. So his personal assistant had postponed the event by a day over the phone.

Because of that phone call, the officers of Livingstone, Bottomley and Goenka hadn't slept all night. Every single guest had to be informed of the delayed arrival, owing to unavoidable reasons, of the eminent guest. The multicoloured card couldn't be reprinted at such short notice. At first it was decided to black the date out with ink, but because Rai Bahadur Sadasukhlal didn't approve, the menu was printed on our special cards instead. Typing it out was my job—and what fabulous fare it was! First, Hors d'oeuvre Shahjahan. The soup, Crème de Champignons, followed by Filets de Beckti Sicilience.

The rest of it went as follows: Jambon Grille Kuala Lumpur, Chicken Curry and Pilao, Pudding de Vermicelle et Crème, Tutti Frutti Ice Cream, Cream Cheese, and finally, Café et Tea (coffee and tea). For vegetarians it was Papaya Cocktail, Potato and Cheese Soup, Green Banana Tikia, Mixed Vegetable Grill, Dal Moong Piazi, Pilao, etc.

I was busy typing out the menu at the counter. Bose-da would arrive any minute to take the cards to the banquet hall. That was when a lady, swinging an airline bag, came up to the counter. Jimmy, who was standing behind the counter, suddenly cried out in joy, as though he had been reunited with a loved one after years.

The moment I saw her, I knew who she was. Ignoring me, Jimmy said, 'Darling Rosie, your grape of a face has shrivelled so; your golden complexion looks burnt to a shade of copper.'

Rosie laughed and said, 'And my teeth?'

Jimmy shook his head and said, 'Your teeth are still just like pearls, though.'

Shaking her head and trying to tame her undisciplined curls, Rosie said, 'Thanks to your hotel job you simply can't tell the truth, Jimmy. When on earth did I ever have a complexion like gold? You are the one who used to say I'd been sculpted out of granite!'

Jimmy seemed a little embarrassed. Softly, he said, 'Where've you been all these days? With not so much as a word from you?'

Suddenly she noticed me. The sight of someone else at her machine seemed intolerable to her. In the usual Wellesley Street style she asked, 'Hello! Who're you, man?'

I was burning with rage and humiliation. Without answering, I continued typing.

Sensing an opportunity, Jimmy attacked me. 'Well, young man, don't you have any respect for ladies in your society? Can't you answer a question put to you by a young lady?'

Rosie was about to say something too, but before she could, Jimmy said, 'You must be very tired, Rosie. Is it very hot outside? Your dress is damp under the arms.'

Throwing a sidelong glance, Rosie said, 'Yes,' and added in an angry, cutting tone, 'But Jimmy, a gentleman doesn't look so carefully at any particular part of a lady's anatomy.'

Jimmy bit his tongue and said, 'Oh dear, I didn't mean to embarrass you, please believe me. But you have to agree that it is very unbecoming of ladies if their clothes are damp in that fashion.'

Rosie looked at me and said, 'Well, man, you haven't answered my question. Who are you?'

I was about to say, 'What concern is that of yours? Mind your own business,' but before that somebody behind me spoke, 'He's Mr Banerjee's brother-in-law. Another cousin of his, Khoka Chatterjee, lives in Bombay.'

It was like setting a cat among the pigeons. 'Ah, dear S-Sata, you're here,' stammered Jimmy. 'I-I was trying to introduce your friend to Rosie.'

By now Rosie had turned quite pale. In spite of the air-conditioning, there were beads of perspiration on her nose. Bose-da came around behind the counter and said, 'So where did you disappear to, Rosie? We were worried out of our minds.'

Rosie stood trembling like a leaf. Jimmy gestured to her to go along with him.

Bose-da said, 'Please give me the cards if you're through with them—we don't want Mr Goenka's honoured guests to be in any difficulty, do we?'

Jimmy and Rosie whispered between themselves, glancing at me. When they returned to the counter, Jimmy said for Bose-da's benefit, 'Poor girl, how sad! So how's your aunt now, Rosie? Better, I hope. The old lady must have suffered a lot.'

'My luck,' said Rosie. 'But how is it that you didn't get my letter? I left it in your room since the manager wasn't there.'

Bose-da said with mock seriousness, 'No surprise there—maybe the rats chewed it up.'

'Yes, quite likely,' said Jimmy. 'The rat menace in my room seems never-ending—the sight of those rats makes my blood go cold. They will be the death of me. If there are all these companies to exterminate termites, why can't they have one to kill rats? Imagine such an important letter disappearing!'

'Don't waste any more time,' said Bose-da, 'go and explain things to Marco Polo right away!'

Jimmy stopped in his tracks. 'But your friend? Poor fellow!'

Bose-da said seriously, 'I've told you before, and I'm telling you again, I have no friends. This boy is not my friend—he's simply my colleague. Anyway, don't worry about him, you go and try to push Rosie's case.'

Overcome with gratitude, Jimmy said, 'Thanks.' He turned to Rosie. 'Let's go—but are you planning to go in this sweat-soaked dress? Dry off under the fan first.'

Roise glared at him and said, 'Even if you dipped me in ice I won't stop perspiring. And if I don't have a job, it makes no difference what I wear.'

The two of them went off quickly in search of the manager. Bose-da smiled, clapped me lightly on the back and said, 'This place should have been named Shahjahan Theatre instead of Shahjahan Hotel. Not that Rosie's going to lose her job, she doesn't lack admirers in this hotel. And heaven knows what's happened to Marco Polo—he's been down in the dumps. I'm sure he's not going to fire anybody—whatever the error, as long as a reasonably logical explanation can be offered, he'll let them off with a warning.'

Marco Polo was prowling around the ground floor kitchen.

Jimmy led Rosie in that direction. A little later Rosie came back with downcast face and stood before the counter.

'What did he say?' asked Bose-da.

Biting her nails, she said, 'Poor Jimmy had bad luck, he got screamed at for his troubles. Marco Polo charged at him with bared fangs and said he hadn't been employed to intercede on behalf of women. And he didn't have the leisure to listen to a lady typist whining. He said he will see me after lunch.'

Rosie's next reaction took us by surprise. Luckily there was no one else at the counter. Bursting into tears she said, 'I know you can't stand the sight of me, Sata, but what have I done to you? You can't stand me, you never could, you've got your cousin a job to ruin me.'

Taken aback, Bose-da said, 'Rosie, this is a hotel counter— don't create a scene here. What was that you said? That I've brought in someone to get rid of you!'

Rosie continued to sob. 'I'd been away four days once before too and no one grabbed my job then.'

'What on earth are you saying, Rosie?'

Wiping her eyes, she continued, 'I know I'm dark as the night, I know I'm not beautiful. People call me a Negro behind my back. You don't like me. You deliberately told the manager about my going off to Bombay—and in front of all those people you said this fellow is Mr Banerjee's brother-in-law.'

Practically transfixed, Bose-da said slowly, 'Rosie, I've never in my life tried to take away someone's bread and butter—and I never will. But I'm sorry about having raised the subject of Mr Banerjee, please forgive me.'

He collected the menu cards for lunch and went out. Rosie immediately came round the counter. Looking me up and down, she said, 'Open that drawer on Sata's right-hand side, will you?'

'Mr Bose will be back in a moment,' I said. 'I can't open the drawer.'

Bending over to scratch her calf, she said, 'There's nothing confidential in that drawer—William Ghosh sometimes leaves chocolates there for me, please take a look.'

I opened the drawer and saw a few chocolate bars inside.

A smile appeared on Rosie's lips. 'William hasn't changed. He's such a sweet boy! He had promised to leave the chocolates, so I'd get them whenever I opened the drawer.'

Breaking off a piece for me, she said, 'Have some—after all, you're an influential person, you've even managed to win over Sata. We had always thought he had no heart—or, if he did, it was a plastic one, but you've conquered that as well.'

I couldn't say no, and nibbled on the chocolate. 'Do you think William spends money on chocolates for me?' said Rosie. 'Not at all—he couldn't be bothered. They get a lot of chocolate at the counter...American tourists don't give tips to people at the reception, they think it's an insult; instead, they give pens or chocolates.'

Bose-da returned to the counter and said, 'The manager's still very busy, Rosie, but I managed to talk to him about you.'

'What did he say?' she asked apprehensively.

Without answering her, Bose-da told me, 'Go upstairs, take your things out of Rosie's room and put them in Pamela's.'

'What?' I was about to exclaim, but Bose-da broke in, 'Pamela's act won't do in Calcutta. The police have served notice. She's vacated her room and is leaving today.' He continued gravely, 'I'd meant to show you the ropes at the luncheon party today, but the steward isn't willing. He's a new man, he says, might make mistakes. Anyway, there'll be plenty of opportunities later on. Go on upstairs, I'll inform Gurberia over the phone.'

Rosie practically fell on Bose-da now and said, 'Sata dear, what did the manager say about me?'

Bose-da smiled and said, 'You needn't worry any more—

go and settle into your room. I've explained to the manager why you were absent.'

Her face lit up with joy and gratitude.

Once on the terrace, however, she started hissing like a wounded cobra, as I quietly got Gurberia to move my things out of her room and into the empty one. 'My turn will come too,' she said, 'I'll take it out on Sata then, I've seen many great men here at Shahjahan—all of them are either Jesus Christ or St Peter!'

My East Bengal blood began to boil. I'd already had a taste of the filthy heart of this squeaky clean hotel, and digested it— after all, I was employed here, and beggars can't be choosers. But I wasn't willing to hear these dirty people talk about Bose-da that way.

I glared at her. 'I think you're overstepping the bounds of civility,' I said sharply.

'What? What did you say?' Rosie burst into flames. She swooped down and grabbed my wrist. I had no idea that in this very Calcutta a woman one wasn't related to could grab an unknown man's wrist in this fashion. I even felt a little scared. Suppose I sparked off a scandal trying to free myself? What if this dangerous woman started screaming and shouting and attracted a crowd?

Gurberia was standing at a distance—he knew his Rosie, and over the past few days, he'd come to know a little of me, too. Though he had seen my precarious situation out of the corner of his eye, he did nothing. Rosie pulled me into her room and slammed the door shut. The whole thing happened in a flash, before I could react. But before I was dragged in, I thought I saw a mysterious, obscene smile on Gurberia's face.

It was pitch dark inside—not even a window was open. Rosie locked the door from inside, panting. Freeing myself with a jerk, I moved towards the door to get out, but she stood before the door, like a madwoman, her bosom heaving violently.

Softly, she said, 'I'm not letting you go, you have to sit down here.'

When I tried to push her away and open the door, she coiled around my arm like a snake and spoke in a well-rehearsed, staccato voice, 'If you try to get out, my lad, I'm going to scream that you tried to molest me. If necessary, I'll go further and say that you locked the door and tried to assault a defenceless girl.'

I wasn't prepared for such a situation. The experienced reader might pity me for my lack of presence of mind and mental strength, but I have no qualms about admitting that I was really scared at the time. I thought Rosie would start screaming, 'Save me, save me,' at any moment. And from what I knew about the law, imagining the subsequent events sent a shiver down my spine. By then the power and courage to push her aside and open the door had evaporated.

Abandoning any attempt to open the door, I simply stood there for a while trying to figure out what I had let myself in for in my quest for a harmless typist's job. Meanwhile, Rosie tried to bring her heaving bosom under control. Clenching her teeth, she said, 'In fact, you have outraged my modesty—you've said I'm not civilized, that I've overstepped the bounds of decency.'

'Please,' I said, 'you're getting worked up.'

'You have insulted me,' she said.

'I met you barely half-an-hour-ago—I've hardly even spoken to you.'

'You're Mrs Banerjee's cousin,' she said, 'you must have heard a lot.'

What a scrape Bose-da's sense of humour had got me into!

In the dark, Rosie said, 'All of you must be telling people I've milked a lot of money out of Banerjee—that I ran away to Bombay with him for money.'

What could I say? I kept quiet.

'And now you're standing there innocently as though you wouldn't harm a fly, as though you've never even seen Mr or Mrs Banerjee in your life.' Panting, she added, 'You can tell your cousin the poor thing has married an animal. He lied to me—he told me he wasn't married. And that devil Byron must have said that the two of us were at another hotel before leaving. We were, but I didn't take money for it. I couldn't get him over to this room, we're not allowed to.'

Tears streamed down her cheeks. Wiping her eyes and pushing her hair back with her left hand, she said, 'You, your brother-in-law, your cousin—all of you have outraged my modesty.' Between sobs she muttered, 'Do you know that I have a mother, a paralyzed father, and two unmarried, unemployed sisters? We're locals, but you Calcuttans make us out to be Negroes. Abroad, you talk big about apartheid but the fact is that you hate us. I'd thought of marrying Banerjee and going away, and asking Jimmy to give my job to my sister. Do you know how badly she wants to have dinner at the Shahjahan? They live on bread, potato and onions, while I eat full course meals here, thanks to Jimmy.' After a pause, she added, 'I could have pushed off with your brother-in-law, but suddenly I learnt he has a wife—and now I see she has a brother, too. I feel sick!'

'May I leave now?' I said.

'Yes, you may,' she said, 'but I still haven't told you what I wanted to.'

Without trying in vain to explain that I wasn't related to the Banerjees, I simply said, 'What is it?'

Even in the darkness, I could tell that Rosie's face had assumed grotesque proportions. 'Your sister's been telling people that Banerjee has run away with a dirty hotel girl,' she said. 'That's a lie—an utter lie. And tell your sister, I spit on her husband's face.' And Rosie really spat on the floor.

Grinding her heel over it seemed to have bought her back

to her senses. Making a face, she said, 'I'm sorry—what's the use of telling you? I only wasted my spit, I should have kept it for Banerjee.'

She opened the door a crack and pushed me out, then slammed it shut behind me.

6

Even as Rosie slammed the door on my face, a window to the world opened as that very day Bose-da began introducing me to the rudiments of the work at the reception counter. 'If only you could have been at the luncheon party, you'd have learnt a lot,' he said. 'Anyway, there'll be many more opportunities— Calcutta is well known for its banquets; people here go bankrupt feasting and hosting.'

Explaining the intricacies of the job he said, 'Standing here for hours on end and listening to two thousand complaints from one thousand people is hardly pleasant, so I tell myself that I'm standing at a window to the world. How many people have the good fortune of standing at the Shahjahan counter and seeing the world in this fashion?'

'The world?' I asked.

'What else but the world?' Bose-da reiterated. 'I've seen passports of a hundred countries at this counter. Except for cannibals of the jungles, there's no race on earth whose members Sata Bose of Shahjahan hasn't met.'

'But is that all there is to the world?' I asked.

Placing a hand on my shoulder, Bose-da said, 'Beware! You're just allowed to observe, not ask questions—the latter only leads to unhappiness. Those who listen quietly are much happier. Whereas those who wonder why this should happen, why that is tolerated, inevitably get into trouble, and many of them have gone to their graves worrying about it.'

Arranging the registers on the counter, I smiled. Bose-da

continued, 'Of course, that doesn't mean I'm not going to answer your questions. I keep praying to God that the real world be different, that the people we see here are the exception rather than the rule. Poor Karabi Guha once told me, "One can't judge the world from one's home—the pet lamb at home turns into a tiger in a hotel." She should know—her experience isn't bookish; everything she says about hotels is worth its weight in gold.'

I didn't know who Karabi Guha was. Seeing the look on my face Bose-da asked, 'You haven't met Karabi Guha yet? That's both good and bad news. Of course, she seldom goes out—and even if she does, it's through the backstairs. She isn't allowed to sit in the lounge—Mr Agarwalla doesn't like it at all.'

All this was gibberish to me. 'Suite number two,' he clarified. 'In other words, Mr Agarwalla's guest house. He's a permanent client, and that suite is not given to anybody else. Miss Karabi Guha is in charge of it so you could say she is a colleague of ours.' Bose-da refused to divulge anything more. 'You'll get to know everything in good time,' he said. 'Suite number two isn't any old room, the future for many of us depends on the mood in suite number two.'

It seems Karabi had once asked Bose-da, 'Have you any idea when it was that people realized they could leave their homes and live in hotels? When did it occur to them to build a home away from home?'

Bose-da couldn't answer that one, but he did tell her that some of the primetime scenes from real life he'd witnessed had taken place, both by daylight and under cover of darkness, in hotels.

'At least a dozen novels about hotels are written in this country every year,' Bose-da said. 'I've read some of them, but most make me laugh. If only living in a hotel for two days, spending three evenings at the bar and going through police reports for four days, could reveal everything that goes on within a hotel, it would have been simple enough. But...You may not believe me, it was just such a book that inspired me to become a hotel receptionist.

'I'd barely arrived in Calcutta from Sahibganj and had put up in a hostel. I was enrolled in a college and my father faithfully wired me money. But I didn't study at all—I only read novels, watched films and listened to Western music. That was when I laid my hands on this novel. It was about an American millionaire who was keen on wooing some sheikh floating on billions of gallons of oil in the Middle East. But the sheikh wasn't particularly favourably disposed towards foreigners. Meanwhile, another oil magnate was also trying to entice the sheikh who had checked into the largest hotel in an American city along with two assistants for negotiations. Two other suites in the same hotel were occupied by members of the rival American groups. When one of them went into the sheikh's room, the other became depressed. And when the second group went in, the first chap's blood pressure shot up. If anybody gained from this tug-of-war, it was the hotel receptionist and his faithful hall porter.

'One of the Americans had a beautiful daughter. After her father's blood pressure shot up, she forced him to go home and took over his job. It didn't take long for her to get friendly with the receptionist—the rest of the novel dealt with how their joint strategies eventually won the sheikh over.'

After a pause, Bose-da continued, 'But it wasn't only this that attracted me to a hotel job. There was one more chapter—in which the receptionist and the millionaire's daughter got married, the sheikh joined the dinner party and then insisted that the couple visit his kingdom on their honeymoon. But they didn't return from the honeymoon because the sheikh announced that the young man would be made resident director of the newly formed oil company. So I decided that the surest way of getting a princess as well as half the kingdom was to take up a hotel job—I too might get into the good books of a sheikh.' Bose-da laughed and continued, 'I often stood in front of Calcutta's best hotels, after saving up enough money to enter one of them. Once, the porter showed me the way to the restaurant—but that was the last thing on my mind. The person I really wanted to talk to had his nose buried in his desk—he didn't seem interested in anything else. Another time I saw an old man working at the reception counter—I felt rather bad; the best years of his life were behind him, but he was still stuck there. Had no oil magnate's daughter laid her eyes on him? But I comforted myself that perhaps he wasn't very intelligent; or perhaps he was already married, forced to remain thirsty despite an abundance of water...I tried to use an uncle's influence to get a job but as soon as he heard it was with a hotel, he practically beat me up and threatened to wire my father.'

Bose-da had tried hard to persuade his uncle but to no avail. 'How can a bright young fellow enter the hotel business out of choice?' the uncle asked. 'There are no holidays, no future and, to tell the truth, no self-respect even.'

Bose-da had tried to placate him. 'I want to understand people; I want to serve them.'

'Then why kill yourself serving these fat, healthy pigs? Get through the ISC and into medical college—you can serve the sick, do some good and help people.'

Realizing that his uncle would not relent, Bose-da had gone directly to Shahjahan Hotel, carrying a letter from Hobbs, whom he had met a few days earlier. Seeing how eager the young lad was, Hobbs had agreed to write a letter of recommendation, adding, 'My dear boy, you're a handsome young man, you won't need any recommendations. Aristotle has said a beautiful face is better than all the letters of recommendation in the world.'

Even as we were talking, the hall porter came running towards us. A middle-aged woman followed him, much of her face concealed behind huge dark glasses. The vanity bag she was carrying was also black. Though she must have been around fifty, the flowing magenta silk sari, sleeveless blouse and a spring in her step refused to acknowledge the years.

'Mrs Pakrashi,' Bose-da whispered.

Mrs Pakrashi stood at the counter. It was obvious from her expression that she wasn't very comfortable at this confluence of a thousand passers-by. She would probably have been happy if she could have proceeded directly to a room without having to wait—and happier if she didn't have to use the front door. If there was a dimly lit passage at the back which she could have taken, so much the better.

Without beating about the bush, she whispered to Bose-da, 'Can I get a room tonight?'

Bidding her good evening, Bose-da said, 'Why didn't you just telephone, ma'am, I'd have made all the arrangements.'

'I thought I wouldn't be able to make it. My daughter and son-in-law were supposed to have come over, but Khuku telephoned half an hour ago and said Sabyasachi's got a cold so they wouldn't be coming.'

Chewing her lower lip, she said, 'So Robertson isn't here yet? I thought he'd have come by now.'

'No, he hasn't,' said Bose-da. 'I haven't heard from him, either.'

Mrs Pakrashi said a trifle embarrassedly, 'He is a Commonwealth citizen, you won't face any police trouble.'

'Mrs Pakrashi, what a surprise!' A man in a suit about to leave the hotel spotted her and came over to the counter.

Mrs Pakrashi's face turned pale. She had no idea what to say, and somehow forced a response. 'Fancy seeing you here!'

Oozing politeness, he said, 'I had quite forgotten it's a dry day. I'd been working hard at the office, and came here directly. When I saw the bar doors closed, I realized I'd miscalculated. This silly rule makes no sense—the government is losing its own revenue. And that too at a time when we need money for national development, when we need to increase excise revenues. I can't even make arrangements at home, my wife keeps telling me the children are growing up.'

We had expected him to be too caught up in his own trouble to ask Mrs Pakrashi any questions, but he said, 'Never mind me, what are you doing here at his hour?'

'I-I came to find out something,' Mrs Pakrashi stammered.

Bose-da took the cue right away. 'I keep telling you, ma'am, the banquet room isn't free that evening. Perhaps you could postpone your women's council meeting by a day?'

The gentleman now came forward to take up Mrs Pakrashi's brief. 'What are you saying? Do you know who you're talking to? How can Madhab Pakrashi's wife not get the banquet hall when she wants it?'

Bose-da said, 'I'm sorry, sir, I'll try.'

'Shall we leave together, Mrs Pakrashi?' the man asked.

Bose-da said with a straight face, 'Since you have waited so long, ma'am, please wait a little longer. Our manager, Mr Marco Polo, will be here any minute.'

'Many thanks, Mr Chatterjee,' she said. 'I might as well wait a little. Why don't you go along home early—never mind your drinks for one evening.'

'That's the problem, all women sing the same tune—don't drink, don't drink...' He bade her good night and strode out.

Mrs Pakrashi heaved a sigh of relief and looked gratefully at Bose-da, though she couldn't say anything. Examining the register, Bose-da said, 'Why don't you carry on to suite number one, ma'am, I'm sure Robertson will be here shortly.'

She hesitated. 'What about signing the register?' she asked.

'Don't worry about that,' said Bose-da, 'I'll get him to sign.'

Mrs Pakrashi was again moved to silence, and gazed appreciatively at Bose-da. 'What about some supper?' he asked.

'Not a bad idea,' she said.

'Would you like to come to the dining room?'

'No, we'd rather have it in our room. I want a little privacy. Please put the extra service charge on the bill.'

'Just a minute,' said Bose-da, 'I'll get you the menu card.'

'Oh, only some hot chicken soup, please.'

'What! At least a little fish...'

'Are you mad! The way I'm putting on weight...' She moved away from the counter.

After a short, pregnant pause, Bose-da said, 'Alas, the way they aspire to be slim!' Looking at me, he added, 'Believe it or not, Mrs Pakrashi used to be rather orthodox once upon a time...and she came from a very poor family.'

Robertson appeared on the scene within fifteen minutes. He started to go upstairs after signing the register when Bose-da asked, 'Would you like some supper? Mrs Pakrashi has ordered hot chicken soup.'

'No, thanks,' he said, 'but could you arrange for some drinks? Please don't hesitate to tell me if it'll cost a little extra.'

Expressing his regret, Bose-da said, 'Impossible. Today's dry day and an internationally renowned hotel like the Shahjahan cannot afford to break excise rules.'

Disappointed, Robertson disappeared into the lift.

'Surely Mrs Pakrashi needn't have made an appointment on a dry day?' I asked Bose-da.

'You're a fool—she chooses the dry days deliberately. On these days the hotel goes to sleep, very few people pass through—it's the safest day for her. There's one dry day a week now, but I believe it's going to increase soon; one will become two, two will become four. And eventually all seven days will become dry, and God alone knows what will happen then.'

The dry day was followed by a wet one—I was on special duty from four in the morning that day. I stood alone at the counter, my only task being to welcome a few guests from Japan. A well-known travel agency in the city had made arrangements for them at the hotel earlier and a chap from the agency accompanied them.

Travel agencies sent us many guests, but in his heart of hearts the manager didn't like them very much. The reason was simple: those who referred guests to us were entitled to a commission of ten per cent of the billing amount. What's more, the payment wasn't usually made by the guests—they would have their meals, their fun and laughter and depart, while we would tot up the accounts and send the bill to the travel agents, who would deduct their commission before paying up.

When the chap from the travel agency left, it was a few minutes after four. Soon afterwards Mrs Pakrashi came down to the counter. She probably hadn't combed her hair after she'd woken up, but she had put on her dark glasses all right.

Advancing slowly, she glanced at the counter, possibly looking for Bose-da. 'Good morning, ma'am,' I said, but she didn't seem to have heard me and walked out in a preoccupied manner, swinging her vanity bag. The doorman's whistle, used to summon taxis, shattered the silence of the dawn.

The person I met next was an employee of a flower shop in New Market, a bunch of different varieties of flowers clutched in his hand. I didn't know it then, but I learnt later that these were samples he wanted to show the lady in suite number two. I sent him to Karabi, who chose the flowers for the day.

Over time I became familiar with the daily routine followed in that room. The difference in status between a hotel room and a suite was the same as that between a general bed and a cabin in a hospital. If there was only a bedroom, it was just a room, but whenever a sitting room was added on, it became a suite and suites merited special treatment from us. Suite number two was extra special—it had a personal phone, and several rooms within it. It took a lot of flowers, which Karabi chose herself, to decorate the suite. Early in the morning, linen clerk Nityahari Bhattacharya went to meet her with pencil and paper. He was the emperor of the sheets, curtains and table linen that were needed at Shahjahan. People said he was a lucky man.

'Not so,' Nityahari contested the claim. 'A Brahmin's son being reduced to work as a dhobi—what is that but bad fortune? My father told me many times, study hard, Netto, but Netto didn't pay the slightest attention. He was busy with his football and his theatre and music and his paan and beedi. Now he's paying the price—he has to cart around clothes used by the world, keep track of them, clean the soiled ones and send them back to the rooms. This is what comes of disobeying your elders. As you sow, so you reap. I must have stolen some washerman's laundry in my last life, why else would God punish me so?'

The bearers couldn't stand Nityahari. 'In that case who knows what you will be in your next life—you've cleaned the place out,' they'd say.

The Englishmen called him Nata. Sata and Nata were both favourites of the bosses. Marco Polo sometimes referred to them affectionately as Satahari and Natahari. When it came to classified news, Natahari's influence was even greater than Mata Hari's. Tucking his pencil behind his ear, the first thing that Nityahari did when he saw Karabi was to bend and touch her feet in the traditional Indian gesture of respect. She retreated hastily each time, saying, 'No, no.'

But Nityahari wasn't put off so easily. 'Oh no,' he'd say, 'You are the goddess incarnate. For years I suffered from asthma, and then, thank god, she appeared to me in a dream and said, the medicine's right there in your hotel—and since I touched your feet, I've been very well, the asthma's practically cured.'

A melancholy smile spreading across her face, Karabi said, 'The flowers I've asked for today need to match with a light saffron. I want curtains, table linen, bedspreads and towels all in the same shade. I hope you have it in stock...'

Pulling his pencil out, Nityahari said, 'Of course, as long as Nityahari is around you'll get everything you need. I admit I complain every minute, but how else could I have kept two hundred and fifty rooms in order? But then, times have changed. When the British were here, they appreciated these things. Sheets used to be changed every day; now it's every other day.'

Karabi didn't enjoy this conversation, but she did indulge him good humouredly, saying, 'Please send them quickly.'

'Right away! I know exactly where everything is. They don't understand now, but if I leave, or stay away, that's when they'll realize my true worth.'

Meanwhile, the hotel was beginning to hum with activity. Rosie came downstairs and started typing Jimmy's breakfast menu cards.

Robertson was probably still snoring his head off in suite number one. I had expected him to make his escape at the same time as Mrs Pakrashi.

The very next moment the thought crossed my mind that if our superstitions were anything to go by, he'd have a long life, for just then a bearer came and said, 'The gentleman in suite number one is calling for you.' I couldn't leave the counter, but Rosie behaved very well that day; she seemed to be coming round to the idea that I wasn't really Mr Banerjee's brother-in-law.

'Don't gape like a fool, man,' she said. 'If the guest in suite number one complains, you won't have a job.'

'That would suit you,' I said.

A flush spread across her face. 'I was unemployed for a long time, both my sisters are unemployed, my father doesn't have a job—I know what it's like to not have a job, man. Just because I ran away with a man I hardly knew, doesn't mean I have no feelings...' She smiled. I discerned a subtle hint of pain in her smile and for some reason, in the light of early morning, Rosie seemed beautiful to me.

Pushing me out, she said, 'Go and meet him, I can mind the counter until then.'

When I arrived at suite number one, taking the bearer along with me, I noticed the other bearers cleaning shoes in the corridor, first marking the shoes with white chalk on the soles. I didn't know it then, but unless the room numbers were thus written, the shoes got mixed up, and the pair belonging to room 200 turned up in number 210 instead. The stout gentleman found a lady's slim high-heeled sandals waiting for him, while the beautiful lady woke up to the shock of her life, spotting heavy rubber-soled boots lying by her single bed. In this very hotel an unmarried young lady had once cried out, 'Help, help!' on spying a pair of clumpy boots in her room, afraid that their owner was hiding somewhere in there. The bearer came running, understood what the problem was as soon as he entered and quickly corrected the mistake. Luckily the matter never reached Marco Polo's ears, or else the bearer might have lost his job. The system of marking the room number on the soles of the shoes was instituted after that incident.

We knocked on the door of suite number one and waited. A voice filtered out: 'Come in.' The person we said good morning to on entering was stretched out on the bed, dressed in a pale, sleeveless vest and a pair of briefs. He betrayed no emotion at seeing us, merely asking, 'Where's Mr Bose?'

'He isn't on duty yet,' I replied.

A little embarrassed, he said softly, 'We...my companion...both of us tossed and turned in our beds all night—there weren't enough pillows; just one pillow in a double room. I was going to complain last night, but she prevented me.'

'Extremely sorry,' I said. 'We would have arranged for pillows at once if you'd only let us know. I'll get them sent to you immediately.'

Getting up, he pulled out a pair of trousers from the cupboard and said, 'That's not necessary. My companion left a long while ago, and I'm about to leave, too. I called you for a different reason—she's left this envelope to be given to Mr Bose. Please make it a point to give it to him.'

I asked whether the suite should be reserved for them for one more day. Putting on his shirt, he said, 'I don't know yet—please ask Mr Bose to telephone me.'

Returning to the counter, I saw that Bose-da had already taken charge of Shahjahan Hotel.

'The lady's left this envelope for you—and there weren't enough pillows in the room, they had an uncomfortable night,' I told him in one breath.

Peeping into the envelope, Bose-da said, 'The lady's embarrassing me. People all over the world do as they please, so why should Mrs Pakrashi be any different? I'm not such a cad that I will put her name down in the register unless she gives me twenty rupees.'

Turning to me he said, 'It's essential to enquire into guests' complaints. If Marco Polo finds out, he'll give Nityahari hell. You'd better inform Nityahari—after all, Mr Pakrashi has his eyes on this hotel, he could join the board any day.'

I had no idea where Nityahari was, or where his stores were. Parabashia was roaming around so I took him along and went back upstairs. On the way up I saw Mrs Pakrashi's companion coming down, empty-handed. He had come in the night before without any luggage.

The building was like a city in itself. There were so many rooms, so many corridors and so many lanes and by-lanes that it took ages to know them, and you could never be sure you'd got to know them all. We walked along the corridor on the second floor, rows of rooms on either side, till the carpeted passage came to an end. There was a closed door to the right— I thought it was another room, but when Parabashia turned the handle, I saw that it led to yet another corridor. We were walking south to north; again there were rows of rooms on either side of the corridor, but these rooms weren't air-conditioned, and the corridor seemed a little narrow.

Parabashia told me that this was the oldest part of the hotel. Mr Simpson had built it himself, and he still frequented it more often than the rest of the hotel.

A few doors were slightly ajar, but you couldn't see much through them as you walked by. Only the swinging shadows made it clear that fans were whirring overhead. The muted sound of radios could also be heard from one or two rooms. In one room there were two Japanese gentlemen, each with a mug of beer; next to them was an American family. In the next room was a Sikh who had taken off his turban and beard-netting to give them an airing, and further on, judging from his garments, was a Burmese. I caught snatches of conversation in various languages—it was as though I were a child tuning a shortwave radio—and fragments of languages from different parts of the world drifted up before drowning in the flow of some other tongue.

In the midst of all this, a little Chinese boy was trying to relieve himself of his clothes with philosophical detachment. He had already taken off his shirt, and was trying in vain to pull off his shorts as well. Suddenly he tottered over to me and grabbed my hand, smiling. I couldn't make out what he was saying, but his gestures were clear—the poor thing had wet his pants, and even got part of the carpet sopping wet.

Parabashia burst out in protest, 'These rascals will destroy the carpets!' It seems that a German boy had once answered nature's greater call on the carpet—and it was Parabashia who had had to wrinkle his nose and summon the sweeper. Ever since, he has been afraid of little boys.

I was about to scoop the child up in my arms, but Parabashia hastily stopped me as though I were about to touch a live bomb. 'I don't trust these Chinese children,' he said. 'He might be up to more mischief—perhaps the sweeper will have to be called.'

The little boy was stumbling around, trying to find his room but, being unable to locate it, started crying. Accompanied by Parabashia, I eventually tracked down the boy's parents. They didn't know English, and were a little scared at not being able to find their son. They hadn't realized that the young man had walked out of their room and arrived in this part of the hotel. They thanked us profusely in Chinese—and, guessing at their meaning, Parabashia proceeded to scold the mother in his own patois, trying to explain that Calcutta wasn't safe and that there was no dearth of kidnappers here.

Back in the corridor, Parabashia said solemnly, 'I suspect Mr Lenin.' How on earth had Comrade Lenin arrived at Calcutta's Shahjahan Hotel? But Parabashia's next statement clarified that Mr Lenin was none other than the linen clerk Nityahari. Apparently, he loved children and often lured them to his room whenever he got the chance. As he counted his bedspreads, pillows, sheets and napkins, he made faces, tickled them, bounced on his bed—antics which the children enjoyed immensely. He had even been pulled up a couple of times for doing this.

Nityahari was seated amidst a mountain of linen, a pair of spectacles perched on his nose. The washed linen was piled high on one side, and the soiled linen on the floor. When he saw me, he flew into a rage. 'Just a minute! Just when I can't account for twenty-two towels, you have to have a word with me.' He paused, then continued in a calmer voice, 'Try to understand my predicament—if I have to buy twenty-two towels with my own money, they'll have to sell me to raise the cash.'

'There's a complaint against you,' said Parabashia.

'Complaint? Against me? Who has the audacity to criticize me? I've spent thirty years in this hotel, I've kept track of the governors' bedclothes and pillows, they haven't said a word against me, and someone dares complain!'

'There weren't enough pillows in suite number one last night,' I explained.

'Impossible!' he screamed.

I was about to leave when Nityahari stood up, picked up his notebook and said, 'Suite number one. Not enough pillows. Impossible. Nityahari Bhattacharya is not quite in his dotage yet, he cannot be accused of not putting enough pillows in the special suite. Let's go and take a look.'

In his half-sleeved shirt, dhoti and worn-out slippers he practically dragged me all the way to suite number one.

On the way he said, 'You have some nerve, trying to catch me out. The number of pillows, mattresses and towels in every room in this hotel is at my fingertips. Two of the pillows are feather ones, which Simpson himself used. Suite number two has eight pillows; suite number one, four. And you come to tell me there aren't enough pillows?'

When we unlocked the door to suite number one and walked in, there was only one pillow visible. Nityahari seemed taken aback at first, but the next moment he exploded, 'Impossible! They must have been rolling around on the floor in a drunken fit and forgotten it afterwards.'

'Yesterday was dry day,' I pointed out.

He brushed aside my objection. 'You tell me! As if Calcutta becomes a chaste widow on dry day!'

He suddenly crouched on the floor and peered beneath the bed, crying out in triumph. Crawling underneath and pulling out three pillows, he said, 'There you are, sir—I nearly lost my job. No one would have believed that I had put in the pillows and that they were playing around with them on the floor. Even after thirty years of service, supplying pillows to the likes of the Governor-General, I would have lost my job.'

As I saw for myself, the pillows had indeed been lying beneath the bed. Relenting a little when he saw my face, Nityahari said, 'You're young, you don't know a thing about hotels yet. Do you suppose people get drunk only on liquor? Rubbish—when old women get stars in their eyes they're drunk most of the time. Of course, it's none of my business— you've booked a room with your own money, you have every right to play with the pillows.' He swallowed. 'But why drop the pillows on the floor and then bay for my blood?'

Sensing that things were going wrong, Parabashia had made off, leaving me alone, wishing I too could make a getaway. Nityahari was still at it. 'You may think grown-ups can't behave this way—but that's nonsense! Even adults become babies when the spirit gets them. Mark my words: I don't delegate, I've been supplying pillows with my own hands for thirty years.'

I tried to leave, but he grabbed my hand. 'Where are you off to?'

'Downstairs,' I said.

'What's the hurry—no one gets away from me so easily.' Even at that early hour his eyes were glowing like embers.

'What do I have to do?' I asked him.

The fire in his eyes dimmed—he seemed to be bringing himself under control. Softly, he said, 'Will you pour some water on my hands?'

'Whatever for?' I asked.

'I have to wash their sins off, haven't I?'

There was running water in the toilet, but he wouldn't touch the taps in suite number one—as though the so-called sins had permeated everywhere. I discovered a mug in the bathroom and poured water from it on to his hands. There was some liquid soap above the basin, but he didn't even look at it, taking out a bar of carbolic soap from his own pocket instead. There was no telling when he would have to wash his hands after rummaging through the linen, so he always had a few bars of soap on him. Washing his hands carefully, he said, 'I must have stolen millions of clothes from washermen in my previous life.'

Returning to the room he sat down on the edge of the bed. 'Can you tell me how many pillows there are in this hotel?'

'How should I know?' I said.

'Nine hundred and fifty,' he whispered. 'There were a thousand originally, but fifty have been torn. The stuffing's in a corner of my room—sins!' He brought his mouth close to my ears and distorted his face. 'A thousand sins!'

He had my full attention by now. I asked, 'Why sins?'

'Didn't your father give you an education? Didn't he pay your school fees?' he admonished.

'He paid to the best of his abilities—he never cheated anyone,' I said.

'Well then? What did the teacher teach you? Don't you know that millions and billions of sins are committed every moment in hotels and bars and drinking joints?'

'Thousands of people come here on business—have they all committed sins?' I asked naively.

'Of course they have. If they hadn't, would they have needed to get out of their homes, or even spend the night outside?' Nityahari's eyes were glowing again. 'How long have you been working?'

'Not very long.'

'Not gone to the dogs yet, I hope?'

'I beg your pardon?'

'Have you met Rosie?'

'I have, but I don't know her very well.'

'That woman had asked me for an extra pillow once. I said no to her face, and then thought, who am I to say no? Give pillows to whoever wants them, as many as they want—what do I care? I took the pillows myself to her room and she returned them the next morning. But I have to say I haven't fathomed two of the people here yet. One is Satyasundar Bose—he has never asked for an extra pillow, even by mistake—and the other is Mr Marco. I've seen him hit the bottle and get high, but that's it—he's never asked for an extra pillow either, as though women are the plague.'

I looked at him in surprise.

'To ask for extra pillows, you first need liquor—what our learned men refer to as booze. You do frequent the Shahjahan bar, don't you?'

'I haven't been on duty there yet,' I said.

'I always tell the girls, give your husbands all the freedom, my dears, but don't let them leave home. The moment they step out there's going to be trouble—there's no telling whose fences they will break down or whose garden they will attack.'

All of this was pretty confounding. I was discovering a bizarre persona within Nityahari. Softly he said, 'Snakes! I've discovered at last that every person has a cobra in him. For some people the snake stays asleep all their lives; for others, it hisses and sticks out its tongue as soon as they get out of their homes.'

I was feeling uncomfortable and didn't fancy staying in that room any longer. He probably wasn't enjoying it either which is why he got off the bed and said, 'Let's go to my room.'

'This is where I live,' he said when we arrived in his room, 'and little Shahjahan is where I eat.'

'Little Shahjahan—where on earth is that?' I asked.

'Behind the real Shahjahan. Can you tell me how much the most expensive dinner at Shahjahan costs?'

'Everybody knows that—thirty-five rupees.'

'In little Shahjahan it's fourteen paise—a four-course dinner for fourteen paise: rice, a curry, two vegetables. They'd planned to raise the price to four annas; the entire Shahjahan staff protested—how could we afford to pay four annas? So they were forced to keep the price at fourteen paise—only, they made the curry a little more watery and we have to wash our own dishes,' he said. 'It's different for you—you've got your stripes before your commission; breakfast, lunch and dinner at Shahjahan immediately on joining.'

I was silent. What could I say? He continued, 'Of course, Juneau doesn't give you much; the leftovers from lunch make up your dinner, and the leftovers from dinner go into the next day's lunch. Do you know what's for lunch today?'

I marvelled at his ability to gather information.

'Madras curry—wonderful to eat, but don't touch it. How good is your constitution—can you digest steel?'

'Not at all—my digestive system is no obedient servant of mine.'

'Then you'd better give the Madras curry a wide berth. Veeraswami of London—gold medallist, honorary cooking advisor to the Secretary of State for India—invented it. In 1924 he went to the British Empire exhibition, and then started a restaurant in London. Juneau claims to have learnt Indian cooking from him, but in fact Veeraswami threw him out. If it hadn't been for our cook, Deben, the skeleton in Juneau's cupboard would have been exposed by now. As I was saying, the day when the meat is bought, it's served as cold meat; it's the same the next day. On the third day it goes into the biryani and on the fourth it's Madras curry for the staff.'

I was about to bid him goodbye when he said, 'Just a

minute. Since you're practically a child, I'm going to arrange
it so that your mind stays pure—or, even if it does get impure,
you realize quickly that it has. Since Rosie has occupied your
room, all your stuff has been transferred next door. I'll arrange
for everything in there to be white.'

Carrying a bundle of linen, he insisted on coming up to
the terrace with me. Rosie was in her room, grinning from ear
to ear. She told me, 'I'm through for the day. I'm going to sit
on the terrace now and fry myself to a crisp. Then I'll have
lunch. And then, you know what? I'll go to the cinema for the
matinee show. Jimmy was supposed to go too, but he's got
banquet duty; there's an extra ticket—would you like to
come?'

I was amazed at Rosie's invitation. 'Many thanks,' I said,
'but I'm on duty.'

'All right, I'll take my sister then,' she said. 'But if I take
her to the movies without notice, her boyfriends will be
disappointed, they won't find her home when they call on
her.'

After one more round of thanks, I went into my room.

Nityahari had somehow kept his expression under control
all this while, but as soon as he entered the room he made a
face. 'You seem to have made a lot of progress,' he said. 'But
remember, the higher you climb, the harder you fall. And
don't forget, either, that there's temptation everywhere; unless
you are careful you'll succumb to it.' Glancing around with an
eagle eye, he went on, 'I'll make sure everything in this room
is white—white curtains, white bedclothes, white towels,
white table linen. If necessary, I'll make arrangements for them
to be changed every day. I have to go, there's lots to do—three
hundred guests at the banquet, which means three hundred
napkin flowers.'

I didn't know what napkin flowers were. It was he who
told me that in the olden days, napkins used to be changed

with every course at the Shahjahan—but now they were laid
out just once, placed in the glasses before the guests entered.
'I've made many arrangements,' he said, 'fans, bishops, boats,
lotuses, orchids. This time I'll make something new—it's much
harder work, but I'll do it, only for the name. A boar's head!
From now on I'll make nothing but a boar's head for banquets
at the hotel,' he muttered to himself as he left.

7

What test matches are to cricket, what the IFA Shield final is
to football, the banquet is to hotels. The top brass of the hotel
don't really know what a banquet is all about, nor do they have
the time to find out.

The person who was happiest when enquiries for a
banquet came was the manager. He told the customer quite
categorically that no hotel other than Shahjahan could possibly
manage such a large party. 'Of course, we do charge a little
more, but the guests are happy, and the hosts are assured of
success.'

Earlier, there used to be more than one banquet per week,
but even now there was at least one every week. Bose-da told
me that there was a time when they had banquets on five
successive days. You couldn't get the hall unless you booked
it two months in advance. But those days were gone, he
added. It wasn't as though the fun-loving population had
declined or that socializing had diminished—it was just that
Calcutta's clubs had taken to organizing banquets. The liquor
in the clubs was cheaper, and so was the food. Besides, the
prestige was by no means any less, since the city's top socialites
preferred to throw their parties in the privacy of clubs. The
clubs' managers were pleased, too—they didn't have to employ
extra staff, and banquets made for a handsome source of
income.

Considering the state the country was in, one never knew when newspaper headlines would announce that Calcutta had also gone down the drain like Bombay; that the city had gone dry overnight. Without a bar licence, a club was like a cake without the icing. God forbid that the dark day be at hand! But if indeed the ominous dry cloud hanging over Bombay made its way to Calcutta, against everyone's wishes, the clubs would have nothing left but their banquets.

If only banquets were a cakewalk! Especially if they happened to be for 350 or 400 guests. There were people at Shahjahan whose skills at handling such events were unmatched. Their services were even sought by official circles in the government. It was they who preserved India's fragile reputation among international guests. Consider Parabashia—he had gone to England in 1924 to work at the Indian restaurant put up at the British Empire exhibition. Since then, there was no counting the number of times he had saved the day at banquets. Banquets pleased him—they did mean working much harder for a couple of days, leading to backaches and aching feet, but still he enjoyed them.

Whenever a banquet was scheduled, Marco Polo increased the frequency of his rounds, and he became rather good-tempered, rather like a stern patriarch who starts treating younger members of the family as friends under the pressure of duties at a family wedding.

Marco Polo said, 'This is a very important affair, Jimmy, the prestige of this poor country depends on this banquet.'

'We'll arrange a banquet the likes of which has never been seen in Calcutta,' Jimmy promised.

Marco Polo turned to Juneau. 'What about you?'

'Oh no, no, sir,' Juneau said, 'these are simple parties, not banquets.' It was his firm belief that Calcuttans didn't know what banquets were. 'This is a stingy Scotch city,' he said. After having learnt his cooking in Paris, he claimed to have forgotten most of it in this small-time ant-swatting metropolis. After all, he hadn't picked up his skills from some Tom, Dick or Harry—Monsieur Bordeaux, before whom every chef in the world bowed in reverence, had taught him personally. And Monsieur Bordeaux was himself a disciple of the Beethoven of cooking—Monsieur Escoffier, who used to say, 'To cook is to search for God.' Juneau had learnt from Bordeaux that you couldn't have a banquet with less than seven courses.

'What?' Marco Polo screamed.

Wiping his hand on his apron, Juneau elaborated, 'Yes. Hors d'oeuvres, soup, fish, entrée, roast entremets, dessert and coffee.'

'My dear friends,' said Marco Polo, 'our banquet is no laughing matter. As far as I know, the guests will be discussing many vital problems of the country and the world. Naturally, they'll want a plain and simple dinner—about fifteen rupees per head.'

Sensing the opportunity to prepare a seven-course dinner slipping through his fingers, Juneau said, 'As you order, so I will cook. If you like, I'll serve just cold mutton and bread. But I have to say that cooking brings you satisfaction nowhere except Paris—there are no real connoisseurs of cuisine anywhere else. In Calcutta you'll get your everyday cook, but never will Calcutta be able to create a Monsieur Bordeaux or an Escoffier.'

Marco Polo rose, saying, 'I'll be back in a moment. I need to make a phone call, I want to discuss the menu with them.'

Bose-da, who had been listening to the exchange, told Juneau, 'Poor Juneau! Don't fret, when I get married I'll let you cook to your heart's content—we'll see what menus you can dream up then.'

Juneau smiled and said, 'French, English, Spanish, Italian, African, Turkish, Chinese, Indian—we'll have a dish of each at your wedding.'

'O God Almighty, O Lord, please make Juneau live very

long. And, as soon as possible, please send a perfect bride for me from the UNO,' Bose-da laughingly prayed on bended knees.

'The soup for the bridal night will be named *La Soupe des Noces oy Tourin aux Tomates*!' Juneau said happily.

Still laughing, Bose-da moved closer to him. 'That's an enormous name—what is it actually, Juneau?'

'We call it the honeymoon soup for short. You have to make a lot of it, and then do what one does with it in our country.'

Jimmy said, 'You Frenchmen can think of nothing but love.'

'Don't talk rubbish,' Juneau said angrily. Turning to Bose-da, he continued, 'On your wedding night we'll eat, drink and make merry till very late. Then, in the dead of night, we'll bang on the door to your room with two bowls of honeymoon soup. We'll keep playing music, shouting and banging on the door. When you or your wife—fed up with the ruckus—finally open the door, we'll burst in and force the two of you to eat the soup. Well—Mrs Bose will feed you, and you will feed her, and until you finish the soup, we won't leave the room.'

'You're welcome to stay,' Bose-da said with a smile, 'but what's the soup made of? Will you get everything you need for it in Calcutta?'

'Of course! I need twelve tomatoes, six onions, some pepper and an ounce of butter.'

'What! *La Soupe des Noces oy Tourin aux Tomates* is made of just onions and tomatoes! I refuse—I'm not going to get married. No woman will tolerate a husband who reeks of onions.'

That Juneau loved Bose-da was obvious from the way they bantered. He was about to respond when Marco Polo came back and said, 'It's all settled. I'm going to dictate the menu to Rosie right away. The only thing we can't find out right now is how many are vegetarian and how many not.'

'We never can find that out,' said Jimmy. 'Might as well make it ten per cent vegetarian.'

'Hell!' said Juneau in anger. 'If Paris is paradise for chefs, Calcutta is hell. Why don't Calcuttans devour fruit at home instead of going to parties? Could Monsieur Bordeaux ever have imagined vegetarians and non-vegetarians together at the same table? One set of vegetarians who eat eggs, and one set of non-vegetarians who don't eat beef, and another set that eats beef but starts throwing up at any reference to pork?'

To provoke Juneau further, Bose-da said, 'So where do I go, my goddess?'

'Eh?'

'That's why our great Ramprasad asked, "Where do I go, mother star?"' said Bose-da, doing a literal translation of a devotional song addressed to the Goddess Kali.

A smile appeared on Juneau's face. 'Was Mr Prasad a great cook, Sata?'

'Very very great—he cooked only for God.'

Parabashia had been present all the while. He whispered something to the manager, who asked Jimmy, 'What about waiters? Can you manage with the people from the main dining hall?'

'I need at least twenty,' said the steward.

There was inevitably a shortage of manpower whenever there was a banquet. Anyone who was available was put into uniform and asked to work as a waiter. Apparently even sweepers had been pressed into service once, at some hotel or other, Parabashia had told me in confidence. Even former employees were sent for—those who had retired (in other words, those whom Jimmy had forced to retire) were summoned if they lived close by.

'Parabashia, go and inform Abdul, Gafoor, Mayadhar, Joy

and company immediately—they'll be paid two rupees each.' As Parabashia rose, Marco Polo added, 'And send Natahari to me before you go.'

By the time Nityahari arrived on the scene in his sandals, most of the gathering had dispersed. Juneau had gone to the kitchen, while Jimmy had gone out with the contractor to arrange for the shopping.

'Banquet, Natahari,' said Marco Polo.

Nityahari knew right away what that meant. 'How many extra hands, sir?'

'About twenty.'

'I'll have forty uniforms and forty pairs of gloves ready. Should I add turbans, sir? Well-known people are coming— maybe the Governor, too?'

'Quite possible, one can never tell,' said Bose-da.

'In that case the musicians should be dressed up too,' said Nityahari.

'Yes, their costumes should also be arranged for.'

'That will be done, sir, as long as I am around. But that doesn't mean I'm going to arrange for uniforms for Gomez's musical instruments also. Instruments are like one's own children—the parents should take care of their clothes, why should I have to do it? As it is, what is it that the five of them really do, sir? They drone a little at lunchtime and flop down in their beds, then drone some more in the evening; the rest of the time they snore their heads off.'

For some unknown reason, Marco Polo tended to indulge Nityahari. Smiling, he said, 'You carry on. Mr Bose will arrange everything.' Drawing me aside, he said, 'I have to go out for a while. Byron has sent a message—maybe there's some news of Susan. Ask Bose to make all the arrangements for the banquet.'

The entire day passed in the throes of excitement. Nobody had a moment to spare. Putting William on duty at the reception, Bose-da ran around frantically with me in tow. In the pantry waiters polished the knives and forks till they gleamed. Parabashia lorded it over them: 'I'm going to count everything. If anything is lost, it will be deducted from your salaries.'

It was amidst all this anxiety that Shahjahan Hotel gradually arrived at the confluence of day and night. Bose-da had the hall ready by then, and the 350 boar's heads crafted out of cloth by Nityahari were waiting in the banquet hall.

The Philanthropic Society was an international organization. Those who were hosting the banquet had recently started the Calcutta chapter. Mr Agarwalla, Mr Langford and Khan Bahadur Huq stood before the counter to welcome the guests. Agarwalla was in national dress—bandhgala and churidar. Langford was in formal Western evening attire, while the Khan Bahadur had not ignored his Mughal tradition. They were all here out of their concern for humankind. They were all busy people, with lots of problems of their own. They did not want for places to enjoy themselves either. But they had put aside their personal problems, sacrificed their individual pleasures only to spend the evening in the hotel for the greater good of society, the nation and the world.

'Take care of him,' whispered Bose-da, pointing at Agarwalla. I was about to ask why, but before I could Bose-da said, 'It's his company that has a permanent lease on suite number two as a guest house. You know Karabi, don't you? She's *their* hostess. She earns a fat bonus on top of her salary.'

What I'd read about the freedom movement—the tyranny of the British, the differences between Hindus and Muslims— all seemed untrue. Guest list in hand, Agarwalla whispered something in Langford's ear, who burst into laughter and leaned heavily on him. It didn't take long for the wave of that laughter to reach the Khan Bahadur, with the result that three civilizations became one before my very eyes.

The guests started arriving. Back from his meeting with Byron, Marco Polo stood in the hall in a freshly ironed sharkskin suit. He seemed worried, but I couldn't ask him anything in the crowd. We were all wearing freshly laundered suits too. Bose-da straightened my bow, saying, 'You have to be the epitome of style, there'll be trouble if you look sloppy.'

Bose-da probably knew everyone worth knowing in this distinguished gathering. Pointing out one of them, he said, 'Mr Chokhania, the cotton king. He's here alone, he never brings his wife.'

All three members of the Philanthropic Society went towards Chokhania. He clapped Agarwalla on his shoulder and moved towards the hall—he too hadn't objected to wasting his valuable time on service to humanity, and had turned up punctually.

'I can reel off the names of all those who will come,' said Bose-da. 'All parties in Calcutta have the same guests—because everyone uses the same list of names to mail invitations. The same people are invited every day, and every evening they dress up and set out—either to different hotels, or different clubs, or to someone's house in Alipore or on Burdwan Road.' He continued in a whisper, 'Watch Calcutta and its philanthropic citizens carefully because when the report of this session appears in tomorrow's papers, the real stuff won't be in there. They'll only carry an account of the speeches and summaries—and those have already reached the newspaper offices. The Bible's been written even before Jesus is born.'

A slim lady with a camera in her hand entered all by herself. 'Shampa Sanyal,' said Bose-da, 'patron goddess of anorexic French beauty! First she became Ghosh, then she married a Marathi named Valenkar or something, then Saha, then Mitra. Now she's gone back to her maiden name— Shampa Sanyal, society reporter.'

'What's that?' I asked like a fool.

'You know these society journals, don't you? Who's throwing a party, who's doing social work, how to do up your home, how to cook...all that kind of stuff. Her magazine sells thousands of copies, and she's to be found at every party in Calcutta. In fact, no party is complete without her—because if you throw a party and don't have it written about in the society journal, it's all in vain.'

Swinging her camera, Shampa Sanyal strolled up to the counter. 'Good evening,' said Bose-da with a nod.

'This time I'll run your photograph,' she said. 'Half the beautiful parties of Calcutta are held at Shahjahan.'

'Thank you.' Bose-da smiled politely.

'I don't feel like going in at all,' said Shampa. 'You know what I'd like to do? Sit in a room with you—alone.'

Bose-da went red with embarrassment; he didn't say a word.

'Where's your room?' she asked. 'Which floor?'

Bose-da probably smelt trouble and said candidly, in his usual manner, 'On the terrace. Three of us share a room—Shankar here, me and someone else, and that poor chap is confined to bed with dysentery.'

Shampa shrugged. 'Poor boy! They don't even give him a room to himself.'

'Fate, Miss Sanyal. God hasn't granted anything called privacy to hotel employees like us.' Bose-da sighed deeply, and then, with a smile on his face, said, 'Are you coming from another party?'

'Yes, there were two cocktails. Delightful affairs—but they would have been much better if there had been a handsome young man like you to escort me. Believe me, I'm telling you the truth.'

Bose-da signalled to William, who ushered Shampa Sanyal to the hall with a courteous 'Should we go to the hall, Miss Sanyal?'

'It's criminal,' said Bose-da gravely. 'Why do they let Bengali women drink whiskey? She isn't in her senses tonight.'

Others at the party included the barrister Sen, the radiotherapist Mitra, the gynaecologist Chatterjee, the sporting politician Basu, the political sportsman Pal, the kings—the kings of jute, oil and butter. Not even the kings of iron, aluminium and lime had been left out. There were even a couple of representatives of the zamindars, as specimens of a disappearing past.

Bose-da whispered to me as soon as the next gentleman walked in, 'Ah! There he is—fortune's favourite son, our only hope in industry, Madhab Pakrashi. The son of a poor man, he has risen from very humble beginnings to the pinnacle of success.'

Madhab Pakrashi made a beeline for our counter. I was shocked to see the lady next to him—it was Mrs Pakrashi! She was dressed in a traditional Bengali sari, the vermilion glowing in the parting of her hair. Mr Pakrashi was in an evening suit.

As soon as he saw him, Bose-da said, 'How do you do, sir?'

Pakrashi was famous for his cordiality. Smiling pleasantly, he said, 'I'm very well, but my wife isn't—she falls ill frequently.'

Mrs Pakrashi shook her head like a demure bride. 'What rubbish! It's you who work so hard and don't take care of your health.'

Madhab Pakrashi smiled and said, 'There wasn't a day last week when there wasn't a dinner invitation. Add to that twelve cocktails and fourteen lunches, and all that after turning down about fifteen. But you can't refuse every time. The problem's with my wife. She's so busy with her prayers all day that she refuses to go out. But everywhere—even in Bombay— it's the wives who act as public relations officers for their husbands. Whenever she doesn't accompany me to a party I have to give explanations…I'm not going to get my son married to a shy girl.'

Mrs Pakrashi was looking at her watch. 'Let's go, they'll start the meeting.'

'Oh, let me be with ordinary people for a while,' said Madhab Pakrashi. 'Let me get some fresh oxygen into my brain. Agarwalla's in there, he'll start talking about the share allotment of Madhab Industries any moment.'

'Let me carry on, then; as it is the industry has started thinking you've become snooty.'

'Please do, that's like a good PRO,' he encouraged his wife.

Mrs Pakrashi looked at Bose-da and went towards the hall. Bose-da must have read the message in that fleeting glance; I felt that I too had become cannier over the last few weeks— the meanings of many quick glances were becoming clear to me. Watching his wife's retreating back, Madhab Pakrashi said, 'I wouldn't have been able to build this kingdom without her—she's a wonderful wife.'

He hadn't come to the counter in search of only fresh oxygen—he had other business as well. He quickly raised the subject. 'Before I forget, two guests of mine will probably be coming to Calcutta from Germany next week. I want two suites for them—the best. I could have put them up at the club, but word gets out. I don't want anyone to know right now why they are coming.'

'Check the register,' Bose-da told me.

I did, but there were no suites available—all of them had been booked in advance. 'I'm afraid a foreign cultural mission is due—they've booked all the suites two months in advance.'

'What do I do then?' Pakrashi asked.

'What's the matter? What's the matter?' Agarwalla suddenly appeared on the scene.

'I wanted two suites—but Calcutta's hotels are in such bad

shape that unless you make your bookings a month in advance you can't even get a cot,' complained Pakrashi.

Agarwalla was indignant. 'How can you not get a suite when I'm here? We have a permanent suite for guests, by special arrangement with the Shahjahan. I'll send for the hostess.'

Bose-da turned towards me, 'Fetch Miss Guha from suite number two immediately.' I hurried off.

Karabi was probably halfway through her toilette when she opened the door—she was putting flowers in her hair. Seeing me, she smiled, her doe-black eyes radiant.

I have been deprived of the rare gift that God has given some people—of being able to tell a lady's age from one look at her. I get by with two words—young and old—and I'd have been happier not to use them. Nobody worries about the age of a man, but in the case of women it has, for aeons, been accorded the status of essential information. Karabi wasn't very old; I could say with some assurance that her young body didn't give a damn about age. With her lovely eyes, sharp nose, smooth neck and level shoulders she resembled a work of art. She was a little plump about the breast, but had kept her waist under strict control.

'Aren't you Bose's assistant?' she asked with a slight smile.

'Yes, ma'am. He's asking for you.'

'Bose is asking for me?' She seemed a trifle irritated.

'Mr Agarwalla and Mr Pakrashi are also there,' I said.

'Oh, I see.' She seemed to have gauged the importance of the matter. Just as a brand-new car has an effortless rhythm of its own as it comes to life, Karabi, too, rose from her chair with a unique rhythm all her own.

Back at the counter, I saw William standing alone. 'The meeting's probably begun,' he said. 'They've all gone inside.'

The two of us rushed off. 'Mr Agarwalla himself called for me?' asked Karabi. 'He said nothing to me when I spoke to him over the phone at three o'clock.'

The Pakrashis and Agarwalla had occupied a table in the banquet hall by then, while Bose-da had drawn the microphone from the corner of the room and placed it before the chief guest. The respected chief guest had flown to Calcutta only for the noble cause of serving mankind; dressed in national attire, he rose and, adjusting the cap on his head, said, 'Ladies and gentlemen.'

Karabi looked at him and chuckled. 'Good god! So that's who it is. No wonder he was being given the royal treatment this afternoon.'

Before I could hear any more, the speech began. 'Calcutta's illustrious citizens, I congratulate you for the pains that you have taken to spend your precious time here this evening. All these days, we have been thinking only of our nation, but now the time has come to think of man in a wider context. Especially since a son of this very Calcutta has said, "man is above all, nothing transcends man".'

Reporters were sitting at a separate table, taking down the main points. Suddenly they put their pencils down and exchanged glances. The famous writer Nagen Pal was seated next to the chief guest. He rose and whispered something in the latter's ear. The chief guest paused and said, 'The leading light of Indian literature, Nagen Pal, has just reminded me that the poet Chandidas had nothing to do with Calcutta. But my point is that Mr Das was born in Bengal, and who can think of Bengal without Calcutta?'

There was mild applause. The speaker continued, 'The main problem of the world is that of food—particularly rice. The amount of rice produced in the world is not enough to provide a square meal for every person in it.' Taking out a piece of paper, he started throwing statistical figures at the gathering.

Karabi was still standing by the door. 'What a bore,' she said. 'How long do I have to wait here?'

'You can go to Mr Agarwalla as soon as the speech is over.'

Karabi grimaced. 'You think he'll ever finish?'

'Well, this isn't a soapbox, it's a banquet hall, the speech is bound to end soon.'

Meanwhile, the speaker droned on, 'The key to the success of human civilization lies in distributing scarce resources in proportion with people's needs. People around the world and all of us here in India—the country of the Buddha, Ramakrishna, Vivekananda, Tagore, Mahatma Gandhi—have to make sacrifices. We will not use rice at any of the banquets of this society. Besides, twenty of our members have announced they will not eat rice at home either for the next few years. Among them are Mr Agarwalla, Mr...' He rattled off the names.

Karabi chuckled. 'What kind of place is this? Does everyone here have diabetes?'

'Meaning?' I whispered.

'How can Agarwalla have rice? He's diabetic. I have syringes and insulin stacked in my room too. When he spends the night here, he takes a dose himself.'

Every table had a menu card or two. Everyone was studying it. A short, squat, roguish character seated at a table with three friends summoned me. I approached with measured steps and bowed before them. Transferring the memo pad and menu to my left hand from my right, I whispered, 'Yes, sir?'

'Is this a vegetarian dinner?' he asked.

'No, sir,' I replied. 'There are several non-vegetarian items as well.'

'That's not what I'm talking about,' he snapped. 'Maybe there's a rice crisis—so drinking stuff made from it looks bad. But what about other kinds of liquor?'

I didn't know what to say. Bose-da was close by. He appeared in an instant and, nudging me aside, said, 'Excuse me, sir, I will request Mr Langford or Mr Agarwalla to explain.'

Crossing his legs, the gentleman said, 'Never mind Langford, ask Agarwalla to see me.'

Walking off towards Agarwalla, Bose-da said, 'Dangerous man, this Phokla Chatterjee. His real name is R.N. Chatterjee, used to be a boxer. Someone knocked his front teeth out. Alcoholic. His eyes are perpetually red, his crew-cut looks like a wire brush.'

Apparently, Chatterjee's presence is enough to make a party a smash hit. At least, that's what many people believe. He is invited to every cocktail and party in town. Only movie parties are a strict no-no. He had thrown up on actress Sreelekha Devi once at this hotel—Sreelekha Devi now refuses to attend a party where he's invited.

Agarwalla stood up as Bose-da approached him. 'Mr Chatterjee is asking for you,' Bose-da said.

'Oh my lord,' Agarwalla exclaimed and set off towards Chatterjee's table.

Phokla Chatterjee said, 'Agarwalla, what kind of joke is this? You aim to serve humanity, but you're forcing so many of God's creatures to suffer. There is no liquor on the menu.'

The chief guest was still speaking. Agarwalla was in a spot. Phokla Chatterjee grabbed his hand and said, 'Don't try to run away. I can create a scene right now. I don't care for any president or chief guest.'

Agarwalla said, 'My dear fellow, we were very keen on serving cocktails. But the chief guest was unwilling. He refused to give a speech if alcohol was going to be served.'

Phokla uttered an obscenity. 'So the bugger's going to be a disapproving aunt. You mean to tell me he's acquired that round shape without drinking?'

Agarwalla tried damage control. 'For them drinking in public is…'

Phokla rose. 'I get it. Fine, I'm going to drink privately. I'm off to Mumtaz.'

Bose-da said, 'The bar's open till ten, you'll get anything you want.'

'Pass me some cash. Forgot my wallet. Better still, tell them to add my bill at the bar to yours over here.'

'All right,' said Agarwalla. Heading off towards the bar, Phokla Chatterjee muttered, 'Damn it, I had two other cocktail invitations. Who'd have come to listen to sermons if I'd known it was going to be dry?'

'Tell them at the bar to not ask him for money,' Bose-da instructed me.

By the time I returned after settling Phokla at the bar, the chief guest was congratulating the people present for the memorable precedence they had set by pledging their love to all mankind. He had no doubt that the road to success for Indians lay in love, devotion and compassion.

And so to dinner. Or, given the time by the clock, you could call it supper. Since there was no rice, the cost was two and a half rupees more. Thirty bearers and the five of us had our hands full trying to serve 300 guests.

In the midst of all this, the chief guest shouted at me, 'So many of you, and yet you can't serve the guests in time.'

I was silent. Agarwalla said, 'In India five people can serve five hundred.'

Performing surgery on the chicken, Madhab Pakrashi said solemnly, 'This is supposed to be English service.'

'It's becoming obvious that in many respects the West is falling behind us.'

Nagen Pal addressed the chief guest, 'Sir, why don't you write a book, *Decline and Fall of the West*?'

'I could. The publishers of Nehru's *Discovery of India* have requested me several times.'

I had often seen the chief guest's pictures in the papers and read his speeches. So I didn't take his rebuke to heart. The respected gentleman had initially said he was vegetarian but would eat eggs. The aroma of chicken probably made him change his mind. 'Is the chicken tender?' he asked Pakrashi.

'Quite...I've been all over the world, but you can't beat Calcutta chicken for tenderness and taste,' Pakrashi replied with a smile.

The chief guest said, 'Get me a plate of chicken.'

I held out a tray to him. Without wasting words, he emptied it on his plate. Abandoning his fork and knife, he grabbed a piece with his hands and started crunching the bone. At the sound, foreign consuls sitting at nearby tables turned his way in surprise. Wiping his nose with the handkerchief in his left hand, he declared, 'I started this the last time I was abroad. They were stunned. That half-foreign Bombay writer Miss Postwalla tried to stop me, but I'm a pure Indian, why should I bother? I ate the stew with my hands and licked my fingers too.'

The dessert service had started. Taking two ice creams for himself, the chief guest observed, 'These help digestion, I'm going to have them later. Get me some more chicken quickly, preferably boneless.' As I retreated in search of chicken, I heard him telling Nagen Pal, 'This is a foreign concern, don't hold back. These fellows will wring us out with their charges, make fat profits, send them abroad in the form of foreign exchange. Make the most of it. Don't worry, I am fully equipped. Digestives, soda, mint, I have them all, don't worry at all.'

As I extended another plate of chicken towards him, he said, 'Doesn't quite sate the appetite without a little rice. But what to do, we have to make these sacrifices for India, for the world.'

Agarwalla belched and said, 'I must say your speech was wonderful.'

The chief guest belched even more grotesquely. 'True. But even better than that was tonight's menu. These buggers do wring every last penny out of you, but they give you great stuff. That's why foreign firms are doing so well in India.'

Karabi had organized things meanwhile. Everything had been arranged for Madhab Pakrashi's guests to stay in Agarwalla's guest house. But she hadn't been able to return to her quarters—she had had to dine with the others at Agarwalla's request. I ran into her as she got up to make her way out. She looked down the hall and smiled. Gomez's band had struck up by then. The advantage of the music was that you couldn't hear at one table what was being said at the next. Everyone felt safe in the privacy this afforded.

Karabi said, 'I couldn't get over this chief guest of yours! The suite had been reserved for him tonight. He asked for a photograph to see what I look like! He said it wouldn't look good for him to spend the night here—he'd go back to his regular place—but he had no objection to a few hours' rest in my room.' She laughed out loud. Before I could comprehend what she had just said, she quickened her steps and said, 'Goodbye. I'd better go and make arrangements for the respected guest.'

The implication of 'making arrangements' for the respected guest was not difficult to gauge from Karabi's forlorn yet resigned expression. The guests left one by one. Discussing humanitarianism with her husband, Mrs Pakrashi climbed into a waiting car. Mr Agarwalla and his English guest didn't linger either. The only person to stay behind was the honourable chief guest who wanted to revive his tired body, exhausted in the line of duty, in the quiet, cool refuge of suite number two. It was not a long sojourn though—he left soon enough, in fact even before the date on the calendar had changed. His hasty departure, as witnessed from the reception counter, is well-preserved in the album of my memories. Finding no resemblance between the furtive figure darting past me and his photographs in the newspapers, I was taken aback for a moment. Perhaps all news was about suppressing part of the truth; perhaps this was how the illustrious names of remarkable people were written in the pages of history.

I am not a cynic. I have faith in the greatness of man. Yet, when in moments of leisure I relive the events of that night, I cannot help question my inherent faith. I recall Karabi seeing off the distinguished guest, glancing at me on the way in the manner, I thought, of a sophisticated hostess. But after he was gone, on her way back, she paused for a moment. I still cannot fathom why she looked at me like that. I wasn't experienced enough at the time to comprehend everything, but in dark Karabi's eyes I discerned a fatigue accumulated over a lifetime. I didn't understand much, but her hurt eyes seemed to think that I had grasped it all; my silence seemed to publicly insult her tortured body.

As she stood before me, weary to the bone, I couldn't help noticing how the grace and poise I had witnessed earlier in the evening when I had gone to summon her had deserted her. For some reason she felt like a kindred soul. She asked, 'How much longer?'

I smiled. 'A long way—I have to be up all night.'

'Poor thing,' she said softly, and almost staggered towards her room.

I still feel embarrassed thinking of the events of that night. The intelligent, experienced reader will forgive this naïve employee of Shahjahan Hotel. For a moment that night I felt I wasn't a 'poor thing' at all. I was extremely fortunate. By God's grace, I had been born as myself, and not as Karabi Guha. I felt that in his scheme of creation, God had made men the more fortunate species. Whoever the creator of women might be, he had not been partial to them. The same thought was to occur to me once more the day Mrs Pakrashi told Karabi, 'I wonder how God could have created a woman like you!'

But that was a few days later. There were still a few days to go before Madhab Pakrashi's guests arrived to enjoy the hospitality of suite number two. In the meantime someone else arrived at the hotel, someone I became well-acquainted with: Connie. If it had not been for her I wouldn't really have become familiar with Shahjahan Hotel. Rather, if Connie is omitted from this memoir, there wouldn't be much left in the sum total of my experiences at Shahjahan. Even now when I meet a woman I don't know, or when I have to form an opinion about someone, I try to bring Connie to mind. She no longer seems a flesh-and-blood creature to me, she's more like a dream. I do not know how exactly to describe her. It was as if she shone with an incandescent light; her dazzle a momentary flash, like that of a camera, illuminating briefly, with great clarity, the darkness of this urban jungle.

It was from Marco Polo that I first heard of Connie. He came to the counter one day with her photograph. Rosie was sitting next to me, clipping her nails and saying, 'This nail-clipper's blunt.'

'Why don't you use a blade?' I said.

Sticking her tongue out, she said, 'What kind of young man are you? When a young lady tells you her nail-clipper's blunt, you should be running out to buy her a new one, instead of which you merely tell her to use a blade!'

'My dear girl, this young man has given you good advice. You won't have any trouble with a blade.' Both of us jumped at Marco Polo's voice—we hadn't seen him come. Smiling, he said, 'Rosie, I need the airlines letter right away—if they introduce a new service to Calcutta, we'll need many more rooms. The letter's in my office, please fetch it quickly.'

Rosie hurried away from the counter. Marco Polo turned to me. 'Now to business. Strictly speaking, this isn't your job—it's Rosie's. But I have heard from Jimmy that she can't stand women; it gets her back up when she hears another woman is coming to Shahjahan.' He handed me a photograph, and said with a laugh, 'Young men shouldn't be looking at these pictures, either, but since you work for a hotel, it's different. The ideal hotel worker is neither masculine, nor feminine!'

The girl in the photograph, as he had said, was a blue-eyed beauty with platinum hair. 'I want you to put an advertisement in the papers: CONNIE, THE WOMAN, IS COMING.'

Many of you must have seen that advertisement in the leading dailies.

Later that day, Bose-da handed me a heap of photographs and said, 'You'd better learn how to display pictures too— you'll soon be juggling many roles.'

The photographs were all of Connie. I arranged them as artistically as I could on the two boards near the entrance, with the caption 'Connie is Coming'.

Bose-da was very pleased. 'Wonderful, a real artist's touch— looks like you used to arrange pictures of half-naked cabaret dancers at the Shahjahan in your previous life.'

I smiled. 'I don't believe in rebirth—it's just that pupils learn faster if the teacher's good.'

Bose-da read the advertisement again: 'Connie is coming. Coming, yes, but do you know from where?' Then, answering his own question, he went on, 'Many people think these beauties arrive straight out of the blue to the cabaret at Shahjahan. She's just conquered the Middle East and is doing a show in Persia—from there it'll be straight to Shahjahan.'

He was in a good mood. He told me that Connie was charging a lot. 'Cabaret girls usually do,' he said. 'If they knew how much, many top-notch barristers and surgeons flaunting FRCS degrees would breakdown in despair. All their pride and commitment and expertise would be ground to dust under the feet of the dancing beauties of the cabaret!'

'That sounds more like a football metaphor than a dance one,' I interrupted.

'Right you are. What else do these dancing queens do but play football with the male brain? Guests often come up to the counter and ask how much the girls are paid,' he warned me. 'Your standard reply should be, "I am sorry, I don't know." The cabaret documents are absolutely confidential.'

Bose-da had already filled me in on cabaret dancers. Their engagements were normally fixed six to eight months beforehand. There were special companies in Paris that arranged these performances. In hotel parlance, these were called 'chain programmes'. The cabaret girls danced their way around the world, marking out a few select cities in which to perform. Starting their journey eastwards or westwards, they moved ahead, doing two-week programmes here and three-week ones there. Before the programme in one city ended, the dancer's photographs were sent on to the next venue and ads were released. In this fashion, they eventually made their way back home.

The world had become smaller these days, an enormous mass of land named China having been wiped off the cabaret map. China alone used to take up five months or so of the itinerary—now Hong Kong was the only saving grace, but how much time could one spend there? Besides, it was a free port now, which meant that there was considerable freedom everywhere, and the night guests expected that much more; satisfying the guests of a free port was rather difficult for most dancers.

The most priceless commodity in the cabaret market was youth. Dancers' rates varied according to the ebb and tide of this fluid quality. As a result, dancers had to get themselves photographed every three months and produce a certificate to prove that the picture was a recent one. Connoisseurs scanned these photographs carefully and fixed the rate. Marco Polo said it was a very treacherous business—passing off four or five-year-old pictures as recent ones was common practice. The hotel had, therefore, made arrangements with a few well-known studios around the world where the dancers had to get themselves photographed. I believe a couple of studios in Calcutta were also part of the list. Dancers got themselves photographed and then sent the pictures to Kuala Lumpur, Tokyo, Manila or, girdling the Pacific Ocean, all the way to distant America.

'These night-blossoms cost a lot,' Bose-da smiled and said. 'For instance—the German girl named Hydrogen Bomb used to charge a hundred and eighty pounds a week, besides board and lodging and passage money. Or take the Egyptian, Farida, who was advertised as the butter-breasted beauty—she and her sister charged three thousand pounds a month between them; that's nearly forty thousand rupees. Then there was Lola, the Tomato Girl, from Cuba, who used to have ten tomatoes hanging around her body every day, selling them at hundred rupees each. If you paid for it, you could tear off a tomato from anywhere on her body—she would bite it, suck a little of the juice and give it to you; you could suck a little and give it back to her. She charged five hundred dollars a week. But Marjorie, a fabulous singer, used to get just hundred dollars a week, and she didn't attract much of a crowd, either. She was a Negro. I've never heard a lovelier voice in my life.'

These huge payments to the cabaret beauties were also a great gamble. No one could tell whether Calcutta's discerning citizens would be pleased enough to throng the hotel every night, drinking bottle after bottle and paying up. For six days a week, they'd make the night as bright as day; only on the dry day, when no liquor was sold, was there no show. Who wanted to listen to music or watch dances holding empty glasses? Instead, there were special programmes at lunchtime on Sunday, but those shows were much more restrained, much more civilized.

Discerning circles responded quite favourably to the

advertisement for Connie. 'The language has a lot to do with it,' Bose-da said. 'Between the movie chaps and ourselves, we've exhausted all the words in the dictionary that describe feminine beauty. However explicit, nothing is provocative enough. After days of spicy food, you long for plain home cooking, which is why I thought of "Connie, the Woman, is Coming to Calcutta".'

People started enquiring over the telephone the day after the advertisement was published: rich fathers' sons, contractors who needed deals, sales officers who wanted to keep purchase officers happy. I had to take many of those phone calls.

'Hello, is that Shahjahan Hotel?'

'Good afternoon, this is the reception.'

'Could you tell me something about Connie the Woman? Is she starting her shows on Saturday?'

'Yes, sir.'

'I'd like to book a table for the first night.'

'I'm sorry, sir, we're full on opening night. We have only three hundred and fifty seats, you see...'

'Hello, is that Shahjahan Hotel? What's the admission fee for Connie's show?'

'The admission fee is five rupees, and dinner is seven and a half rupees.'

'What about the dress code?'

'There are dress restrictions, sir, evening formals or national.'

Phokla Chatterjee telephoned, too. 'Is that Bose? This is Chatterjee.'

'Mr Bose is not available right now, sir, this is Shankar.'

'Look, I want three tickets on the opening night, booked for Mr Ranganathan.'

'We don't have a single ticket, sir. We're all sold out.'

'What? What about at black-market rates?'

'No sir, we haven't given more than five to anyone.'

Phokla wasn't willing to let go so easily. 'I have to have

the tickets,' he said. 'By hook or by crook. Ranganathan is leaving the very next day. Tell me the names of those who have booked tables—you're Bengali, we expect some consideration from you. Is it fair for all of Calcutta's pleasures to be monopolized by non-Bengalis?'

'I can do nothing, sir,' I said. 'I'll read you the names: Mr Khaitan, Mr Bajoria, Mr Lal, Mr McFarlane, Saha, Sen, Chatterjee, Loknathan, Joseph, Lang Chang Sun. There's more: Singh, Sharma, Ali, Basu, Upadhyay, Jajodia, Motiram, Hiraram, Chuniram, Chhatawala, Whiskywala.'

'All those buggers are having fun on the house, and genuine parties like us can't get tickets.'

'I beg your pardon, sir?'

'Those bloody pigs have expense accounts—they'll submit even the bills for their pleasure women to their companies. And we who want to pay our own way in can't get a seat. The government's snoring its head off. All right, check if Agarwalla's name is on the list.'

'Yes sir, against two tables for five each,' I said.

'Thank god, I might as well ask him to let me have a table. That bugger Ranganathan is a south Indian. Has nothing but tamarind and sambar at home in Bangalore, and a harridan of a wife. The poor chap's here on business for a few days, and wants a little titillation. But he's new here, knows nothing, and he's full of fears—fear for his life, fear for his heart, fear of diseases—which is why he doesn't dare go anywhere he wants to. So I'm his guide.'

I was about to put the phone down when Chatterjee asked me a question I'd never heard before. 'By the way, I forgot the most important point. Why didn't you put the statistics in the advertisement?'

'Statistics, sir?'

'You'd better find out from Bose, I'll call you later.' Chatterjee rang off.

Bose-da explained the meaning of the word 'statistics' to me. 'And to think you used to work at the High Court,' he chided me. 'Don't you know the yardstick of modern civilization? In today's world a man is measured by his bank balance and a woman by her figure: 36-22-34, 34-20-34—that is all our patrons need to get the picture.'

We didn't have Connie's statistics yet. 'I have ones that are six months old,' said Marco Polo, 'but we can't give out those.'

Phokla Chatterjee phoned again.

'Yes sir, we've sent a reply-paid cable for the latest statistics,' said Bose-da over the phone, 'but we haven't got an answer yet. It'll be a very nice show, sir, it's not just a dance routine, there's more.'

'Really? Please give me a hint...it will help me keep Ranganathan warm. Poor fellow—his wife gives him hell every day.'

'Sorry, I'm not allowed to tell you now, sir, you'll see it all live.'

From eight in the evening, the road in front of Shahjahan was jammed with cars, as though someone had scooped up the most beautiful automobiles of the country in a giant net and brought them to the hotel. As car after car drove up and stopped for a moment at the gate, the doorman opened the door and saluted the passengers stepping out.

Attired in evening dress, I dropped in on Nityahari—to remind him to change my bed sheet. Seated amidst a pile of dirty linen, he said, 'I'll send you a fresh one. What's the crowd of cars like?'

'Huge,' I replied.

'Everyone in this country's become an Englishman,' he grumbled. 'Those who claim that the English won India in an orchard in Plassey in 1757 know little about history. Actually, victory came many years later, right before our eyes, on 15

August 1947, our Independence Day. The country went English overnight.' Pausing briefly, he continued, 'When Gandhi was leading the freedom struggle, when people were going to jail, singing "Bande Mataram" and wearing khadi, we used to be scared that our hotel jobs wouldn't last long. My brother-in-law was a film projectionist in an English cinema hall in Chowringhee. The two of us were under the impression that all this would stop with Independence, that not even a fly would enter an English cinema hall, that Shahjahan Hotel would become a desert, and Mumtaz Bar would close down. Sending Christ, cricket and the cabaret packing, the Englishmen would also push off, leaving us old men in the lurch.'

He rose, saying, 'I have to visit your lady Connie.' Then, almost as an afterthought added, 'And yet, strangely enough the demand for pillows seems to be rising, liquor sales are increasing, and hotel rooms are full. But I have to go, I can't stand here talking to you all day. I'm going to find out if Connie wants extra pillows. I'll even offer her a bolster,' he said, rubbing his nose with his left hand. 'Those foreigners don't use them. I sometimes feel like getting them addicted to bolsters. Just revenge for what they did to us. I've even done it with one or two of them. The Nata pillow, they call it. Once you acquire the habit you can't shake it off! The bolster has ruined the Bengali race.'

Cars were still arriving outside. Old men got off young cars, and young men got off old ones. The very essence of male Calcutta seemed to have gathered at Shahjahan—barely a couple of miles from where Tagore and Vivekananda were born, where Aurobindo and Subhash Bose joined the quest for an independent India, where William Jones sowed the seeds of Western thought in this country, where David Hare taught children how to read and write.

There wasn't an inch of space at Mumtaz bar. William Ghosh was lording it over the crowd at the restaurant door, seated at a table with the ticket book and a cashbox. Many people were buying advance tickets. Phokla Chatterjee and his companion Ranganathan had already occupied chairs in the front row. He was in national dress that evening. Parabashia stood at the door, keeping a watch on people's attire.

When a man in shirtsleeves was about to enter, Parabashia stopped him. William rose and showed him the notice in front of the door (Rights of Admission Reserved), saying, 'We're terribly sorry, but you can't enter in that dress.'

The guest's face reddened, and he said, 'Even in independent India it's still a South African regime, I see.'

I told him, 'There's plenty of time, you could change and come back.'

Growling with rage, he disappeared, only to return in fifteen minutes, looking the perfect Westerner. When I nodded to him he said, 'Two hundred and fifty rupees down the drain—I had to buy a ready-made suit. I'll teach you people a lesson. I'm going to write a letter to the papers about this.'

Alcohol was flowing like water; Tobarak Ali and Ram Singh had started whipping open soda bottles from eight o'clock, and the beer, whisky, rum and gin, free of the confines of bottles, were dancing about inside glasses. When Marco Polo went to Ram Singh to find out the situation, Ram Singh said, 'Very hot. We'll sell six or seven thousand rupees' worth.'

After downing two White Labels, Phokla ordered a large peg of Dimple Scotch, while the salt-and-pepper haired Ranganathan sat nursing a shot of Cinzano vermouth. Chatterjee said to us, 'Mr Ranganathan's put me in a real spot; I keep telling him, when in Rome do as Romans do—Connie's from Scotland, and so is Dimple, but he keeps sitting there with Italy on his lap.'

Ranganathan shook his head and said morosely, 'Blood pressure.'

Chatterjee said, 'Try a peg—that pressure will climb down from the rooftops to the basement. And Connie will work as the sedative—put your nerves to sleep. This is her first appearance in Calcutta, but a friend of mine saw her perform in Cairo, he went from Damascus to Cairo for her show.'

'I'm not particularly used to whiskey,' said Ranganathan.

'Don't say that before these young men,' said Phokla. 'They'll start laughing if they hear that even at fifty-two you haven't got used to whiskey. Such things are unimaginable, even in our wildest dreams, in Calcutta.'

Ram Singh, Tobarak Ali and the other 'wet' boys had worked up a frenetic pace by now. The hall had become pungent with the foul smell of tobacco, as though teargas shells had been thrown inside. The hands of the clock were gradually creeping up to ten, and the clink of the dinner crockery sounded like part of an orchestra.

'How much longer?' shouted Phokla.

It was my turn now. Bose-da could barely speak, thanks to a bad cold, and kept coughing. Marco Polo had agreed to 'give the young man a chance'. Over in the corner Gomez's band played on indefatigably. Bose-da signalled to me from the door, and, as in a cinema hall, the bright lights in the corners went out. With a beating heart I went and stood in front of the stage, the mike in my left hand. At my signal, the orchestra fell silent. 'Cheerio,' said Gomez softly.

I saw before me seven hundred eyes suddenly come alive with expectation. Almost without my knowing it, the words slipped out: 'Ladies and gentlemen.' Though I couldn't find a real lady in the hall that evening, I repeated, 'Good evening, ladies and gentlemen. On this splendid evening at Shahjahan Hotel we hope you have been savouring the cuisine of our French chef, and the wines carefully chosen from several countries. I now present to you Connie—you have seen many women in your eventful lives, but she is *the* woman, the only one of her kind created by God in this century.'

All the lights went out at once, and a soft hum of anticipation rose in the hall. But under some invisible influence, it suddenly died out, though for just a moment. By some strange chemical reaction, the fading sound was unexpectedly transformed into light. Piercing the darkness, a needle-sharp beam of light fell on the stage, seeking someone in its inebriated wandering. Someone had even appeared onstage, but the drunken beam simply couldn't stay still long enough. Was the figure on stage, wearing a veil of darkness, Connie herself?

Without teasing the patrons' curiosity any longer, the beam grew stronger. But where was Connie? She was nowhere to be found. Instead, a two-foot-tall dwarf in evening dress was strutting about on the stage. He had a three-foot-high top hat on his head and a cane in his hand.

Without giving the disappointed audience a chance to express its disapproval, the dwarf took off his hat with his left hand and, twirling his cane, climbed on the chair, saying, 'Good evening, ladies and gentlemen, I am Connie the...' Then, as though he had forgotten, he started muttering, 'Man or woman, woman or man...no, I am the woman Connie, Connie the woman.'

The audience started shouting. A few among them couldn't sit still any longer. Rising from their chairs they started screaming, 'We want Connie—where did this blasted dwarf turn up from?'

According to our plans, I had to do some acting, too. Pretending to be dumbstruck by the appearance of this dwarf instead of Connie onstage, I stood before the mike and said, 'Pardon me, ladies and gentlemen, I cannot quite understand. Barely five minutes ago I was in Connie's room. She had finished dressing and was just about to take a vitamin pill. You go ahead and make the announcement, she told me, I'm ready. And now this two-foot-tall gentleman has arrived out of nowhere!'

The dwarf wasn't put out, though. No sooner had I finished than he raced up to the mike, brought it down to the level of his face and said in a thin, feminine voice, 'Believe me, I am, I am Connie—I took the wrong pill by mistake. All the same, I'm delighted that all of you have stayed awake for me till eleven at night.' After that he started dancing like a cabaret girl, at which the entire hall burst out in protest.

I went up to the mike and said, 'Don't be impatient, ladies and gentlemen, I'm sending for a doctor right away. It's the wrong tablet that's led to this unforeseen mishap.'

The dwarf said, 'Five minutes ago I was a woman, I was young—but now?' He started feeling about his body, as if searching for something, pulled out another tablet from his pocket, gulped it down and started muttering an incantation. Suddenly the lights went out once again, and a Marwari businessman in the front row screamed. 'My God! There's someone sitting on my lap!'

In the darkness, I said, 'Don't be scared, what does it feel like?'

He had got over his fear by now, having realized just who it was. 'Very soft!' he replied.

Now a single beam of light came on, and it revealed Connie sitting with her arms draped around the man in the front row. She had on a tiara and a necklace, besides the soft, multicoloured fabric covering her from neck to ankle. A few more lights came on, and, dragging her captive up to the stage, Connie bowed to the audience.

The prisoner freed himself, along with his enormous paunch, with great difficulty and went back panting to his chair. I announced, 'Ladies and gentlemen, we present to you Connie; she has been on television several times, she has even appeared before His Highness King George VI, but tonight each one of you is her king—the king and emperor of Connie, the Woman!'

Connie began her dance now—but in that long, flowing outfit, there wasn't much pace to her routine, which deflated the audience a little. 'My darling Calcuttans,' said Connie, 'I believe some of you have been asking for my statistics. I'm sorry, but I never can remember figures—maybe one of you could measure them for yourself? Any mathematics professors among you?'

There was no reply from the audience. 'A chartered accountant perhaps?' asked Connie, making a face. No reply.

'A tailor?' The hall was still silent. 'Dear, dear,' she wiped her eyes in simulated grief, 'are there no tailors in this great city? Don't your girls wear anything that's stitched?'

Everyone burst out laughing, but I felt my stomach churning, my head reeling. I thought I would collapse any moment. Gomez tugged at my jacket and said, 'Cheer up, it's going very well.'

'Anybody with a head for figures?' Connie sent out another appeal. Phokla was apparently waiting for just such an opportunity—he rose immediately and approached the stage, while I threw a measuring tape at Connie.

Meanwhile, the dwarf had returned to the stage. He seemed a little taken aback at the sight of the beautiful Connie and kept biting his tongue and scratching his head, not sure what to do. At the other end of the stage Connie stood with her face averted, handing the tape to Phokla and saying, 'Measure for yourself—yesterday it was 38-24-36.'

The dwarf stood at the mike and whispered to the audience, 'I was mistaken; I'm not Connie. My name is Lambreta, Lambreta, the man.' Then he looked at Connie and screamed, 'Hello, miss. I'm an expert statistician, a qualified accountant, and a famous tailor, and I can do complicated sums in my head.' He pulled out a handkerchief from his pocket and started wiping his face. Seeing that Phokla was all set to start measuring the long-limbed Connie, he loped towards them

awkwardly. His eyes seemed to be on fire. Trying to push
Phokla aside, he said, 'Get away, I'm going to measure her.'

Phokla paid no attention to him at first, but soon Lambreta
pushed him with all his strength. The hall-full of people were
laughing fit to burst, and Chatterjee was forced to hand the
tape to the dwarf and return to where he'd been sitting.
Meanwhile, Connie had begun humming a song, and couldn't
hear what Lambreta was screaming from around her knees. She
was standing with her legs slightly apart, and twice the dwarf
passed between them, at which some members of the audience
whistled obscenely. But Lambreta had no time for them. He
tried his best to attract the lady's attention, while the proud,
tall Connie appeared not to have seen him at all.

Failing in all his attempts, Lambreta suddenly got hold of
a ladder from somewhere. But as soon as he propped it up
against Connie's back and started climbing it, she walked off;
he wasn't going to give up, though—he clung on to her dress.
Now it became clear that the ladder was on wheels, because
as Connie moved away, so did the ladder, taking Lambreta
with it. The faster the ladder moved, the more scared he
looked—in desperation he pretended to clutch her around the
waist. In the midst of all this, Connie did an about-turn,
whereupon he spun around, too. By now he had grown
bolder, and climbed a little further up the ladder, saying, 'Miss
Connie, I've brought you a rose.'

Overcome with gratitude, Connie said, 'Oh what a lovely
rose! Really, there's nobody like you!'

As soon as he heard this, Lambreta fell off the ladder in
excitement, but Connie paid no attention. Struggling back to
his feet, he brushed the dust off himself and, propping the
ladder back against Connie, tried to kiss her. Failing to express
his passion physically he tried to show it verbally, but the
attempt backfired. As soon as he had climbed up the ladder to
whisper something in her ear, Connie grabbed him and

dangled him by his ears. Swinging his legs wildly, he cried out pathetically, 'Please, please, pardon me, miss, I'll never propose to such a tall girl again, it was a big mistake.'

When Connie threw Lambreta down on the floor, a few people rolled on to the carpet from their chairs, laughing. For a moment the lights came on very bright, and showed Lambreta running away.

Going up to the mike, I said, 'Now that we've got rid of the dwarf with great difficulty, the dance is about to begin.'

Smiling sweetly at me, Connie took off her voluminous robe. Gomez's band was busy trying to awaken the animal passions slumbering within the depths of the human mind, with a teasing rhythm. Dancing her way off the stage, Connie went over and sat on a guest's lap, as she laughingly took his neighbour's handkerchief to wipe off her perspiration. Another man called out, 'We're waiting back here.' Connie floated off in that direction, sitting on his lap for a while. Then she pulled Mr Ranganathan up, caressed him and said, 'Hello, my boy, come sit on my lap.'

Ranganathan was about to object, but Connie brushed his murmurs aside and forced him down on to her lap. He had probably been somewhat softened—under the effect of alcohol he caressed her dress and said, 'Lovely.'

Putting her arms around him, Connie said, 'I'm like a mine, the deeper you dig, the more jewels you will find.'

Who knew what Ranganathan made of that, but Connie had no more time to spare. Pushing him away, she began her act. One by one, her clothes came off—the tiara bid farewell, the gloves on her hands disappeared, and then the skirt slid off, whereupon Calcutta, hungry for feminine flesh, raised a cheer. But the very next moment their hopes were dashed to the ground as they realized that Connie was dressed in several sets of clothes, one beneath the other.

After that, I remember nothing. I saw Gomez's face distort

with loathing and exhaustion, while his assistants played on furiously, like machines. All of a sudden there was nothing covering Connie, and at that instant, the hall went dark. Picking up a diaphanous piece of cloth from the floor, she preserved her modesty somehow and disappeared.

The lights came on and the crowd burst into a frenzied, prolonged applause. Standing on the stage, I saw numerous items of clothing strewn about, the midget Lambreta picking up the skirt, panties, blouse and brassiere slowly, one by one.

'Ladies and gentlemen, there will be a few minutes' interval,' I announced into the mike.

Wiping his face with a handkerchief, Gomez said, 'It's the death-knell of civilization—can't you hear it?'

The band struck up once again, and the guests took advantage of the break to consume a few more pegs. I even saw Ranganathan trying out the whiskey.

The lights went out once again, and the tinkle of anklets filled the entire hall. A strange wave of sound emanated from Gomez's instruments. I felt as though I was sitting in a dense forest, where the doe had been calling all night long—all the stags heard her, but only those who could identify the sound approached her. On that strange evening, it was time for love.

The lights came on slowly, revealing Connie on the stage. Amazing! She had no clothes covering her, only balloons, hundreds of them. The coloured lights mingled with the coloured balloons to create whole new shades of the spectrum. Connie started dancing and as she danced, she strolled among the guests, handing a small metal pin to one of them, saying, 'Go on, burst one.' He plunged the steel pin into a balloon near her breasts, and it exploded with a grotesque bang.

After dancing a few more steps, Connie went up to another guest, who also burst a balloon. As the number of balloons decreased, more and more of her body could be seen. And the madness in the hall reached a crescendo. Clearly the

stags were fearless tonight. There was unbridled excitement in
the air. Lust, desire and craving were palpable everywhere.

There were only three balloons left on Connie's body
now. A few old men rushed forward together to pierce them,
and as the balloons exploded, all the lights went out. Trying to
make her escape in the darkness, poor Connie tripped on the
carpet and fell. I helped her up, and heard her gasp, 'Please get
me my robe.'

I gave it to her, and she ran out of the hall.

The lights came on again, and with it I seemed to have
regained consciousness. Next to me lay a pair of Connie's
shoes. Gomez packed his instruments with the help of his boys,
his eyes studiously downcast. Going up to the mike, I managed
to speak: 'Ladies and gentlemen, I thank you on behalf of
Connie and Shahjahan Hotel for being present at this pleasant
gathering. Goodnight.'

But there was no respite yet. Phokla came up to me and
said, 'Mr Ranganathan wants to meet Connie.'

A few more people made the same request.

Swaying in his inebriated state, Phokla drawled, 'That's
why I like coming to the first show. She won't be as free in
the next one. The lords of law and order in Calcutta will never
allow so much—at least, they'll never allow the last three
balloons to be burst.' Before leaving, he said, 'Another thing—
I'm asking you because you're Bengali—they're never
completely nude, are they? That's not allowed in Calcutta, is
it? They probably have something thin on—nylon or silk, isn't
that so?'

I could feel my ears burning; I couldn't speak. Looking at
him, I somehow managed to say, 'Honestly, I have no idea.'

Gomez was standing in front of me. 'Come on, let's go
back to our rooms,' he said.

Phokla and Ranganathan exchanged a few words, after
which Phokla grabbed my hand and whispered, 'I have

something to say to you in private—strictly private and confidential.'

I went out with him to the car park. Standing by his car, he said, 'This is a very nice place, there isn't another hotel as respectable in the country. They have shows elsewhere too, but those have no dignity. As I was saying, you are a Bengali, it's your duty to take care of my needs. And it's my duty to ensure that you make some money over and above your salary.'

I still couldn't make out what he was getting at. He now leaned towards Ranganathan and, taking a few ten-rupee notes out of his pocket, held them out to me, saying, 'You know what the problem is? Mr Rangnathan is feeling very lonely, he's all alone in Calcutta. I have to go back home right now, my wife is waiting for me. If you could get Connie to agree— it's not very late yet, and besides, they're used to staying up nights, they can always sleep all day.'

I was in no frame of mind to reply; I quickly drew my hand back as though an electric current had passed through it, and stared at him. Phokla burst out laughing. 'Too young...you're very raw, very green.' Putting the notes back in his pocket, he said, 'You've put me in a spot. If I'd known I would have made arrangements elsewhere. He's a very important purchase officer—I can't possibly ask him to spend the night in any old place.'

His car left with Ranganathan in it, as did the other cars with their owners sitting in them.

I hadn't enjoyed a single moment of the evening. Though I hadn't had time for dinner, I didn't want any now. I went out of the hotel on an impulse, almost against my instincts.

Buses and trams had stopped plying long ago; it was as if someone had injected the indisposed city with a strong sedative and put it to sleep. Never before had I seen this calm and yet terrifying face of Calcutta by night. Walking down Chittaranjan

Avenue, I went and stood before Sir Ashutosh Mukherjee in
his judge's robes. The stout Sir Ashutosh remained perpetually
at the crossing, the illuminated globe atop the head office of
the Calcutta Electric Supply Corporation still rotating according
to its own sweet will.

I have to beg your indulgence once more. Bose-da had
told me only to observe and not ask questions, and yet, in the
middle of the night I was forced to ask myself: Was this
Calcutta? Was this the city of our dreams? Or was I standing
alone and helpless in, as the poet had put it, the dense forests
of Libya? I recalled the words of a poem by Bose-da's favourite
poet. It was he who had made me read the poem many times.

> Turning on the hydrant the leper licks up the water
> Or perhaps the hydrant was always on, being out of order
> Midnight descends on the city in droves...
>
> ★
>
> Yet from the window above
> In a voice all her own
> Sings the half-awake Jewish girl...
>
> ★
>
> Smart young foreigners walk by
> Leaning against a pillar an old Negro smiles,
> Cleans the briar-pipe in his hand
> With the faith of a toothless gorilla
> The generous night of the metropolis
> Seems to him like a Libyan forest
> Yet its animal denizens are unique,
> In fact they wear clothes only out of shame.

'You here, sir?'

With a start, I found two waiters from Shahjahan looking
at me.

'What are you doing here?' I asked.

'This is where we sleep, there's no space in the kitchen—
the cook's mates don't let anybody get in there.'

There was plenty of space in the hotel lounge—a few people could easily sleep on the carpet if they allowed it. But that would mar the beauty of the hotel. The portico was also out of bounds—if employees were found lying there it would lower the hotel's prestige. So there was no choice but to seek shelter at the feet of Sir Ashutosh and Victoria House.

'Have you had dinner?' I asked.

'Yes, I have a permanent arrangement with Little Shahjahan—fourteen paise per meal; only Mayadhar hasn't eaten.'

'Why haven't you eaten, Mayadhar?'

Mayadhar had flopped down on the grass by then, clutching his legs in agony. The other bearer said, 'The pain in his leg has worsened, his veins are hurting badly today.'

Kneeling, I saw by the light provided by the Calcutta Electric Supply Corporation that the veins in his leg had swollen up like knotted cords, as though several blue snakes had entwined themselves around his legs. Bose-da had told me that these were varicose veins.

'We feel like cutting our legs off at the end of the day, sir. That's how we all end up. After years of standing the veins start swelling up. We have to hide them from the boss, sir, if the steward gets to know he'll throw us out immediately.'

'Don't you ever go to the doctor?'

'It costs a lot, sir. And the doctors say, give your feet some rest. How can you work in a hotel and still give your feet some rest, sir?'

'Haven't you been to a doctor yet?' I asked Mayadhar.

'Bose sahib had given me a letter for a doctor he knows,' he said. 'But I haven't been to him—I'm saving money. It's expensive. But now I have to go, or else I'll become like Bharat. After this there will be sores all over the legs, and they'll burst and bleed, I won't be able to stand any more. I'll lose my job, my children will starve to death, sir.'

'It's very late, you'd better go to sleep,' I said and started walking away.

Where could I go? I had no idea. Tramping through the darkness, I entered Curzon Park. There were a lot of people sleeping there, too. Who knows, some of my colleagues from Shahjahan may have been among them. The paved area at the feet of Sir Hariram Goenka was tempting, but it had already been taken by a few lucky souls. The street light filtered through the railings on the west and bathed his feet. The inmates of 'Hariram Inn' had devised a clever way of shielding themselves from its glare. The light distributed free of cost by the Corporation had been stopped in its tracks by dried leaves that they'd placed over their eyes. There was darkness beneath. And it was there, it seemed, that my India slept.

9

By the time I returned to the hotel, it was very late. I don't know why, but walking down Calcutta's deserted streets, I felt that I had at last come of age. All this time, I had been seeing the world through inexperienced eyes; I had not matured. But that night I crossed over into adulthood and entered a new world.

On my way into the hotel, I saw Bose-da at the reception counter. There was no one else. He probably read something in my expression—perhaps my eyes were a little red. Taking my hands, he said, 'Are you feeling ill? Where did you go off to? You didn't even have your dinner—I asked Juneau, he said he hadn't seen you eat. I got hold of some sandwiches from the old man and put them in the drawer here. No one's going to turn up, so you can break the rules and eat them here, like a schoolboy.'

'I'm not hungry,' I forced the words out.

Bose-da could read people's minds very easily. He probably

sensed that the obedient, well-mannered schoolboy inside had been displaced by an unfamiliar, frightening grown-up. He continued in his light-hearted vein, trying to cheer me up.

'That's why I asked for sandwiches! If you'd been really hungry half-a-dozen sandwiches would have been no good. Besides, I want to give you a treat—you did a great job as a compére. Connie's very pleased, too. She just couldn't believe that you've never presented cabaret artistes in your life. I can see clearly that one day you will be indispensable to this hotel; the counter, the bar, the cabaret won't survive a moment without you.'

Tears had started rolling down my cheeks by then—I couldn't understand why those tears, oblivious of my reluctance to let them flow, were bent on making a fool of me.

The next moment Bose-da embraced me affectionately. He had been burning in the same fire for ages. In a voice choked with emotion, he said, 'I'm very happy; I can't tell you how happy your tears make me. Just keep observing, Shankar, you'll never get a chance like this again. But don't change, my boy, never change. May you never lose this ability to weep.'

He went back to being impersonal. 'Connie was looking for you at supper. She's a very sociable girl...talks beautifully. She told me a lot of interesting stories—she's been a wanderer all her life. She says there's only one season for sportsmen, actresses and dancers—and that's spring. The only gift they have is youth. She'd have told more stories, but Lambreta spoiled the party. As soon as the dwarf appeared at the bar, some women shrieked in horror. Lambreta was most offended and promptly sat at one of their tables. There was a pregnant lady sitting with her husband. Lambreta told her, "Don't look at me like that, the child you'll have will be even smaller than me!" Whereupon she practically fainted, so we had to take care of her. Connie had to forcibly take Lambreta to his room, and the whole session fizzled out.' He paused briefly. 'Go along to bed now. I might as well doze off on a chair, too. There's nothing to do except wake some guests who're leaving at four in the morning.'

Going up to the terrace, I opened the door quietly. I didn't expect to find anybody at this hour—Gurberia should have been asleep too. But as soon as I set foot on the roof I found Lambreta, still wearing his suit, on the dirty floor, a liquor bottle in his hand. He was taking swigs from it. When he saw me, he stood up and said, 'Have you seen how lovely the moon looks?'

I was in no state to gaze at the moon. 'Aren't you going to bed?' I asked.

Bottle in hand, he followed me to my room, entering without so much as a by-your-leave. His eyes were terrifying— the clown who had made 350 Calcuttans laugh just a while ago seemed to have vanished.

'I heard this is where you sleep,' he said. 'I was waiting for you. I'm warning you—from tomorrow you'd better not invite anybody to sit on Connie's lap, or there'll be trouble.'

I couldn't follow him. Was the man completely drunk? Without waiting for my reply, he went on, 'All Calcuttans are animals. None of your fathers or mothers or grandfathers or grandmothers was a human being, they were all animals.' He started dancing in his characteristic style, singing, 'Everyone in this world is an animal. If you don't believe me, come with me to a brothel, or at least to a hotel.'

I was almost falling asleep on my feet and here was this lunatic raving and ranting! 'It's very late, Mr Lambreta,' I began.

He started abusing me. 'So what if it's late? As if this is the holiest of holy hotels, where every man falls asleep at nine o' clock.'

'Mr Lambreta, I'm very tired from the day's work,' I pleaded.

Jumping on to the bed and dancing on it, he retorted, 'You don't feel tired when sitting on Connie's lap, do you?'

'Why are you saying all this to me? I didn't sit on Connie's lap.'

'No, why should you? You people are the people of Rome, the Archbishop of Canterbury, the direct descendants of Lord Buddha, you citizens of Calcutta don't even know Connie has a lap.'

Lambreta looked all set to start breaking things in my room. Left with no alternative, I went looking for Gurberia. He was sleeping, but he woke up with a start and said, 'What is it, is the god creating trouble?'

God indeed! Gurberia was convinced that the dwarf was an incarnation of the creator himself, in his vaman avatar!

'Never mind your god,' I told him, 'tell me how to get that drunkard out of my room.'

Gurberia didn't give a damn about me—his job didn't depend on keeping me happy. Besides, the damage had almost been done—Parabashia was about to finalize his daughter's marriage with someone else. I realized I had no choice but to send for Connie.

'Where's Connie?' I asked Gurberia.

'Downstairs,' he replied.

I was forced to telephone her. She answered on the first ring though she couldn't possibly have expected anyone to phone her at this hour. 'Who is it? What's the matter?' she asked.

I explained the problem to her as briefly as possible, apologizing all the while. 'I shouldn't be disturbing you at this hour, but Lambreta has left me no choice.'

Connie seemed quite upset; I could make out the shock in her voice as she said, 'I'm coming upstairs right away.'

Hearing that Connie was coming up, Gurberia jumped to his feet. 'Why does the naked lady have to come up to the terrace so late in the night?'

A few moments passed before the door to the terrace opened. The person who stood there, her body wrapped in a nightgown, her head in a silk bonnet, was the same person who had been entertaining Calcutta's crème de la crème a few hours earlier. Then she had been sensuous, wild. But in the darkness, the woman before me was someone else—whoever she might have been, she was not Connie the Woman. There was no fire in this Connie. It may sound rather clichéd, but her face had the radiance of the moon.

'Where is he?' she asked. 'Did he attack you?'

'No,' I said, 'but he refuses to leave my room. And he's spilled whiskey on my bed.'

Acutely embarrassed, Connie whispered, 'I am so sorry.' Going into my room, she called out in an undertone, 'Harry!'

It hadn't occurred to me that Lambreta could have had another name. Hearing his name, he looked at the door in surprise. As soon as he saw Connie, he held his bottle close to himself, as though that was what Connie had come for. Then, realizing what she was there for, he summoned up enough courage to protest. 'I won't go, I simply won't. I'll squash these animals to death like insects—what business is it of yours, and what business is it of this chubby-cheeked balloon-face?'

Through clenched teeth Connie said, 'Harry, it's very late. You've ruined this poor gentleman's bed.'

'I'm sorry about that, I didn't do it on purpose, the bottle slipped while I was trying to squash some bugs. But what harm has it done him—I'm the one who's suffered the loss.'

'Harry!' she said in a soft but sharp voice.

Lambreta exploded. 'I'll do as I please, what business is it of yours? I'm going to get a mug of beer and wet this fellow's pillow. I'll launder my jacket in two bottles of rum, what's it to you?'

Connie probably wasn't prepared for such a turn of events; Lambreta had clearly gone berserk. Embarrassed and humiliated, she stepped forward, about to do something, but stopped short—she suddenly seemed to remember I was also in the room. She turned to me and said, 'If you could please wait outside for a moment.'

I left immediately without a word, but I didn't have to remain outside for long. Connie had worked her magic in less than a minute and Lambreta had miraculously returned to his senses. Connie poked her head out of my room and said, 'You can come in now.'

I saw that Lambreta had cooled down completely. 'Please,' he said, 'I realize my mistake. I'm really sorry.'

'No more,' she admonished, 'I've had enough.'

He almost burst into tears. 'I'll go to my room and go to bed right away.'

'Yes, do that, at once,' she said.

He suddenly looked at me. Pouting like a hurt child, he said, 'You only blame me, but what about the time they called me a chimpanzee? You didn't say anything then!' Sobbing like a child, he went to his room. She followed him to say something, but he slammed the door on her.

She stood outside like a statue. I hadn't been prepared for such an uncomfortable situation either. She went slowly to a corner of the terrace. I noticed she was crying. Connie the Woman was wiping her eyes on the sleeve of her nightgown. Softly she said to me, 'Brutes. The people of this world are brutes. A man came up from the bar and asked me in front of Harry: Is this clown of yours a man or a trained chimpanzee?'

'I am sorry to have bothered you. If he only drank in his own room, I wouldn't have gone to all this trouble of calling you up. But he left me no choice.'

'No, that's all right,' she said. 'You've been working hard all day, and Harry upset you.'

'He didn't do it on purpose. You can't blame someone when he's drunk.'

'I'll go and have another look at him,' she said, and tiptoed into his room.

I knew I wouldn't get any sleep that night. I asked Gurberia to get me a glass of water and stood at my door. But what had happened to Connie? There was no sign of her coming out of Lambreta's room. I couldn't even make out if the light was on for she had shut the door. Were they talking? Didn't look like it. Even if they were whispering, one would have heard them through the wooden partition.

My throat was parched. I drained the glass of water Gurberia gave me in one gulp. Gurberia sensed trouble—he alone was responsible for the rooms on the terrace at night, and if something went wrong he would be the first to lose his job.

'Has the naked lady gone downstairs?' he whispered.

I shook my head.

'What! She hasn't?'

I pointed to Lambreta's room.

'As far as I can make out, the light is out, isn't it, sir?'

'So it seems,' I replied.

Gurberia went towards Lambreta's room and peeped through a crack in the wood to satisfy himself that the light was indeed out. I kept standing there like a fool. He came back scratching his head and stood before me.

'Disaster, sir, the blue light is on.'

'What's the problem with that?' I asked.

'What are you saying, sir! I wouldn't have been so scared if the room had been completely dark. Parabashia told me the very first day, if the light is on there's nothing to fear...even if it's out, it's all right. But the blue light is danger.' He was almost in tears. Wiping his eyes, he said, 'The devil's got his eye on me, I'm going to lose my job.'

Tearfully he explained, 'I have orders to keep a strict watch on the naked ladies. They're not allowed to enter the bar, men are not allowed to enter their rooms, and they're not allowed to enter men's rooms, either. Even if they do, they have to keep the door wide open. I'll lose my job tonight, sir.'

'Don't worry,' I reassured him. 'Who's going to come up to the terrace at this hour?'

'You never know—there's no telling when Markapala sahib will show up in his rubber shoes. He won't listen—he'll throw me out immediately, just as he threw out Karim—the naked lady had asked him to let a gentleman through at night, and he did it, too. For five rupees he lost it all.'

He was about to go and knock on the door. I stopped him, saying, 'All these tired people are asleep after a hard day's work, Gurberia, don't disturb them now.'

Who knows what Gurberia read in my words? I thought he suspected that I had a hand in Connie going into that room and switching on the blue light. He was about to say something, but the grim expression on my face deterred him from speaking his mind.

The night sky seemed rather depressing to me, as though whatever joys there had been in the storehouse of creation had been squandered away by the spendthrift people of this world. There were only sorrows left. There was no peace to be found.

At last the door to Lambreta's room opened. The blue light was no longer shining inside. Connie emerged from the darkness within and shut the door softly behind her. As she walked towards the stairs, lost in thought, she saw me. Perhaps she hadn't expected me to be standing there; she ignored me and walked away.

10

'I can smell it! I can smell it clearly, it's very difficult to fool Nityahari Bhattacharya's nose,' Nityahari screamed as soon as he entered my room. The darkness hadn't lifted yet when he had left his room to come up to the terrace. He couldn't sleep at night; he had come up to my room for a chat. Seeing the state of my mattress and bedclothes he said, 'That's the way it is—as they say, when in Rome...'

I told him what had happened.

He made a face. 'Oh yes, even I told my father once that I had been kidnapped.' His words showed just how implicitly he believed me. 'I made up that story about being kidnapped,' he said. 'My father was a simple man, he believed me. But the one up there saw everything. There's no way to fool Him, He's always ready to make us pay for all our mistakes. Why else should a high-born person like me have to work as a laundryman, rummaging through the sins of the world? Why else should I have to clean up the transgressions of the night in every corner of this hotel, the sins that permeate every pillow and mattress and bed sheet?'

Then, as if to warn me, he continued, 'Things needn't have turned out this way. I'm a Brahmin's son. I could have been well educated and taken up a professorship like my father in Bangabashi or Ripon College. The blood of professors runs in my veins.' He stopped suddenly, and then in utter despair continued, 'There's not a drop of that blood left in me, it turned to water long ago. If you cut my veins now all you will get is soapsuds and soda. I went to the dogs when in school, you know. One night I got drunk, then joined a bunch of good-for-nothings and even visited a brothel. But my father was an innocent soul—he knew nothing outside of books—and so was my mother. The next morning they asked, "What happened? Why didn't you come home last night?" I lied, saying we'd gone for a stroll on the maidan, but on my way back a gang kidnapped me and that they let me go because I had been crying all night. I was stinking of liquor, yet my mother thought it was because I had to spend the night with those criminals. And now you tell me the dwarf messed your bed up—better be careful.'

I smiled weakly.

'The government doesn't keep track of the many young men that are ruined thus in hotels, restaurants and other places. But why blame the poor government, when even their own fathers can't or don't keep track—they all think their sons are being kidnapped,' he said. By then he had rolled up my bedspread. 'I'd better change the mattress too. Try to avoid sin.'

'Would you like to wash your hands?' I asked him.

'How many times should I wash them,' he shouted. 'The skin's peeling off from so much washing. I'd find peace only if this entire hotel were immersed in a huge tub of Dettol.' His mood didn't encourage me to say anything else. But he hadn't finished. 'What you did isn't right. You were the shorthand man, fine; then you became the welcome-please-take-a-seat fellow at the counter—even that's acceptable. But why does the country bumpkin want to become a gentleman? What did you have to go to that dance for?'

'You think I had a choice?' I said. 'I have to hold on to my job, don't I?'

It was like cold water being poured on the flames of his wrath. The fiery Nityahari went out without a flicker.

'That's true,' he said softly, 'there's so much we have to do to keep this damned stomach full! If it hadn't been for that, Nityahari wouldn't have been killing himself over the world's dirty linen.'

'Yes, and if it hadn't been for the stomach Connie wouldn't have had to dance around the world without a stitch on.'

Nityahari became grim. 'There's something else besides the stomach there, and that's habit. I don't like this lady of yours.'

For a moment I thought he had learnt of the previous night's incident, but he was referring to something else.

Straightening the spectacles on his nose, he said, 'Yes sir, I've been supplying pillows all my life. If you want a couple of extra ones I can understand. But no, of all people she has to pick on me! All I went there for was to enquire whether she wanted extra pillows. Instead of giving me a straight answer, the lady in the cold room gets red hot with anger and says that her assistant must also be given an air-conditioned room next to her. My eyes popped out.

'I told her I was in charge of pillows, not rooms. And that though Shahjahan had given her an air-conditioned room, it wouldn't give one to her assistant. "Where will he stay, then?" she asked. "Where every other employee stays," I replied, "on the terrace."

'The lady seemed distressed. There have been so many dancing girls in Shahjahan, month after month, but I've never seen any of them worry about their assistants. All they ask about is their own rooms, whether there are proper locks on the door, whether the beds are soft, and whether there are enough pillows.'

'And so?' I asked.

'And so?' he said, slapping his forehead, 'Oh lord! Hasn't God given you an ounce of brain? Can't you see for yourself? Such a lovely lady, pretty as a picture, and that dwarf! But as they say, circumstances make strange bedfellows. On the one hand you have the famous dancer, for whom our gentlemen are ready to spend thousands of rupees, and on the other you have her hanger-on dwarf, who's irrelevant to the show. But what a nerve shorty has! He tells her, you can stay here, Connie, I'm off. And the woman's face falls and she says, please don't be angry, I'm doing what I can. The dwarf knows he's got her under his thumb, so he loses his temper some more and says, you can stay here and dance and get people to clap, I don't need all this. And do you know what Connie says to that? I could hardly believe my own ears. She asks me, "Can't you get me a room on the terrace as well?"

'I've been killing myself over the dirty linen of Shahjahan Hotel all these years—I can see through everything. A room next to his, no doubt, I said to myself. To her I said, "I don't know. I'll call Jimmy." I don't know what Jimmy did, but I saw Lambreta go upstairs, and the lady stay on in her air-conditioned room. Elephants fight, and the poor ant gets squashed. I only went to ask whether she needed extra pillows for the night. She doesn't answer, instead flies into a rage, and then she asks like a hypocrite, "Pillows? There are two pillows already. What am I going to do with more pillows in a single room? Roast them and eat them?" Kali! Kali!' Nityahari rose at last. 'I'd better go, my staff must be idling away, having a smoke.'

He picked up my bedspread and pillows himself. I tried to stop him, saying, 'Let the bearer take them, or else send one of your people, why should you...'

Instantly his demeanour changed, possibly without his even realizing it. His eyes blazed for a second as he said, 'Just because I don't have children you think God hasn't granted me kindness either? How could you say this to me? Do you know how much older than you my son would have been?' And on that note he hurried out.

Gurberia hadn't been prepared for such melodrama so early in the morning. 'Your tea's getting cold, sir,' he said.

Finishing my cup of tea, I went out to find Connnie on the terrace, dressed in the briefest of outfits. She was trying to attract the attention of the sun atop Shahjahan Hotel. The early morning rays were supposed to contain secret elements that made lovely women even more beautiful. Maybe—who knows? Connie didn't seem bothered that this public worship of the sun at dawn could cause minor problems to other creatures present.

A well-dressed Rosie emerged from her room. Marco Polo normally dictated some letters at this hour. She looked daggers at me.

'Good morning,' I said.

She didn't return my greeting, and chewed on her nails instead. I teased her, 'Even Mr Marco Polo told you the other day that you should use a blade.'

Maybe I shouldn't have said that, but I couldn't resist the urge to needle her every time I saw her. She turned a flaming red. 'I'm going with Jimmy to Marco Polo right away. I'll take Bose along too, if necessary.'

Now I was really scared. Jimmy wasn't exactly enamoured of me. I needn't have gone out of my way to provoke Rosie unnecessarily first thing in the morning. But it had happened, and she was not going to let it pass easily. If she got half a chance to get rid of me she wouldn't let it go.

'What will you tell Marco Polo?' I asked.

'I'll tell him this chap just cannot be kept on.'

'Why? What harm have I done you?'

Rosie smiled saucily, threw a sidelong glance at Connie, and whispered, 'Not to me, but to yourself. No man your age should be put up here on the terrace.'

I felt a little better. Twirling her keys, she said, 'Don't be smug, I can tell that witch is ready to gobble you up.' Without giving me a chance to reply, she made her way lightly down the stairs.

I looked around in wonder. Was I dreaming? Standing on the terrace of Shahjahan Hotel, was this the same person who once lived in Kashundia and who used to count Patterson, Chini, Kanai, Pulin, Keshto and Robi among his colleagues and friends? Was it the same fellow who had once lost his way going to watch a film at Metro Cinema? For a moment I thought it was indeed a dream. I must have had a glass too many of the festive brew back in Kashundia and taken leave of my senses. But the very next moment I noticed Connie—there she was, bathing her Scottish body in the rays of the Indian sun. This was real; it was Kashundia that was a dream. I must

have downed a few stolen pegs of whiskey from the bar at
Shahjahan, then dreamt that there was a place called Kashundia
which I once used to frequent.

Slowly I walked to the middle of the terrace. Connie
wasn't basking in the sun, I thought, she was purifying herself
in its all-cleansing glow. She started when I stood beside her
and said, 'Good morning.'

She acknowledged my greeting. 'Why are all of you such
fools?' she asked. 'Why don't you rent out this lovely terrace
for sunbathing? You could earn plenty.'

Before I could reply, a gramophone was switched on in
one of the rooms. 'Who is this philistine?' Connie screamed
immediately. 'I can't stand any kind of noise early in the
morning.' I knew it was Gomez. Connie said impatiently,
'Must be a colleague of yours…will you ask him to switch it
off? I have to drown in music all night, do I have to bear it
even now?'

Gomez was in his room, sitting on a chair in his shirt and
pyjamas, his eyes closed, a gramophone record playing before
him. I wondered, why twilight music at dawn? It seemed as if
the tired sun would set any moment on the western horizon,
as though the time to say farewell was upon us. I understand
nothing of music, but it felt as though someone was giving me
a cocaine injection to numb my senses.

A sad smile spread across Gomez's face when I entered.
'Listen carefully,' he whispered.

I wanted to but was worried that Connie might start
shouting again. 'Connie's calling you,' I whispered to him.

He went out, rather irritated. Connie covered herself with
a Turkish towel and said softly, 'Mr Gomez, I don't like any
kind of sound early in the morning.'

An electric current seemed to pass through his body.
Gomez had no illusions about his status in the hotel. Connie
was its centre of attraction now. Thanks to her, sales would go

up by eight or nine thousand rupees on a single night—he knew that. Compared to her wishes, the opinion of an ordinary musician amounted to nothing. He stiffened for a moment. She sensed the change in him. Removing the towel and preparing to enjoy the sun some more, she asked Gomez, 'What is it?'

'Many thanks, Miss Connie,' Gomez forced the words out somehow. 'I am extremely sorry for causing you discomfort. But it's only because this is a memorable day.' He hurried back to his room and switched off the gramophone.

Connie realized something was wrong. She rose from her mat and, putting on her nightgown, ran after him; I followed and heard her ask, 'Why is this a memorable day?'

Gomez feared nobody now. Even Connie, the management's pet, Connie the darling of the audience, could do him no harm. His eyes blazed as he said, 'You're a singer and a dancer, and yet you don't know what happened on this day?'

She looked scared, as though hypnotized by his fury. Somehow she mumbled, 'Pardon my ignorance, but do tell me...'

The musician said, almost to himself, 'The king of melody, our emperor, died on this day, unknown and unsung. But he is still my king. I may play rock-and-roll, I may compose tunes for cabarets, but he is still my God.'

I couldn't remain silent any longer. 'Who is it? Beethoven?'

Shaking his head, Gomez said softly, 'My king is someone else. He was poor. He found fame, and he lost it. He used to play in a priest's home. One day the priest kicked him out. Our impoverished king faced only misery after that, which is perhaps why he could understand others' miseries. But who values that? Amidst apathy and contempt and neglect, the king of melody ran through his earthly life in just thirty-five years— but ah, how exquisitely beautiful even that death was. "Do you want to say something?" whispered the young wife of the genius on his deathbed, placing her mouth close to his ear. Yes, he tried to say something but it was not about the world or about music. Gathering his strength, he said, "Promise not to announce my death immediately. Poor Albrecht is out of town. It will be a few days before he returns. If word gets out now, someone else will get my job, and you know how badly my dear friend needs the job." Only Mozart could have said something like that when he was face to face with death. It was because he had a heart like that that he could create the kind of music he did.'

Gomez fell silent. He seemed to have returned from Mozart's funeral only moments ago. 'He knew what it was like not to have a job, that's why the king of melody couldn't forget his friend. Nor was he able to forget the music of his own death. Mozart's *Requiem, K. 626*—he had started composing it barely a month before his death, commissioned by someone who had paid a pittance in advance. Sick as he was he sat day after day at the altar of the goddess of music, saying, this is my own requiem. It's clear to me that I'm composing the score for my own death. But will this wasting body allow me to finish it? I must complete it.

'Shortly before his death Mozart summoned his favourite disciples and friends to his deathbed. He no longer had the strength to speak—he could only signal. Begin the requiem, he indicated. Then, in the climactic moment of the composition, he burst into tears. He lay unconscious, but even in that condition he seemed to be singing the melody.

'Do you know his last words?' Gomez asked me. I noticed that even Connie was affected. She was gazing in wonder at the humble musician. Putting Mozart's *Requiem* on the gramophone, Gomez said, 'His last words were: "Did I not tell you that I was writing this for myself?"'

The melody began grieving its way to its painful finish in

the heart of the machine. Some unexpressed agony seemed to be struggling to free itself from the prison of the body and mingle with space. In the morning of life we were face to face with the evening of death. It was like seeing one's bride in widow's weeds at the moment when one was exchanging vows.

Gomez appeared to have left his earthly body behind on the terrace of Shahjahan Hotel and set off on a voyage to a distant land. Suddenly aware of herself, Connie wrapped her body in her nightgown. She was visibly moved. I rubbed my eyes in disbelief—Connie, our lady of the night, had tears rolling down her cheeks. She apologized to Gomez and left the room. I followed her out.

All this time, I hadn't quite understood Gomez, assuming he was simply another musician who played in restaurants and hotels. Someone had said about his breed long ago, 'Just because they play in hotels or restaurants, it isn't as though they lack knowledge. In Calcutta's hotels I've even heard musicians who could have earned worldwide fame if they had had the opportunity and the right breaks.'

Bose-da had also said, 'You don't know what these Goan Christians are like—they know nothing but music, as though they have no other purpose in life. All day long they sleep with their cellos and violins and clarinets by their sides, dress and go downstairs like machines at the appropriate hour, come back upstairs after playing for the entertainment of the guests at Mumtaz, and then undress and go to bed, as though they know no other way to live.'

But Prabhat Chandra Gomez was an exception. Admittedly, he conducted the music at Shahjahan Hotel as mechanically as the others, but in his spare time he dreamed of another world—a world inhabited by the kings of melody.

From Gomez's room Connie went back to the terrace to sunbathe. But she seemed to have mellowed. He had demolished her hauteur and pride.

Sitting with her back to the sun, she told me, 'If we had
a sun like this in Europe, I'd have lost my bread and butter.'
I looked at her blankly. Seeing my uncomprehending look she
smiled and explained, 'If they had a sun like this to get a tan,
every girl would have been beautiful. Now, the attractive ones
are nature's exceptions, but then everyone would have been
beautiful and I wouldn't have had a market.'

If I hadn't talked to Connie, I wouldn't have believed that
cabaret dancers also had an ordinary, everyday existence, that
one could talk with them comfortably. 'I think I'll try to make
it to India once a year,' she said, 'I'll get a decent complexion
then. Why are you standing, take a seat.' She extended an easy
chair towards me.

I sat down. 'Have you seen Harry?' she asked.

Like her, I was also under the impression that Lambreta
was still asleep after his exertions the night before.

'I'll find out if he is still in bed,' I said.

'If he's asleep, don't disturb him.'

I felt a little peeved. Surely, a dancer's companion wasn't
so important that he couldn't be disturbed even for breakfast.
To her, however, I said, 'We hotel employees are trained in
the art of not disturbing people.'

The door to Lambreta's room was shut, but the moment
I peeped through the window, I grew apprehensive. The bed
was empty. I opened the window wide for a clearer view.
Where was Lambreta? He wasn't in his bed. Perhaps he was in
the toilet, but there was no sound from there either. I moved
towards the door. Connie came up to me. She seemed
supremely unaware of her body. It existed, that was all,
whether it was covered or bare was immaterial.

'Isn't he in there?' she asked. She looked shaken. 'Where's
he gone?' My silence made her impatient. 'Why don't you say
something? What's the use of keeping quiet?'

How was I supposed to know where Lambreta was?

Her eyes were brimming with tears. 'It's all your fault,' she cried. 'Why did you have to call me at night? If a harmless little fellow did create a little trouble in your room, couldn't you have taken it in your stride?'

This was real trouble. Her tirade continued. 'I take a lot, don't I? Harry and I have to silently put up with the onslaught of hundreds of people day after day, night after night. We don't complain, do we?'

I didn't know what to say. She went on, 'Do you know he was sobbing last night? I tried to explain, to apologize, but he wouldn't listen. He was so hurt he wouldn't even look at me.'

I was about to respond, but the telephone on the terrace rang. It was Rosie.

'Hello Rosie, what's the matter?' I asked anxiously.

'No young man, I'm not talking to you as Rosie. The telephone operator's got an upset stomach—I'm filling in for her.'

'Your willingness to help others is indeed praiseworthy,' I said.

'I didn't want to disturb you,' she retorted, 'but there's a call—someone's determined to talk to Connie. I'm transferring the line.'

'Hello,' said a voice on the other end.

'Yes?' I answered.

He had been prepared for the sweet voice of Connie the Woman; a male voice disappointed him considerably. 'I want to talk to Connie,' he said.

'Who's speaking, please?'

'I'm a member of the public, I need to discuss something with her.'

'Sorry,' I said, 'she is not available on the phone. She doesn't talk to strangers.'

The 'member of the public' was a little put off. 'What kind

of logic is that? How can we get to know her unless we meet her?'

Expressing regret politely—those who had tempers couldn't survive as hotel employees—I said, 'Nobody can meet Connie, or even talk to her on the phone.'

'One can talk to even the prime minister on the phone, but not to your Connie?'

'Exactly, sir,' I said. 'However, if you wish to pass on a message, I will do so.'

The man sounded peeved. 'I've been to many hotels around the world, but I've never encountered such bad manners anywhere.' Then he added, 'What I wanted to know is whether she has received my present.'

'What present?' I asked. I could see Connie getting impatient.

'I sent some flowers and fruits this morning,' he said. 'Hasn't she got them yet?'

'If you've sent them, I'm sure she'll get them,' I said and put the receiver down.

Connie came up to me and asked, 'Bad news?'

'No,' I said.

No sooner had I spoken than Gurberia came up with a huge bouquet and a basket of fruits and deposited them at Connie's feet. There was a card with the name and telephone number of the 'member of the public' on it.

Connie didn't even glance at it. She was crying like a little girl by now.

Gurberia was startled by her tears. 'What's the matter? Doesn't madam like the flowers?'

'Have you any idea where the short gentleman is?' I asked.

Gurberia saved the day. 'The short gentleman? He's gone out for a walk.'

Early at dawn, Lambreta had asked Gurberia where he could take a stroll nearby. Gurberia told him that Esplanade was just a short way down Central Avenue, and then, a little further along Chowringhee was the maidan, the ideal place for a stroll. Lambreta had given him a tip and left immediately.

Connie seemed to regain her composure. 'Let's have some fun,' she said. Picking up the bouquet from her feet, she threw away the card and, asking me for a piece of paper, wrote a few words on it. Entering Lambreta's room, she looked for a vase, saying, 'What kind of a hotel is this? There isn't even a flower vase in every room!'

'All the rooms downstairs have them; only the ones on the terrace don't.'

'Why? Aren't these rooms occupied by human beings too?' She placed the bouquet carefully on the bed. Shutting the door behind her, she said, 'Harry will be surprised. He'll wonder where Connie managed to get hold of flowers for him in this strange city!' She seemed very happy that she'd had a chance to please him.

But her happiness was short-lived. Glancing at my watch, she became fretful once again.

'Don't worry,' I said, 'he'll be here any minute.'

She wasn't reassured. 'I feel scared—he's a dwarf, after all. Suppose he has an accident trying to cross the road?'

'He'll be here any minute, take my word for it,' I told her once again. To myself I said, 'Aren't you overdoing the concern bit? The longer that ill-tempered fellow stays out, the better. He'll start a row the moment he gets back.'

I hadn't expected my prophecy to come true so soon. In a moment, Lambreta opened the door to the terrace and entered. He was humming a song whose words I couldn't make out. Connie couldn't either. She looked at him and asked, 'What are you singing, Harry?'

I followed his English pronunciation carefully to identify the song he was singing, clapping to keep time: *Jai jai Raghupati Raghava Raja Ram*. Had he gone mad! 'Wonderful song,

Connie,' he said, and sang with his twisted pronunciation, dancing along, his hands raised, 'Patito pavano Sitaram.'

'Where were you?' Connie asked him. 'I was worried sick.'

'That's the problem with you,' said Lambreta. 'You can't sleep for worrying about me! Your concern for me is upsetting the rhythm of your nude dance.'

Connie wasn't prepared for such a response. With a hurt look she said, 'Harry! You say that to *me* of all people!'

The pleasant morning had indeed had its effects on Lambreta. He realized his mistake and, taking Connie's hand, said, 'I was only joking! You're still a little girl, can't you get a joke? I didn't realize I had reached the river front. There I saw a group of people on the pavement, singing. Very sweet song, very nice people—real gentlemen, they stopped singing and greeted me when they saw me. What song is that, I asked, is it for your sweethearts? They couldn't make out what I was saying. They said, "Only God at this hour of the morning— only Sitaram, Sitaram." One of them was a little cleverer than the rest. "Right you are, sir," he said in English, "Sitaram also has a very sweet heart."

Lambreta hadn't been able to help himself after hearing that wonderful song. There by the Ganga, next to the Calcutta Swimming Club, he joined them. Calcutta's pavement dwellers had no idea what to do with the foreigner. They felt bad about keeping him standing, but where could they offer him a seat? He, however, was caught up in the music and made a place for himself on the ground. He picked up the tune soon enough and, clapping along in time, he sang blissfully, without understanding a word, 'Raghupati Raghava...'

His singing partners treated him well. 'May we offer you some flowers, sir? they asked.

'Of course,' he said, whereupon they gave him some marigolds.

'Will you be able to find your way back by yourself?'

'Yes,' he said.

But they weren't as confident as he was, and said, 'Calcutta, sir, is a very bad place.' Then one of them had escorted him to the gates of Shahjahan Hotel.

Lambreta pulled out a few of the marigolds from his pocket and showed us. 'Lovely,' he said.

Humming his newly learnt song, he went into his room, putting the marigolds carefully on the table. And the bouquet, sent by a member of Calcutta's public smitten by Connie's beauty, paled beside them.

I went to my room and prepared to report for work, but there was yet another interruption. As I was about to head for the toilet, Gurberia came and said, 'Madam is looking for you.'

Back I went. As soon as I entered Lambreta said, 'I have an idea—I'm going to give Connie lessons all afternoon, and tonight both of us will sing *Raghupati Raghava Raja Ram*! A pleasant surprise!'

'What do you think?' asked Connie. 'Is it a good idea?'

I was appalled, but said, 'You are the performers, you can do as you like.'

'We know that,' said Connie, 'but will the guests at Shahjahan be pleased?'

'Everyone is bound to be pleased,' said Lambreta confidently.

'Nobody visits a hotel for devotional songs,' I said.

'You have to mould their taste,' said Connie.

'Mr Bose says their taste was moulded long ago,' I replied. 'Each generation hands over part of its cultural preferences to the next before departing, and in turn, the next one passes them on, which is why there's been no change at Shahjahan Hotel. The original arrangements for entertainment are still in place here.'

'So this song won't go down well?' asked Lambreta, disappointed.

'No.'

'Why?' asked Connie.

'There's a line in the song which might offend our guests,' I said.

'Which line?' Lambreta shouted.

'Give good sense to everyone, O God,' I said. 'What would our guests think? That they don't have good sense?'

Suddenly Lambreta lost his temper. 'Get out of my room right now! I want to rest.'

Connie got scared and glanced at me hurriedly before leaving the room. I didn't linger either. Lambreta slammed the door.

'He's normally good-tempered in the morning,' said Connie, 'but these days there's no accounting for his mood. Sorry, I've taken a lot of your time. See you tonight—at Mumtaz.'

Mumtaz was chock-a-bloc with people. Not only had all the tables been booked well in advance, but Bose-da had also squeezed in a couple of extra tables under pressure from well-connected circles. Sometimes requests came from people who just could not be refused. Besides, Jimmy had made arrangements for people to buy their way to the front row. 'People are even willing to bribe you to get seats up front,' said Bose-da. 'There's nothing Jimmy isn't capable of doing.'

Liquor sales were even higher than the day before. The excise inspector peeped in and was very pleased with what he saw. Plenty of money would be deposited under excise duty and entertainment tax, swelling the government's coffers.

Upon arriving at the hall, I noticed there were women in the audience that night. This floor show was part of Calcutta's culture, after all. So the well-educated and modern women of the city were hardly willing to pass over this pilgrimage.

Bose-da was there too. Smiling faintly at me, he said, 'The zeal with which we are embracing modern civilization will ensure that in the not-too-distant future Indians too will show up with their wives and children to watch belly dancers. The West has opened its doors wide. No wonder the poet had written, "Give and take, mix and mingle, by the shores of Shahjahan's great human sea".'

A few days ago, an academic friend of Bose-da had aptly described the outfits of the women who frequented this predominantly male bastion. His name too was Bose and he had come to the hotel to satisfy his curiosity. About Calcutta's middle-aged modern women, he had said, 'Their dresses follow a completely new tradition—beyond the wildest dreams of our forefathers. Mere suggestions masquerade as blouses and non-existent wraps pretend to be saris.'

Bose-da had smiled and told his friend, 'Observe by all means, if that's your mission, but don't follow in the footsteps of these people. When Nagen Pal visited us for the first time he said it was only to add to his experiences, but he's trapped now—so he's still gathering experience; he can't do without a daily visit to the bar.'

There he was that evening too, nursing his whiskey at a corner table, awaiting the cabaret dancer. He had a small notebook open before him. In case the liquor stimulated his brain, he wanted to write the idea down immediately.

'Hey, you there,' Phokla Chatterjee summoned me. He was in attendance again, accompanied by a shy young man with wavy hair and a face that still held the innocence of youth. He was in formal evening dress and was drinking orange squash.

'Does this make any sense? Can you watch a cabaret on orange squash? Tell him,' Chatterjee said. 'Go ahead and have a drink, nobody needs to know. I'm advising you as your uncle—not a soul will find out. They know at home you're out with me. If you're still worried, you can always spend the night at my place. What's the most expensive cocktail in the house tonight? Might as well baptize my nephew with it.'

'Silver Grade,' I said. 'Twelve-and-a-half rupees.'

'What does it have?'

'Vodka, fresh lime, syrup and egg,' I said. 'But if you're looking for something ideal for a baptism, why not try a Manhattan, instead? Whisky, vermouth and sherry shaken with ice.'

'This is my nephew,' Chatterjee snapped, 'not my niece. I've never heard of a man being baptized with vermouth. I see it costs only four-and-a-half rupees—how much real booze could you get for that?'

After I had ordered the Silver Grade, I came back to stand next to Bose-da and found him chuckling. 'Do you know the young man being baptized tonight? That's Mrs Pakrashi's son—the prince of the Pakrashi empire.'

It was time for the show. I would have to go up on stage soon and present Connie the Woman. But Lambreta hadn't shown up yet, and neither had Connie. I hurried into the lift and saw Nityahari grinning from ear to ear near the door.

'Seen Connie and Lambreta?' I asked.

'Don't bother me now,' he said. 'Your dwarf tore up two of my pillows last night, the stuffing's all over the room.'

I knocked on Connie's door. The door was open, but where was she? I was worried at first—where had she disappeared just as the show was about to begin? If the people ensconced in Shahjahan's soft chairs, already drunk, were to be told, after having purchased five-rupee tickets and drunk their way through another fifty, that the floor show had been cancelled...I shuddered to think what lay in store for us employees at that hour of the night. The price of the tickets could be refunded, but what of the liquor? It couldn't very well be extracted from the stomachs and sealed back in the bottles. Which meant that glasses would be smashed, tables and chairs would be upturned, and we would have no choice but to call for the police.

I'd heard this had happened before, and the police had, with great difficulty, managed to rescue the hotel employees from the drunken mob. But the real trouble had come afterwards. The police, who served the King of England, had expressed their wish to be served at Shahjahan Hotel; having driven out the drunkards, they had themselves proceeded to get drunk, occupying all the tables at Mumtaz, ordering the most expensive dinners on the menu, picking the choicest items on the wine list and barking out their orders. Bottles of Black Label, Black Dog, Dimple, Vat 69 and Johnny Walker, lovingly collected in the darkness of Shahjahan's cellar, emitted wretched cries of distress in apprehension of imminent disaster. When Ghengiz Khan's troops had finally left after having plundered the jewels of the treasure-lined Shahjahan, the manager had almost been in tears. But there hadn't been a murmur of protest, for it had only been on the manager's personal request that they hadn't arrested any of the customers. Arrests would have led to the courts, and the courts would have led to bad publicity.

This was what I was thinking about when I found Connie's room empty. Not sure of what I should do, I went up to the terrace. As I was about to enter my room, I heard a familiar voice next door. Lambreta was saying, 'Go. If you're all that concerned, why don't you go by yourself?'

'Please don't be so stubborn,' pleaded Connie. 'Please come.'

'Don't touch me,' he exploded. 'You think I'll succumb to your touch?'

'Quiet,' she whispered. 'People will hear.'

'Never! I won't go.'

I left my room and knocked on his door. Connie emerged, dressed in her costume for the show, exuding a whiff of expensive French perfume. When she saw me she realized they had been overheard and went back inside.

'The guests are getting restless, please get dressed quickly,' she said to Lambreta who was sitting on his bed, his hands cupping his face.

In a grim, irritated voice, he said, 'Leave me alone, woman, don't disturb me.'

Connie was clearly wary of the dwarf's mood swings. She seemed to have no idea about what to do next, so I said, 'If we wait any longer they might set the hotel on fire.'

'For God's sake come along,' said Connie sharply.

'All right, but this is the last time,' said Lambreta. 'I'd like to see who can get me out of my room tomorrow.'

Connie and I left the room while he dressed. Connie's face was ashen. 'How unreasonable can you get,' she said. 'It's a cabaret, after all. What's acting got to do with real life? Harry is such a baby—I just cannot get him to understand. He forbids me to sit on anyone's lap during the show.'

I hadn't said anything till then, but now I spoke. 'Someone like him in your troupe will affect your ratings. You don't owe anyone any explanation for what you do during the show.'

'Exactly,' said Connie. 'I can't stand it that a member of my troupe should make life so difficult for me.' Then, hearing Lambreta's footsteps, she added softly, 'He mustn't hear us.'

'Ladies and gentlemen!' That night I was an experienced compère. 'Good evening. On this beautiful evening at Shahjahan Hotel we hope you've enjoyed our French chef's cuisine and our specially selected drinks from around the world. I now present to you Connie—Connie the Woman. You have seen many women in your lives, but here is *the* woman—one of a kind, exclusively created by God for this century.'

As on the previous night, the lights went out once again. The audience seemed to be the same too, or perhaps they were just behaving the same way. The same murmur rose in the hall, and then came the familiar anticlimax, the disappointment, the dashed expectations. No Connie the Woman, instead, Lambreta the Dwarf.

But look at Lambreta. Who would have said the man had been sulking on his bed a few minutes ago, refusing to take part in the show. The exhausted, bad-tempered individual had vanished; in his place was a dwarf holding a three-foot-high top-hat in his hand saying, 'Good evening, ladies and gentlemen. I am Connie the Woman. I am honoured that you've waited for me so late into the night.'

Then the previous night's events repeated themselves. The lights went out and Connie materialized from nowhere. A man in the front row screamed: 'Someone's sitting on my lap!'

In the dark, I said, 'Don't be afraid.'

But Connie had made a bad choice that evening; the lap belonged to someone who knew the game. 'Got her,' he shouted, 'don't turn on the lights!'

Bose-da had warned me repeatedly to be prepared for just such an eventuality, so, without a moment's delay, I signalled for the lights. All the lights in Mumtaz came to life immediately, blinding us. Connie struggled out of the man's lap, panting, but nobody paid attention to that.

Her performance began. The primal rhythms of her dance were designed to arouse the beast lurking within each guest. A feral force caged in suits and ties strained at the leash, seeking to break out, brooking not a moment's delay. Lambreta's bizarre display of passion for Connie tickled the audience's fancy even more. It was obvious the poor fellow was besotted with her and was bending over backwards to impress her. Even the ladies present exclaimed 'Oh lord' in dismay at the sight and leaned against their male companions, even though their gently indulgent smiles betrayed their enjoyment. They were not overtly bothered about the lack of good taste.

I got off the stage and was standing by the front row, when I heard a lady say, 'Poor fellow.'

Her companion said, 'Don't waste your sympathy—they're acting.'

The lady held his hand, snuggled close to him and said, 'What rubbish! You could spot it a mile away if only you had eyes to see, darling. That passion in his eyes isn't acting—it takes a woman to know.'

Seeing me, she quickly whispered something to her companion. 'Excuse me,' he said. 'What's the relationship between Connie and that dwarf?'

'I don't know,' I answered.

'Do they spend the night in the same room?'

'No, they have separate rooms,' I said.

The lady continued her conversation. 'That doesn't prove anything, darling. These hotel people are experts at all this— ask them and they'll tell you.'

I didn't want to answer this middle-aged woman's tasteless question. Did working in a hotel make us criminals? Didn't we have families? A sense of right and wrong? Didn't we know what was proper and what wasn't? As I walked away, I could see other things that were lacking in decorum. Unmindful of probing eyes, a sari-clad leg had recklessly wrapped itself around a trousered one under a table.

Connie was dancing, and so was Lambreta. As her movements gathered pace, so did Lambreta's. He tried to match her rhythm, but he was clearly running out of breath. For every stride that Connie took with her long legs, Lambreta had to take three. Connie could sense that her partner was losing steam. Suddenly, her handkerchief floated down to the floor. The dwarf retrieved it and returned it to the beauty who became livid and said something to him. Those at a distance thought the dwarf had made an indecent proposition. Still dancing, Connie began chasing Lambreta, saying, 'Get away from me, devil. How can someone so small have such evil intentions?'

Lambreta left the stage. Having got rid of him, the sensuous Connie began her dance of desire. But I was looking at Lambreta. The night before, he had danced for much longer. No one else realized, but I knew he was tired and couldn't stay on his feet any longer. That was why Connie had dropped her handkerchief and, taking advantage of his clowning, given him an opportunity to take a break. The poor fellow's breast was heaving like a pair of bellows; his clothes were drenched in perspiration. But Connie wasn't remotely tired—she kept dancing like a mechanical toy. The lights in Mumtaz had gone out long ago. Just a single beam lit up her half-naked body, lending her a deeper aura of mystery.

Lambreta pulled himself together. He looked at me and, in the darkness, his eyes glowed like headlights. He whispered, 'Can you recognize the fellow on whose lap Connie sat? I'm going to smash a bottle on his head. You don't know me—that fellow scratched Connie.'

'Don't be angry now,' I said. 'Please, be quiet.'

'Oh yes? People will go ahead and torment Connie, and you expect me to do nothing about it?'

'Mr Lambreta,' I said angrily, 'I haven't the time for a debate with you. My job depends on the whims of the people you see in this hall. If they lose interest and stop eating, we will die of starvation.'

'If they fast, we starve. But if they eat they'll feast on Connie—what about that? I'll show you,' he gestured. 'I'll show the whole lot of you.'

Oh God, what kind of madman's clutches had I got myself into? You've come here to perform, and you're getting paid a fortune for it, I wanted to tell him. Because they're paying you so much, the owners are charging more for the food and drinks. Where do we poor employees come into the picture? Just let me work, let me scream into the mike, Ladies and gentlemen, I welcome you on behalf of Shahjahan Hotel.

SANKAR

We've made a few humble arrangements to relax your tired minds and bodies. Who the hell are you to disturb us?

The first act had in the meantime come to an end. At my signal, the electricians turned out the lights in order to preserve Connie's modesty. By the time the lights came on again Connie was backstage, wrapped in a robe, panting.

'Where's Harry?' she asked breathlessly.

'Mere mortals like us can't keep him under control. Who knows where his rage has taken him?'

Patting her hair back in place, Connie rubbed her right arm near the elbow. 'People here drink so much that they can't control themselves. That fellow must have been soaked to the gills. Could you get me some iodine? That man probably doesn't clip his nails; he scratched me so hard my arm's hurting.'

Lambreta appeared from nowhere. 'Man? Who are you calling a man, Connie?' He had got hold of some cotton wool and iodine and, taking her hand, started cleaning up the wounds.

Connie shut her eyes and said, 'Oh Harry, it hurts.'

Lambreta said grimly, 'May the wrath of God descend on the devils.'

Connie quietened down and, forgetting her own pain, said affectionately, 'Wasn't it you who asked me not to abuse people in God's name, Harry? It's a sin.'

'Rubbish! You can do anything you like to these dirty devils—God will not prevent you. He won't be unhappy with you. On the contrary he will be pleased, he will bless you.'

Even after all these years, as I write this, I can clearly see the beautiful Connie and the ugly Lambreta. By the grace of God, I've come into contact with many strange people in this world, but the Creator's plan behind this extraordinary game of good and bad, right and wrong, isn't clear to me yet. Even now, the scenes from that night float up before my eyes as

vividly as a brand-new print of an old movie. I can see
Lambreta extend his hand towards God and say, 'O Lord, curse
them. Let your condemnation descend like a bolt of lightning
on them.' Who knows whether the half-insane dwarf's desperate
plea reached the ears of the detached Creator? For thousands
of years of human history, humiliated souls from all corners of
the world had sent up similar prayers in different tongues on
thousands of occasions, but had it helped?

Nityahari had once told me, 'God? Don't mention him,
my dear sir, I'm sick of him. He works just like the government
offices. If you went to his office you'd find thousands of
petitions piling up every day, and his employees filing them all
away, having marked "no action, may be filed"; nobody ever
digs them up again. You find it funny? Your blood's still
young, laugh while you can. One day you'll have to shed tears
though, nothing but tears. That's when you'll believe me,
that's when you'll realize there's no more space in God's office.
So many famous people's files haven't moved an inch, and you
expect God to read your file or mine carefully? He doesn't
have the time.'

Perhaps I should never have taken a job at Shahjahan.
Perhaps I was being childish. As I left Lambreta and Connie
backstage, it seemed to me that another file had been deposited
in God's office: Lambreta's petition. But that was probably as
far as it would go, for the plea would die in the file. Lambreta
would keep waiting. Connie would keep waiting, expecting a
response any moment. Eventually the waiting would end.
Connie's youth would start ebbing, affecting Lambreta's
livelihood. Leave alone Shahjahan, they would no longer be
seen at any cabaret anywhere in the world. A new Connie,
along with a new dwarf, would strike a playful pose before the
footlights, greeting the inebriated guests, 'Good evening, ladies
and gentlemen.' The men would lose control, and one of them
would scratch the new Connie with his wild, lustful nails. And

perhaps the dwarf of the evening would lose his patience and send up another plea. But nothing would come of that either, just another file would be opened, while he counted the days, waiting eagerly for justice.

But what rubbish was all this? I was a hotel receptionist— and I had a lot on my plate. A few moments of rest for an exhausted dancing girl, away from prying eyes, didn't mean I could take a breather too. The hotel wasn't paying me to ruminate. I should be standing at the mike, dripping with politeness, announcing to the guests present, 'Connie the Woman will be here soon. Please be patient a little longer and, meanwhile, order your drinks.'

That wasn't all. The compére at Shahjahan's cabaret had more duties, which I would now have to perform with care, and as expertly as a circus clown. My future depended on how well I could carry out all those responsibilities. On them hinged how much longer Shahjahan Hotel's free bread would arrive at my table.

Completing the necessary announcements over the mike, I went on to the floor. It was time to supervise the guests' needs.

A familiar voice hailed me, 'Hello, sir, this way, if you please.' I went to Phokla Chartterjee's table. 'Maybe we're not at a front-row table,' he said. 'Does that mean you're not going to look after us?'

'We're here only to carry out your commands, sir,' I said.

Phokla said, 'I'm in a real spot with my nephew—he wants to go back.'

I looked at Pakrashi junior. The poor fellow's eyes were heavy with sleep. 'I brought him for his baptism, you'd better look after him a little,' said Chatterjee, 'or else he'll form a bad impression of Shahjahan.'

I greeted Pakrashi junior and said, 'I hope you're having a good time. Our relationship with your uncle goes back a long way—please treat the hotel as your own.'

The uncle told his nephew, 'That's right, son, enjoy life with a sporting spirit. After all, how long do you suppose we'll bat on earth—so long as you are at the crease, hit all round the wicket.' The boy laughed at the cricket metaphor. The uncle continued, 'I shouldn't be criticizing your father, but he's got eyes only for his business. He's never tried to play an attacking innings.' Noticing the empty glass, he said, 'But the glass is empty. No wonder the conversation isn't flowing! How is the car to run on an empty tank? Let's have your suggestion, quick.'

'Pure, original whiskey—nothing like it,' I said.

Phokla didn't seem satisfied. 'It's been plain and simple whiskey practically since I learnt to read. Recommend a special cocktail.'

'Pink lady,' I said.

'Gin and egg white? No, I don't care much for that.'

'White lady, then,' I ventured.

'That's gin and lime—oh no. Whatever happened to your imagination, you don't seem capable of moving beyond gin. Call our friend Sata Bose.'

At my signal Bose-da appeared. Laughing, Phokla said, 'Your disciple's as bad as my nephew—still a novice, can't recommend a suitable cocktail. The uncle is going to lose face before his nephew.'

Bose-da's eyes danced with inspiration. 'These young fellows have new-fangled ideas, while we're getting outdated,' he said. 'Which is why I'd suggest an Old Fashioned— Canadian whiskey with lots of fruit soda.'

'Wonderful,' said Phokla.

'And,' said Bose-da, 'if you prefer something else, I'd recommend a Moscow Mule.'

'What! A mule at my age—what will people say?' Phokla guffawed.

Pakrashi said softly, 'I'm not having any more, Uncle.'

'What a bore. Look, you're no longer a baby, examine your birth certificate when you go back home. You were born in the year of the earthquake—your father was going through a bad phase, about to lose everything in the Depression. When I heard you were born I sent him my congratulations from England, and you know what he wrote back? Ha, ha, ha.'

Phokla exploded in laughter. Pakrashi junior stared blankly at him. Reining in his laughter, Phokla said, 'Your father wrote, I have no idea what the family will live on. Can you imagine, Madhab Pakrashi writing in his own hand that he cannot afford a child. What a mistake I made tearing up those letters. Bose, you might as well give me the second drink—I'm not old-fashioned, nothing but the Moscow Mule for me; if you have anything called the Calcutta Donkey you can give me that, too.'

'And for him?' I indicated Pakrashi junior.

Bose-da said, 'These are young men, Mr Chatterjee, life to them is like sparkling wine. With your permission, I would like to serve Mr Pakrashi some sparkling hock. Wonderful stuff—bottled the year I was born.'

'Wonderful, wonderful! That's why I can't do without Sata Bose. Shahjahan Hotel minus Sata Bose is equal to Madhab Industries minus Madhab, *Hamlet* sans the prince of Denmark, Bengali literature with no Tagore, Ramakrishna Mission without Vivekananda and last but not the least Phokla Chatterjee minus liquor.' He was laughing uproariously, but even as he laughed he changed visibly. 'I can't stay without my drink, I simply can't. At sundown, as soon as the faint darkness of the evening draws a veil over Calcutta, I simply can't hold myself back. The sun has set, lead us to the river, someone seems to sing to me.'

It wasn't just I who had become uneasy at this unexpected change in Phokla; his nephew had too. 'Uncle!' he cried. Uncle had by then grabbed Bose-da's hand. 'Can you tell me why this happens to me? Beg, borrow or steal, I have to hit the bottle every day.'

'Don't get upset, Mr Chatterjee.' Bose-da was at his solicitous best.

But Phokla Chatterjee's eyes were brimming with tears. Trying his utmost to control himself, he said, 'I'm not a man, I'm an animal—I'm a Moscow Mule. Would anyone else have urged his own nephew to drink? It was I who christened him, you know. Tired of being vilified all my life, when I got my sister's letter asking for a name for her son, only one came to my mind: Anindo, the one beyond reproach.' Phokla looked lovingly at Anindo Pakrashi. Taking his nephew's hand in his, he sighed, 'He's still so innocent.'

Bose-da was about to ask the bearer to get Chatterjee's drink, but Phokla stopped him. The toothless man seemed to be totting up something mentally. 'Just a minute, let me think,' he told Bose-da, and then suddenly got up. Putting some cash on the table for the drinks he had already had, he said, 'Anindo, let's go.'

Anindo Pakrashi promptly stood up, surprised. Had Phokla Chatterjee completely taken leave of his senses? He wasn't one to be bowled out by the few pegs he'd consumed so far. Why, just a moment ago he was advising hitting all round the wicket.

'Mr Chatterjee, don't you want to watch the last act of the cabaret?' Bose-da asked.

Phokla shook his head sadly. 'I'm sorry, Sata, I should never have brought Anindo here.'

When, having both amazed and overwhelmed us, Chatterjee left the unfinished show holding his nephew's hand, the lights of Mumtaz started to dim again. The bearers were trying to get the drinks across to the guests' tables for the last time.

'How's your arm?' I asked Connie before she went onstage.

'Don't remind me of these unpleasant things just before

going on, it might spoil my mood. Anyway, I'm never bothered by these things; it's Harry who gets worked up.'

The dance began again. In an orgy of coloured lights, Connie the Woman's balloon dance began. Unless one saw it with one's own eyes, one wouldn't believe that someone who had been upset a moment ago could become so titillating and sensuous the next. The guests were euphoric, the cheers started, as did the wolf-whistles. It was a repeat of what had happened the night before, what would happen the following night, and what had been happening at the pleasure house called Shahjahan for decades. And yet I couldn't understand why the rhythm was clearly missing. The Connie who had danced the previous night was no longer there. Her dance may not have lacked prehistoric wildness, her eyes may not have lost the hypnotic gaze of the venomous snake, but the dancing girl was indeed tired, her spirits were visibly flagging.

That night, too, the audience burst the balloons. A single body was the focus of the entire sex-starved gathering at the historic Mumtaz bar. But it was brief. The despondent dancer eluded the audience's predatory eyes much earlier than on her first night and disappeared into the darkness. The lights came on once again, murmurs floated across the hall, there was a stampede as everyone wanted to be the first to leave and get back home.

After putting the mike back in place and giving the necessary instructions to the bearers, I met Bose-da on my way out.

'Where's Connie?' he asked.

'I don't know,' I said. 'She ran away as soon as the lights came on.'

'We have trouble on our hands. Marco Polo's displeased. Jimmy was present during the last sequence, he must have complained to him.'

Apparently, the manager had noticed Connie's lack of

concentration, and he'd discussed it with Jimmy. 'It's a competitive market, if we get a bad name we're finished. Three girls will be dancing together at the same time at the other hotel from tomorrow—they're saying it's three sisters. Sisters my foot! These women never saw one another till they were eighteen—but now the advertisements have turned them into three sisters,' Jimmy had said.

'How did the manager hear about Lambreta?' asked Bose-da. 'Did you tell him anything?'

'Me?'

'They think it's that short fellow who's the root of all trouble,' said Bose-da. 'It's because of him that Connie's not dancing well.'

'What could the poor fellow do? Someone in the audience scratched Connie and messed up everything.'

'Marco Polo wants to do something—that's why he was calling for me,' he said.

'What will he do?' I asked.

Bose-da smiled. 'Why are you getting so upset? The management has to do many things to run a hotel as large as this.'

For some reason, I was worried that Connie would come to harm. Bose-da seemed to read my thoughts. He smiled and said, 'Haven't I told you this is only a hotel? Nobody will be here for ever, don't feel too much for anyone.'

Unable to look him in the eye, I averted my gaze.

'The fault is Connie's,' he said. 'Even the bearers are joking about the dwarf—Jimmy said Connie had demanded an air-conditioned room even for him.'

I didn't want to hear all this; all I wanted to know was what the manager and Jimmy were up to. But Bose-da refused to divulge anything—and seeing the expression on his face, I didn't dare ask.

11

The next day the whole thing was out in the open. I was in Karabi Guha's suite on some work. She had completed her morning chores, the representative of the flower shop had been given his orders. Nityahari was there, waiting to be briefed on the colour scheme of curtains and bedclothes for the day.

Karabi said, 'People have such lovely curtains in their homes, such wonderful new shades, and you only keep old-fashioned colours in your stock.'

Nityahari looked worried. 'How can homes and hotels be the same? Even a sack hung up at home is a pleasure to the eye.'

'I have to keep this suite well decorated. If the colours don't match, what will this guest house amount to?'

'As long as I'm here you needn't worry,' Nityahari replied. 'I'll find a way to get matching colours every day. But must this game of different colours be played on a daily basis?'

After he left, I told Karabi, 'If there are problems I can tell the manager. Is Nityahari finding it difficult to give you the kind of linen you want?'

She said, 'Please don't say anything to anyone. He'll be hurt...he's such a nice man, don't ask me why but I like him very much. Pure gold, unblemished even after all these years.'

'When are Pakrashi's guests due?' I asked. 'Let me know if there are any special arrangements to be made.'

'Mr Agarwalla wants no stone left unturned in our hospitality. So I've decided to give them the two cabins, and convert this space into my bedroom—I don't think that'll be a problem, we've had four or five guests at the same time before.'

When I asked again when they were due, she said, 'Oh yes, thank you for reminding me. It'll help to know when they're arriving.' She picked up the telephone. 'Why are you standing? Do sit down.'

As I sat I noticed that her feet were exactly like lotus petals, her toes lined with alta peeping out of a pair of golden sandals. Smiling, she said, 'Do you know what that chief guest of yours did? He sent this pair of sandals by post—I wonder when he managed to find out what size shoes I wear.'

'They suit you,' I said.

Karabi chuckled. 'I don't know about that, but I like the fact that there he was at the head of the gathering, and then here, he was at my feet. He got so drunk he was clutching my feet!'

She spoke briefly over the telephone and then turned to me. 'I couldn't get the boss—he's off to the factory. But the wife took the call and handed it to Pakrashi junior. Nobody has a clue, but the son has kindly consented to call and let me know.'

'Please let us know, too,' I said, and was about to leave, when she said, 'What's your hurry? Have some Ovaltine.' Nobody in this hotel had ever offered me anything as warmly. 'I may live in a hotel,' she smiled, 'but I've set up a small household. I've made a few cooking arrangements—I don't like the hotel coffee all the time, so I make my own tea, coffee or Ovaltine.'

'That's not a reflection on Shahjahan's coffee,' I remarked. 'All it proves is that Bengali girls can't sleep unless they get a chance to cook occasionally.'

'Quite right.' Sipping her Ovaltine, she asked about Connie. 'You see quite a lot of them, don't you? What's the story?'

Not quite getting the drift of her question, I said, 'Why should I be seeing a lot of them? Mr Lambreta's room's next to mine, that's all.'

'And that's where Connie is to be found most of the time!' Karabi said meaningfully. 'He's her fellow performer, they travel around the world together. But does that mean she has to be at the dwarf's beck and call?'

'What do you mean?'

'In the show the dwarf begs for her favours, her sympathy, but in real life, it's just the opposite. Connie is the dwarf's lady-in-waiting. She doesn't dare protest even against his temper.'

'So what? What matters to us is their act.'

'It's your customers who're concerned about the act,' she said. 'Since we stay in the same hotel, what matters to us is what they do outside of their act.'

There was nothing I could say. I didn't even understand why we were discussing them.

'This is a sort of indulgence,' Karabi continued. 'Cabaret dancers don't have to worry about money, after all. For a few minutes' pleasure, kings and emperors, the rich and the famous, all place gifts at their feet. So without a hobby they get bored—some have monkeys as pets; others indulge dwarfs.'

'Don't you feel bad that the poor fellow's a midget?'

'I can see they've influenced you as well,' she said. 'It's because he's a dwarf that he's earning his bread. If he had been as tall as you, would he have appeared onstage with Connie? I've been in this business for a long time, and I can tell you, the deformed and the ugly have a lot of opportunities when it comes to begging and entertainment; artistes pay a lot to get hold of such people.' She paused. 'Pay them by all means, but don't let them get above themselves.'

From Karabi's suite I went to the counter and, after finishing my chores there, went upstairs. Connie was on the terrace, sitting with her back to the sun and smoking. When she saw me, she took one long drag, threw away her cigarette and said, 'Good morning.'

I knew the morning hadn't really been very good for her, but returned her greeting nevertheless. She stood up and, throwing a sidelong glance towards Lambreta's room to check whether he was watching her, walked into my room without a word. I'd meant to change my clothes and rest, but now that was ruled out. Taking a chair, she asked, 'Are you through with work?'

'For the moment,' I said. 'The new round begins in the evening.'

She hemmed and hawed, as though she wanted to say something but couldn't quite get round to it. 'Is something the matter?' I asked.

'If you don't mind, I'd like to go out with you for while.'

She knew nothing of Calcutta—and besides, it wasn't safe for someone like her to go out alone, so I agreed, though reluctantly.

By the time she was ready for her Calcutta tour, no one could say that this girl turned into Connie the Woman at night. The young woman in a straw hat, dark glasses and tight knee-length skirt looked like a tourist from Europe who had set out on a world tour with her father—an eager tourist, naive, who had not yet got over her fear of an unknown, unfamiliar place. Hobbs had once told me a story about two young American girls who were accompanying their father on a world tour. They left him in Bombay to attend to some urgent business and went off by themselves to Delhi. Apparently, they put up at Maidens Hotel. They went on a buying spree as tourists usually do and spent all their money. Having no options left, they sent an express telegram to their father. He was foxed by the cable his daughters had sent: 'All money spent. Can stay maidens no longer.'

Walking down Chittaranjan Avenue, Connie and I reached Chowringhee. 'Where would you like to go now?' I asked. 'To Victoria Memorial, or the museum, the zoo or the Governor's house?'

She shook her head, took out a slip of paper from her handbag and showed it to me.

'This is where you want to go?' I asked in consternation. It had the name of an obscure lane in a suburb written on it.

'Yes, that's where I have to go. Do you suppose I've come out to admire Calcutta's beauty?'

I hailed a taxi. Connie said, pronouncing the name with great difficulty, 'I want to meet the great man—Professor Shibdas Debsharma the Great, who had predicted that Lord Curzon would never become Prime Minister of England; who, despite being praised highly by Lord Kitchener, didn't hesitate to inform him that he would die in a shipwreck.'

She had memorized Shibdas the Great's glorious achievements. Among his sensational predictions were Tagore's renunciation of his knighthood, Lord Brabourne's untimely death, the decline and fall of Germany, Goering's suicide, Subhash Chandra Bose's exile from India and marriage to a foreigner and, above all, India's independence. Shibdas had also predicted that India would not be able to free itself from the clutches of the Commonwealth in the near future.

It was Professor Shibdas who had secretly informed Kasturba Gandhi, through Mahadev Desai, that there was great danger in store for her husband but that she had no reason to worry, for when she finally gave up the attractions of earthly life, it would be with her head in her husband's lap. If only Edward VIII had worn the amulet that Shibdas had advised him to wear and sent by express mail, the history of the English royal family would have been written differently. To take even an anna more than the seventy-three rupees and four annas that it cost to prepare this amulet was, to Shibdas the Great, a sin, tantamount to eating beef.

Connie pulled out a pamphlet from her bag. In one corner it said, 'Private and Confidential'. That's how I learnt that this 'saint' did not believe in publicity. And that he considered it sinful to accept payments of any kind.

I asked Connie to turn back, but she paid no attention.

Shibdas's laboratory was in a tiny lane in a remote corner of the city. When we arrived there, he was dispensing advice to his clients. His assistant ushered us in a little later. Connie had taken off her shoes at the door and a pair of nylon stockinged legs advanced towards the sage. Shibdas the Great took out his sacred thread and blessed her. Arranging her skirt, Connie sat down on the floor. No one could tell from her rapt, devout expression that she didn't belong there. Had our mothers and aunts dressed in skirts, they would probably have presented themselves at temples in the same fashion.

Shibdas the Great tried to size her up with his sharp, probing eyes. Placing his hand on her head, he seemed to meditate for a while, and then said in his Bengali-accented English, 'Ma, ma, no fear. Shibdas will save you.'

Connie turned around and looked at me. 'He's telling you not to worry,' I said.

She couldn't say a word. She just took Shibdas's hand and held it in utter trust, as her eyes clouded over.

Shibdas's speciality was that he asked no questions at first. He discerned the stranger's past and future merely from their expressions. But that was the problem. He had to win the disciple over with his very first utterance, and there was no denying that it was a risky affair.

He tried to hazard a guess about Connie from her age, manner and clothes. One didn't have to be an astrologer to know that she wasn't here for tips on B-Twill, handicaps or Indian iron. Still, he ruminated for some time, his eyes closed. Meanwhile, she took a ten-rupee note out of her bag and laid it reverently at his feet.

Allowing a meaningful smile to spread across his face, he said, 'Don't worry, your wish will be granted. You will get what your heart desires.' Her face lit up like a hundred-watt bulb. It was as though she had travelled this far only to hear this.

'Spread your palms out,' he told her. She obeyed. Gazing at them for some time, he turned his eyes back to her face. 'You have suffered a great deal, but you'll have to suffer more.'

'More?' she said tearfully. She had quite forgotten that I was standing behind her. Each of the astrologer's blind arrows was scoring direct hits. But then, even I knew that she had suffered a great deal. 'If something good for Harry comes out of it, I'm willing to suffer a lot more, sir,' she said.

Realizing that the prey had fallen into his trap, the great soul's face grew brighter. Shutting his eyes and abandoning his physical self, he launched his astral self on a voyage into Connie's future. She stared in wonder at him, agog with anticipation, though she dared not speak.

Shibdas the Great opened his eyes, smiled and said, 'I know exactly what you want. But still, I want to hear it from your own lips—the goddess will be pleased if you make your demands yourself.'

Connie couldn't bring herself to say what she wanted. Her speech was slurred. It was as though the entertainer of the night had suddenly been afflicted by the shyness of the child-bride, her face hidden behind a veil. But she would speak; she would reveal to Shibdas the Great everything that she had not said so far.

Forget me, I don't think even Shibdas the Great was prepared for what she said.

Perhaps it would have been easier for her if I hadn't been present. Her lips trembled as she said softly, 'My lord, you can achieve anything if you want to. I will happily give whatever I have to the service of your God, as long as you make Harry taller. I don't want happiness or property or riches. I'll be thankful if Harry could become ordinary. Let him be short, I don't mind that, but don't let people call him a dwarf.'

My heart has hardened after years of watching the world; sorrows and agony, humiliation and neglect no longer overwhelm me, but I confess that even today my hair stands on end when I think of that extraordinary prayer.

Finally, I understood Connie. That explains it, I said to myself. You stupid, silly girl, that's why you brought me here, wasted my time. Never mind, I'm glad you did. I'm not angry at all. Though it's silly, though people will call both you and me mad if they knew, still, I'm ready...I'll drop everything and take you wherever you want to go.

Not even Shibdas, the seer, could contain his surprise. 'What is she saying?' he asked me.

'She has a companion named Harry, who's a dwarf. With him...'

'You don't have to tell me any more, I've got it,' he said. 'The dwarf will have to be made taller—he'll have to be stretched to normal proportions.'

'Yes, my lord, I'll give you whatever you want.'

The great man hadn't come across such a golden opportunity in a long time. His eyes spoke his joy at having found a willing victim. Shaking his head, he said, 'This is nothing new; from dwarf to giant, or from giant to dwarf— changes like these have taken place in our country many times in the past.'

Professor Shibdas had by now surmised that I wasn't on his side. Avoiding my eyes, he spoke, almost to himself, 'It's called the *vamanavatar yagna*. Very complex, needs hard work. The priest will have to perform the rites for seven days and seven nights.'

As Shibdas got ready to roll out the costs, I realized he was planning to make a killing on this hapless girl. I couldn't take it any more. I couldn't be a silent witness to the swindle.

He saw my annoyed expression. 'Yes?' he asked me defensively, to gauge my mood.

I spoke sternly, giving him the benefit of my Kashundia dialect. 'Please remember, I work at the Shahjahan Hotel,' I concluded. 'I'm sure you'd like our guests to visit you in future. This lady is my colleague.' Unable to understand what I was saying, Connie looked at me. 'I'm explaining Harry's problems to him,' I said.

'Thank you,' said Connie. 'I don't know just how to thank you.'

Shibdas the Great had no problems understanding what I had said. Keeping the future in mind, he changed gears. 'I'm probably the only person alive who can conduct the sacrifice.'

'Then make the arrangements, lord,' Connie said impatiently. 'I'll stop my shows at the Shahjahan and stay with you here. I'll beg and plead with Harry to come too.' Connie turned to me. 'Ours is a weekly contract. I'm not going to extend mine any more. You'll have to explain to Marco Polo.'

But Shibdas the Great started shaking his head. 'There's an unwelcome side effect to this sacrifice. When the dwarf becomes taller, there'll be no difference between him and normal men. But...'

'No more buts, all his troubles will be behind him if Harry can become taller,' Connie interrupted.

Shibdas the Great threw me a poisonous look and said, reluctantly, 'But he won't live for long after the sacrifice. I haven't seen anyone survive this beyond six months.'

The colour drained out of Connie's face. She shivered. 'Harry, my dear Harry, dead! No! No, I don't want that to happen!' Connie swept up her skirt and stood up.

Shibdas said, 'We are what God wants us to be. If we try to bend his will, he becomes angry.'

Connie listened attentively. She bent down and touched his feet.

Shibdas opened a box and pulled out an amulet. He said, 'This is extra-powerful. It runs on atomic power. Wear it on your bare feet after a cleansing bath. No drinking and debauchery on the day you put it on.'

Connie accepted the amulet respectfully and said, 'I don't drink.' She gave Shibdas another ten rupees and asked, 'If I wear it, Harry will find peace, won't he?'

'Of course. That's why the extra-special amulet,' Shibdas sighed, obviously distraught at losing his quarry.

Connie was sombre on the way back. She didn't say a word. She had lost her last hope of getting Harry to be normal. All she said was, 'I'll probably find peace too now, won't I?'

The atmosphere seemed extremely tense when we got back to the hotel. Bose-da was at the reception counter. He looked right through Connie. I joined Bose-da at the counter while Connie took the lift upstairs.

Rosie was sitting at the typewriter. She finished typing a letter and read through it. Then she said, 'Hello man, so the morning was fun, eh? Jolly good time?'

I didn't respond. She came up to me and whispered, 'Poor fellow, however hard you try, it won't work. The person in Connie's heart is Lambreta. You'll have to be much shorter to compete.'

Bose-da said, 'Rosie, Mr Marco Polo has been waiting half an hour to sign these letters.'

Rosie realized she couldn't intimidate me in Sata Bose's presence. So she sashayed off with the letters, flouncing her skirt and tip-tapping along on her high heels.

Bose-da said grimly, 'You shouldn't have gone out with her. Harry created a scene. He's screaming, abusing the bearers, asking for liquor. Gurberia told him it was dry day, but he paid no attention. Finally, he made the worst mistake—he went to Jimmy. Jimmy was waiting for precisely such an opportunity. He told him, go meet the manager, he'll organize something. Like a fool Lambreta knocked on the manager's door. You can guess what happened. Marco Polo had no idea that a cabaret girl's dance partner could create a scene in the manager's room. Maybe nothing would have happened. But

Jimmy had information that the other hotel had sold out the floor show for ten days. The demand for our show isn't that high, he said. Some advance bookings have even been cancelled.'

'Now what?'

'It's all the dwarf's fault. Connie's only problem is that she indulges him. The manager hadn't paid attention to Jimmy's original suggestion. But they've probably been discussing things since then. Maybe he'll send for Connie right away.'

That Bose-da's fear wasn't unfounded was clear when Rosie returned. Breaking into peals of laughter, Rosie said, 'It's happened. Marco Polo the man has sent for Connie the woman. He asked me to leave. When I'm here, you tell me the manager wants me. When I'm there, he tells me to go help Bose at the counter. I'm caught in the crossfire. Nobody likes me.'

I said, 'Enough of work. Take a break.'

'All right,' said Rosie. She went round the counter, pulled out a bar of chocolate from her handbag and started sucking on it.

Bose-da asked, 'Rosie, why do you like chocolates so much?'

'Because chocolates and I have the same complexion,' she snapped.

I told Bose-da, 'I'd better go, then.'

'Yes, you'd better. We need to find out what's happening to the girl. She's in a foreign land, after all. I'd come along, too, but there's a lot of pressure here.'

Though he asked me to leave, I could not. I was anxious to find out which way the clouds gathered around Connie's fate would blow. Bose-da probably realized how I felt. Writing something in the register, he said, 'There's no point hiding anything now. They've decided not to let Lambreta dance. Connie will have to do the show on her own. They don't have a contract with Lambreta. He will be sent back as soon as possible.'

I was shocked. But Bose-da explained, 'You cannot blame anyone. People are paying to see Connie, nobody cares about Lambreta's performance.'

Absent-mindedly I went towards the lift. Then, on a whim, I took the stairs instead. I shouldn't have barged into Connie's room in the melancholy afternoon of that dry day. Well versed in the grammar of etiquette as I am now, I wouldn't display such audacity today. However, I was inexperienced; I could do it then. I was dying to know what the management had told Connie.

I don't regret it though. It hasn't caused me any harm. On the contrary, it proved beneficial. Immensely so. I consider myself blessed for what I learnt.

I was surprised by what I saw. Sitting with her chin in her hands, Connie looked like a statue carved by a Renaissance sculptor. Her hair fell all over her face. She said nothing even after she saw me. Suddenly, everything became clear to me. If only I had displayed such sagacity in school, my life might have been different. I could have been well educated, well dressed and in an important job. I would not have been seen anywhere near Shahjahan.

I had understood. But what could I have said? 'I am sorry, believe me, I am very sorry.'

'I'm going too,' Connie said. 'I can't let Harry go by himself and still keep performing. I have asked for just one favour. Harry mustn't get to know any of this. I'll tell him I've had a fight. And that I've cancelled the contract in a rage. I hope they keep their word. I'm sure they won't push Harry to the edge. He's trying. He's trying with all his might to improve his lot in life, but he's not able to. Believe me, he's not able to. If he gets to hear of this, he will lose the battle forever.' Connie paused. 'They probably think I've gone mad. Jimmy laughed so peculiarly, I wanted to throw up. For a dwarf, he seemed to say, I was giving up my prospects for a dwarf. But they don't know, why blame them?'

What was Connie saying? What did she mean? I hadn't noticed the small photograph in her hand. She had probably concealed it the moment she saw me. Now she had nothing to hide any more. At least, not from me. She examined the photograph closely. So did I. A nondescript woman's photograph. On the other side of the ocean, surrounded by water and mountains, in an unknown town. A newborn baby in her arms. A boy next to her—seven or eight years old.

'Recognize anyone?' asked Connie. How could I? Connie's voice was heavy with unshed tears. 'My mother.' She hesitated. 'Harry's mother.'

'What?'

'Yes. That's me in her lap. Harry, my brother Harry, by her side. Did anyone know then that Harry wouldn't grow?' Connie could contain herself no more. 'Harry didn't grow,' she said through her tears, 'but he's done so much for us.'

Connie told me of a mother, a brother and a sister in faraway Scotland. They had no one to look after them. It was the dwarf who took a job in a restaurant. The short waiter couldn't reach the tables. So he had to be stationed at the gate. He would bend low and welcome the guests, opening the swing doors for them. Amused, the guests would tip him. That was how Harry had supported his widowed mother and sister.

But as he grew older, Harry changed. He became difficult. He started drinking. Only his mother could restrain him. She would rescue him from bars late at night. Connie hadn't been to school, she didn't have the chance. But she learnt to sing from her brother. When he was in a good mood, he would teach her. Sometimes he would show her how the girls danced at the restaurants. Others would laugh at his antics. But Connie and her mother never did.

Connie chose a dancer's life for herself. She didn't let her brother work any more. Stay at home, she told him, keep mother company. Harry agreed. He didn't enjoy holding the restaurant doors open on a road where thousands of people passed by.

Harry would ask Connie for money on the sly. He used the money to drink himself into a stupor before returning home. Their mother wouldn't say anything. Yet, Harry was afraid of her. He would take her hand and apologize. Sobbing, he would say, 'I'll never disobey you again, Mother.'

'Mother is dead,' Connie said. 'She called Harry and me to her as she lay dying. She told Harry, "You'll be a good boy, won't you? You'll listen to Connie, won't you?" Harry agreed like a child. Mother said, "I'll be watching everything." Then she told me, "If Harry disobeys you, if he doesn't listen to you, shut your eyes and talk to me."

'Even now, when I can't cope with him any more, I threaten to tell Mother everything. It works like a charm. Harry starts behaving immediately. It's almost as though he's jolted back to reality. But then he gets angry. He goes off in a huff. Doesn't talk to me. Sobs on his bed. I have to cuddle him then. It takes ages to placate him. I have to say, aren't I your little sister? How would I know what to do? If I'm wrong, you should scold me. If necessary, you should box my ears. He is transformed. He kisses me. He says, who dares box my little sister's ears? Who's got the guts? My sweet sister, my darling sister, your eyes look as though you're going to drop off. Go to bed now. I say, I won't go to bed till you do. He laughs. All right, he says. And then he does fall asleep.'

At that moment, the mystery of the other night, when Connie had gone into Lambreta's room, became clear.

Connie had regained her composure by now. Patting her hair in place, she said, 'Where can I go leaving Harry by himself? I wouldn't be at peace anywhere in the world if I left him in Scotland. That's why I've included him in my act. But Harry can't do it. He becomes insane with rage at what I have to do onstage. He does not understand that acting is just that.'

Breaking into tears again, she said, 'My own brother, and yet I can't explain to him. That's the kind of profession we're involved in.'

She would have said more, but suddenly Lambreta came in. I stared at him for a moment before leaving the room.

Later, I met Lambreta on the terrace. He was packing. Like a little boy he called out to me. 'Listen up, my lad. You got us angry, now you can face the music. We're leaving, we don't care for your Shahjahan. Mark my words. We'll never return to this rotten city of yours.'

Indeed they didn't. But I do keep thinking of Connie. It wasn't just one Connie I had seen in the light of dawn, in the silence of the afternoon, in the cacophony of the evening and in the darkness of the night. Connie—the woman, the girl, the mother and the sister—is still a wonder to me.

Who knows in which corner of the world Connie is spending her days with her brother now? Surely there is no room for her at any well-known hotel any more.

On some exhausted evening, in some obscure bar, should a reader of *Chowringhee* see a dancer past her prime dancing with a dwarf, please ask her whether her name is Connie. If indeed it is, please write me a letter. I will be happy. I will be very happy indeed.

12

Life at Shahjahan went on as before after Connie left. After all, she was only one among the many who came and went every day. People arrived from different parts of the world, but how long did they stay? A week, three days, one day—there were some who stayed only a few hours. That's how it was— welcome and farewell, reception and goodbye went hand in hand here. On arrivals there was at least a modicum of expectation; on departure, nothing at all.

'On an average, our guests stay three days,' said Bose-da. 'If one stays a fortnight, we feel he's been with us for an eternity. And the one or two who stay on a monthly basis practically become one of us.'

But this person who had left wasn't just another guest—she was one of those whose lives revolved around the hotel guests. Much like us. And if indeed she had been one of us, her absence would surely have left a mark on our lives. But it left nothing. For most of us at Chowringhee she might have never existed.

One day, while he was shaving on the terrace, Bose-da remarked, 'We hotel employees are very detached, but even more dispassionate is this building. She will remember no one, not Connie, not you, not me; take my word for it. She isn't bothered that we silently serve here from early morning till late at night. Even when we are dead and gone, she will continue standing here, decked up in fresh paint and plaster, to entertain an endless stream of visitors. Not once will she think of us.'

I found his words rather depressing. 'And why only us,' he went on. 'Many others have served Shahjahan Hotel before us. So many other Nataharis have run from room to room carrying pillows, other Sata Boses have stood at the counter day after day, night after night, innumerable Connies have dazzled the guests with their dances, so many other Gomezes have made the silent night come alive with music. But nobody remembers them, and nobody's supposed to, either.

'You think I'm being poetic, don't you? Even Hobbs, who is so passionate about old Calcutta, who is just about the only person I know who has maintained a link between the past and the present, says it's today and tomorrow that make our hotel. We have nothing to do with yesterday. We're not bothered about it at all.' Bose-da finished shaving, wiped the blade on the towel and continued, 'I don't have a way with words or else I could have expressed my thoughts beautifully.

To put it simply, our good morning starts with today and when at the end of the day, in the darkness of the night, the dregs of today are left behind in the dining hall, we start planning for tomorrow. We don't keep track of how and when today became yesterday.'

Not just the employees of Shahjahan Hotel, even its patrons had no time for yesterdays. Reading advertisements in the paper about the arrival of a new dancer, they started making enquiries again. Not one of them asked where Connie had gone. The phone started ringing as soon as the new advertisements appeared.

'Hello, Shahjahan Hotel? At last you've seen sense, you're getting a belly dancer!'

This time a dancer from Central Asia was expected.

'Yes, I am sure you'll enjoy the show,' I said.

'I hope she's a genuine belly dancer,' the voice at the other end said. 'There's so much adulterated stuff going around these days, you can't trust your own grandmother.'

I didn't understand what he was trying to say. Bose-da, who was standing next to me, grabbed the receiver from my hand. 'Sir, this is Shahjahan Hotel—not some cheap restaurant where a local girl will be passed off as an Egyptian.'

The caller was probably a little annoyed. 'You can't blame us...we are naturally wary after the number of times we've been tricked. We buy tickets for a genuine belly dancer's show and find a dancer as square as a packing box—no body movement whatsoever. Do you know how many times a minute the stomach muscles of a genuine belly dancer move?'

Bose-da slammed the receiver down. But that didn't mean respite. Like the poor deer which thinks closing its eyes will mean respite from the hunter, we sometimes believed that ending a call would mean the end of our troubles.

Once again the phone rang. 'I'm not going to take it,' said Bose-da, 'you'll have to manage. Let's see how much you've learnt after all these days at Shahjahan.'

It was the same person. 'What happened?' he asked. 'We were cut off in the middle of a conversation.'

'Very sorry,' I replied. 'I wonder how it happened.'

'Lodge a complaint,' he said.

I promised to take appropriate steps immediately and asked, 'So when can we expect you, sir?'

'Book two seats for tomorrow.'

'We have a new rule, sir, we can't reserve seats for anyone over the phone during the first week,' I said. 'Please send someone to collect the tickets.'

'Heavy demand, eh? Naturally. Calcuttans are bound to appreciate a genuine belly dancer.'

As soon as I put the phone down, Bose-da smiled. 'You'll do just fine. You'll be able to stick if you try.'

'And some of us can't stick despite trying!' commented someone from behind us. It was a man in a short-sleeved shirt, cigarette in hand and a smile on his face.

'Oh, how fortunate we are! How is it you haven't visited us for so long?' Bose-da welcomed him effusively.

'What's the use?' said the man, extending a cigarette towards Bose-da. 'You're a miserly lot—you don't let even water slip through your fingers. Despite thousands of requests, you never open your mouths.'

Lighting the cigarette, Bose-da said, 'If you want to hammer both my impoverished self and the hotel, go ahead, but please remember, this slave is always at your service.'

Brightening up, the man said, 'Never mind your Shahjahani politeness. Any interesting consignments?'

I was intrigued. Was there some mystery behind this? Why was Bose-da talking so effusively, and what was the consignment all about?

Bose-da thought for a while and then, tucking his pencil behind his ear, said, 'Nothing right now, but there may be one tomorrow.'

The man laughed. 'No, Mr Bose, I'm a professional, I'm not interested in your belly dancer Laila.'

Bose-da laughed too. 'No, no, not her. Do you think we don't know what you want? Something you'd be interested in is turning up tomorrow.'

The man left. Bose-da looked at me. 'What are you staring like a fool for? Be careful. He comes here for information. His name's Bose too. He's as well-behaved as he's charming and he has the uncanny ability of managing to glean information— things that happen right under our nose and we never notice. We read it in his reports the next day. According to him fifty per cent of the news in India is created in airports and hotels these days. He might be here again tomorrow—help him if he comes.'

'Help him? How?'

I had forgotten, but Bose-da hadn't. 'Aren't Mr Pakrashi's guests arriving tomorrow?'

Their schedule must have been sent to Karabi and she must have done up her suite for them. I telephoned suite number two to find out. Karabi took the call.

'Shankar? Nice man you are, phoning from one room to another. Can't you come over?'

'You were supposed to let me know when you're free,' I said. 'What if you had a guest?'

'I wish I knew when I would be free,' Karabi sighed. 'Can you tell me when business transactions of all sorts will disappear from the face of the earth?'

'Why ask me? Besides, if business transactions and cultural tours and international conferences came to an end, we'd go bankrupt.'

'Maybe we won't have jobs,' Karabi said, 'but we'll have peace. If only you could have seen some of the guests.'

'Why! You have select guests—you don't have to hold out a welcome tray before all and sundry like we do.'

'Come over to the suite,' said Karabi, 'let's chat here.'

Duty hours were over. For eight hours I had welcomed guests with a smiling face and bade them goodbye with a sad one. I had also organized a tea party, a regular feature at our hotel. I had become used to them. Adjusting the mike or giving a hand to the host at such parties was part of our daily routine. So a little rest was not unwelcome. Without wasting further time I arrived at Karabi's suite.

She had had her evening bath and smelt of expensive perfume. She was relaxing on a rocking chair, but as soon as I entered, sat up.

'The things I see every day make me want to throw up,' she exclaimed. 'In independent India it's as if the earth revolves around the sun thanks only to contracts, contractors, purchase officers, accounts officers. And what can I say about Mr Agarwalla—he has no taste in selecting his guests. He invites people who have never been inside a hotel, who wouldn't know how to spell liquor, brings them over to suite number two, and takes them to the bar.'

Karabi rose from her chair and put the kettle on to make coffee. Then turning to the mirror to look at herself, carefully scrutinized her red lips. She removed the carefully arranged flowers from her hair and put them carelessly on the table. 'People who don't know how to use a knife and fork, people who slurp their soup, people who belch loudly after their meals—these are the people Agarwalla fawns over and calls sir,' she said sadly. 'It's a shame.'

I waited for the coffee without replying. Karabi continued, 'Of course, some of them have perfect manners—but I have no idea what substance God has fashioned them out of.'

Gravely I replied, 'The day we unravel that mystery, Shahjahan Hotel will become unbearable for us, and Mr Agarwalla probably won't be able to hold you back either.'

'If you could watch this room through an invisible hole,

there'd be very little about human nature left to know. I would have written another Mahabharata by now if only I could write. As a child I used to think human beings were capable of greatness—I believed with my heart and soul that God lives in every individual. Do you know what I think now?' she asked, turning off the electric kettle.

'You probably think people are becoming decadent with every passing day,' I said.

Karabi laughed. 'Whether or not God lives in every individual, a canny purchase officer certainly does. He wants to make every purchase in this world without paying. You can't beat these people when it comes to surviving on free samples.' Stirring the coffee, she said, 'The man Mr Agarwalla brought today doesn't talk very much. He wanted a drink, but was scared of getting drunk. He did drink, however, and now he's gone to another hotel to watch the cabaret, courtesy Mr Agarwalla. This man comes frequently from south India, and buys a lot of stuff to take back. I say, guzzle down what they're offering you to buy their stuff, stay in the suite since you are here, but don't be such a hypocrite. Believe it or not, even as he was drinking he took off his shoes to say his evening prayers. Only a moment before, he was making enquiries about the cabaret girl. To please him Mr Agarwalla said, "This is what we must learn from you, Mr Ranganathan...wherever you might be, you cannot forget God." Ranganathan was high by then. But in response to Agarwalla he said, "I've got into the habit out of fear of my wife. Dangerous woman—she doesn't give me dinner unless I've said my evening prayers."'

I was surprised to hear Ranganathan's name. I remembered Phokla Chatterjee having introduced him to me. Karabi said, 'He's through with Phokla and attached himself to Mr Agarwalla. Mr Agarwalla reminded me that Ranganathan's a tough nut to crack, he needs to be reminded of hinges every now and then. He holds the key to an order for one lakh hinges, and if this one is bagged there are bound to be repeat orders.'

Sipping her coffee, Karabi went on, 'It's really funny. Agarwalla says Ranganathan understands everything, controls the ups and downs of the market. He knows there's plenty of this stuff available, so he's trying to squeeze as much out of Agarwalla as he can. Agarwalla wasn't able to make much headway with him, so he sent him to me.' Karabi adjusted her sari. 'That's why I feel it would have been better if there were no buying and selling in the world.'

'And what does Ranganathan say now?' I asked.

'He's agreed. They've finalized a deal for him to pick up Agarwalla's entire stock. Do you know what he said before he left? "This is why Calcutta and Bombay are flourishing— business runs on much more scientific lines in these two great cities; businessmen here know how to sell, they haven't learnt their salesmanship from grocery stores." He was sozzled.'

'What did you give him to drink?' I asked.

'Just as I use matching linen, I try and match the drinks to the person. For him I got Old Smuggler—he was definitely tottering. In that condition he said, "Why doesn't Mr Agarwalla open a school? Even in Calcutta many businessmen don't know how to sell—my blood pressure goes up trying to deal with them, it's just like dealing with my wife."'

From Ranganathan we moved on to Madhab Industries. 'All the arrangements have been made,' Karabi told me. 'I only need to confirm everything over the phone. Do you know Mr Anindo Pakrashi?'

'Slightly.'

'Did you know him before?'

'No, I met him here.'

'Really! In this hotel? Is he a regular here? What kind of a person is he?'

'Why do you ask?'

Karabi smiled. 'I have my reasons. I have urgent business with him.' She picked up the phone. The call yielded more information on Anindo Pakrashi. He was busy those days—one day he would be the emperor of the industrial empire Madhab Industries, for which he needed a lot of education. 'Not education, acid test,' Anindo had once told us himself.

Many of you must have seen Anindo Pakrashi, one of the country's youngest industrialists. Looking at his face—hard, devoid of feeling—in newspaper photographs these days, I find it hard to believe that this is the same person who would often seek us out for a simple chat. He would sneak out of home to come to Shahjahan. 'I'm not even allowed to smoke,' he would say, 'my mother doesn't like it at all. My father wasn't very keen when I took this on—he says there's no peace of mind in business. He wanted me to enjoy my freedom for a few more years, to roam around at will in the worlds of history, geography and literature. But my mother didn't agree.'

Another time he had said, 'I love to paint, you know, but I simply don't get the time. When I see some artist painting on the maidan as I am driving by, my mind wanders off. Reading Eliot, Pound and Auden was like an addiction for me; I used to read Bengali poetry too—I loved Jibanananda Das, Premendra Mitra and Samar Sen. Sen's poetry made me sad sometimes. Do people in our country really suffer so much? I even asked my mother once. She explained it all to me. They're poets, she said, they probably have to weep when they write, that's the convention, a rule of poetry. Unless you condemn those who are happy and affluent, why should ordinary people spend money on your poetry? If you meet them, she told me, you'll find they lead ordinary lives just like we do.'

This was the Anindo I knew—and the Anindo whom Karabi knew much better than I did.

After the call Karabi said, 'The rich man's darling is coming on a tour of the hotel to check if the arrangements for the foreign guests are adequate. To satisfy his whims he'll probably order for this chair to be moved there and that one to be moved here—we must learn from these people how to entertain guests!'

Anindo Pakrashi arrived from New Alipore a little later, in a multicoloured T-shirt and charcoal-grey trousers, swinging a tennis racket in his hand. Welcoming him, Karabi said, 'Though this is a suite on paper, actually it's an entire wing of the hotel—I can accommodate quite a few guests.'

'Shelter, you mean, not accommodate,' Anindo said with a smile. Running his eyes over the arrangements, he said, 'Believe me, I've never lived in a hotel—my mother doesn't like it at all. When I was at the Bombay branch for a few years, she made arrangements for me to stay at my aunt's instead of a hotel. My uncle's the agent there, I worked under him.'

Laughing like a little boy, he went on, 'The people who are coming own a huge factory in Germany—we're negotiating with them. My father's put all the responsibility on me. If the slightest thing goes wrong, I will be blamed. What can I do? Do you suppose I understand any of this? You'll have to make sure I don't lose face before my father.'

He was least bothered with the arrangements, happy to thrust all the responsibility upon us. Sitting down in Karabi's rocking chair, he said, 'I hope I can get through the next few days. My mother tells me that once when Father wasn't very well-off, he had to skip lunch for three days to wangle the agency of a firm. Let's see what fate holds in store for me—I don't like skipping lunch at all.'

'Times have changed,' said Karabi, poker faced.

'Absolutely,' said Anindo, 'I'll make sure my mother hears that. I'll go to the airport early tomorrow morning, and then come here. I'll stick to them like a leech. After that, we'll see what happens.'

'Your mother won't have anything to complain about,' I said. 'But it's not a bad idea to let her know your point of view beforehand.'

He didn't agree. 'You don't know my mother—she'll think her Kajol hasn't been concentrating. Oh I forgot to tell you, my nickname is Kajol. At Presidency my friends used to call me Kajla-didi. Whenever they saw me they would shout, "It's evening at the bamboo grove and the moon is out, but where's Kajla-didi, the poet, up and about?"'

Karabi's expression remained deadpan, but I couldn't help laughing.

'Did you recite a lot of poetry?' I asked.

'Of course not, but I knew many quotations by heart and I loved answering in rhyme. Though all that's over now. It's one thing to live in your father's hotel—but working in your father's office is rigorous imprisonment. Mother wanted me to stay outside Calcutta for some more time; she feels your work improves if you've had your training elsewhere. Father had considered calling me over, but Mother held him back. Now he thinks it's time for me to get familiar with Madhab Industries. Big industrialists have two major enemies you know, the public sector and coronary thrombosis, as my father often says.' Glancing at his watch, he said, 'Time to go. My mother's orders, have to go to the club and play some tennis.'

I remember even today that both of us were silent for some time after Anindo left. His nickname 'Kajol' may have signified black, but in the stale corrupt air of Shahjahan, he came across as a whiff of scented mountain breeze. Eventually, Karabi said, 'How could Mrs Pakrashi keep someone like him away from her for so many years?'

'Like the mother of the future king, the mother of the future managing director also has to make sacrifices,' I answered.

Almost involuntarily Karabi said, 'Let's hope so.'

I was very happy that day. At last I had seen someone good—not everything about a hotel was bad. Good people came by too.

I woke up early the next morning. Someone was already

sitting on the terrace like a statue. Prabhat Chandra Gomez. The empty cup beside him revealed that Gomez, following in the footsteps of Brahms, had been drinking the bitter black coffee he had brewed himself. Who knows what he was waiting for in the corner of the terrace?

He beckoned to me. 'This is the only luxury in my life— looking at the eastern horizon and waiting for the sun. This is when I find food for new thought.'

'You might catch a cold,' I said. 'All you've got on is a vest.'

He paid no attention, muttering to himself, 'If I catch a cold and die, the world won't be the poorer for it. A long time ago someone paid no heed to the cold and paid for it with his life. That day the world indeed became poorer, and that loss hasn't been made up yet.'

The melancholy harmony in his words moved even a tuneless person like me.

'He was the Shakespeare of music—his name was Beethoven,' he explained. 'If I had the means, if I had a record library worth its name, I would have played Beethoven's *Ninth Symphony* for you. It's the most awe-inspiring musical work in existence.'

'May you have everything one day, by the grace of God,' I said.

'His grace? His judgement?' A pleasant smile flitted across Gomez's face. 'Then how could Handel and Bach have gone blind? How could Beethoven go deaf? In the long history of human civilization there hasn't been another Beethoven. If you want to hear the sweetest symphonies in the world, you'd have to listen to the nine left behind by him. If you want to listen to a piano sonata that's unparalleled, you'll have to choose one of the thirty-two he wrote. And string quartets? There, too, you'll have to fall back on his seventeen compositions. If you want to unravel the mystery of how to create extraordinary harmony through ordinary means, lock yourself in your room and pay homage to Handel. He may not answer your prayers at first, but you mustn't lose heart. Be patient and one day, at just such a time, at the confluence of light and darkness, you'll understand why Beethoven had said, go and learn from Handel how to achieve greatness through simplicity.'

Gomez fell silent, and, seemingly oblivious to his surroundings, turned his gaze back upon the eastern horizon, as though the key to grasping the extraordinary through ordinary means was written with invisible ink in one corner of the sky.

I went back to my room without another word. Everyone else in the hotel was still wrapped in deep sleep, but my work had begun, and so had Karabi's. She and Agarwalla had spoken to Marco Polo. I was to be on special duty for the special guests for a few days.

As I went down the stairs, I could think only of Gomez. All of us seemed to be sitting like beggars by the roadside, trying to grasp the extraordinary through ordinary means.

Karabi opened the door as soon as I knocked. Her suite was almost ready for the guests. She had placed lovely bunches of flowers in the corners and on the table—every shade matching the room.

'Sometimes I think I should work as an interior decorator. How do you like it?'

'Wonderful,' I said.

'I made poor Nityahari slave yesterday,' she said. 'I rejected every shade he showed me for the curtains.'

Eventually, Nityahari had been forced to say, 'Forgive me for saying this but I've made the Governor's bed; when a member of the royal family came to India, I was summoned to provide his bedclothes and pillows. Lord Reading was so comfortable in the bed made by my unworthy self that he overslept by an hour—all the morning programmes had to be postponed. And now...I can't get approval for curtains for a room for two Germans. Such is my fate!'

Karabi had told him, 'Someone's future depends on these arrangements—if anything goes wrong he'll lose face before his father.'

Nityahari had assured her, 'If it's so serious, let me tell you something: it's no use worrying your head off over the curtains and table linen; focus all your attention on the bed. Forty years of experience in the linen department tells me that the bed is the most important item. If the bed is comfortable, nobody will say anything even if the food is bad—the bed must be made in such a way that the person feels he is sleeping in his own bed at home. It is, after all, the most important thing in life. It is where we laugh, where we lie down and cry, where we are born, where we die. And yet, you don't pay any attention to it. Heaven knows what will happen to this hotel when Nityahari isn't there any more.'

Then he had brought a sample of every shade of curtains he possessed to Karabi's room, and she had chosen one.

'How does it look?' Karabi gave me a cup of tea and asked once again.

I was still thinking of Handel. I said, 'Simple, and yet beautiful.'

Karabi smiled. 'That's the secret of all beauty. Anindo Pakrashi, for example. Why are the two of us slaving so hard on his behalf? Because he's simple and yet beautiful—isn't that so?'

A little before breakfast that day, the huge Chrysler belonging to Madhab Industries drove up to Shahjahan Hotel from Dum Dum Airport with the important guests Dr Reiter and Herr Kurt.

Karabi was dressed in a Murshidabadi silk sari, her hair bedecked with flowers. How lovely she looked! Simple and elegant. She was at our counter when the guests arrived, and greeted them in the traditional manner. Anindo transferred the responsibility for their luggage to me and went ahead with Karabi.

When I arrived at suite number two with the porters bearing the luggage, I was in for another surprise. Sometime between now and when I had met her at dawn, Karabi had had traditional Indian patterns painted on the floor of the suite.

'What's this?' the visitors asked.

'*Alpana*. Traditional decorations,' said Anindo. 'Our housewives paint these patterns to welcome respected guests.'

'Wonderful!' said Dr Reiter and focused his camera on the floor. After he had finished, he said, 'You mean ordinary housewives do such artwork—it's not done by professional artists?'

'That's right,' said Anindo. 'Of course, you could call Miss Guha a talented artist.'

Tapping his foot, Kurt said, 'May I have a glass of beer?'

'Certainly,' said Anindo.

I had to remind him reluctantly, 'It's dry day.'

'What?' Kurt said sharply.

'I'm extremely sorry,' Anindo explained, 'you've arrived on a bad day. One day every week, selling liquor is prohibited in our state—bar and restaurant managers have to keep all spirits locked up that day.'

Kurt had never heard of such a thing in his life. 'You mean to say you're completely dry for a whole day?' he exclaimed. 'You deliberately cripple normal life in India for a day? And you mean to tell me that your country is going to start an industrial revolution in this manner, with leftover ideas from the last century?'

I realized from Anindo's face that he was dismayed with this inauspicious beginning. If only he knew what was to follow.

Assuming full responsibility for his country's transgressions he stood with his head bowed before his foreign guests, and begged their forgiveness.

Dr Reiter tried to calm his friend down. 'Calcutta is still the best among the worst. I believe, in Bombay every day is dry. I've heard you need a permit for even a bottle of beer.'

Disgruntled, Kurt sat down. I thought Karabi had discreetly disappeared so that Anindo wouldn't feel embarrassed in front of her, but I soon realized my mistake. She came back to the drawing room shortly. The guests looked at her in surprise. The bearer stood behind her, with two tender coconuts in his hands. The Germans had never seen such a strange fruit before.

'What's this?' Kurt asked.

Karabi laughed. 'Nature has arranged this drink for us in India—the *daab*.'

'*Daab*? Never heard of it!' Reiter said.

Karabi held the coconuts out to them. 'Indians drink a lot of this,' she said.

Anindo felt a little reassured at seeing the change in his guests' expressions.

A bewitching smile spread across her face as Karabi said, 'Drinking *daab* is also an art. I could have poured the juice into glasses for you, but I want you to drink it the way our villagers do.'

Kurt looked intrigued. 'Tell us how to drink it,' he said.

'We put our mouths to the holes cut on the top and tilt it in such a way that not a drop is spilled. But that's quite difficult.'

Kurt took this as a challenge. He wanted to prove that he too could drink the same way. He handed the fruit to Karabi while he took off his jacket.

'Wait, Mr Kurt,' Karabi told him. 'If you try to drink that way you'll get your clothes stained and our country's reputation, too. I've arranged for straws for you.'

'Give me the straw,' said Reiter. 'I have no objection to taking know-how from your country on subjects I have no experience about.'

Kurt, however, was not going to give up easily. 'We're Germans, o lovely Indian lady—very stubborn. Now that you've got me interested I'm going to try it.'

Karabi said, mimicking him good-naturedly, 'O foreigner, thank you for the compliment, but for your stubbornness you have only my admonition.'

Kurt insisted on trying it out. But the liquid splashed on to his clothes; then, he drew in his breath too quickly and started coughing. Karabi snatched the coconut out of his hands, while he laughed and coughed at the same time.

'That's enough,' she said, 'no more. Eventually it will be rumoured that there was a plot to kill you in India.'

Kurt finally gathered himself. Looking down at his wet clothes, he realized his mistake and said, a trifle embarrassedly, 'I'm really sorry, Miss Guha, I shouldn't have lost my head over a drink.'

Reiter said gravely, 'You've already been punished enough for bad behaviour—maybe Miss Guha has some more punishment in store for you.'

Everyone laughed and then Kurt and Reiter went into their rooms.

Anindo's grateful eyes, as he looked at Karabi, are still etched in my memory. 'Really, you're one of a kind,' he said, unembarrassed by my presence. 'Our relationship would have soured right at the beginning, but you miraculously saved the situation.'

Karabi blushed for a moment and, plucking at the end of her sari, said, 'Would you like something to eat? They're going to rest for some time.'

Anindo said, 'Yes, but on one condition. You must accompany me.' He looked at me. 'You come too...we can chat over breakfast.'

'Thank you,' I said, 'but I have a lot to do.'

In his naiveté Anindo may have believed me, but Karabi let the cat out of the bag. 'That's not true. He belongs to the hotel staff...how can he eat at the same table with guests?'

'So what?' said Anindo. 'He's my guest.'

'The management doesn't like employees hobnobbing with guests.'

He said with his typical childishness, 'What nonsense! I'm going to talk to the manager at once.'

Pleading urgent duties, I excused myself while they went down for breakfast.

Who knows where that Anindo, who got upset at a hotel employee's inability to share a table with him and wanted to protest against it, has disappeared. His speeches today give the impression that he's lost all respect for ordinary people. He now thinks that everyone is conspiring to cheat Madhab Industries; that workers are interested only in their salaries, their overtime payments and their bonuses, but give nothing in return. He believes that the entire state is hell-bent on destroying industry with the indulgence of the government and the encouragement of the communists.

The Anindo I knew had once recited lines from one of his favourite poets to Karabi and me:

Men have been born and in their time on earth
Gathered at ever-new confluences of history
But still, where is the fulfilment of that unique dream
The fresh dawn of virgin humanity?

'Just you wait,' Karabi had said, 'I'm going to call your mother and tell her that her son is roaming around with volumes of poetry instead of concentrating on work.'

Anindo had replied, 'I'm going to give you some poems and then I'll see how you can stop yourself from becoming an addict too.'

After having his breakfast with Karabi, Anindo came to our counter. 'Both of them are snoring their heads off,' he said. 'Whatever we have to do can wait, meanwhile I have some time to kill.'

He wasted a lot of it standing around after that, watching us as we worked. 'Really, what an interesting job you people have. You get to meet so many different kinds of people…now I understand why English novels are so absorbing when they're set in hotels.'

'Why don't you start a new hotel, Mr Pakrashi,' said Bose-da. 'A unique hotel, in a completely Indian style, with Indian dances instead of cabarets, and popular Indian musicians to entertain guests. I have spoken to many well-known artistes who stay at our hotel…they would all be willing to help.'

Anindo shook his head. 'My father has his eye on the electrical and mechanical industries now,' he said glumly.

He might have said more, but Karabi appeared suddenly in the lounge. 'Nice man you are,' she said to him, 'I go to my room for a moment and you come away without a word!'

'But you need some rest too,' he said.

'Me? In the morning?' she exclaimed. 'And you needn't stand outside—you can always use the suite like your own room.'

'That's why you are so renowned as a hostess.'

I had no idea that Anindo's response would offend Karabi so much. Her smile disappeared. Raising her eyes slowly, she said, 'You think I'm asking you in only because I'm a hostess?'

He didn't understand, but from her face I knew she was hurt. The ever-smiling 'welcome' girl of the firm had forgotten for a moment that she was on duty. But it doesn't take long for girls on duty to remember their obligations. 'Your guests are ready,' she said. 'You're probably going out with them now, but will you be back for lunch?'

'There's no need for lunch,' he said. 'Father will be coming to the club too, I'll take them there.'

After they left, Bose-da told me, 'In the olden days it used to be kings—these days it's trade representatives, and they merit better treatment than kings even, because they come with the crown jewel: know-how.'

I didn't quite understand what he meant. He started laughing. 'You don't get it? The key to Alibaba's treasure trove. We don't have the initiative to use our brains and brawn to fabricate this key, so we're trying to open doors by borrowing the keys from someone else. Don't worry,' he said. 'It's good news for the hotel. All the rooms will be occupied. We'll be able to raise our rates again, we'll be able to put more money into belly dancers.' Pausing, he added, 'Remember to send the police reports today.'

Anindo returned with his guests late in the afternoon. They'd probably had plenty to drink somewhere, which meant that they were in no condition to stand or even sit; they tottered off to their rooms.

I went up to Karabi's suite with Anindo to discuss the police reports.

'How was business?' she asked him.

'Couldn't have been better,' Anindo replied. 'They were taken to our office and then to Mrs Chakladar's flat within half an hour. I had no idea that so many households in Calcutta are converted into bars on dry days. I knew nothing about this; it was my uncle Phokla Chatterjee who told me—he phoned Mrs Chakladar to let her know. She doesn't entertain unknown parties. I daren't ask, but may I have some tea?'

'Why are you hesitating?' I said to him. 'I'll tell the bearer to get some right away.'

Karabi stopped me. 'Let me prove today that even in hotels you can get home-made tea.'

She made some for Anindo. After he had finished drinking it, she asked, 'What now?'

'I'm going to drive to the river front,' he replied. 'My

parents are under the impression that their son is escorting our guests around the city. But I simply love watching the onset of dusk over Calcutta. It's as if someone drapes the city in ornaments of light, which are locked away carefully in a box during the day.'

She asked, 'Where did you learn so much about jewellery?'

'Just because I'm not married you think I shouldn't know anything about jewellery?'

It was Karabi who told me later that they talked a lot over tea. Though I wasn't supposed to know, she was probably keen to share everything with someone. She seemed bubbling with happiness. I had always known her as reserved, but this was a pleasant change.

'What's the hurry? Where are you off to so soon?' she asked me.

'I have to go to the counter. I've promised William Ghosh,' I said.

'Why do you have to be there during his duty hours?'

'He's made a special request, so I've promised to stand in for him for a couple of hours.'

I didn't want to say anything more, but under her cross-questioning I had to come out with the truth. William was taking Rosie out that night, having got this extraordinary opportunity after months of coaxing and cajoling. The two of them would go to a restaurant on Chowringhee for dinner. They could have had free meals at the hotel, but poor William had agreed to spend his own money.

Karabi smiled and said, 'Then you'd better go. If you can, drop in before you go up to your room.'

William was fidgeting, waiting for me at the counter. 'I can't find the words to thank you,' he said as I approached.

'That's all very well, but where's the one for whom I am doing overtime?'

'She refuses to be seen going out with me,' William

whispered. 'She'll wait for me in front of the Grand. I'll take a taxi and pick her up on the way to Park Street.'

'Excellent plan,' I said.

Before leaving, he came to the counter once more, saying furtively, 'One request: no one should get even a whiff of this. If it gets to Jimmy's ears, you know what will happen.'

I nodded. 'Of course I do. Have a wonderful evening.'

Every job has its own addiction—one in a hotel certainly does. Once you get absorbed in the work, everything else slips out of your mind. As I got busy directing the flow of guests at the counter, the two of them had been forgotten. I remembered them only when Rosie threw a sidelong glance at me and walked straight into the lift. She looked different under the fluorescent lights.

William returned after another quarter of an hour. 'Thank you, o pilot,' he proclaimed. 'Let me take the controls now.'

'Why so late?' I asked.

'Rosie wouldn't let me return with her. "You must wait at least fifteen minutes before setting foot in the hotel," she told me. I spent some time walking across Central Avenue, enjoying the night breeze.'

I handed over charge to William and knocked at the door to Karabi's suite on my way up. I wasn't too keen on visiting her at this hour, but I had promised. She might have been up and waiting for me.

'Come in,' she said softly. I entered to find Karabi Guha hunched over a table in a corner of the dimly lit room. Slowly she turned towards me. I was shocked by her appearance. It seemed as if I had left someone else in suite number two when I went to relieve William Ghosh. This was a different woman.

Even in that air-conditioned suite, I felt beads of perspiration on my forehead. Why was Karabi seated like this? She didn't ask me to sit. She just looked at me. Then her eyes turned to the telephone in the corner.

'Is there something you want to tell me?' I asked. She looked as though she did but then, on second thought, changed her mind.

'No,' she said. 'I was thinking of asking you to call him, but maybe I shouldn't.'

'Where are your guests?' I whispered.

'They wanted to go to Mrs Chakladar's again,' she said, 'but some top-level government officers had booked the place for the evening. She could have accommodated the two of them, but the contractor, Mrs Kanoria, didn't agree. She had promised her guests that there would be nobody else at Mrs Chakladar's. Officers are very careful these days...What if someone wrote a couple of paragraphs in a newspaper?' She paused, and then added, 'I may have to ask you for a favour—but not now. I've managed for today.' She was pale.

'I don't like the look of things,' I said. 'If I can be of any service, please don't hesitate to tell me.'

But she didn't say anything. I went back to my own world on the terrace. There was a dazzling festival of stars in the sky, as if some inhabitant of the heavens had arranged a banquet up there.

On dry nights, hotel employees usually went back to their rooms and fell asleep early. But Gomez wasn't one of them. He was sitting on a stool outside his room. I was worried about Karabi. Why had she been so overwrought? I found it puzzling. It felt like a play was being enacted on the stage of suite number two, and I was a silent member of the audience. Who knew what other plays were being staged in the different rooms of Shahjahan, in the dark of night, away from the public eye? Who kept track? I did not care where the lives of those I did not know were headed. But suite number two was different. The thought of Karabi as the heroine of some tragic play made me apprehensive.

Gomez beckoned to me. 'Still up?' I asked him.

He smiled. 'I can't sleep—my habits have changed after years of treating night as day, so I spend dry nights in the company of the stars. Nice feeling.' I drew up another stool next to him. 'You're young, you should sleep well,' he said. 'Once you get older you'll also have to do a lot of coaxing and cajoling to get sleep to visit you.'

'There's so much you reflect on, Mr Gomez. The stars, the sun—they seem to be in communion with you. Can you tell me why we are always apprehensive about something or the other? Why irrational anxieties affect us so?'

'I believe the Hindu scriptures have the answer to that,' he said. 'But I'm an uneducated Christian, I don't know. I can give you the answer through a song though, an ordinary song from a film. That's where I found the philosophy of life: que sera sera.'

'What does it mean?' I asked.

Gomez started singing softly, 'Que sera sera, whatever will be will be, the future's not ours to see...' Finishing the song, he said, 'An American guest who had come to this hotel gave me the record. I'll play it for you some time. It reminds me that it's not our job to worry about the future—que sera sera.' His words helped me regain some of my composure.

Anindo returned the next day. That morning the front page of leading newspapers had carried a report under the headline, GERMAN INDUSTRIAL REPRESENTATIVES IN CALCUTTA. It had mentioned Madhab Industries and that Madhab Pakrashi wasn't present at Dum Dum Airport because he was unwell, and that his wife couldn't make it either, busy as she was tending to her husband. Karabi had read the report and looked at Anindo. I was also present, but only because she had insisted on it.

Anindo shook his head. 'I don't know,' he said. 'These are all mother's plans. She got hold of our PRO, Mr Sen, and prepared the press note. Father wanted to go to the airport, but she insisted that I be given a chance. He had no choice but to

fall ill.' Then, turning to Karabi, he said, 'If you don't mind,
I'd like to ask your permission for something.'

'I'm your friend Mr Agarwalla's hostess, which practically
makes me part of your staff. So it's not for you to make a
request, you have only to order,' she replied.

Anindo wasn't prepared for such an answer, but he smiled
and said, 'I see, this is revenge for yesterday. But I'm not angry.
I didn't spend much time by the river yesterday—I went
straight to a bookshop. You're a prisoner all by yourself in the
hotel. So I thought my favourite poets' works might bring you
some joy.'

'How did you assume that your favourite poets would also
be mine?'

'Jibanananda or Samar Sen won't have an answer to that,
but it's easy for me to give you the answer. Speculation. We're
businessmen, speculation runs in our blood.'

'You could really have done a lot for Bengali literature.'

'Wait. For now let me improve the lot of Madhab
Industries by being in the service of these two Germans,' he
replied, laughing. 'But I can also tell you that I'm not going to
stay this way all my life. I'll break free of this madness and
devote myself to poetry and history.'

Karabi wanted me to stay on. But I had other tasks to
attend to. I was on special duty at the suite, but I hadn't been
released from all my other responsibilities.

I went to the counter and had just begun work when
Bose, the reporter, appeared. 'How are you?' he said. 'And
where's your guru Sata Bose? I need some more information
about these Germans.'

'I'm sure the PRO of Madhab Industries will send their
press release to your office well in time.'

'If such press releases were all that was needed to run a
newspaper, the owners wouldn't need reporters like me. I
want the real stuff, not artificial flavouring. Now tell me where
I can get some unadulterated news.'

I was silent. But he was apparently quite well informed. 'Miss Guha from your deluxe suite could help me if she wanted to,' he said.

'She has guests now,' I said. 'If you could come back a little later?'

'No problem. I'll pay a visit to the railway publicity office at Esplanade in the meantime.'

As soon as he left I called Karabi. 'Here is your chance to get famous—a newspaper representative wants to meet you,' I told her.

'I don't understand...why don't you come over to the suite?'

Anindo was still there. I repeated my conversation with the reporter. She said, 'Hostesses should always stay in the background. Anindo will meet the press.'

Anindo immediately became uneasy. 'Neither my father nor my mother talks to the press without the PRO around.'

'There's nothing to be nervous about,' she reassured him. 'I'll be there.'

She did not invite the reporter to suite number two. The number of people privileged to go in there could be counted on the fingers of one hand. They met Bose in a corner of the lounge. Karabi asked me to arrange for some tea.

As I went back to the counter after ordering the tea, I heard Karabi say, 'Mr Pakrashi's going into a new industry. He loves Bengal, and the future of our country depends to a great extent on this collaboration between Indian and German industries.'

Anindo said, 'If you give these guests good coverage, it'll help us. If we can set up this factory for manufacturing electrical equipment, we'll be able to give jobs to lots of unemployed young people—all those unemployed youngsters whose woes you write about in your papers.'

Bose left after promising to help as much as possible. He

kept his word. The next day a long account of the interview with Anindo Pakrashi, spokesman for Madhab Industries, was published in Calcutta's most influential English daily.

Anindo arrived at Shahjahan with the newspaper in his hand. He was ecstatic. 'Both my parents are amazed,' he told Karabi effusively. 'They're wondering how junior managed to organize such publicity. It's thanks to your foresight. I came here right away—you know why? So that I could—'

'Thank me, right?' Karabi snatched the words out of his mouth.

He smiled. 'You think I'm always being polite and formal, don't you? Have you ever considered that we too can feel like expressing gratitude from our hearts?' Karabi was quiet. 'My guests must be troubling you a lot,' he said.

'Not at all. Compared to the VIPs from our own country, these are demigods. They drink at the bar, watch the cabaret and go to sleep in their rooms. They don't bother me very much.'

'Where are they now?'

'Having their breakfast in the hall.'

'Fine, I'm not worried any more. All these days I've been thinking about them all the time—now I will try to be normal. And the day they sign the agreement, I'll be a free bird.'

I had just got back to my room after the day's work, and was lying on my bed, when there was a knock on the door. Opening it, I stood transfixed for a while. I had never imagined Karabi would come to meet me at that hour.

She entered and sat down on the chair, her face clouded over with anxiety. Her breath came in short gasps.

'What's the matter?' I asked. 'You could have sent for me.'

'No, we couldn't have spoken in my room. I need your advice.' Her voice quivered as she spoke. 'I didn't realize it that day, though I did suspect it. But at that time I thought Mr Agarwalla was showing interest on Mr Pakrashi's behalf.'

She told me that the owner of suite number two had called her. 'This is top secret,' he had said. 'Reiter and Kurt will have to be observed. How do you assess their state of mind?'

'I haven't spoken to them about business,' she'd told him.

'You must. What's the point in having a beautiful hostess otherwise?'

Even at that point, she had thought Agarwalla was making enquiries on Madhab Pakrashi's behalf. Before ending the call, he had said, 'They must be given the best possible treatment, a great deal depends on their being kept happy.'

I still couldn't make sense of what she was saying.

'Only a moment ago I realized that Agarwalla is planning to meet them separately. Having obtained the detailed plan of Madhab Industries, he wants to get into the act himself. The Germans don't care if they build their factory in collaboration with him instead of Pakrashi. Agarwalla wants to meet them secretly. He wants to come when the Pakrashis aren't around and quietly get his job done. He has rung me up several times to find out how long Anindo stays here. Even last night he phoned to find out today's programme. I lied and told him that as far as I know, Anindo would be here till late. But there's somebody called Phokla Chatterjee who feeds secret information to Mr Agarwalla; he's promised to arrange it so that Anindo doesn't come to the hotel this evening. Mr Agarwalla has promised to pay whatever is needed. Mr Chatterjee shouldn't skimp on expenses for a drive or drinks or anything else.'

'Phokla Chatterjee, did you say?' I asked.

'Yes, that's the name I heard,' she said. 'I've never been in this kind of situation before. All these days I thought my loyalties lay with the person I work for...but now things are different...I have been reading the poems Anindo gave me and they made me realize that I have an identity too, that I have to account for my actions.' Trying to say all this coherently, she seemed to run out of breath. 'Will you please call Anindo?'

'I can,' I said, 'but you'll have to do the talking.'

Had we called a little later we wouldn't have found him in. 'What's the matter?' he asked.

'Please speak to Miss Guha,' I said.

To her he said, 'I'm not going to the hotel this evening, I'm going out with my uncle instead. He's promised to introduce me to Jibanananda Das—he's going to read his own poetry. Then I'll go the river front. My uncle's suddenly developed a wish to listen to poetry—I'm going to read, and he's going to listen. He's such an unromantic sort of chap, I may not get another chance like this.'

Karabi's lips were trembling. 'Go some other day,' she said. 'Today you'd better come here. Immediately.'

'But why?'

'I want to see you right now,' she said and hung up.

Karabi went downstairs without wasting a moment. I couldn't sit still either. I went down to the counter and chatted with William. I was in his good books now, and he wanted to keep me happy. Who else would cover for him if he got the chance to take Rosie out to dinner again? Bose-da was present too.

I hadn't expected the whole thing to play out before our eyes. It happened because Anindo and Mr Agarwalla entered the hotel practically at the same time. Agarwalla was in a good mood, but the sight of Anindo gave him the shock of his life. Hitching up his trousers which had slipped below his navel, he asked Anindo, 'You here?'

Anindo was a little embarrassed. 'To check on my guests,' he said.

Agarwalla gulped. 'You needn't have bothered. By your grace no guest in Agarwalla's guest room lacks for comfort. I don't pay Miss Guha so much for nothing!'

'I wish I knew how to thank you,' said Anindo. 'Not one suite was available in any of the city's good hotels—and these people couldn't have been put up in ordinary rooms.'

'Not at all. If one business concern doesn't look after another, how will we operate? After all, your father is an old friend.'

Now it was Anindo's turn to ask why Agarwalla was there. 'I've come looking for a friend,' said Agarwalla. 'He's supposed to be waiting at the bar. I'll be going out with him in a minute. Do let me know in case your guests have any problems.'

Anindo went in. Agarwalla went straight to the lounge telephone, but couldn't get through to whoever he was trying to contact. Then he came over to the counter and told us that if Phokla Chatterjee came looking for him, we should tell him that he had gone to Mrs Chakladar's.

Phokla Chatterjee arrived at Shahjahan soon after. Coming straight to the counter, he said, 'Sata! This is getting too much for me. At my age I'd be happy with a ten-to-five job.'

'What's the matter, Mr Chatterjee?' asked Bose-da.

'All in good time,' wheezed Phokla. 'Right now I'm dying of thirst—can you organize some booze?'

'Why do you want to get us into trouble? You know very well we unworthy people are helpless. Drinks cannot be served in the lounge.'

'Wonder when this damned government will be voted out! These are the bastards for whom we fought the British! For them our martyrs gave up their lives!' Phokla was quite agitated. Bose-da merely smiled and went on with his work. But Phokla continued, 'Damn it! There's no objection to selling booze, but you're not allowed to drink it in public— what kind of law is this? I really feel bad for you fellows, you're decent people, you've come into this line, but the future's bleak. Some day the bastards will declare that you cannot drink anywhere except in the loo.'

Bose-da said, 'You have a lot of contacts, why don't you tell them to protest?'

'That'll be the day,' Phokla said. 'The buggers grumble in

private, but they won't say a word in public. All of them draw veils over their faces and become nuns when they walk down the road. They're the kind of people who would actually drink in the loo without making a fuss, if the government passed the order. One person could have made a difference—my sister, Madhab Pakrashi's wife. But she's very old-fashioned, she can't stand alcohol.'

'Is that so?' Bose-da feigned surprised.

'All day she is busy with her women's society, her literacy society, her preservation of moral health society, or her gods and goddesses. If only she'd say just once that it's better to drink openly than to drink furtively, the government might pay attention.'

Bose-da suggested, 'If you need a drink so badly why don't you go to the bar?'

'I can't,' said Phokla. 'I have to wait here for someone.'

'Do you mean Mr Agarwalla?' I asked. 'He's left a message for you.'

'Yes, that's who I'm waiting for. He phoned me, but I wasn't in, so he asked me to come to Shahjahan.'

'Mr Agarwalla's gone to Mrs Chakladar's,' said Bose-da.

'Mrs Chakladar's?' Phokla started laughing loudly. 'Never show a starving man a dinner table! I was the one who first took Agarwalla to Mrs Chakladar's. You can have a peaceful drink in a nice homely set-up. Sheer heaven for people like us. The rates are a little on the high side—the minimum admission charge on dry days is twenty rupees. But these chaps are hell-bent on milking it for all it has got. Agarwalla's started taking guests there even on other days. He goes there every day. Some day it's going to get into the papers and the honeycomb will be exposed.' Glancing at his watch, Phokla continued, 'All my life I have been doing other people's dirty work. So many bloody businessmen have become filthy rich by entertaining clients through me—and all I have to show for it is a bad liver.

I drink the booze for free, and occasionally earn a couple of hundreds. No capital, you see. If I had some, I'd have shown them; hundreds of unemployed young fellows would have had jobs with the Phokla group of industries by now.'

'Mr Agarwalla is waiting there for you,' I reminded him.

'Let him—it's not as if the world's coming to an end!' For a moment he paused, hand on brow. 'If you don't mind my saying so, Bengali girls are good for nothing. No race can be great without the help of its women. Never mind me, even Swami Vivekananda said women are the source of our strength. But Bengali girls will not make the least bit of effort. You remember Mr Ranganathan, don't you? He controls contracts worth lakhs. He used to think highly of Bengal, he was very keen on becoming friends with a Bengali girl. He was ready to foot all the expenses. But, such a shame, nobody would agree. And as luck would have it, Mrs Kapoor had no qualms about being friends with him. The order that should have come to us went to Mr Kapoor instead. And yet we keep lamenting the lack of opportunities.'

Phokla Chatterjee glanced at his watch. 'I'd better go now.' As he was about to leave, he wheeled around suddenly. 'Seen Anindo?' he asked.

Bose-da looked at me. 'He's come to call on the German visitors,' I said.

'Hmm...' He hesitated a little and then asked, 'By the way, did anyone staying here telephone Anindo a short while ago?'

My heart missed a beat as I looked into Phokla Chatterjee's eyes. 'Yes, Dr Reiter did,' I said.

'Sure?'

'He used this very phone.'

'I see...I thought I heard someone speaking in Bengali.'

I almost lost my nerve. 'You're right,' I said. 'I spoke first—Dr Reiter had asked me to connect him.'

'All right,' he said.

I heaved a sigh of relief after he left. Who knows what I might have said had he asked more questions.

Bose-da looked at me. My expression told him all he needed to know. He knew Dr Reiter hadn't been to the counter all afternoon and evening. But he asked no questions.

'The gurus of the hotel business have a maxim,' he said softly. 'Never forget that there's a counter between you and your guests. Sita fell prey to Ravana because she crossed the line.'

I met Karabi that night. She was sitting by herself. I'd meant to tell her about Phokla Chatterjee, but I could not bring myself to do so. She said, 'I feel so relieved now. Anindo's left, they're asleep. Agarwalla can do no harm even if he were to turn up now.' I heard from her that Anindo wasn't pleased by the summons. Karabi was unable to explain why she had called him. All she'd said was that he was needed and that she wouldn't be able to manage the two of them by herself. 'He'll be here in the morning again. I'm not letting him go. I'm scared.'

Bose-da's warning was still ringing in my ears. I didn't want to get involved; my only concern ought to have been my job. And yet, I couldn't remain a silent witness and watch Agarwalla stab the Pakrashis in the back.

We weren't supposed to know, but I learnt later that the Pakrashi business empire wasn't as powerful as it appeared from the outside. Without this German collaboration its foundations would have been shaken. Anindo never got to know, but by ensuring his presence beside her that evening, Karabi had managed to protect the Pakrashis from Agarwalla.

The newspapers carried the photograph: Madhab Pakrashi signing the memorandum of understanding with the German company. Anindo Pakrashi could be seen to his left. The photograph made Karabi cry with joy.

It could have ended there. Anindo Pakrashi could have faded out of Karabi's life and Shahjahan Hotel. At least, that would have been the natural outcome. But no one had reckoned with the events that followed.

I was surprised at Anindo, though. Had it not been for Karabi, the papers would have carried Mr Agarwalla's photograph instead of Madhab Pakrashi's. But Anindo didn't even express his gratitude to Karabi. And, more surprisingly, Karabi didn't seem upset about it either. I had expected her to discuss the matter with me, to show her disappointment, at least. But nothing.

As a matter of fact, I had understood very little of what was happening. But one evening when Mrs Pakrashi entered the hotel, dressed in a silk sari, wearing dark glasses and carrying a white vanity bag, everything became clear to me. Mrs Pakrashi hadn't been seen in the hotel for a while, perhaps the German guests' presence had made her visits impossible. Now that they had left, and perhaps because Madhab Pakrashi was in Delhi or Bombay with Anindo, she was here. And fortunately, suite number one was unoccupied, too.

Mrs Pakrashi seemed disappointed to see me at the counter. 'Where's Mr Bose?' she asked.

'He's resting in his room. May I help you?'

'I need to talk to him.'

I went to fetch Bose-da. 'Why didn't you ask when she wants the room? Why bother me?' he complained.

'She's your client,' I said. 'She doesn't want to deal with me.'

Mrs Pakrashi walked towards us as soon as she saw Bose-da. I left them and came back to the counter. After sometime Bose-da came up to me and said, 'Give me the key to suite number one.' Both of them disappeared upstairs.

The hands of the clock turned slowly, as I waited anxiously for them. Almost an hour later, Mrs Pakrashi left, hissing like a wounded snake. As soon as she departed Bose-da sent for me.

'Sit down,' he said.

'Any special arrangement for Mrs Pakrashi?' I asked.

'Nothing like that,' said Bose-da, looking worried. 'What's going on? I'm sure you know, though you haven't told me.' I looked at him blankly. 'I'm asking about Karabi and Anindo. How did they manage to go this far?'

'Meaning?'

'I'm sure you've seen everything so there's no point concealing anything from you. Anindo wants to marry Karabi. The Prince of Madhab Industries is madly in love with the hostess of suite number two at Shahjahan Hotel.'

I cannot explain why, but I felt elated. Anindo and Karabi! Why ever not? If there was one person who could offer Anindo some shade from the searing heat of life it was Karabi. And if Anindo could water the arid desert of Karabi's heart and make it bloom, surely this world would be a more beautiful place.

Bose-da said, 'We're going to be in trouble. We've never been in such a sticky situation before. Mrs Pakrashi thinks Karabi is trying to blackmail Anindo. She believes Karabi has taken advantage of his naiveté to get him into a compromising situation, and is now trying to cash in on that.'

'But where do we come into the picture?' I stammered.

'Mrs Pakrashi has a soft corner for us. For whatever reason, she's partial to this hotel. Besides, she's come to us in a crisis—you must help even your enemies if they are in trouble.'

'Help?'

'She's requested us to have a word with Karabi. I told her that is neither possible nor appropriate. Now she wants to talk to Karabi herself.'

I was silent. Bose-da said, 'I've told her. You're the only one in this hotel Karabi talks to.'

'Why, what about Nityahari, he's so much older than we are,' I said, trying to wriggle out. But without success.

'Are you mad?' asked Bose-da. 'Nobody but you, me, Karabi and Mrs Pakrashi must know about this.'

I had to agree. Karabi was alone in suite number two. She had a volume of poetry on her lap. Raising her eyes she asked, a la Banalata Sen, 'And where have you been?'

'Where do you suppose?' I laughed. 'Running up and down the six storeys of Shahjahan.'

'After ages, I'm not busy,' said Karabi. 'I don't have a single guest. Since his failure to checkmate the Pakrashis, Agarwalla hasn't visited. I telephoned him but was told he's reeling from a simultaneous attack of high blood pressure and diabetes. So I'm going to spend some time happily reading poetry, singing, going out, doing as I please.'

I had to get to the point. 'I have a request.'

'Request?' She looked surprised.

'Yes, you're free to say no. But there's a condition. You can't tell anyone—not even Anindo.'

Her face grew pale on hearing Anindo's name. She forced the words out, 'I have no idea what you're talking about, but I accept your condition.'

'I haven't much idea either. All I know is that Mrs Pakrashi wants to meet you.'

Mrs Pakrashi had suggested that they meet not at the Shahjahan but somewhere else. Karabi didn't agree. She wasn't used to leaving the hotel, she said. Mrs Pakrashi had burst into peals of laughter when she heard this. 'I see. Since I'm the one in a spot, I have to accept her terms. But I hope she will keep this meeting a secret.'

'You remember your promise, don't you?' I asked Karabi.

'We're infamous hostesses of famous hotels. We work for Marwaris to ensure square meals for our families. How can our word be worth anything?' she said sadly.

Mrs Pakrashi's arrival at the hotel that day is indelibly inscribed in my memory. The very same Karabi who had made others' fortunes by playing host to the rich and famous was a pale shadow of herself. 'I don't feel comfortable,' she told me. 'I want you to be present.'

'That's impossible,' I said. 'I'd rather wait for you outside.'

The resident goddess of Madhab Industries turned up at the hotel not in her own car, but in a taxi. She hadn't expected to run into the reporter Bose at the entrance.

'What's the matter?' he asked. 'PTI says you've changed your plans to attend the social work seminar in Paris at the very last moment.'

Mrs Pakrashi chuckled and said casually, 'Don't worry, Mr Bose. Mrs Lakshmivati Patel of Bombay has agreed to represent India at the seminar.'

'That's all very good, but who will compensate for your presence and how it would have glorified this city of ours?'

'It's your love and affection that sustain me. Do pray that I recover quickly.'

Getting rid of the reporter, Mrs Pakrashi asked me anxiously, 'I hope that bitch is there.'

In just ten minutes, maybe even less, Mrs Pakrashi emerged from suite number two. Bose-da escorted her outside and saw her into a taxi. He came back and said to me, 'Tell Karabi she had better listen to Mrs Pakrashi—or else. The lady wanted me to let her know.'

Karabi was waiting for me. She had nobody to call her own. I was lonely, too, but for some reason Karabi's condition upset me no end. Why did she have to get herself embroiled in this unpleasant situation? And wasn't there anyone else she could have turned to for advice? What counsel could the youngest clerk at Shahjahan offer to solve this oldest of problems?

Karabi looked at me and couldn't contain herself any longer. Breaking down she said, 'What have I let myself in for?'

Have you ever heard the cry of a lonely woman hurt in love? It's not a very uncommon sight in this misery-infested world. I've heard it many times and, remarkably, it's the same each time. I do not have the words to describe the despair, the helplessness. Only Beethoven or Mozart or Wagner could have given it form in melody; perhaps Saratchandra, Tagore or Dickens could have described it in words. The bricks in the walls of suite number two seemed to echo her anguish: what have I let myself in for?

What indeed? You fell in love. Unknown to all of us, you gave your heart to a decent and handsome young man. You had assumed that he too was enamoured of you—that he too felt the same about you. And then? You didn't realize that things had gone this far. Anindo did not tell you that he had spoken to his family, informed them of his intentions to take this relationship further. But Mrs Pakrashi, unaware of your ignorance, had proceeded to give you that most unexpected piece of information, in her own inimitable manner.

'I'm warning you,' she had threatened, 'I will not tolerate the slightest harm to Pakrashi Industries. Anindo is young, he doesn't understand. But you are old enough, experienced, don't you realize the consequences? Heaven knows why the Germans had to be put up here. How much money do you need to forget all this?'

Karabi had stared at Mrs Pakrashi in shock. 'Money?' she had stammered.

'Yes, that's all there is to it, isn't it? That's why you created this situation; that's why I couldn't go to Paris,' Mrs Pakrashi had replied. And then theatrically she had cried out, 'I wonder how God could have created a woman like you!'

Karabi couldn't believe her ears.

And as a parting shot Mrs Pakrashi had added, 'Don't forget, you've promised not to let Anindo know any of this. And don't raise the price because I came all the way to see you. Think it over. I'll be in touch.'

A bewildered Karabi, hurt by the accusations, sobbed her heart out. 'How come he never told me? Shouldn't he have discussed this with me? How did he know I would agree?'

'Perhaps your eyes gave you away,' I tried to comfort her.

'I saw it in his eyes too.' Even at the time Karabi could only think of Anindo, she had no time to consider Mrs Pakrashi's warning.

I couldn't offer any advice. I knew how powerful the Pakrashis were. Who knew what fate had in store for Karabi. I went back to my room. The gramophone was playing in Gomez's room, which was surprising because he was supposed to be playing at Mumtaz.

I found Gomez in bed. 'I'm not well, I've been throwing up,' he told me. 'So I couldn't go and play. I'm listening to Mozart's violin concerto. He wrote just five of those.' I felt his forehead. He had a high fever but oblivious to that, kept talking. 'All five were composed in Salzburg, in 1775. Would anyone believe that a nineteen-year-old boy composed this?'

'Don't work yourself up, please rest,' I told him.

'Listen,' Gomez whispered. 'If you want to discover the most secret sorrows of this planet, listen closely to Mozart's concertos.'

I didn't have to listen to a record. The sorrowful song of the heart in suite number two still resounded in my head.

Nityahari asked me the next day, 'What's the matter? Karabi devi didn't bother to approve my linen today; she didn't even scold the flower man.'

'I don't know,' I said.

He shook his head. 'I don't like it. After all these years at Shahjahan I can sense trouble before it gets here. You may not believe me, but I can smell it.'

Later, when I went to the reception, I ran into Phokla Chatterjee. 'Is that person in Agarwalla's guest house a woman or a cobra? She doesn't care for anybody. Agarwalla himself asked me to escort a gentleman to her, but she kicked us out. This is the problem with Indian firms—no such thing as discipline. There are so many guest houses like this in the UK and the US—would any call girl there dare to do such a thing?'

Since we did not respond, he went away in a huff.

'Any idea what's going on?' Bose-da asked.

'I don't think anybody does,' I said.

Karabi didn't, either. She hadn't even found the time to comb her hair. When I met her in her room, she said, like a child, 'If someone loves me and I love him, what's wrong with marrying him?' I was silent. Almost to herself she continued, 'What do we care what people say?' Then turning to me, 'They'll condemn it, they will mock us—the prince of the Pakrashi empire has married Agarwalla's hostess, they'll laugh.'

She paused for a while before continuing defiantly, 'Let people think what they want to, right? And why does Anindo's mother have to meddle in our personal affair? I'm taking the responsibility of making her son happy, am I not? Why are you silent, why don't you say something?' I still didn't say a word. 'I'm not going to listen to anyone,' she said. 'We'll go ahead.'

Had I ever known this defiant, uninhibited Karabi?

I met her again some time during the day. She smiled when she saw me. 'Have you heard? Mrs Pakarashi's threatening me. She says she can get Agarwalla to sack me, and many more things besides.' She burst into laughter. 'You're the one who got me into trouble—I could have managed everything on my own.'

'I?'

'Yes! You made me promise not to tell Anindo anything.'

'So break your promise—what business is it of mine?'

'How can I do that? That'll harm Anindo,' she said gravely. 'I cannot tolerate anybody threatening me. Right from childhood, nobody's been able to get the better of me by intimidating me. Anindo was here. He asked me why I was so upset. I couldn't say anything to him.'

Mrs Pakrashi had threatened Karabi all right, but now it was she who came to meet Bose-da that very night, her face pinched with worry. Karabi had contacted her over the phone, telling her that she had weapons—one that could destroy Mrs Pakrashi's lovely family.

Mrs Pakrashi was no longer the proud lady we knew. She seemed devastated by Karabi's threat. She lamented her fate: why had the phantom of suite number one in Shahjahan Hotel attracted her? 'I'll never be able to trust anyone again,' she whimpered.

Bose-da stood at the counter like a statue. He didn't utter a word.

Later that night Karabi sent for me. She was glowing with happiness. I knew Mrs Pakrashi had been to see her. Karabi had an envelope in her hand. 'She's agreed!' she burst out. 'She had no choice. How else could she save face in front of her family? She said she won't raise any more objections. At first she had some doubts—she thought I had no proof. Then I showed her these.' Karabi waved the envelope in her hand. 'I can't show them even to you—negatives of photographs taken inside suite number one.'

Mrs Pakrashi had been stunned at first. She couldn't believe Karabi had documented proof of her secret liaisons. 'O God, where did these come from?' she had asked nervously.

Karabi had merely said, 'It's better they stay with one person rather than do the rounds, don't you think?'

I was curious. 'Really, where did you get them?' I asked. 'I had no idea that anyone could take photographs inside a locked room.'

'Someone in this hotel gave them to me,' said Karabi. 'How else would I have got them? Just because Mrs Pakrashi doesn't care for me, you think nobody else does?' Again there was a peal of laughter. 'She's agreed—she won't stand in our way any more. So, now what?'

Like a fool I said, 'Now goodbye to Shahjahan and hello to New Alipore.'

She placed her hand on my shoulder—I had become a friend. 'Now all of you will forget me—you never did think of me as a colleague, did you?'

'You are the one who will forget us. Even if you come to Shahjahan for dinner or a banquet, you won't spare a glance for the counter—you'll walk straight to the hall with the other eminent guests. And we will still be making out receipts, drawing up bills, filling in the registers, attending to phone calls and getting ticked off by the steward.'

'Don't you like this job?' she asked.

'Not at all. You'll get me a ten-to-five one, won't you—you'll have so many jobs to dispense.'

'Of course I will. You've done so much for me, and you think I won't do this one little thing for you?'

'Good night,' I said.

'Good night,' she replied.

I must have dozed off, for it was quite late when Gurberia knocked on my door. The lady in suite number two wanted to see me, he said.

Splashing water on my face, I went downstairs again, and saw that something was wrong with Karabi. She was trembling.

Clutching her head, she cried hysterically, 'What have I done? Save me.' Her eyes were popping out of their sockets.

I tried to calm her. 'You mustn't carry on like this! What is it? We met just a while ago; nothing was wrong then.'

Karabi was like a frightened child. 'I thought I wouldn't tell anybody...no matter what anyone says, I won't give Anindo up. I've got nothing from life—if someone offers me his love, why shouldn't I take it?' She paused, and then continued, 'Why is Mrs Pakrashi so worried? Does she think I won't take care of her son, or that I won't love him?'

Trying to comfort her, I said, 'Why these thoughts all of a sudden?'

'How can I not have them? When Anindo's mother left my room...you didn't see her...she was shaking like a leaf. You won't object any more, will you? I had asked her. No, she said. She also said, you're probably a little older than my son, still I won't say anything. Then she started sobbing. She pleaded with me, "You'll tear up those negatives before the wedding, won't you?" Clutching my hand, she said, you won't tell anyone, will you?'

I couldn't make out what was happening. Karabi was almost in tears. 'It wasn't supposed to be like this. How can I marry a person like Anindo by blackmailing his mother and taking advantage of her weakness.'

She reached inside the envelope to check if the negatives were in it. Then suddenly, right in front of my eyes, she tore the envelope and its contents to shreds. 'Impossible,' she said. 'Anindo's mother, his father—they are my elders. I can't take such an immoral path into Anindo's home; it'll be sinful, and bring harm upon him.'

After a few minutes she calmed down. 'I'm losing my mind,' she said, wiping her tears. 'I have no one to talk to here, that's why I sent for you.'

The next day I woke a little late. By then there was a great commotion in the hotel. The police had broken down the doors of suite number two and brought out Karabi's lifeless body.

'She took an entire bottle of sleeping pills,' said an inconsolable Nityahari.

When her body was sent to the morgue I didn't go.

On his return, Nityahari said, 'Not even a last goodbye? I put my best linen in the police van. Why did she have to come to this hotel? The first day I saw her, I told everybody, this isn't a hotel girl, this is my daughter. Nobody listened to me then—now look what's happened.'

13

I often find the past impinging upon the present, memories intruding on my pleasant, personal thoughts. Even though I can scarcely afford the luxury of indulging in solitary ruminations, the painful memories of Shahjahan Hotel cloud my thoughts every now and then. I do not know, nor want to know, the whys and the wherefores. But I do realize that without my sojourn at Shahjahan, my education in the school of life would have remained incomplete. If you want to know the real individual lurking inside a person, you must come to this magnificent roadside inn.

Years ago when I set foot in the world of law and justice, there was someone experienced and sensitive enough to guide me through its mysterious lanes and by-lanes. I did not have to seek anything out for myself; whatever I needed to see, to know, was arranged for me personally by my affectionate British employer. At the Shahjahan, however, there was nobody to point out to me the extraordinary hidden deep within the crowded human jungle. And yet this insignificant employee, with no one to guide him, has been fortunate enough to receive priceless gems from this incredible treasure-laden world. I tip my hat to the supremely talented artist who can create ever-new characters on the canvas of literature with the help of his imagination. But I am a slave of experience. I am not free to indulge my imagination. So many flesh-and-blood men and women are imprisoned in my memories. They try to escape whenever they can; they demand their freedom. I do not have the opportunity to create characters out of nothing.

But what is an ordinary hotel employee like me capable of? I became painfully aware of my helplessness the day Mrs Pakrashi hosted a party at Shahjahan—a cocktail party, a reception for Anindo and Shyamali.

The dinner to celebrate the marriage of Anindo and

Shyamali had already taken place at Pakrashi House. The uniformed bearers of Shahjahan had waited on the guests. I had been ordered to go, too, but Bose-da had probably guessed my state of mind. That is why he bailed me out, saying, 'Forget about telling the manager; I'll go instead.'

It was very late when Bose-da came back to the hotel, his shirt soaked with perspiration. He was angry when he saw me sitting on the terrace. 'Why on earth haven't you gone to bed?' I merely smiled. Loosening his tie, he said, 'Special catering for fifteen hundred guests is no simple matter—I've worked my fingers to the bone.' I said nothing. 'What are you thinking about?' he asked.

'Nothing,' I said.

Bose-da lit a cigarette. 'As children we used to sing that song—*Bhabite paarina tomari bhabona*—I cannot take care of your worries.'

'Well, you have been doing just that all your life, taking care of other people's worries,' I reminded him.

Putting his arm around my shoulder, he said, 'How can you be "other" people?'

'Those you think of as nearest to you will all become "others" one day,' I told him.

In the dim glow of his cigarette, Bose-da probably couldn't see me clearly. 'Wouldn't you help me if I were in trouble?'

What could I say? I knew my abilities only too well— didn't you see how effectively I came to the aid of the person in suite number two?

After years of ingesting and digesting the poison of Shahjahan, Bose-da had probably become immune to everything that went on around him. Blowing a smoke ring into the night, he said, 'One can't really serve another in the hotel of the world. We can at best hold out the tray, like good waiters. People will have to pick out their own rewards. Anyway,' he continued with a laugh, 'you don't have to hold out that tray for the time being. What you have to hold out are drinks, because Mrs Pakrashi has arranged a cocktail party here, in this hotel. No auspicious occasion in Calcutta is complete with just dinner these days. It has to be the glass after the plates; in other words, a special treat at a good hotel for specially selected guests. You will have to organize all this. Tomorrow onwards that's where you'll be on duty, and Mr Sohrabji will be your lord and master. But all that can wait. Now go to sleep like a good boy.'

'And you?' I asked.

'I'm going to take a shower; then go downstairs for night duty.'

Night duty after such a hard day! I tried to dissuade him. Since he had filled in for me at Mrs Pakrashi's, I could take his place at the counter. But he refused. 'Who's the boss here? Is the responsibility for drawing up the duty chart yours or mine?'

He practically forced me into my room.

I had no idea when I fell asleep. Suddenly I was awakened by a loud knocking on the door. I opened it to find Bose-da standing outside with a torch. Placing his hand on my shoulder, he said, 'Sorry to wake you at such an hour, but you'll have to vacate your room right now. I'll explain later; let's tidy up your bed first. Go splash some water on your face.'

As I went into the toilet, I heard him tell someone, 'Please come in. You're very tired, you'll collapse unless you get some rest.'

When I came out, I saw a man sitting on my bed and taking off his shoes. 'What about Miss Mitra?' he asked.

'Don't worry,' said Bose-da, 'I'll make arrangements for her right away.'

In the dim glow of the night, my eyes heavy with sleep, I saw a young woman in a blue silk sari, a bag in her hand. Taking the bag from her, Bose-da said, 'This way, please.'

'You can't carry my bag,' she protested.

Not paying any attention, Bose-da said, 'Come along, please.'

We went and stood before his room. Handing over the bag to me, he said, 'Just a minute, let me get the key.'

The lady seemed to cringe with embarrassment. 'Why should you be carrying my bag,' she said, 'I feel every embarrassed.' Yawning delicately, she added, 'I wouldn't dream of putting anyone to such trouble at this hour of the night.'

I didn't say a word. The girl who stood before me was breathtakingly beautiful, with incredibly sad eyes. Even her voice was distinctive. If a dancer's anklets were a little softer, if the rumble of trams were absorbed somewhat by the velvet green grass, if they had been a little more subtle, a little more restrained, they might have been somewhat like Miss Mitra's voice.

Bose-da unlocked the door, saying softly, 'You'll have to rough it out here tonight.'

Looking around her, she asked, 'Whose room am I forcibly occupying?'

'You can find all that out later,' Bose-da said. 'Why don't you go to bed now?'

'Unless I'm told whose room it is, I won't get any sleep,' she said adamantly.

Bose-da was silent, so I said, 'Mr Sata Bose's.'

'What Bose?' Now there was a smile in her melancholy eyes.

Bose-da was forced to provide the answer. 'I used to be Satyasundar, fate has made me Sata.'

'We could have stayed on the bus, or spent a few hours in the lounge. But you've gone and taken matters into your own hands—now where you going to sleep?'

'There's no question of my going to sleep, Miss Mitra, I'm on duty. And this young man also has to report to work in a short while.' Bose-da opened the toilet door and said, 'The key's a little tight, turn it with a little extra force, the door will open. The towel's fresh, so you can use it.'

I accompanied Bose-da downstairs. 'I had no choice,' he said apologetically. 'I couldn't take the liberty of waking anyone else up. She's an air hostess. They had to come to the hotel because their plane developed a technical snag. Normally we have separate arrangements for airline crew but tonight we're in bad shape. All the rooms are occupied, and they seemed exhausted. She did say she could rest here on the sofa in the lounge. But how could I allow that? So I woke you. A couple of rooms will be vacated in the morning, I'll move them there then.'

I was probably trying to suppress another yawn. Bose-da put his hand on my shoulder and said, 'If you're going to work in a hotel, it's a good idea to get used to staying up nights. Do you know who stays up nights?'

'When I was a child I was told that naughty, disobedient children do,' I said.

'Exactly. It's the naughty, disobedient, grown-up children who don't go to sleep at night. After the excesses of the night, they fall asleep the moment dawn breaks.'

There was nothing to do but stay awake. The two of us went to the counter. Bose-da began doodling on a piece of paper, trying to replicate the Shahjahan lounge with strokes of his pencil.

Unexpectedly, I found myself suffused with the joy of a delicious freedom. There wasn't a soul in sight—we were the lords and masters of Shahjahan Hotel. The occupants of the countless rooms here had reposed their faith in us and were sleeping through the silent night. Like the driver and attendants of a night train, the two of us were ferrying a group of long-distance pilgrims towards a golden dawn. I had no idea what the pilgrims of this sleeping continent would discover, but we wouldn't be awake to share in their joy. Having entrusted the responsibility of the hotel to someone else, we would, by the light of day, try to woo the night into our tiny rooms.

Mr Agarwalla had employed a new hostess. In the still of night, I saw a man emerge from suite number two. I couldn't recognize him, but Bose-da whispered in my ear, 'He's a well-known labour leader, head of the union in Agarwalla's factories.' A taxi drew up and the man disappeared inside. The doorman took out his notebook and wrote down something in it as the taxi sped off towards Shyambazar.

'At night, we take down the number—there's no telling what lies in store for people who move around so late,' Bose-da told me.

I realized that night was coming to an end when, wearing a short dhoti, Parabashia's Lenin-babu approached the counter, chanting hymns. It was just as well that rules weren't observed that early in the morning or else he would have been reprimanded for wandering around dressed like that.

'Where to?' I asked.

'To my mother—she will forgive all my transgressions. Whatever sins I have committed, sifting through dirty linen all day long, will be washed away at her feet.' Glancing at Bose-da, Nityahari said, 'You're an Englishman, it's no use telling you, but allow this Brahmin's son. If he develops the habit of taking a dip in the Ganga at dawn, he'll be spared eternal damnation.'

'Am I holding him back?' asked Bose-da good-humouredly. 'Let him go if he wants to.'

'Come along, then,' said Nityahari turning to me. 'At this hour on the riverbank you can see hundreds of men and women washing away their sins. Our head barman Ram Singh has probably completed his ablutions by now and is sitting down to his prayers.'

'I'm sorry,' I said. 'You'll have to excuse me.'

After he left, Bose-da said, 'Quite mad! He'll bring back

a pitcher of water. First he'll sprinkle it in front of the hotel, then he'll enter through the back gate and sprinkle some on the mountain of pillows and linen, muttering his prayers all the while.'

A room was vacated early that morning by an American couple leaving for Ranchi. Bose-da said, 'We simply must have a room to ourselves now. Go and check if either of them is up.'

I went to the terrace. Bose-da's room was still locked. The air hostess, Miss Mitra, was probably still asleep. The door to my room, however, was open. Gurberia said, 'The gentleman's up, he's even had his tea.'

When I knocked, he said, 'Come in.'

'You must have had an uncomfortable night,' I told him. 'A room's been vacated downstairs, please come with me.'

Handing his luggage to Gurberia, I took the airline officer down to his new room and then reported to Bose-da. He smiled ruefully. 'My luck's run out after all these years at this counter. I envy you; who knows when I'll be able get rid of the lady and get some sleep.'

Today it amuses me to recollect those words. Thinking of Sujata Mitra and Sata Bose makes me feel warm inside and at the same time an overwhelming emptiness assails me. On lonely evenings, I can, as it were, see Sujata Mitra in close-up. My ageing eyes yearn for that distant past. Then I realize this kind of restlessness is quite unbecoming of someone as old as I am. A very dear person chides me good-naturedly, 'I like you, but for this childishness. Even after all these years, you remain a little boy, you haven't grown up.' The person who makes this accusation probably wants my mind to overcome its adolescent fancies and indulge in the preoccupations of adulthood. But I believe that I've gone straight from adolescence to old age.

I remember telling Sujata-di, when she and Bose-da were

back from their scooter ride, one day: 'You remind me of this
poem by Jagannath Chakraborty:

> Matching steps are two evening stars
> On a scooter,
> Red ribbons in her flowing locks
> Her back bared by her flying scarf
> Bold and undaunted the young scooterist

Sujata-di didn't let me recite any more, she tweaked my
ear instead. 'It hurts,' I cried. 'Let go.'

Bose-da said, 'Come on...let him have his say.'

'Where did he get the scarf?' Sujata-di asked.

It all seems like a dream so many years later. I will
eventually have to get to Sujata Mitra's story. But before that,
the cocktail and Mr Sohrabji.

Sohrabji was our new bar manager—an old gentleman, with
skin the colour of ripe apples, stooping a little under the
weight of his age. Folding his hands in a namaskar and speaking
in pure Bengali, he said, 'Welcome, welcome. With you at my
bar I fear nothing.'

'You know Bengali?' I asked in surprise.

'Of course!' he said, tightening the buckle on his white
trousers. Patting my shoulder, he explained, 'I came to Calcutta
when I was just fourteen. You probably weren't even born
then.'

'The thought of the excise registers scares me. They have
to be maintained properly, I am told,' I said.

Removing his thick glasses, he smiled pleasantly and said,
'I'm not afraid of them. As long as I don't try to avoid taxes,
don't mix water with my drinks, don't let dubious women sit
alone at the bar, why should I fear the excise department?'

Sohrabji had arranged all the bottles in the bar himself.
While Ram Singh looked on, he held up a bottle to the light

with a practised hand. Then he checked the stock against the records and looked up suspiciously. 'The books say four pegs, Ram Singh,' he said, 'but it looks more like five pegs to me.'

Ram Singh was taken aback. 'We measure it by hand, sir, maybe it gets a little less or a little more at times.'

'That won't do,' he said. 'No one should be served either more or less.' He turned to me. 'When we came into this line nobody cared for a peg or two more or less. But what cost six rupees then is not available at eighty-six rupees today. So giving a customer even a drop less now is to cheat him.' Grimly, he started rummaging among the bottles himself. Then, leaving me alone at the bar, he went to the cellar.

The cellar was a hundred-and-fifty-year-old room in the bowels of the earth, closed to the public. In the corners of that dark cellar were some bottles which Simpson had put in there himself.

Hobbs had interesting stories to tell about the cellar and its contribution to Calcutta's hoary past. A young English commander in a solar hat and khaki shorts had disembarked from his ship at Chandpal Ghat and spent his first night in Hindustan at Shahjahan Hotel. To provide the lonely soldier company, a bottle of Scotch was brought out from this very cellar. Even after the sailing boats on the Ganga gave way to mechanized ships, the festive nights came alive with liquor from Shahjahan. Then, a group of people arrived in Calcutta with maps in their hands. Their leader, McDonald Stephenson, put up at Spencer's Hotel while the rest of the team stayed at Shahjahan. They sat at the bar all day and night, and drew up their plans. The barmen whispered among themselves that those mad Englishmen were going to bring mechanized transport from their country. They would put shackles on the feet of all Indians and build iron roads, on which enormous giants would run about one day. The Englishmen had captured the giants and imprisoned them in iron safes, so they wouldn't be able to do anything except sigh occasionally—and their dark breath would burn India's lovely villages and golden crops to a cinder. The Englishmen knew this would happen, and felt sad about it sometimes, which was why they were drunk from morning till night. The Englishmen left, and a pall of gloom descended on the bar. Then the unthinkable happened. Palmer and Company went bankrupt, turning many emperors into paupers overnight. To comfort the hordes of bankrupt kings, bottles of liquor—brandy, whiskey and gin—emerged once again from the cellar of Shahjahan. Under its spell, Calcutta forgot everything once again. New governors came, and the old bottles were opened to drink to the newcomers' health.

Then one day, the top brass of the Shahjahan found themselves in despair. A new machine had come to Spencer's—a lift. Nobody would have to climb stairs any more. Of course, at Spencer's it was only for the ladies. Laughing merrily, they entered a cage and sat down, and two bearers pulled them up with ropes and pulleys. Would anyone visit the old-fashioned, lift-less Shahjahan any more? While they fretted about this, whiskey was placed before them, specially bottled in Scotland for the Shahjahan.

Thus it was that the new century dawned over Shahjahan. Times changed, viewpoints changed, fashions changed. The king, the owner of the hotel, the barman, the barmaid—all of them had gone, but the whiskey hadn't changed. 'The sun and the moon in the sky above and whiskey below—these are things that will never change,' Hobbs had once said to me. He was the one who told me that one bottle from the case of red wine that Simpson had left in Shahjahan was opened when Lord Curzon had set foot in our hotel. The remaining bottles were still enjoying their century-long slumber, awaiting the arrival of another illustrious guest.

By the time Sohrabji returned from the cellar it was afternoon. The lunch crowds had thinned. A few men from

Clive Street were sitting in a drunken haze in one corner. They had come for lunch, but after drinks, had forgotten their office addresses. Summoning the bearer, they asked him, 'Do you know? Got it all mixed up.'

'How would I know where you work, sir?' the poor bearer said to them.

Still in a haze, they sent for me. 'Why do you employ these good-for-nothing fellows?' one of them said.

Sohrabji came forward and told them where they worked.

One of them started in surprise. 'Of course! I'm the managing director there. I've been sitting here for an hour and a half trying to remember where I work.'

After he left, I asked Sohrabji, 'How could you tell?'

'I know practically all of them. We have to know not just their office addresses, but also their home addresses, since they are frequently unable to go home at night on their own. There's no problem if they have chauffeurs, but many of them drive themselves. In that case the cars are left behind and they're dropped home in taxis.'

There was no more time to chat; there was too much to do for the evening party.

If one wanted to get a taste of old-world culture one had to get invited to a cocktail party at Shahjahan. Mrs Pakrashi's party offered me that experience.

Sohrabji whispered in my ear, 'There are four chapters to a cocktail party. In the first hour, it's breaking the ice; in the second, beginning to feel nice; in the third, tongues become loose; in the fourth, the senses feel the booze.'

During chapter one everything's hunky dory. The guests are easy and normal. 'How do you do?' 'Where's Mrs Sen, has she gone and joined a monastery?' 'Poor Mr Sen, this is a dangerous age for women—a little indifference and the lady of the home gives her heart to a mission.' 'Unbearable! Anyway, Mrs Pakrashi has finally managed to pull it off! She should have got Anindo married two years ago. Look at the West, the average marriageable age is continuously going down, sixteen–seventeen-year-old boys and girls are getting married, setting up home and going straight off to maternity homes, whereas here in India, the age for marriage is going up. Soon an anti-spinster act will have to be passed.' 'Congratulations, Mrs Pakrashi, what about a drink?'

'In a minute, Mr Banerjee, I'll have an orange squash, but that shouldn't hold you back. Please drink to a happy life for the two of them. Do carry on, there's a champagne cocktail as well. Ah! Mr Agarwalla's over there all by himself, he's done so much for us, a real friend.'

As soon as she left, I heard Banerjee say, 'Hello PK, I can't make head or tail of Mrs Pakrashi's parties. They should have insisted on evening dress—but no, it's lounge suits. Bad. After all, the dignity of a party can't be maintained unless you're in a formal suit. Calcutta's going down the drain. Any day now you'll find a clerk from your office drinking next to you, but you won't be allowed to protest.'

Chapter two is a little complicated. At that point it's 'I could have danced all night.' 'Heaven knows why we're letting ourselves be boiled in these suits and ties, what's all this formality in aid of?' 'Boy, barman, come here—make two Rob Roys: Scotch, brandy and ABT. Quick, barman.' 'Seen Mrs Anindo?' 'Ah, yes...the doe-eyed beauty...flaunts her sublime curves as she speaks.'

Chapter three opens when, thanks to the whiskey, sons and families have been renounced. There are verbal pyrotechnics all around. 'Do you know how silly my wife is? She starts crying if she hears I've been drinking. What kind of stupidity is that? Honestly, She's a complete a–double-ess!' 'So is Madhab Pakrashi, which is why he's gone for a Bengali girl—this fragile doll will make the young fellow's life miserable. Yes sir, if you have to marry it should be someone from up north. They are wonderful! Those girls realize the value of liquor. Tagore understood them, why else would he have chosen Punjab of all states to lead the rest in the national anthem? Punjab, Sindhu, Gujarat, Maratha, Dravida, Utkal, Banga—he's arranged them perfectly according to merit. There you are, see how Rajpal is downing peg after peg happily with Mrs Rajpal right next to him?' 'What are they drinking? Paradise? Wonderful— gin, apricot and orange—heavenly! The person who christened it had fire in his belly, and that solitary beauty, what is she having? She'll write an article about Anindo's wife in a Bombay fashion magazine.' 'What? A White Lady—gin and lime? Poor girl, she looks heartbroken! May her lonely eyes find someone, may her lips grow redder, give her a glass of Pink Lady. It'll glow like fluorescent paint.' 'What's happened to you, brother? Why have you retired? Don't tell me you've also joined the ranks of the fashionable lime juice brigade? Don't be stupid, you don't often get chances like this, people don't invite you to champagne cocktails every day. Remember, twelve rupees a peg—knock it back; forget the invitations in those eyes and the smile on those tempting lips and take a dip in the sea of champagne.'

In the fourth and final chapter, the number of players is much smaller. Many have been bowled out during the third innings. The hosts want to leave, too, but can't make their escape. Some guests show no sign of abandoning their glasses. In their drunken stupor, some have chosen the path of non-violent non-cooperation, while others resemble a bull in a china shop. Glasses are being smashed, empty bottles are being thrown around, nobody knows what's happening. Mrs Pakrashi had already left with her husband, while the PRO of Madhab Industries had stayed back to clear the bill and, if necessary, handle the police. One by one, they depart, leaving the hall nearly empty. But there are still a couple of people who don't want to go.

'It's time to close the bar, sir,' said the PRO.

'Shut up! What kind of etiquette is this? Inviting guests and then not giving them what they want?'

The poor PRO stood by quietly, while the guests, to wrap up their evening, downed a few more drinks rapidly before tottering out. Clearing up the shards of glass, a bearer discovered a guest under a table in one corner. When I went up to him I recognized the man immediately—Phokla Chatterjee, sozzled to the gills. Staggering up somehow, he slurred on his way out, 'Very careful batsman—but since it's my nephew's wedding, I chose to throw my wicket away.'

So this was what a cocktail party was like. When Mrs Pakrashi had entered that glittering evening, flanked by her son and daughter-in-law, I hadn't quite imagined the rest of it.

Anindo Pakrashi was a changed man. He paused briefly on seeing me. Perhaps he wanted to say something, but Mrs Pakrashi told him, 'You don't have time to waste chatting, Anindo. The guests are waiting for you.'

I didn't get another chance to talk to him. I didn't want to, either. And yet, amidst the waves of light, laughter and the golden haze of sparkling wine, a melancholy woman's face floated up repeatedly before my eyes.

I may not have profited from Mrs Pakrashi's party, but the hotel had—it earned a cheque for ten thousand rupees! The excise inspector who had come to examine the accounts said, 'Wonderful! The more cocktails you have like this, the more both you and the government gain.'

'The bearers, too,' said Sohrabji, laughing.

'Everyone, in fact, except the liver.' Hearing a new voice I turned around. It was Hobbs.

I hadn't met him in a long time and was very pleased to see him. Taking off his hat, he said, 'I came to meet Marco—I need a room for a friend, but he isn't in.'

'Why do you need the manager—what are we here for?' I said.

'Arrange it, then.'

Hobbs now looked at Sohrabji. He seemed surprised. 'What are you doing here?'

Sohrabji smiled wanly. 'It's all God's will, what can we do?' Hobbs stopped. Guessing that he had something to say in private, I went on ahead and opened the register at the counter to check whether Hobbs's friend could be given a room. Hobbs came up and, placing his hand on my shoulder, said, 'From what I know of Calcutta's hotels, the receptionist can always find a room if he wants to.'

Bose-da was also at the counter. 'Once upon a time it was indeed like that,' he said. 'But now, thanks to foreign tourists and business tours and conferences, receptionists no longer wield that kind of influence. The manager himself keeps a hawk's eye on the bookings.'

However, there was no problem where Hobbs's friend was concerned. A room was available.

'How long has Sohrabji been here?' asked Hobbs.

'A few days,' I said.

'How is his daughter?'

I had no idea what he was talking about.

'Where's Marco?' he asked.

'He's gone out.'

'Ah! He's probably gone for a Macaulay on Corporation Street.' I didn't know there was a drink named after Lord Macaulay. Hobbs smiled and said, 'If Macaulay, the author of the penal code, had been alive he'd have been shocked. You Bengalis have ruined his name by christening the Ma Kali brand of country hooch Macaulay. Many of your top people prefer Macaulay to Dimple, John Haig and White Horse.' He glanced at his watch. 'I may as well wait for a while—I do need to see Marco.'

The two of us sat in the lounge. Bose-da came up to us and said, 'Should I send for some tea or coffee? What else can ordinary hotel workers like us offer?' Then turning to me, 'Listen closely to him...there are very few people in the world who know more about hotels than he does.'

'Fine, let's have some coffee,' said Hobbs. 'I've eaten here so many times since the eighth decade of the nineteenth century—one more occasion might as well be added to the list.'

Bose-da ordered coffee for us and went back to the counter. Hobbs leaned forward a little. 'If some of the best novelists of Europe had stayed here for a few years, they could have written an amazing novel. I've seen many hotels of the West, but they cannot be compared to those in the East. From Simpson, Silverton and Horabin to Marco Polo, Juneau and even Sohrabji—all of them are like characters from a sprawling historical novel.'

Since both of us had some time to spare, the story-telling session warmed up. Sipping his coffee, Hobbs said, 'I would never have dreamt that Sohrabji would take a job at your hotel. I've known him since before World War I—he used to serve at Hafezji's bar. His real name isn't Sohrabji—it's Madan or something like that. He took this name from the Indian word for liquor. I remember a friend of ours reporting him to the excise department.

'He couldn't have been more than fourteen then. The poor fellow came crying to me. Boys of that age weren't allowed to work in bars, so someone had reported him and he was going to lose his job. I felt sorry for him so I managed to get the report suppressed. That's how long I've known him. But he surprised me. Parsis are not normally so poor. They have so many trusts, so many ways to avail of charity that no young lad needs to roam the streets. Which is why I was a little suspicious as well.

'After the whole thing blew over I went to Hafezji's bar one evening. There wasn't much of a crowd. I ordered a small peg. Sohrabji came running when he saw me and said softly, "If it hadn't been for your help, I'd have been begging on Chowringhee now."

"'Why do you have to work at such a young age?" I asked.

'In broken English he said, "I am have no one. I was brought up at orphanage. I have no brains...they try so hard, but I couldn't learn anything." Some Indian grammarian had been an absolute imbecile in childhood, but with effort he became a scholar. Sohrabji had tried too, but it didn't work, nothing would get into his head—so he had finally run away.

"'You could take the help of a trust," I said.

"'I can't," he said somewhat agitatedly. "How can someone who didn't get help from his own parents ask others for help? It doesn't seem right. I'm sure God wants me to help myself, so that's what I'm going to do."'

Hobbs paused, turned to me and said, 'In independent India women have equal rights as men, don't they?'

'Yes sir,' I said.

Hobbs started laughing. 'Let me ask you a question. Tell me, in which field has women's freedom not yet been acknowledged?' I looked at him. He said, 'Ask Sohrabji, he'll tell you immediately that the last bastion of anti-feminism is the hotel. The bar licence says that no unaccompanied woman will be allowed to enter. In your country, women can go anywhere alone, even if they climb Mount Everest no one will object, but even today no woman is allowed to enter a bar by herself. There's no problem if she has a man with her—then she can enjoy her drinks as long as she wants to.

'Some woman should protest against this law which denies the freedom promised in the Constitution. But it's an old law, and those who drew it up had a different objective in mind. There are women who frequent bars for a different reason. They do it even today, as you can tell if you go into any of those seedy ones. Displaying their wares, women from all over the world wait to net the big fish. It's probably not a bad law, but some people are making a living off it. Poor young Anglo-Indian men stand around in clean clothes, waiting to catch the girls. "Hello Dolly, you must take me in this evening, I'll wait as long as you want me to." Dolly says, "I've promised Peter's mother I'll take Peter as my escort. I'll have to pay only a rupee." "I'll come for twelve annas, I need the money," says the young fellow. "That's shameful," says Dolly. "Your rates are even lower than a woman's. You're willing to spend hours with me in that den of hoodlums for twelve annas?"

'According to the excise laws, a woman can't enter many of Calcutta's bars without such escorts. And that's how Sohrabji earned his first meal in Calcutta. He told me once that an Anglo-Indian fellow had given him his first break. He was young and the law stated that one couldn't go into a bar with an escort his age. But Hafezji wasn't such a stickler for the law—he didn't worry about the escort's age. He knew very well that younger escorts came cheaper, which meant smaller expenses for the poor girls. All he said was don't do that one horrible thing, don't share a lemonade. That ruins our reputation—so make sure you have at least two bottles in front of you.

'One day while he was roaming the streets of Calcutta looking for a job, Sohrabji met a young chap on Dharmatala Street who was looking for a substitute. This fellow used to take a young girl called Cynthia to the bar every day, sit with her until a customer swallowed the bait and the rate was fixed, whereupon he settled the stranger in his chair and disappeared. That day, however, he was going to Kharagpur to request someone he knew in the rail factory there for a job.

'The young man told Sohrabji, "This is just for a week, though. You'll have to push off when I get back. Better not make a fuss then. A couple of fellows tried to play dirty in the past. Just because the girl spoke to them sweetly or gave them a cigarette, they started getting ideas. Don't make that mistake or I will thrash you proper—remember, if a couple of your teeth are knocked off, they won't grow back."

'Sohrabji agreed. At least he'd have a meal for the next few days. So he was introduced to Cynthia and he escorted her to a bar, feeling a little apprehensive at first. He had never been in such an environment in his life. There was so much smoke, it felt as though the place was on fire. In the distance a three-member band played some music, occasionally signalling to the girls: "Don't just sit there guzzling lemonade, come here and dance; our bar can't afford to employ dancers."

'Sohrabji noticed many other couples like themselves. Looking at the clock on the wall, Cynthia crossed her legs, blew a cloud of smoke and said, "This is how it'll be till nine o'clock, and then the customers will come. Let's see if you're lucky for me—maybe I'll get a customer right away. I didn't even get a good spot today—come a little late and the best spots are taken by the other girls. The sailors prefer the corners. Only when those are full will they come this way." Blowing out more smoke, she continued, "But to get the best seats you need to come here by seven-thirty. I don't have much patience, I can't sit for hours. Maybe I could give a little money to Rahim—but I have to pay him one rupee a month anyway, how much more can I give?"

'Sohrabji's throat was parched. He took another sip of his lemonade. Cynthia tapped his arm. "Are you planning to ruin me, man? Who knows how long we'll have to wait, and you've finished half a glass already. If we have to get another one you'll have to pay for it—I don't earn enough to blow it up without a customer in sight."

'Sohrabji didn't say another word. He was most uncomfortable. The smell of tobacco was making him sick. Finally, a couple of sailors, enormously tall, their heads almost touching the beams of the ceiling, walked in. Cynthia left her chair and rushed towards them, but the fish didn't take her bait. Back at her table, she waited till her breathing had returned to normal, then blew some smoke in Sohrabji's face. He paid no attention, he kept watching his glass.

'Cynthia said, "All right, you can have another sip. From tomorrow, drink two or three glasses of water before you leave home, there's no telling how long you have to wait. If you're lucky you can leave with your money in an hour." She would have said more, but suddenly she turned pale. Someone seemed to have corked the wild enthusiasm in the hall. The bearers quickly went around the tables making sure all the girls had companions. Otherwise the government officials would get them into trouble. They turned up sometimes, acting on a whim, just to check if there were any girls sitting alone.

'Sohrabji heard the manager say, "You can see for yourself, sir, everyone has an escort, genuine customers."

'The inspector came and stood beside Cynthia and Sohrabji. Cynthia was used to all this. She casually blew out a cloud of smoke and started playing with Sohrabji's fingers. "What happened after that, John?" she said as if they had been having a conversation.

'The poor fellow had no idea what to do. Cynthia hadn't warned him either. She looked at him and winked, and somehow, he managed to nod. The inspector probably guessed what was going on. "Absolutely fresh, eh?"

'The manager said, "What are you saying, sir? Genuine customer...he comes quite frequently."

'The inspector whispered to the manager, "Of course, there's no better place for a bottle of lemonade in Calcutta, is there?" and moved away.

'A little later Cynthia got a customer and Sohrabji left with his payment, as the newcomer to Hafezji's bar took his place.

'The next day he met Cynthia again. "You're lucky for

me," she said. "That chap last night let me drink to my heart's content and didn't skimp on his payment either. He made it worth the effort. If I got such customers every night, I would have nothing to worry about."

'Sohrabji went back to the bar, sipping his lemonade by Cynthia's side and praying for a customer. That evening, too, his luck held. No sooner had he taken his first sip of the lemonade than a stranger arrived and chose Cynthia as his drinking companion. Sohrabji was about to abandon his glass and walk off when Cynthia said, "Finish your lemonade before you go."

'The next day when Sohrabji met Cynthia she said to him, "You're really lucky for me. You know what happened last evening? I left with the customer in a taxi, but I was back in an hour—he had a train to catch. I was sorry I let you go, I could have gone in and sat down once more. Anyway, I thought I would go in alone, but the manager lost his nerve. The excise inspectors were turning up frequently, he said, and they could create trouble. Besides, you've had one round, give your sisters a chance, he told me and sent me home."

'Then Cynthia took out some money from her bag—it was more than was agreed on—and said to Sohrabji, "Don't be such a wimp. Ask the customer for a tip before you leave. Even I will tell him, give my man some money—we're decent people, our parents don't know we're here, if you don't pay him he'll tell them and I won't be able to face them after that."

'But Sohrabji couldn't bring himself to ask for a tip. He simply sat and watched the bar. He got acquainted with the owner and saw how some police officers came to the bar under the cover of night. Hafezji would rush around, attending to their needs, asking them if they wanted a drink. The officers would then ask for the bar inspection book and make an entry: Inspected the bar at 11 p.m. Mr Hafezji was in personal attendance. Place full of customers. All ladies had escorts. Nothing unusual to report.

'Even today the same comment is put down in the record books of Calcutta's bars.' After that aside Hobbs continued his tale. 'A few days later Cynthia's former companion came back, but Cynthia refused to give up her new escort. "I'm not letting such a lucky fellow go," she declared.

'But Sohrabji wouldn't agree. "It's not right. If I take away his job God will be displeased."

'And the gods must have looked his way for Cynthia's lucky escort got a job at Hafezji's bar. When the bar opened in the morning, he hardly had anything to do, since the bar was more or less empty. Even if a couple of people turned up, they left after a peg or two. In the afternoon some more people came—mostly from the suburbs. They didn't have the time to enjoy lovely Calcutta in the evening. But at night, when Hafezji sat at the counter himself, the atmosphere of the bar changed dramatically.'

Suddenly, Hobbs looked at his watch. 'I'm not holding you up, am I?'

'Of course not,' I said. 'If it hadn't been for you I'd never have got the chance to know Sohrabji.'

'I can't say I know him myself,' said Hobbs shaking his head. 'If I hadn't seen him here today, he might have remained just another person I knew. But now he's made me curious.'

'You're turning Sohrabji into the hero of a novel.'

'You never know…every brick in this hotel has a novel in it.'

He picked up the threads of the story again. 'People get garrulous in their old age. When the ability to think disappears, they begin to quote others. It's like an illness. I feel like doing the same. Sata once told me, "A bar is a bank where anything you deposit, you lose: whether it's your money, your time, your character, your self-control, your children's happiness, even your soul." Everything is written off. But one person profits, and that's the bar owner. The money that others spend is deposited in his bank.

'I didn't know when Madan became Sohrabji. I didn't meet him for years. Then, many years later, I ran into him at the Dharmatala crossing. When he saw me he rushed towards me and took my hands. He told me he had left Hafezji's bar.

'"Why? Did you have a fight?"

'"No, God has smiled upon me—I've opened my own bar."

'"A bar? But that costs a lot of money."

'"If you have God's blessing you need nothing. I got a bar on Dharmatala Street itself. The owner was ill, he had to go back to England, so he made me his partner. I'm going to look after the bar, and send him a share of the profits."

'He persuaded me to go to his bar with him and showed me around. "This is a much quieter place," he said. "Not like the other one." I saw many people sitting around, drinking, but without any noise or trouble at all.

'"I've also changed my name," he said. "Since I'm going to be involved with the liquor business, sharab as we call it, I'm Sohrabji now."

'"But it's not enough to be involved with the business, you have to be involved with liquor too," I said jokingly.

'He looked embarrassed. "Oh no, I've never touched alcohol in my life. I've poured out thousands of pegs for others, but I don't know what it tastes like."

'I met him again when he invited me to his wedding. "The girl I'm marrying is a little scared, poor thing...after all, I work in a bar," he said shyly.

'I used to see his wife frequently at the market—nice girl. "You do the shopping yourself?" I asked her one day.

'Mrs Sohrabji replied, "Who's going to do it if I don't— the poor man just doesn't have the time. It's because I do the shopping myself that the stuff is fresh, the customers praise it, and besides, the prices are low. If I leave it to someone else, they will charge more and cheat on the weight."

"'Do you help your husband at the bar too?" I asked.

"'That's the problem," she said, "He just won't allow it. I do the shopping and fix the menu, then he takes everything over to the bar. The days he's held up, he sends a helper over. If nobody comes I telephone him, but I do not take it myself. You can go anywhere in the world you like, he says, but not to my bar."

"'And you've accepted that without a murmur?"

'She was probably a little embarrassed, but because she knew what my relationship with her husband was, she whispered with a shy smile, "I protest. But he says, you're going to have a baby, the air in the bar might harm our soon-to-arrive guest."'

Hobbs was getting a little breathless. He took a few deep breaths before continuing. 'I heard that Sohrabji had had a child; I also heard that he had bought the bar. His partner wasn't coming back so he had bought out his share with his meagre savings and by selling his wife's jewellery. I met him again at the bar one evening. Like always he thanked me profusely, "All this was possible only because of you, please treat the bar as your own. My bar is not like Hafezji's. I give good stuff, I don't mix water, I don't allow women either, and yet I get no peace," he said almost sadly.

"'Why?" I asked.

"'My bar closes at ten-thirty. But those who park themselves here in the afternoon warm up as the evening progresses. With the first drink it's health, with the second it's happiness, with the third it's shame and with the fourth it's madness. I don't like it. Some problem or the other crops up every day. My bar has a fairly good reputation—only those who want to drink in peace visit it, but in spite of that there are rows sometimes."

'I was a witness to one incident myself. While we were talking, a bearer came up and said, "A gentleman in the cabin is asking for you." Sohrabji went to find out what it was all about. I followed. The brown sahib scowled and said, "Dis drink not good—got water."

"'What do you mean?" Sohrabji was indignant. "I don't cheat my customers. If you like I'll send the bottle; the bearer will pour the drink in front of you."

"'Had five pegs already," the customer replied, "but still feel like a monk."

"'I'm familiar with such cases—we get one or two every day. Of course, newcomers won't know what's going on," Sohrabji said as we went to the bar counter.

'He picked out a bottle of whiskey and carried it to the cabin. "We get our stuff directly. If you like, I'll take the seal off in front of you and serve it."

'I was standing outside. Now the customer came to the point. "Want girl."

Hobbs laughed. 'Sohrabji's reply, in broken English, would have earned worldwide fame if it had reached the ears of a writer. The customer was persistent. He grabbed Sohrabji's hands and said, "Please...pleasure girl."

'Sohrabji began to advise him. "Girls here no good. House girls, in your family, far, far better; hotel girls take all money." To make his point clear he started gesticulating, "Street girls don't love you, they love your moneybag. House girls—my sister in your house—she love you. If she hear, she weep." He even contrived a few tears. The guest seemed a little embarrassed. He hurriedly settled his bill and walked out without leaving a tip.

'Sohrabji looked at me. "You see?" he said. "Earlier when I was alone, I could take it. But now I'm getting older, I have a daughter. I find it very hard to bear."

'I left without a word. Later I heard that his bar was doing well. It had a huge stock—liquor you couldn't get anywhere else was available there. And that too at fair prices. "I do my business honestly," Sohrabji would say. "The good lord above will look after me." The next time I saw him he was standing forlornly on the road; I was driving by. I stopped the car and asked him, "What's the matter?"

"'Can you tell me why people lose their heads when they drink?" he asked.

"'The effect of the chemical reaction from the alcohol, perhaps," I said.

"'I've learnt my lesson!" he cried. "I'm never going to say anything to those drunkards again. They come to the bar together, they sit and drink together, then they start quarrelling among themselves. The other night, at about nine o'clock, two men were shouting at the tops of their voices, banging their glasses on the table, singing songs. And another group—they're my best customers, their bills amount to three–four hundred rupees every day—was sitting in the next cabin. One of them came up to me and said, 'Your bar's becoming a hooch joint— decent people will stop coming here. You've started entertaining people from Hafezji's pick-up bar. Unless you keep them under control, we won't come here again.' I had no choice but to go up to the two rowdies. By then they were broadcasting cricket commentary over the radio. India had scuttled out the MCC in one over and put Australia in the next. One of them was saying that wasn't allowed, while his companion said he would do as he liked, no one need interfere. This was followed by a barrage of filthy abuses. I was forced to say, you can't behave like this, you're disturbing other customers. The man burst into tears immediately, called all the others and complained, he's threatening to throw me out because I'm drunk—look at the nerve of this man, just because he's the bar owner! Some of the other customers took his side immediately and started shouting, 'How dare you, we are leaving right now. What does he expect us to do after drinking—read the scriptures instead of enjoying ourselves?'"

'Sohrabji's eyes brimmed over. "You know what the

funny thing was? Those who had originally complained also
left their tables and walked out. I pleaded with them, told
them it was because of their complaint that I had warned him.
Do you know what they said? 'We're drunk, even if we did
say something you cannot insult one of our brothers. Who do
you think you are? Do you think there are no other bars in
Calcutta? We'll make sure no one visits your bar—we'll resort
to picketing if necessary.' My bar's been closed for nearly three
weeks now—nobody comes any more. Finally, I decided to go
to this gentleman's house. I managed to get hold of his address
and visited him today. I apologized to him profusely, saying, if
I've made a mistake I beg your pardon for it—but you asked
me to stop the noise, that's why I requested them to quieten
down. The man was satisfied and has agreed to bring his group
again. But he's warned me, never trust a drunk again and insult
anyone at his behest.'"

Hobbs returned to the present. 'This was the Sohrabji I
knew—he was doing business decently and profitably. He put
his daughter into a good school outside Calcutta. I saw them
at the zoo once, he had brought her with him. That's as much
as I know. I have no idea how he got from Dharmatala to
Shahjahan.' He looked at his watch again. 'Your manager
doesn't seem to have any intention of returning today. What's
up? He goes out very frequently these days. Is Sata Bose
expected to run the place all by himself? Well,' he said as he
rose, 'at least I got to meet Sohrabji—I'm happy about that.'

When I met Sohrabji later at the bar, it was as if I was
seeing him in a new light. He was a man of few words—yet
I felt I had known him for ages. It was almost as if I had
discovered a kindred spirit in the bar manager of Shahjahan.
Just like me, he had come a long way, been through a lot, seen
incredibly hard days. The head barman told me, 'He's a
wizard, sir, has every cocktail at his fingertips. He knows so
many different kinds of mixing.'

You couldn't get a toehold in the bar at this time of the day. Even the machines of business need oiling, and the most effective lubricant was whiskey. It was quite a sight—people pouring whiskey down their throats with complete concentration, their eyes closed in rapture, and then, like clockwork, calling for a refill. Sohrabji told me, 'If you want to preserve a corpse put it into whiskey, and if you want to kill a living man, pour whiskey into him!'

My acquaintance with Sohrabji gradually turned into friendship. I realized that he was not what one would call sharp, but he did have a keen desire to stay honest. Besides, he had an unshakeable faith in God.

Every evening Sohrabji would stand in a corner of the bar and keep looking at the clock, waiting for the bar to close, for the wine lovers to remember that they had homes to return to. The customers would pay their bills, the barmen would rearrange the chairs, I would shut the cash box and do the accounts—and then we would be through.

But even after all these years, Sohrabji seemed to be dogged by an inner conflict. And I found out more about that when I heard the last part of his story in his own words.

'I am not educated, but I like those who study, who think. You know a lot; can you tell me why people drink?' Sohrabji asked me one day.

'Sata Bose thinks that cowards seek courage in liquor, the weak seek strength, the miserable seek happiness—but nobody finds anything but utter ruin.'

'Hasn't anyone said anything about people like us, who sell liquor? I'll tell you my story, maybe you'll understand. Maybe because I'm uneducated, I haven't found the answer. I could have asked my daughter, she's educated—but can anyone ask one's daughter about things like this?'

He loved his daughter very much. 'You don't know my daughter,' he said. 'You won't get a girl as intelligent and knowledgeable as her. She's beautiful too. She reads such thick books; she writes letters to me every day. I'd like to write to her, too, but I feel embarrassed, my spelling is all wrong. Of course, she says, don't worry about all that, you must write long letters to me. She's studying abroad now, you know.' The daughter of an uneducated orphan—Sohrabji's breast swelled with pride.

Some great man has said that of all the loves in the world, the one of a father for his daughter is almost divine. I remember the exact words: 'He beholds her both with and without regard to her sex.' Behind our love for our wives lies lust, behind our love for our sons lies ambition, but our love for our daughters is free of all selfish motives. I saw the truth of the words in Sohrabji that day.

It was also the day that I heard his sad tale.

He had never allowed his wife or daughter to visit his bar. He would be home till nine in the morning, then leave with the groceries for the restaurant. Around noon his lunch would be sent from home. Once in the afternoon he would go back for a cup of tea. With evening the bar started to fill up. As night advanced, the problems increased. Closing the bar at ten-thirty was always difficult. Many customers refused to leave, others insisted that the bar be kept open till later. He was forced to tell them that the licence did not permit that, whereupon the customers would shower abuse and break glasses. He couldn't stand it. For some of them he would call taxis or rickshaws—they were too drunk to go home safely on their own.

When they arrived at the bar the next day, though, they would smile and greet one another, asking after each other. But gradually the atmosphere changed. Sohrabji was sorely tempted to say, have a few and go home, your womenfolk are waiting for you. But he didn't dare.

One day his daughter said, 'I want to go to the bar with you.'

'No dear, you cannot. I have lots of work there, I'm always busy.'

'Why, what's wrong with my going there?'

'Don't be impertinent, dear, I'm telling you, you shouldn't.'

His daughter was growing up, blooming like a flower with the beauty of spring—intelligent, educated, and yet simple. She knew nothing about life. So many times she had said, 'I'm also going into business like you, Father.'

'No, my dear,' he would say hastily, alarmed. 'You're going to be a professor, a great scholar. People all over the world will marvel at how much the uneducated fellow's daughter knows.'

Everything was arranged for her to go abroad. He couldn't imagine getting by all those years without her, but what could he do? He thought about the day when she would return as Dr Sohrabji and the papers would carry her photograph.

But something happened to his daughter a few days before her departure.

There was chaos at Sohrabji's bar that night. One of the customers was lying on the floor, foaming at the mouth, a few were creating a ruckus, having had one too many, others were sitting sullenly around with their glasses, saying, 'One more peg, bearer.'

The bearer said, 'The bill for this peg, sir. What can we do, sir, it's the excise rule—bills to be made out for each peg, and to be settled immediately.'

The bearers couldn't manage by themselves, so Sohrabji was forced to lend a hand. He went up to one of the tables and asked, 'What can I get you?'

'Pure whiskey, so it burns everything as it goes down the throat.'

Suddenly there was a hush followed by a murmur around the bar. A new arrival.

'Who's that?' Sohrabji said as he looked up. With a shock he realized it was his daughter.

'What are you doing here?' he forced the words out.

She had come to give her father a surprise. She wanted to take him back home with her. After all, in a few days she'd be gone for a long time.

The young woman had never seen so many dishevelled men in various stages of drunken stupor. On seeing her, the peg measure in Sohrabji's hand jerked and quite a lot of liquor spilled on the table. The man who was lying on the floor rose and shouted, 'I want a large peg too.'

The girl's face clouded over. In a whisper she said, 'Aren't you coming with me, Father?'

Her father came out on to the road with her, holding her hand, trembling. 'Go home,' he croaked. 'I can't close the bar yet, they'll smash everything.'

When he got home, he found his daughter had gone to bed.

The next day he was afraid to meet her. He had been found out. The day of her departure was fast approaching, but she remained aloof, despondent. She hadn't quite recovered from the sight of her father in the bar. Sohrabji wanted to put his arms around her and say, 'Why are you worrying about all this, my dear? Just carry on with your studies—you'll do so well.' But he could say nothing.

Early on the morning of her departure, when the mother was still asleep, the father entered his daughter's room quietly. 'Is there something you want to say?' he asked her. 'You look as though you do.'

Her lips quivered. She said, 'I'm frightened, Father. Those people I saw in your bar the other night—their mothers and sisters and wives and daughters must be weeping. Will they ever forgive us?'

He had never thought of it that way. What can I do? he was about to say. How is it my fault? I don't drag them to my bar—I do business honestly. But he couldn't speak.

His daughter left for Bombay on a train, and then for England on a ship. But Sohrabji was trapped. All he could see was his daughter's sad face, and the question in her eyes: Will they forgive you, Father?

He was stricken by an inner conflict. He tried to persuade himself that he was not to blame. Do I ask you to order so many pegs? Why don't you leave after one? What can I do—if I don't serve it to you, you'll go to some other bar. But his daughter still seemed to be questioning him. He said to himself, their wives and daughters can always stop them, what can I do? I'm a simple seller of liquor, how can it all be my fault?

But he simply wasn't able to convince himself. The more he tried to rationalize, the more the question kept haunting him. He felt afraid. He started dreaming that the mothers and sisters, wives and daughters of all his customers were cursing him through their tears, that those curses had enveloped not just him but also his family, including his daughter.

He almost went mad. Then in desperation, Sohrabji sold the bar. That same night he sat down to write to his daughter, 'How is it my fault? If they come on their own to drink at my bar and destroy their families, how is it my fault?'

Sohrabji thought he would put the proceeds of the sale in a bank and run his small family on it. But his troubles had only begun. The bank declared bankruptcy two days after he had deposited the cheque. Could it have been the outcome of the curses, the tears? he wondered. What would he do now? He had to pay for his daughter's education. He needed a job, but who would give a job to an uneducated person?

So it was back to a bar. He whispered to me, 'I'm only an employee now. I am no longer responsible for anything. Even if someone puts a curse on the bar, surely it won't affect me.'

His eyes were closed. He was probably asking God, 'Surely I'm doing nothing wrong by working here—I have a family to support too.'

After a long silence, Sohrabji rose and headed home, carrying his turmoil-ridden heart with him.

I was silent, overwhelmed once again by the discovery of yet another star in the firmament of my life.

14

Sometimes I think I am selfish. The joys and sorrows of those who have been part of my working life may have appealed to me, but why inflict them on the readers? And then again, it occurs to me that the Phokla Chatterjees, Mrs Pakrashis and Mr Agarwallas of this world are not part of my world alone. Everyone should be acquainted with them.

And what of the ebb and flow of everyday guests at the Shahjahan? I have not introduced them in my narration. I have only written about the people I got close to, those whose lives became interlinked with mine. From my vantage point I merely watched the stream of people flow past my wonderstruck eyes every day, without sharing that vista with readers. Tomorrow, some gifted soul might be able to do justice to that other scenario. Under the power of his or her pen, the voices of the many others in this hotel will possibly be rescued from the past and be served up to the present. From everything that is ugly and repulsive here an exquisite literary creation might be born.

I told Bose-da one day, 'It's really incredible. I never even dreamt of being part of this hotel, and yet, now that I am, my soul, without my even realizing it, has mingled with Shahjahan and become one with it.'

'You people believe in Western ideas—you have no faith in rebirth, or else I'd have said that I've been here many times before, I've come to know every room in this hotel over my past lives.'

'Perhaps,' I said. 'Perhaps I was here too, perhaps I too had

seen some sad-eyed Karabi Guha, perhaps met many more
Connies and Sutherlands.'

'And perhaps you should have met many more people, but
didn't,' said Bose-da. 'All I can tell you is that a lot of
memorable moments spring to life before our very eyes. Only,
we are far too absorbed in our work at the counter to take
notice.'

I must have looked puzzled by his remark. Laughing, he
explained, 'I think of eighteen sixty-seven sometimes. Not our
hotel, a different one. But it must have taken place in front of
some receptionist just like us. That receptionist, too, must have
been absorbed in his register as we are, and, startled by the
sound of footsteps, must have looked up to see a stranger
standing there. No visitor like this had ever been seen at the
hotel before. He was wearing a dhoti, had only a cloth
wrapped around himself, the sacred thread visible under it, and
red slippers on his feet. A native Brahmin who had lost his way
and wandered in, he must have thought, or, one never knew,
times were changing—maybe the Brahmin wanted to sit at the
bar and strike up an acquaintance with French grapes!

'The receptionist must have said good morning in his usual
manner and must have been surprised by the Brahmin's reply
in flawless English. The receptionist, following tradition, would
then have pushed forward the visitors' slip. He must have
glanced at the bold handwriting of the Brahmin and, even as
the latter said, "I want to meet Mr Dutta," answered, just as
we do, "Oh, Mr Dutta! Our guest who's just back from
England? One moment please."

'The receptionist couldn't have known who the Brahmin
was, or why he was there. Perhaps he was seeking some
donation. Still, he asked him to take a seat. Other people, too,
were waiting to meet the guest who had just arrived from
England.

'Coming down to the lounge, the guest shook hands with

everyone else, but seeing the Brahmin, he embraced him and kissed him and, beside himself with joy, continued to hold him in a bear hug, kissing him and dancing all the while. The discomfited Brahmin could only keep muttering, "Let me go, let me go."

'As a receptionist, the mere thought of that scene, of Vidyasagar and Michael Madhusudan Dutta together, still makes my hair stand on end. Here at the Shahjahan, too, we must have been present at many dramatic moments, but didn't notice them. How I envy that receptionist at Dutta's hotel—he's the only one we remember. Thousands of others have sunk into oblivion, just as we will.'

I too followed Bose-da to that forgotten afternoon of the nineteenth century. I could see Vidyasagar and Michael Madhusudan Dutta in my mind's eye. And I wondered whether the events that were taking place now would ever find a place in history books.

'I read somewhere that there are two kinds of history,' Bose-da said. 'One is written in detail and turned into books, while the other stays unwritten forever. Everyone knows it, but nobody dares put it in words; we are probably witnessing events of the second version.'

'I don't understand,' I said.

'I don't, either. Someone once told me that the characters of history are real, and the events imagined. Whereas in novels and stories and plays, it is the characters who are imaginary, the events are real.' I was about to disagree, but Bose-da himself did so before I could. 'I don't think that's entirely true. But then it is equally true that not every truth of ordinary life is found in history books.'

Just then the phone rang. Bose-da said, 'Just when I was getting into the groove, lecturing like the head of the department of a university, God has to remind me that I'm only a humble receptionist at Shahjahan Hotel!'

Into the phone he said, 'Yes, this is Sata. Of course, rest assured, do come over.'

'Who is it now?' I asked.

'Someone who owns a house in a fashionable neighbourhood right here in Calcutta, with plenty of spare rooms. Yet she wants to spend the night here, and for a night's shelter she's even willing to beg and plead with an ordinary hotel clerk,' he said.

'What's going on?' I asked.

Bose-da shook his head. 'Hundreds of people would throng this hotel if they knew she was here. We all know her name.'

Soon the phone rang again. As soon as I took the call a male voice asked, 'Can I get a room tonight?'

Bose-da took the phone from my hand. 'May I know your name, please?' he asked. Then, after a minute, he said, 'Sorry, we're full up.'

I looked at him in surprise. We did have a few rooms available.

Sometime later the woman 'hundreds of people would throng this hotel for' turned up at the counter. I hadn't ever expected to meet her anywhere but on the silver screen. She was the brightest star of the film world, Sreelekha Devi. I'd seen many heart-stopping photographs of her in film magazines, but had heard of her only once in connection with a party here at the Shahjahan, where Phokla Chatterjee had thrown up all over this paragon of beauty. She had almost fainted in revulsion. Phokla had said in apology, 'Please don't mind, Sreelekha Devi—it was the new cocktail. Those buggers have named it "Filmstar", but the thing looked good only from a distance. As soon as I tried one I threw up.'

But Sreelekha Devi had refused to accept the apology. Declaring loudly that she would not go to any party where Phokla was present, she had walked off. Since then nobody has invited poor Phokla to film parties.

Phokla had once or twice broached the matter with me. 'What a fuss. We're human, can't we throw up occasionally? But Sreelekha Devi thinks I puked all over her deliberately. You know her, don't you? Why don't you explain to her?' He was drunk. So I hadn't bothered to respond. 'All right,' he had gone on. 'My name is Phokla Chatterjee. One of these days I'm going to spit a mouthful of water on her face. Then all the powder will wash off and her real looks will be revealed. She won't get another film after that.'

He didn't believe me, but I really didn't know Sreelekha Devi. I saw her for the first time that night. Bose-da greeted her and gave her her room number after looking it up in the register.

What she said next astounded us to say the least.

'Can you get me a sari?'

'A sari? At this hour? But all the shops are closed,' Bose-da replied.

'I came out just as I was. I couldn't bring any clothes.'

I like to think of it as my one contribution to the world of films: I woke up an employee of a sari shop I knew in Dharamtala, cajoled him to get the key from the owner, and managed to buy a sari for the most famous actress of the time. A very ordinary sari—but she was grateful.

Later that night, we were sitting on the terrace when Bose-da smiled, 'Sreelekha Devi has worn many saris in her life, her saris have sparked off many fashion trends, but I don't think she'll ever forget this one. I'm inclined to put down this extraordinary event in my notebook. It'll come in handy if I ever write my autobiography. Satyasundar Bose will abandon his suit and bow-tie for a dhoti and kurta and turn into a celebrity author overnight. Hundreds of admirers will line up to meet the one and only Sata Bose.'

'Really, why don't you write a book?' I asked.

'Writing never got anyone anywhere,' he said, gazing at

the sky. 'I've been told that the written word has wrought many changes in this world, that civilization has often changed course at the behest of authors. But I don't believe it. I don't think you can change anything about this blind, dumb, unfeeling society of ours. You can shout from the rooftops, you can write a hundred Mahabharatas, you can bathe evil in thousand-watt light bulbs—but it will all be in vain.'

I was more than a little surprised. I had no idea there was a cynic lurking within Bose-da. 'If only we could gaze at the sky for aeons perhaps one day we would find the answer to those eternal questions: why we do what we do, why the so-called pillars of society abandon their souls to crowd our bars and cabarets. Man has devoted himself to conquering poverty and want. Perhaps he reasoned that once the problems of everyday existence were wiped out there would be leisure to address the problems of the soul. And what happened? Those who don't have to worry about two square meals a day, those who have all they need and more, they are the ones who have become morally bankrupt, who make a fool of themselves under the multicoloured lights of Shahjahan. Ridiculous, ridiculous.'

I listened to him in rapt attention. 'In one of his books Aldous Huxley has written about his travels in India,' Bose-da went on. 'In the bookshop of some hotel in Bombay, he saw countless books on a particular science. "Rows of them and dozens of copies of each." Yet it wasn't as though doctors or scientists interested in the subject bought those books. It's ordinary people who bought them, said Huxley, and tried to explain it as a "strange, strange phenomenon! Perhaps it is one of the effects of climate."

'I, too, thought it was the fault of the climate, but later I asked myself, was Huxley's own country any better? I don't know the answer to that, but I did find a partial answer in D.H. Lawrence's writings, for which he can be given at least pass marks, if not full marks: "The God who created man must have a sinister sense of humour, creating him a reasonable being yet forcing him to take this ridiculous posture, and driving him with blind craving for this ridiculous performance.'"

That night Bose-da seemed to be intoxicated with words. 'There's probably no simple answer, though. The question paper of life is filled with conundrums to fool you. You'll go mad if you try to decipher them. It might be better to talk about Sreelekha Devi.'

'Aren't you going to bed?' I asked.

'I will. But you're going down for night duty, so you'd better be warned. Sreelekha Devi's husband might turn up tonight. It seems he's threatened to throw acid on her face. The poor woman is terrified of him. He had called earlier, remember? I did tell him there are no rooms available, but you can never tell with him. He just might come by. If he does, don't let him in under any circumstances.'

He was about to say more, but someone seemed to be approaching us in the darkness. It was Mathura Singh. We had never seen him come to the terrace before. He saluted us and stood there looking forlorn. 'You haven't gone to bed yet, sir?' he asked.

'I can't, Mathura, I'm on night duty.'

'Even if you had, I would have had to wake you,' he said, shaking his head. 'This has never happened before.'

He told us that Marco Polo had gone out earlier in the evening and hadn't returned.

'Did he go out all of a sudden?' I asked Mathura.

'It's a dry day, sir. He usually goes somewhere for a drink. But sir, in all the years I've been here, he's never been out so late.'

Bose-da seemed worried too. 'Now this is a real problem,' he said. 'Have you informed Jimmy? He's the second-in-command at Shahjahan. If anyone is authorized to do anything, it's him.'

Mathura knew human nature. Smiling sadly he said, 'We're lowly workers, sir, we shouldn't be saying this, but you know Mr Jimmy—he'll be the happiest person if the manager were to come to some harm.'

For a while Bose-da sat in grim silence, then said, 'You carry on, we'll see what we can do.' After Mathura went away, he said, 'Mathura's sized up Jimmy perfectly. The man's greed has no limits—he even makes the bearers share their tips with him. Nobody dares blow the whistle for fear they will lose their jobs. And though Marco Polo knows everything, he doesn't say anything either. After all, Jimmy is a veteran, he was here even before Marco Polo arrived. And Marco Polo's lost his old spirit too. He's changed—he sits by himself all day long and mopes over something. And Jimmy has started resorting to daylight robbery. The only person who keeps track of things is Rosie, but she's also under Jimmy's control.'

'Marco's all alone in a strange land. We should do something; it's our city, after all.'

'Go downstairs,' said Bose-da. 'William Ghosh must have pushed off by now, you'd better hold fort at the counter. And about Marco, let's wait a little longer. He might get back on his own.'

'What if he doesn't? You'll be in bed...'

Bose-da laughed. 'I won't go to sleep. Sleep is like a switch for me. Until I turn it on the fellow dare not show up. You carry on.'

I went downstairs. William Ghosh had indeed gone, leaving a bearer in charge.

It was very late. Like the quiet, obedient, well-behaved children of Calcutta, Shahjahan Hotel, too, was asleep. I alone was awake at the counter and, somewhere in the city, so was Marco Polo. Where was he? Had he fallen into the clutches of the police, drinking on a dry day? Drinking itself wasn't a crime, but getting drunk was.

I looked at the reservation register. Nobody was scheduled to leave that night, but some guests were due to arrive. A call from Dum Dum Airport a little earlier had informed us that they would be slightly delayed. At that precise moment, a plane was cutting through the inky blackness, carrying passengers from distant lands to Calcutta.

When the guests finally arrived, the night had progressed considerably along Calcutta's mysterious roads. Against my wishes, and despite my best efforts, sleep had started gathering about my eyes. I was startled by the sound of a bag being set down. Sleeping at the counter was a major transgression. Straightening up quickly, I saw Sujata Mitra.

Dressed in a sky-blue sari, her airline uniform presumably, she was smiling at me. 'Poor fellow,' she said.

Embarrassed, I stood upright and wished her a good evening. 'Good morning is more appropriate,' she said, holding her watch out towards me.

Her companions signed the register and went in. 'You carry on, I'll be along in a short while,' Sujata told them. To me she said, 'I feel bad for you!'

'No, no, I'm not sleepy at all, Miss Mitra,' I said quickly.

Widening her large oval eyes, she said with great affection, 'How sad, you have to talk to me as politely as to a customer!'

Ignoring her remark I looked at the register. 'You've got a very good room this time, Miss Mitra. Number two thirty. It's time to dispel the bad impression you must have got of Shahjahan after staying in Bose-da's room the last time.'

Sujata was very affable—she had no problem standing around talking to an insignificant hotel employee unlike many of her peers who just walked by, their high heels clicking away. My remark had obviously upset her.

'Your face shows you haven't been working at a hotel very long,' she said. 'So how did you manage to pick up all these sophisticated professional courtesies so soon?'

I was enjoying the exchange. Her sincerity touched one in spite of oneself. I smiled. 'The only reason I've learnt so much so soon is because of Sata Bose—'

Sujata didn't let me finish. She laughed and said, 'What a strange name! I remember him telling me that night that he used to be Satyasundar. This hotel of yours isn't a safe place at all. Satyasundar is a far cry from Sata. You'd better be careful. One day you'll find you've become Sanko; maybe foreigners have already started calling you Sanky.'

I believe I behaved quite childishly. 'Indeed! I'd like to see someone mess with my name—it'll be a fight to the finish.'

Sujata burst out laughing. 'But your guru has gone and relinquished his.'

'So what! It's his name—he can do what he likes with it. What business is it of anyone else?'

Changing the subject, she said, 'I caused you a lot of trouble last time…I still feel bad thinking about it.'

She might have said more, but suddenly her expression changed. I hadn't realized that Bose-da had tiptoed up to the counter and was standing beside us.

'Oh, it's you!' Bose-da was the first to speak. 'This chap must be talking his head off in the middle of the night. He likes nothing better.'

'Oh yes, and he takes pride in introducing himself as your worthy disciple,' Sujata laughed. 'He's learnt a lot of lip-service from you. You were the one who opened up your room to let me stay that night and now your disciple oozes politeness and tells me, you must have been uncomfortable, this time we've got a good room for you.'

Bose-da did something I never dreamt he would with a lady. Dead serious, he said, 'And you didn't even say thanks before leaving.'

I still remember the smile that appeared on Sujata's face in reply. It was like the early morning sun spreading its first rays on a snow-capped mountain peak. 'I know I didn't,' she said. 'Those who give up their rooms of their own accord to unknown guests and stay awake all night are either stubborn or foolish—it's no use thanking them.'

'Stubborn, foolish, stupid—you've managed to call me a lot of names, taking advantage of the fact that you are our guest!'

'Such imagination! Where did the word "stupid" come from?' Addressing me, she added, 'Before leaving the other day, I did go up to say thank you, but neither of you was there. Now I see it was just as well—people like you are not worth thanking! You really don't deserve it.'

Bose-da apologized. 'I had no idea you came looking for me.'

I added, 'How would you know? If all day you're bothered only about breakfast, lunch, dinner and banquets or reservations and floor shows, how can you keep track of anything else?'

'Don't you people ever feel sleepy?' asked Sujata.

Bose-da didn't let the opportunity go by. 'As Sade has shown, God has given sleep to the unholy so that the innocent are not disturbed.'

'Do both of you stay up all night?' Sujata wanted to know.

'Bose-da isn't supposed to tonight,' I said, 'but our manager has gone missing.'

Bose-da turned to me. 'I was thinking of informing the police, but that'll lead to complications. Besides, I just spoke to Mathura Singh. He told me that Byron had come by a couple of days ago and the two of them had had a long conversation. Why don't you go and see him? I would have gone, but I don't know where he lives. It'll be very difficult to find his house at this hour. Take a taxi. I'll manage at the counter.'

Sujata was listening to our conversation silently. 'May I say something?' she said. 'If you don't mind, take the airline car. I'll tell the driver—he must be sleeping inside the vehicle.'

Have you ever seen the Calcutta of dark nights and deserted roads? The ferocious trams and buses had fallen asleep, lending the city an unreal calm. A taxi or two could be spotted now and then. I wondered who the passengers were. Only if one of Calcutta's taxi drivers wrote his autobiography would we ever know!

From Chittaranjan Avenue our car hit Chowringhee. The neon lights of the night were still dancing like clockwork dolls on an empty stage. I couldn't help myself. I told the driver to turn right. Behind the iron railings of Curzon Park, Sir Hariram Goenka still stood, the emperor of insomniacs, waiting for dawn to break.

I can't say why, but no living person has held me as much in thrall as he has. For some reason, to me he has always appeared omnipresent. Sir Hariram looked through me with eyes that had uncovered intimate secrets of this ancient city ages ago. There wasn't a trace of affection or pity in his petrified body. From the distance, I felt as though the annoyed gaze of the sleepless, hard-hearted Sir Hariram Goenka Bahadur, KT, CIE, held me, of all the people on earth, responsible for all his unpleasant experiences. He seemed to think that the insolent people of the city had sent me there on purpose to humiliate and insult him and to disturb his peace in the dead of night.

I could have carried on my childish musings on Sir Hariram, but the driver broke my reverie. 'Are you expecting anyone here at this hour, sir?'

'No,' I said. 'Let's go—we have to go to Eliot Road.'

With Curzon Park to its left, the car turned eastwards. Sir Suren Banerjee stood there as if addressing a crowd of thousands under the monument. He had paused for a moment because of a malfunctioning mike and in that brief interlude the unappreciative audience had fled the meeting. In despair, the spurned and insulted Surendranath had turned to stone.

Crossing Corporation Street, the car entered Wellesley Street, and my thoughts turned to Byron once again. I hadn't met him in quite a while. I had seen him from afar in the banquet hall a couple of times, but he had signalled to me telling me not to talk to him. He must have been silently stalking his prey, perhaps shadowing someone. I even saw him sitting quietly at the bar with a bottle of beer one evening, but he had looked through me. I knew he did not want me to recognize him and strike up a conversation.

Still, I should have enquired after him; I should at least have visited him at home to convey my gratitude. But I hadn't. Shahjahan seemed to have swallowed everything I had in one big gulp. Its ravenous appetite hadn't spared even a part of me.

'Which way, sir?' asked the driver.

'Drive on,' I said. 'I'll tell you when we get there.'

'This isn't a safe neighbourhood, sir,' he said. 'There might be trouble if they see a car here at this hour.'

'I came here by daylight a long time ago,' I told him. 'Though I don't remember it very well, I'll recognize the lane when I see it.'

I did spot the lane eventually. If it hadn't been for Sujata's kindness, I wouldn't have had the courage to take a taxi to that place at that hour of the night. The car didn't go into Byron's lane, though; I got off and walked the rest of the way.

I should have brought a torch. The street lights in the city, perpetual targets of the local boys' pebble shooting, didn't enjoy a long lifespan. I practically groped my way to Byron's house. A solitary street light nearby had somehow eluded the eyes of the ace marksmen of Eliot Road and survived to illuminate that broken nameplate.

Byron's door was closed and there was no light on inside. Was it right to wake him at his hour? Muttering a prayer, I rang the doorbell. There was no response. Maybe no one was home. I rang the bell again.

This time someone stirred within and a female voice let loose a volley of filthy abuse. 'Go back to your dustbin, why have you come to disturb me in the middle of the night?' I shrank with fear, while the lady fired a second round. 'Aren't you ashamed of yourself, you swine, no income to speak of, now waking me in the middle of the night? Go sleep with the dogs in the dustbin—you expect me to work all day and earn your bread for you, then stay up all night like a whore? Not a hope. Get out, get out!'

By then I was terrified. Marco Polo was the last thing on my mind. I was debating whether to run away but before I could make up my mind I heard the door open. About to take a swipe with a broomstick, the lady froze when she saw me instead of her husband. She started screaming, 'What is it? Tell me, what is it? Something must have happened to him. How many times have I told him not to be a detective, it won't work in this lousy country. It's better to hawk newspapers, or even sit at home. As long as I have a job what do you have to worry about?'

In any other locality the neighbours would have come running out by now, but in this Anglo-Indian neighbourhood that sort of thing didn't happen. Even at the pain of death, no one intruded on another person's privacy.

Mrs Byron started whimpering. She wanted to know whether I was from the police or the hospital. It was beyond her capacity to imagine that anyone else could visit her at that hour. 'Where's my husband?' she whined. 'I want to go to him immediately.'

I managed to say, 'I don't belong to either the police or the hospital, Mrs Byron. I work for a hotel. Our manager Mr Marco Polo can't be found, so I've come to enquire about him.'

'Oh, I see!' Mrs Byron became her former self again. 'You're talking about that fat fellow who sometimes brings packets of sandwiches for us? That swine is at the root of all the trouble. They ask me to leave the room and then whisper between themselves. My husband says he's a client, but I can recognize a leopard by its spots. All lies! Actually, he's a crony. And now that the two good-for-nothings have gone out, who knows where the hell they are.'

She went on showering filthy abuses on me, but I had regained my composure. I had at least managed to get some information about Marco Polo's whereabouts.

'Did he say when he'd be back?' I asked.

'He said nothing. He went out as soon as that swine came. To hell with them,' she said and slammed the door in my face.

When I returned to the hotel, Bose-da was waiting for me. 'You needn't have gone, after all. Marco Polo has just returned. Byron was with him. It was he who helped Marco out of the cab and entrusted him to the bearers before leaving.'

Marco Polo was standing stock still near the counter, as though he was a stranger at the hotel. Bose-da asked him where he had been and told him how worried we all were. But the Marco Polo who was obsessed with the hotel, who had to have every detail at his disposal, had disappeared into the night. This one stared blankly at Bose-da and asked, 'Why do you stay up all night?'

Bose-da was nonplussed. 'You sign the duty charts yourself every day.'

Marco Polo shook his head. 'Useless...completely useless. When everyone in the world is asleep, it's no use keeping the party going.'

Just then my eyes fell upon Sujata. Marco Polo noticed her too. But before he could say anything Bose-da told him that she was an air hostess, our guest. Marco Polo became wary. He may have wanted to talk some more, but he bade us good night and left.

'I get to see hundreds of people up there in the clouds every day,' Sujata said, 'but you have even stranger creatures here. I wanted to tell your manager the night has ended.'

Bose-da smiled, but then became serious. 'His life is as dark as the night...I feel sorry for him.'

I was not a little surprised to find Sujata still at the counter. Bose-da said to her, 'I should thank you, but I don't have the words. You not only offered your car, you even stayed up with me all this while.'

She looked at me and said, 'Now your guru can't find words—see if you can help him!'

I smiled, 'That too is a way of saying thank you.'

Sujata's pigtail swayed like a snake. 'We don't like formal people very much.'

Without a flicker on his face, Bose-da said, 'There you go again. No wonder, passengers don't like Indian air hostesses very much.'

'Really? If they didn't, why are new girls being taken on?'

'Perhaps those who are new are better and much more polite,' Bose-da answered with a twinkle.

'That's like a lawyer...did you practise at the courts before joining this hotel?'

'Don't bring up the subject of courts,' Bose-da said. Then pointing to me he added, 'This poor fellow feels bad. He had a very close relationship with the courtroom once.'

I looked at the clock. Clouds of sleep were gathering over Sujata's oval eyes. Bose-da probably noticed as well. He said, 'I'm sorry, it's very late, there's no sense in keeping you up any more.'

There wasn't a single porter at hand. Sujata was about to pick up her suitcase herself, but I looked at Bose-da out of the corner of my eye. Interpreting my signal, he took the case out of her hand. Sujata was probably a little surprised, but Bose-da was his usual self. 'Ask this fellow here,' he said. 'What difference would it make if you carried your own suitcase? But he glared at me, as though he couldn't stand by and watch a lady carry her own luggage while an able-bodied porter like me stood around.'

Both of them now looked at me, Sujata shrugged, and then, leaving me in charge at the gates of Shahjahan, the two of them disappeared.

I had got used to Shahjahan's hushed nights by now. The ancient inn of the nineteenth century no longer surprised me in my solitary moments. Having reached an intimate phase in our relationship, this antique palace no longer held back any of its secrets from its dear friend.

But that was only as far as the bricks and mortar went. Who could track the many dramatic acts that were being played out at that very moment in its chambers? Were those mysteries revealed to a dispassionate sleuth, the world's literature would have been richer, helping to develop insights into the human condition.

The most onerous task on a taskless night was to keep sleep at bay with a stick, prevent it from approaching. So this luxury of reminiscing had to be indulged in despite oneself. Or perhaps the disembodied soul of Shahjahan had picked on this poor receptionist to weave a pleasing web of thoughts, using the golden thread of the past.

Suddenly the phone rang. 'Hello, reception? This is Sreelekha Devi.' Hadn't she gone to sleep? Was she feeling uncomfortable in the hotel, away from home?

Sreelekha Devi said, 'What instructions do you have about me?'

'I'm not to tell anyone your room number. And I'm to tell your husband to go back if he shows up.'

She sighed and asked, 'Did anyone come looking for me?'

'It's very late at night, madam. Nobody comes to the hotel at this hour.'

'Don't talk rubbish. How much of this hotel do you know? Ask Mr Sata Bose. Every time I've left home in a rage, my husband has shown up here.' It was my turn to be surprised. 'Would you go outside and check?' she said. 'I'll hold on.'

Sure enough, outside I saw a man in an expensive Indian outfit standing like a block of wood on Chittaranjan Avenue. Thanks to the pictures in the newspapers, I knew it was Sreelekha Devi's husband.

'Looking for someone?' I asked.

He was annoyed. 'I'm not in your hotel, am I? I'm standing quietly on the road—why do you have to come and pick a quarrel with me?'

I went back in and informed the actress. This was just what she was waiting to hear, it seemed. She would probably have been surprised had it turned out differently; perhaps she would have broken down in disappointment.

'You may send him to my room,' she directed me. I was about to mention my inability to do that but she said, 'No buts, please. Charge me for a double room.'

Putting the phone down, I went out again. The man was still standing there holding on to a pillar. I went up to him. 'Excuse me, why are you standing outside? Please come in.'

He looked at me with bloodshot eyes. 'That won't be necessary, thank you,' he said firmly.

I informed him that Sreelekha Devi had asked for him to be sent to her room. I could show him the way.

'Enough,' he said, taking a matchbox out of his pocket and lighting a cheap cigarette. I was a little surprised to see the husband of the city's top film star smoking such a cheap brand.

Glowering at me with his clouded, sleepless eyes, the man with the famous wife said, 'I haven't allowed my habits to change. When I brought Durga to Calcutta, we used to eat at Little Shahjahan—you couldn't get a cheaper meal anywhere else. I used to smoke this cigarette then and I still smoke it now. Durga may have been transformed into Sreelekha Devi, she may have abandoned Little Shahjahan in favour of the real one, but I haven't changed.'

He refused to come in. 'If I could stand here all this time, till four in the morning, it won't be difficult to remain here a little longer.' He turned his face away.

Back at the counter I heard the phone ring again. Sreelekha Devi was impatient. 'Hello, have you sent him up?'

'He refuses to come in,' I had to tell her.

She disconnected immediately. What one earth was going on? First she leaves home in a huff, then the reconciliation drama begins here before the night is over. The man seemed strange. His eyes scared me.

I hadn't expected Sreelekha Devi to leave her room and come down to the counter. I haven't yet forgotten how she looked without make-up. Her hair was tousled and her face mirrored the exhaustion of the night, as though she were enacting an intensely emotional scene in the studio.

'I'm afraid,' she said. 'Please come with me to the door. You never know, he may have brought acid to throw on my face.'

Even hotel employees feel like weeping in despair in such a situation. Who knew what I was getting involved in? Perhaps the first act of a sensational criminal case was about to unfold before my very eyes.

I tried to dissuade her. 'Do you really have to go out at this hour?'

She didn't reply, making straight for the door. I had no option but to follow.

Once we had reached the door she told me not to go any further. From a distance, I saw her approach her husband. He was facing the road now. She went and stood in front of him. I couldn't make out what they were saying to each other, but it suddenly seemed to me that she was sobbing, and that her harassed husband was trying to pacify her.

I was baffled. Before I could figure out what was happening I saw both of them get into a car. Without another word, her husband started the car. I came back to my senses only after the car had disappeared down the road. It suddenly struck me that Sreelekha Devi had gone. Who would pay the bill now?

I started fretting. The tariff for the night would probably be deducted from my salary, because it was my responsibility to ensure that the bill was cleared. It hadn't even occurred to me to ask for payment, given the situation.

I was miserable. Meanwhile, the sky was getting lighter; the sun was about to come up.

'Kali, Kali, o ma Kali,' Nityahari chanted as he came downstairs on his way to the Ganga for his ritual bath. When he saw me, he said, 'Why don't you take a dip in the Ganga every day? Sin will destroy you otherwise. It's only thanks to Ma Ganga that I can still walk around with my pillows, my head held high, even after being immersed in sin twenty-four hours a day. Every day I rinse and wash this dirty body and clean it—let sin do its best to harm me.'

I said nothing. An annoyed Nityahari grumbled, 'Of course, a prophet's words are never heeded till he is dead. I had told her too, whatever you do, take a dip in the Ganga every day. But she didn't listen. It was fate that brought the English-speaking girl from a decent family to this abode of sin.' His eyes suddenly started glowing like embers. 'Who on earth am I? She never knew me all my life. All I did is supply matching linen to her. Why does she, of all people, have to come into my dreams?'

'Maybe you loved her, maybe she loved you too,' I said.

His eyes brimmed with tears. He couldn't keep his pain under wraps any more. 'I've never seen such a stupid person in my life. Taking poison—how does it help? My wife—that hag also took poison and killed herself, all because I didn't get back home at night. I told my mother that some thugs had kidnapped me. She believed me, but my wife didn't. "What are you smelling of?" she asked. "Onions," I had said in English. "Onions? What's that?" the girl had asked like a fool. In anger I had said, "Onions are what you use to cook; your father taught you nothing."

'I used to reek of hooch—it almost made me want to throw up myself. She was a clever girl, she knew what onions were, she sensed everything. And then...the one weapon they have. She didn't even give me a chance to reform myself. Women can't do anything except take poison. Ever since then, I've suffered. The son of a Brahmin spending his days washing dirty linen. But it could have been worse. I could have been struck down by a bolt of lightning, but Ma Ganga saved me.'

Pressing my hands with fervour, he said sadly but affectionately, 'Be very careful, son. Nobody knows what Chitragupta, the superintendent of Yama's office, has written down as people's fates.'

He left, and my mind filled with unease. At last I seemed to have understood Nityahari. I had somehow emerged from a night that was actually one long nightmare; I simply couldn't bear to man the counter any longer.

I woke a bearer. 'Take care of this place for a while, I'll be back soon,' I told him.

15

Dawn had arrived. Our rooms seemed to be blushing like a bride in the tremulous expectation of a meeting with the sun.

With the door ajar, Bose-da was sitting on his bed, sipping tea. He smiled at me. His smile never failed to lift my spirits. It had a strange way of reassuring one that all would turn out well.

I told him about Sreelekha Devi. 'Don't worry,' he said, 'I have her address. We'll send a note for the payment if the need arises. But it won't. She'll send the cheque on her own. This sort of thing has happened before—she's taken refuge for the night, away from her husband, and by morning they have made up.'

Bose-da got up and handed me a glass tumbler. 'Go wash this in the bathroom and have some tea Indian style—you've had a rough night.'

After a cup—or rather glass—of tea with Bose-da, I went to my room and fell asleep. I have no idea for how long I had been in the arms of Morpheus, but suddenly I was woken by Gurberia. Someone had apparently come up to the terrace without permission.

I went to the door and found Byron standing there. Bidding me good morning, he came in. 'I thought you might be asleep, but I came all the same. And I met Marco, too, in the bargain,' he said.

'I was rather worried about the two of you last night,' I said, after ordering some tea for him.

'Last night will probably remain eternally memorable for Marco and me,' he said.

'Why? Did you manage to shed some light on the darkness of poor Marco's married life?'

He peered around suspiciously. Then, settling down comfortably on the bed, he said, 'You remember the whole story, don't you?'

'I do,' I said. 'How can I forget it?'

Byron's face that morning reflected the joy of success. 'To tell you the truth,' he said, 'we're detectives only in name. Our clients come to us when all else has failed, hoping we'll somehow solve their problems. The police view us sometimes with suspicion and sometimes with pity—but they don't help us at all. Why call the doctor when the quack is good enough?

they laugh. So I didn't harbour any hope at all where Marco was concerned. I had never really expected to be able to help him.'

Apparently, one of Byron's sources had brought him the information. In a dank, dark slum in Chhatawala Lane, he had tracked down a woman who once used to sing in a restaurant. The name of the road brought back memories of my previous job. The previous night the two of them—Marco Polo and Byron—had gone to Chhatawala Lane in search of that woman. But she had a guest in her room, so they had waited for ages outside, hoping to meet her after the guest left. But they couldn't.

I was finding in increasingly difficult to keep quiet. Byron gathered from the look on my face that there was something in his narrative that fascinated me. He wanted to know what it was. I asked for the address, and his answer stunned me. It was the same building which housed Magpil & Clerk, the company I had worked for! There was good reason to be suspicious about how the women there earned their living, but they had often helped me out. They would count the baskets and tie them up in bunches. If I was thirsty, I'd ask them for some water.

'Do you keep track of them any more?' asked Byron, excitedly. 'Do you know any of them?'

There wasn't a single woman in the building whom I didn't know; they had been my colleagues, after all. During the afternoons, they would sit on low stools in their torn skirts and sandals, painting our baskets and putting them out in the sun to dry, getting a pittance for their efforts. Whenever it rained, they had to move the baskets away. Though Pillai had fallen on bad times, they helped him out in various ways.

They treated me well, too. 'You've been walking around in the sun—take a break before you go out again,' they'd say, 'or you'll fall ill.' One of them would add, 'We depend on our bodies and you on your health—both have to be kept in good shape, it's a question of one's livelihood.'

A small board outside the building said, 'The gates of this building are closed at ten-thirty. No one is allowed in or out after that.' In that dark building, I had had another strange experience, but that tale will have to wait for another time.

Byron said, 'This is God's will! Will you make some enquiries for me? I'm sure the women will recognize you.'

I went back to the old place later that day along with Byron. He'd wanted to go immediately, but I told him there was no use going before eleven—it was the middle of the night until then as far as the women there were concerned. They'd be sleeping.

When I turned up, the women crowded around me enthusiastically. My clean clothes made it obvious to them that a revolutionary change had taken place in my life.

'Have you won a lottery?' they asked.

'I've got a job at Shahjahan Hotel,' I said.

'Shahjahan Hotel!' they exclaimed. 'I believe you get a fabulous dinner there for eight-and-a-half rupees? We would love to try it—we'd have all gone if we could afford it. It was very easy during the war.'

Those who had joined the profession after the war looked curiously at their senior colleagues.

'Those days the soldiers took you gladly if you asked them, and these days they think you're cheating them even if you ask for a cigarette!'

'Did any of you know Susan Munro?' I asked. 'She used to sing on Park Street.'

'We haven't heard of anyone by that name—why on earth would anyone who sang on Park Street end up here?'

But one of them said, 'Why, what about Elizabeth? That old woman says she used to sing once, that it's fate that brought her to this hellhole.'

'Who's Elizabeth?' I asked.

'Don't you remember her? She used to keep the accounts for your baskets, you used her towel to dry off after getting wet in the rain one afternoon.'

Now I remembered. 'Where is she?' I asked.

'She's in bed, ill,' someone said. They showed me the door from a distance. It was shut. I knocked, and a weak voice responded, 'Come in.'

She recognized me at once and tried to sit up in bed. Everything in the room was dirty, very different from what it used to be. She waved me to a stool.

'Recognize me?' I asked.

She smiled wanly. 'Why should I? After you went, Magpil's business went down—many people cheated him, taking his baskets and not paying for them. He was forced to leave. My earnings have dropped, too—at least I used to make something from those baskets. It's pathetic now. The younger girls have kindly allowed me to stay. They look after me, clean the room, and, if an undemanding customer turns up, they send him to me.'

She tried to move her leg. 'I can't walk any more. I'm all right, but my leg isn't—I fell down a long time ago and broke a bone. I couldn't afford to see a good doctor, and the bone was set awkwardly. Now I'm paying the price.'

Suddenly it all fell in place. Elizabeth was Lisa—the singer Susan had replaced! I knew her quite well when I was at Magpil. If only I had known that it was she who had got involved in poor Marco Polo's life! Maybe I reminded her of the old days, because she started humming a line or two from a song that had once stirred Calcutta's pleasure-seekers.

'I can't stand,' she said. 'I have to hold on to the wall and hobble to the toilet. Sometimes I can't even do that—Barbara and Pamela arrange for a bedpan.'

I gazed silently at her, thinking of her bizarre life. Sadness no longer causes me pain. Sometimes, when I'm really overwhelmed, it reminds me of the slaughterhouse. I feel like a sheep, waiting, watching as one of its kin is led to the abattoir to meet its ultimate, terrible fate.

'Let me call someone,' said Lisa. 'Let them get some tea for you. After all, you're a guest.'

'Don't bother, there's really no need...'

She seemed a little hurt. 'You're probably worried I'll spend too much. I have money now, I earned quite a lot last night,' then added, 'by the way, where have you been?'

'I work at Shahjahan Hotel now.'

'Shahjahan!' The light seemed to return to her tired eyes. 'Ah, what cooking! Once you've tried it, the taste stays with you all your life. Their Omelette Champignon! If they give it to you free, will you please get me a Jumbo Grill from Shahjahan sometime?'

'Of course I will,' I said.

'How much does it cost?'

'About seven rupees.'

'And you people get it free,' she said, amazed.

I would not get it free, but I didn't tell her that. If she knew I'd have to pay for it she'd probably refuse to accept it.

The tea was disgusting. Even if my grateful heart was prepared to cope with the unhealthy environment, my body was close to revolting.

'Did you know anyone named Susan?' I asked.

'Susan? You mean Susan Munro? Who used to sell pastries? Who started singing instead of me on a ten-rupee salary? Of course I knew her.'

She didn't seem very favourably disposed towards Susan. 'How do you know her?' she asked suddenly.

'I heard about her from a friend in the excise department,' I said. 'Apparently she earned a great deal from a flat on Theatre Road.'

'Is Susan back?' she asked me. 'Major Shannon must have kicked her out, then. I knew it would happen.'

An island long buried in the ocean in the aftermath of an earthquake was resurfacing. I seemed to have been given the exclusive opportunity of unearthing something that had been considered inaccessible all this while.

'You could do anything with money those days,' Lisa said. 'Those American soldiers could get just about anything by paying for it. How else could Shannon have transformed a woman of ill-repute into a virgin and taken her to Illinois with him? He even wanted to get the wedding over and done with here, but he didn't dare. In the eyes of the law she already had a husband, but who would have known that in Illinois? In any case, who knows what name Susan Munro's taken on now? But I said, all's well that ends well—and I knew this wouldn't end well.'

I was tempted to reveal everything and ask her if she remembered her evening out with a foreigner named Marco Polo at Shahjahan, but resisted the temptation. I took her leave even though I wanted to stay longer. Having rediscovered a forgotten chapter in my life, I was sorely tempted to examine it closely, but Byron was waiting for me. He must have become very impatient, standing there on the road all by himself.

'Eureka! Eureka!' He hugged me, overjoyed. 'It is God's will—how could it all turn out this way otherwise? Why should you have got a job at Shahjahan? And why should you have been working at Chhatawala Lane before that?' He ran towards a taxi. 'Hurry up! Quick, take us to Shahjahan Hotel.'

He practically ran up to the manager's room, emerging again in a few minutes with Marco Polo in tow. They left the hotel together.

William Ghosh was on duty at the counter. Poor William, he seemed to be having a bad time. Going up to him I said,

'If you're having trouble coping all by yourself, I can give you a hand.'

Adjusting his tie, he said despondently, 'I intend to survive without anyone's help from now on.'

'Not even Rosie's?' I joked. 'When is she taking up residence on Madan Dutta Lane amidst the chanting of the scriptures?'

He looked even grimmer. 'Since you'll get to hear anyway, there's no point hiding anything. If I'd known the outcome, I wouldn't have gone out with her. I troubled you needlessly, forcing double shifts on you while Rosie and I dined elsewhere.'

'And what great harm did that do?'

Looking up from his work, he said, 'Having spent my adolescence and youth roaming the high seas, I had anchored this middle-aged ship at the Shahjahan harbour. After all, how many years do I have left? When Rosie and I became intimate, I thought, having given me a livelihood, Shahjahan was now going to provide me with a wife as well. In spite of all her immaturity and shortcomings, I really was in love with Rosie. But do you know what she's saying now? She says I'll have to wait for at least another five years. By that time her sick parents will have passed away and her sister will have married and settled down. She cannot even dream of marriage and happiness before that.'

Rosie. The dark-skinned, beautiful typist Rosie. I had regarded her with nothing but hatred and contempt all this time, but at that moment she became a member of my family.

'Rosie took me home one day,' said William. 'It's not a home, it's a hovel—the way they live in just one-and-a-half rooms! Three sick people on their cots, coughing and spitting constantly. It's a hellhole. Rosie's parents were probably scared at the sight of me. They didn't want their daughter to fall in love with anyone, for then they would probably starve. I saw other people in the slum too, all curly hair and thick lips and snub-nosed. She told me, "The Rosie you see at the Shahjahan has her roots right here. You probably think of me as Anglo-Indian; that's what I tell people too. But actually, I'm African—almost everyone here is a descendant of old African slaves.'"

William had been surprised. She told him that at the beginning of the nineteenth century, their forefathers were shipped from distant African shores and made to disembark at Chandpal Ghat, ropes around their waists, and sold at Murgighata for twenty-five rupees each. At that time, the aristocracy of Calcutta used to buy slaves of their choice from this market. Many years later, a law was passed freeing all the slaves. But where would they go with their freedom? They stayed on in this city. They didn't have names of their own, either, taking on the surnames of their former owners instead. What the slaves of Rome had done centuries ago, the slaves of Calcutta did as well—Dickson's slave became a Dickson himself, Shakespeare's slave came to the slum as a Mr Shakespeare, and so it went on. Even after a hundred years, that unique stream of Africa hasn't become one with the Indian mainstream. Through their suffering, their deprivations and their uncertainties, they remained African.

William had told Rosie, 'I don't care, we were all slaves once upon a time—millions of Indians were subjugated to another race all these years.' To which she had replied, 'Don't tempt me. Please treat me badly. Or else I'll want to marry you right now—I won't be able to wait another moment.'

'I don't want to wait any more, Rosie,' William had insisted. 'Five years is a long time. What'll be left of me in another five years? Or of you, for that matter?'

As he wrote in the register, William continued, 'We are not getting married. I told Rosie she could carry on working after the marriage. She said, "Impossible! That devil Jimmy won't let me work another day if I get married. He'll sack me. You have no idea."'

I listened in silence.

'Perhaps you'll say I'm selfish. I'm thirty-seven now, in
five years I'll be forty-two. I've had a string of bad deals in life.
I don't want to wait five years for another.'

16

Ask me today which of Shahjahan's treasures has enriched me
the most, and I will say without hesitation that it's my
colleagues' love. You never know just how or when office
acquaintances become close friends. Suddenly one day you
discover that many lives have been linked with yours in the
same chain.

That's probably why I'd forgotten that, initially, Rosie had
been the cause of many of my problems, and that till a few
months ago I didn't know William Ghosh, Gurberia or
Nityahari. At one time they were complete strangers, but now
I knew so much about them.

Nityahari once said, 'This whole business is like marriage,
you know. Say a friend of fifteen years arranges a match
between you and a woman he knows. Soon after the wedding,
your wife will know much more about you than your old
friend ever will. A job is also like a marriage; in fact you could
say it's more important than marriage.'

I didn't probe too much, but Nityahari wasn't to be
deterred. Sidling up to me he whispered, 'What's up, sir? I
heard Satyasundar Bose asking the manager for a few hours off.
Whatever's happened to the man who hasn't set foot outside
for twelve years? I don't like the look of things.'

I was about to protest, but he continued, 'Remember,
smoke, money and love can't be kept under wraps. They're
bound to come out into the open.'

And with that he walked off, without giving me the
opportunity to say anything. I had to agree, however, that
Bose-da was indeed moving away.

Bose-da, I don't mind confessing after all these years that I really felt jealous of Sujata-di at the time. It's true you had given all you could to the young newcomer, the stranger who'd arrived at Shahjahan, but he wasn't satisfied—he wanted more.

Do you remember that evening on the terrace? You were sitting in an armchair, while clusters of stars were lighting up one by one in the sky. You were a different person that evening—not the Sata Bose who had welcomed me at the counter on my first day, who had nurtured me through good times and bad. There was something in the way you asked me to sit down beside you that made me nervous. You were calm. Like a gentle rain-bearing cloud, you had slowed down. I sat silently on a stool next to you for hours.

'Miss Mitra thinks very highly of you,' you had said. 'She thinks you are as innocent as a child.' I had flushed with embarrassment and pleasure. 'She's very down-to-earth too,' you continued. 'I've seen lots of air hostesses since I came to work at this hotel, but I really can't imagine how someone like her can entertain passengers up in the clouds.'

'Some people have this simplicity built in their personalities,' I had said. 'They can't shed it even if they want to.'

What I said probably appealed to you. Unknown to yourself, you had started to hold Sujata-di in high esteem. This esteem is the foundation for real love.

You went on to say, 'I looked rather silly today, I had no inkling she'd ask such a question. She was quite annoyed when she said, "Are you aware of life outside this hotel?" And like a fool I answered, "Of course. That's where the customers come from, and that's where they go back to." Do you know what she said then? "Why are you wasting your life like this? You are obsessed with the hotel—thanks to you, even that young fellow is messing up his present and future."

'Didn't you say anything?' I had asked you.

'I had meant to,' you said, 'but I couldn't. I hadn't expected her to be quite so aggressive.'

I was positively astounded to hear that Bose-da had run out of rejoinders. I wouldn't have believed it possible. Many years later, I found an explanation in Victor Hugo: 'The first symptom of love in a young man is timidity; in a girl it is boldness. The two sexes have a tendency to approach and each assumes the quality of the other.'

I remember Bose-da saying, 'I did protest, but this display of stars does make me feel that in opting for exile in Shahjahan, we are indeed depriving ourselves of many of the joys and blessings of the world.' Glancing at his watch, he said, 'You never know, Sujata Mitra could turn up here.'

'I hope so; it's always a pleasure to banter with her,' I said.

Bose-da lit a cigarette. 'Night duty again tonight—but I don't feel like it.'

'You needn't go as long as I'm here.'

'I must have kept my parents awake late at night in my previous life, which is why I'm paying the price for it in this one. Now if I keep you awake too, the accounts for my next life will get all messed up as well!'

'It will work out to my benifit,' I said. 'If I can be of service now I can spend my next life snoring my head off.'

'Now that I think of it, it's true, you know—I have been so engrossed in the hotel, I have quite forgotten that I have a life beyond it, that one day I too had come in here from the world outside.'

Just then we heard someone say, 'May I come in?' It was Sujata Mitra peeping in at the terrace door.

'Of course. This terrace isn't reserved for us alone,' said Bose-da.

Shielding her silk sari from the assault of the breeze, she came up to us. I rose and offered her my seat, meaning to go to my room. But Bose-da said, 'Get the stool from my room, let's all have a chat.'

'Chat with you!' Sujata snapped. 'You'll bring in breakfast, lunch and dinner to the conversation immediately.'

'Whatever I may bring into the conversation, may I have some tea brought in right now?' Bose-da asked.

She didn't give up. 'Hotel staff enjoy a lot of advantages—it makes me jealous. Whether guests get their food or not, the staff get it all the time. That's why gluttons are envious of hotel employees.'

'That's why every small boy wants to work in a chocolate factory when he grows up,' said Bose-da with a smile.

'Just as I had wanted an airline job.'

Both of us looked enquiringly as her face took on a wistful expression. 'I was in school then,' she said. 'We used to live in Bombay. I remember one time we didn't get tickets for the train so my father decided to fly down to Calcutta; and that did it for me.'

'Why?' I asked.

'As soon as I got into that plane my life took a turn. I stared at the pilot's cockpit throughout. The captain was a nice man—he indulged me and patiently showed me around, explaining everything.'

'What's the big deal?' Bose-da quipped. 'If there were such an attractive woman around, I would have neglected the plane and enjoyed the pleasure of her company too.'

Sujata flew into a mock rage. 'No more stories if you talk that way—didn't I tell you I was a twelve-year-old schoolgirl then?'

'I should quote the ancient Indian poet Vidyapati in response to that but the gentleman's made so many hostile comments about beautiful, well-endowed women that he's better avoided.'

'I wouldn't have been as thrilled if I'd met Tagore himself,' said Sujata-di. 'When the captain signed my autograph book, I was over the moon. I told my father, "I'm going to be a pilot, Baba." He didn't have the heart to object. He may have ruled his office with an iron hand, but he couldn't say no to me. "You're my son and daughter rolled into one," he would say.'

Sujata Mitra took a long dip in the blue pool of nostalgia.

'Despite my mother's protests my father said, "Do well in school, and then, no matter what, I'll ensure you become a pilot." But ultimately it was mathematics that did me in. If you want do anything worthwhile in life, the first question they'll ask you is, do you know maths? You want to be an engineer, they'll ask, do you know maths? You want to be a doctor and cure diseases, they'll demand that you know maths. The way things are going, even to get into art school you'll have to show the principal your maths marks. So I narrowly missed the honour of being Bengal's first woman pilot—but I did get half a loaf. I was determined not to give up. I had to fly up there. The things I imagined: From the cockpit I'd go for a swim in space, with the friendly stars giving me my bearings; Ma, Baba wouldn't need tickets when they travelled with me; during the flight I'd sometimes go up and chat with them. Ma had her own solution. "Since you're so keen on flying I'll get you married to a pilot."'

'That wasn't such a bad proposal, was it?' said Bose-da. 'Can't be a pilot? Marry one!'

'I wonder how an argumentative person like you can work as a receptionist.'

'Ask this chap here whether another receptionist of Sata Bose's ability has been born in India. If I'd been born in England I'd have become the manager of Claridges by now, and if I'd been born in America, I shudder to think what the fate of the present manager of the Waldorf-Astoria would be. Well, young man, how about standing up for me?'

Before I could make up my mind about what to say, Sujata Mitra said mockingly, 'Some ally—the drunkard propping up the bootlegger.' She giggled. 'Please don't mind, I was just joking.'

I had in the meantime decided that it was Bose-da who was at fault. 'It's your fault,' I told him. 'Why do you have to keep interrupting?'

In mock despair, Bose-da exclaimed, 'Et tu Brute! You let down an old friend only because of an air hostess's charming words. You aren't even aware that air hostesses too take tablets to keep smiling, just like we do. It's part of the job profile. We could be writhing with a stomach ache but would still have to put our dentures on display at the counter.'

'So the receptionist and the air hostess cancel one another out; like cures like,' I replied.

Bose-da smiled. 'But you're forgetting that if I'm the bootlegger you're the drunkard. I work in a hotel, we have a bar, so of course I could be involved in bootlegging as a side business, but this lady here has gone and slurred your pure-as-the-driven-snow reputation!'

All of us burst out laughing, shattering the silence of the night on Shahjahan's terrace.

Sujata-di said, 'So that's how things turned out. A nurse instead of a doctor, an air hostess instead of a pilot.'

'An uncle of mine wanted to be a police superintendent but became an office superintendent,' Bose deadpanned.

'You're laughing at me, but what does he know of the agony of the poison who has not—'

Before Sujata-di finished her statement somebody switched on all the lights in the terrace and Gurberia came running towards us in great agitation.

'What is it, Gurberia?' asked Bose-da.

Marco Polo wanted to see me after dinner, Gurberia informed us.

He should have left after conveying his message, but he stood there like a slab of prose in our poetic world. Looking at him I asked, 'What is it?' He hemmed and hawed, whereupon Sujata Mitra took the hint and said, 'I'd better be off, then.'

I stopped her, while Bose-da said, 'Gurberia, my boy, you may reveal the most secret news of the world to this trio. The lady gathers a lot of information flying up there in her plane, and all of it stays secret.'

Reassured, Gurberia told us that when I met Marco Polo, I could be of great assistance to him if I wanted to. And not just he, someone else—Shahjahan's head waiter Parabashia—would remain eternally grateful if I did him that favour. It was very simple. Dedication and patience had made the impossible possible. Parabashia had been won over, and he had adjudged Gurberia suitable for the hand of his youngest daughter. But it was not possible for him to approach the highest authority to recommend a promotion and leave of absence for his would-be son-in-law. Besides, he wanted to test the intelligence and acumen of the match for his beautiful, talented, housework-expert daughter. Desperate to get married, Gurberia had with a pounding heart suggested using the tried and trusted trick—a telegram from a distant village in Orissa: 'Mother serious, come soon.' But his would-be father-in-law had not approved of that. He had to be present at the wedding ceremony, too, and he intended to use the telegram ploy. In this enemy-infested fortress, it was particularly dangerous for father-in-law and son-in-law to use the same excuse for taking leave.

Mortified about having discussed his marriage in the presence of a stranger, Gurberia left hurriedly. Bose-da was delighted. 'This is a memorable day for the inhabitants of the terrace. We shall overcome, we shall overcome, we shall overcome some day! Gurberia's long-standing dream has been fulfilled.'

'Poor fellow,' said Sujata-di.

'Tell the manager and arrange for some leave for him,' said Bose-da. 'We don't have too many people, and Mrs Pakrashi's banquet is round the corner, but tell him we can manage by ourselves here on the terrace for a couple of weeks. We can do without a bearer.'

'I can see you're quite an avid champion of Gurberia's cause,' said Sujata-di.

'All the world loves a lover. Gurberia had vowed he wouldn't marry anyone but her.'

In his enthusiasm Bose-da called for Guberia at the top of his voice. Gurberia sprang up from his perch near the lift, and came up looking a trifle worried.

'You can start shopping for your wedding,' said Bose-da. 'Your leave is assured. If there's anything you want in particular, don't hesitate to let me know.'

Thus encouraged, Gurberia expressed a long-nurtured desire. He wanted a cake from Shahjahan for his wedding, wrapped in coloured foil. He was willing to spend up to one rupee.

'Certainly,' Bose-da said. 'I'll tell Juneau to have a three-pound wedding cake made—with your name on it.'

Gurberia was rendered speechless at this unexpected windfall.

'You'll bring your wife to Calcutta after the wedding, won't you?' Bose-da asked him.

'No, sir, it's too expensive here.'

'I'll arrange for you to be transferred. If you're on duty at Mumtaz, you'll earn a lot more from tips.'

'They make a lot from tips, don't they?' asked Sujata-di after Gurberia had left.

'Yes, they do. Earlier, people tipped to ensure prompt service. Now they do it to show off. And to ensure peace, to avoid squabbles over the sharing of tips, many hotels have simply slapped on a service charge of ten or fifteen per cent and stopped the practice. Marco wants to start the same system here. Had he been in his former frame of mind, he'd have done it by now. Jimmy is a good-for-nothing scoundrel.'

Sujata Mitra looked at him, surprised by the uncharacteristic vehemence in his voice.

There under the starlit sky, I experienced a strange sensation. Each of us had been born in a different place, at different times and yet, floating on the tide of time, the three of us had gathered at the same moment on the terrace of Shahjahan.

Bose-da's life had been flowing at its own pace all this while, like a stream meandering through human habitation. Now, some unknown girl had emerged, to ask a single question and complicate matters: Where are you off to, all by yourself?

None of the people who had accepted the hospitality of Shahjahan all these days, all these months and all these years, had asked Satyasundar Bose of Sahibganj that question. Momentarily disturbed by the simple girl's profound question, the stream had answered: Why, ever since I bid goodbye to college at the dawn of youth and willingly took refuge in this eternally young inn I've been flowing continuously. Drunk on its own rhythm, the river of life has been coursing forward.

But where to?

I have no idea.

Bose-da's mother had died long ago at the Sahibganj hospital, giving birth to another child. Bose-da was in class five then. If she had been alive, she might have asked this question. And his father? He had discharged his responsibility by wiring money every month to his hostel address.

That evening Bose-da revealed to Sujata Mitra what he had not told even me. 'I have a stepmother, you know.'

'Doesn't she worry at all about the future of the gentle, romantic young man?' asked Sujata-di.

Satyasundar Bose of Sahibganj stared at the stars billons of light years away, and then said softly, 'Why blame her? She's only a few years older than I am. She must be caught up in the anxieties of her own dark, uncertain future.'

Bose-da had no one to call his own anywhere in the world—he didn't have an address either. All he had by way of responsibility was to send money to his widowed stepmother occasionally.

Breaking through the silence, the poignant sound of a violin floated into Shahjahan's melancholy sky. Amidst our gathering in the dark of the night, someone seemed to be mourning the loss of his beloved, far from prying eyes.

In his room, Prabhat Chandra Gomez was paying homage to some tragic maestro from the seventeenth century, or perhaps the eighteenth or the nineteenth. In the musical worlds of Handel and Bach, Beethoven and Schubert, Schumann and Wagner, Brahms and Mozart, Chopin and Mendelssohn, there was only anguish. The playful breeze seemed to have carried the cries of torment from some distant land many centuries ago to Shahjahan that night.

I could no longer keep sitting. The suffering, agony-stricken, joyless sages of Western music, snubbed by all, had come to my cottage with their begging bowls. While Sujata Mitra and Sata Bose sat there mesmerized, I went to Gomez's room.

In the dim glow of a light, he was lost in his world, playing the violin. Who are you, blessed child of music? Whose curse has hurled you from heaven and condemned you to the agony of hell in Shahjahan? Did the disembodied soul that took possession of your accursed body to create such melody belong to the rich man's son Mendelssohn? Or was it the infant prodigy Mozart? Or perhaps the blind, dying Johann Sebastian Bach? Or even the luckless, deaf Beethoven? Or Chopin, afflicted with tuberculosis? I have no idea—if I did, I could have given your art the appreciation it deserves. You are presenting music to an audience of deaf and dumb people. You have arranged for fireworks in the land of the blind.

That everyday musician of Shahjahan no longer seemed to

belong to this planet. Transcending the insults, the neglect, the sorrows, the suffering, Gomez paid homage by the light of the five elements, tears coursing down his face.

'Who's that?'

My shadow startled him. With the appearance of the hunter in the sacred grove of music, the birds of melody disappeared.

He spoke slowly, 'No more noisy, loud words from me— such is my master's will. Henceforth I deal in whispers. The speech in my heart will be carried on in the murmurs of a song.'

The god of poetry seemed to have glanced at this ordinary employee of Shahjahan with compassion. Softly I recited the Bengali words of the song which Gomez had referred to.

He picked up his violin again. This time the tune was familiar to me.

> Give me not just your words
> My friend, oh my dear
> From time to time let my soul
> Feel your touch so near

Suddenly, he realized it was almost time for dinner. Putting his violin on the bed he picked up his jacket and went downstairs hurriedly. He had to eat before the guests had their dinner. I wondered whether he wasn't already late and would have to go without a meal that night.

Sujata Mitra and Bose-da were still sitting on the terrace.

'How long will you be here, Sujata-di?' I asked.

'What do you mean, how long?' she said. 'I'm leaving tonight.'

'When will you be here again?'

'I have to come here quite frequently—I'll be bothering you again in a few days.'

'I envy you your life,' said Bose-da.

'So you should,' she replied. 'What a strange life—it's either up in sky, or in a hotel. While everyone's asleep at night, I'm off to a hotel from the airport pulling my bag along, and at dawn it's back to the airport from the hotel. One hotel today, another tomorrow, a third the day after.'

'That's why they say in Arabia: "Mortal, if thou wouldst be happy, change thy home often; for the sweetness of life is variety, and the morrow is not mine or thine,"' said Bose-da.

'I can't match you on quotations or learning,' said Sujata Mitra. 'I'm a simple air hostess. All I understand are accompanied baggage, tea, coffee, chocolate, alcoholic drinks, flights. How do you manage to pick up so much here at the hotel?'

'Where else but a hotel would you get a chance for pickups?' Bose-da punned. Before Sujata-di could come up with a suitable rejoinder, he continued, glancing at his watch, 'We've detained you long enough, you'd better have your dinner and get some rest—you have to be off again at midnight.'

Sujata Mitra rose. I escorted her downstairs. Inside the lift she asked, 'How long have you been here?'

'Not very long,' I said.

'And Mr Bose?'

'He's been here ages—the hotel wouldn't survive without him.'

'I wonder why a man like him is wasting himself within the four walls of a hotel,' she said to herself.

Before getting out of the lift she smiled at me and said, 'See you later.'

I found Marco Polo in his room. He looked dazed. He raised his head when I entered and then welcomed me so effusively, no one would have thought he was the manager and I an ordinary receptionist.

'How long have you known Lisa?' he asked.

'Not very long—before joining the hotel I had to go to their place every day to buy the baskets I used to sell.'

'But she's very fond of you—she spoke highly of you.'

Once again I realized how blessed I was to have the love of so many people. Time and again, such unexpected gifts had turned the desert of my life verdant.

'I took her to the doctor today,' he continued. 'I had her foot X-rayed, too. The doctor says it will be all right, Lisa wanted me to tell you. I have to take her to the doctor again tomorrow afternoon, but I've given Jimmy the day off. Can Sata and you handle the tea party in the banquet hall?'

'Of course,' I said. 'Please do take Lisa to the doctor. She has been in great pain, poor thing.'

Marco thanked me. I could make out that he hadn't been able to get over the meeting in that dark building on Chhatawala Lane. 'I saw Lisa after ages,' he said. 'Her health may have deteriorated, but have you seen her eyes? They still shine like diamonds.'

Bose-da and I handled the meeting of the cultural association quite well. Honoured guests and enthusiastic members turned up in droves. It was a memorable day in the history of the association; its inspiration, Mrs Pakrashi, was being given a reception on the eve of her departure abroad. Representatives of twenty other organizations in Calcutta were there—all of them had the upliftment of children, the betterment of women, the removal of social inequalities and so on as their objectives.

Mrs Pakrashi arrived at the banquet hall with the honourable president, dressed in a white sari with a red border and a white blouse. She didn't have sunglasses on that afternoon, nor did her eyes hold the venom I had seen earlier.

Tea was served at every table; cakes, sandwiches and pastries had been laid out in enormous quantities. The president said, 'It's a day of great pride for Calcutta, as well as for Bengal, and for India. The respect and opportunity we are giving women in independent India are not easy to come by even in England or America. No other woman in the world before Mrs Pakrashi has been elected chairperson of the committee for moral health. She is the epitome of the original ideal of the Indian woman. Despite being a wealthy man's wife, she has devoted herself to the cause of serving the poor, dressed like an ascetic. When I see her working with a smile in the dirtiest of Calcutta's slums, I am reminded of Sister Nivedita. That lady from foreign shores didn't have a family, but this dedicated woman has neglected neither her husband nor her nation in fulfilling her duties.'

There were many more speeches. 'Keep listening,' Bose-da whispered to me.

Drawing her sari to cover her head a little more, Mrs Pakrashi said, 'Like many others, I am also an ordinary housewife—that is my only identity. Whatever free time I get after taking care of my husband and son, I try to devote to my brothers and sisters scattered all over the country. The honour that has come my way from abroad actually belongs to all of you. I am merely receiving it on your behalf. I should have returned immediately after the conference—after all, how long can a housewife stay away from her husband and son? But keeping in mind the conditions in our country, I have reluctantly decided to travel for a few months to see for myself the condition of women in different countries of the world.'

The gathering burst out in fervent applause. She continued, 'Finally, I would like to draw the attention of Indian women to the essence of Indian womanhood. We must never forget that our husbands are everything to us. The creeper lives and so does the tree—neither is less important. And yet the creeper prefers to grow winding itself around the tree. We, too, will grow winding ourselves around our husbands.'

Before she left, Mrs Pakrashi happened to look at Bose-da. She turned her head away, pretending not to have seen him.

After the party was over and Bose-da had seen off the last
of the guests, he returned to the banquet hall and said, 'You
know her programme—now let me tell you someone else's.
Remember the foreigner of suite number one? He's taken
leave from his office; he'll be on the same flight to Paris. Poor
Mr Pakrashi!'

17

Ever since I first set foot in Shahjahan Hotel, awed and
wonderstruck, the clock had begun ticking. Now the time had
come for it to strike. Without my having noticed, morning had
turned into a tired afternoon and spread long, melancholic
shadows; the twilight had pervaded the Shahjahan sky as well.

All this time, the hotel had offered me not just the
exceptional opportunity of learning about human nature, but
the infinite joy of meeting soulmates as well. That is why I had
never felt lonely even in that unfamiliar world. But now
ominous thoughts began creeping into my mind unbidden.
The lights were going out one by one in the brightly lit
auditorium. All of us were waiting for the last ferry at the
Shahjahan jetty.

Changes were coming over me. The constant arrival and
departure of countless guests no longer left their mark. Waiting
at the station, a passenger can only recollect fellow travellers
from the past. My memories had suddenly come alive with a
vengeance, blurred sepia tones from the past becoming sharper
with the dust of forgetfulness wiped off them. Whenever I
passed suite number two, I recalled Karabi Guha; a visit to the
cabaret inevitably brought up images of Connie and Lambreta;
at the bar the stories of a helpless barmaid from many years ago
came to mind; and at the terrace I could see the tall Dr
Sutherland musing on the local boys of Williams Lane.

In the midst of it all life went on. The river that an English pioneer named Simpson had coaxed into this desert of ours decades ago may have slowed down, but it hadn't dried up yet. And that's why Sohrabji's mind was still on his daughter while he tracked the bottles in Mumtaz bar, unable to forget that he once owned a bar himself. William Ghosh had finalized his marriage with another girl—the announcement had been carried in the engagements column of the *Statesman*. And poor Rosie's parents were worse. Unable to pay for their treatment, she was desperately running around for money.

Phokla Chatterjee spoke to her frequently. 'Rosie's a nice girl,' he told me once. 'I've introduced her to Mr Sadashivam. He's a highly placed officer with a lot of power. I used to meet him frequently for business, but he kept putting me off. Eventually, he overcame his inhibitions and came to the point: "I'll give you what you want—but I feel rather lonely in the evenings." So I made an appointment with Rosie for him. Now they meet frequently at another hotel. Mr Sadashivam's wife's been living with her parents for a year now—what business is it of mine! I have to make my living on these quotas and permits and orders. Why should the damned purchase managers and accountants and high officers in bush-shirts alone enjoy the good things of life? Don't ordinary people like us want a drink, too, sometimes?

'The sad thing is, you people talk of poverty, but we can't get girls for our business. I can tell you as a Bengali, everybody wants Bengali girls. They have the opportunity, they have the edge, but they refuse to sign up. I'll be damned for telling the truth—but it should be survival first, ethics later. What's the point of all this chastity when the average Bengali girl is dying of TB and malnutrition? But what a race! They will break but not bend. Tagore and Bankim and Vivekananda, these are the people who've ruined the race. This is a different era, you need practical people. What can Phokla Chatterjee do all by himself? Agarwalla's looking for a full-time hostess—good salary and lots of extra money to be made—but I can't get a suitable local girl. Rosie's after my life to get her a job. The woman claims she desperately needs a lot of money. I think I'll set it up for her. After all, poverty knows no caste. You have to look after people when they're in trouble, no matter what their caste, isn't that so?

'Let me see what I can do. It's Sadashivam who's creating problems—the bugger likes Rosie and doesn't want to let go of her, and we can't afford to antagonize him either. I keep telling him, why not try a disposable cup instead of using the same cup and saucer for your daily tea?'

Before leaving, Phokla Chatterjee added, 'Let me give you some good news. I'm going to be a director in Agarwalla's company. Just proves one can still be successful through sincere effort, without resorting to dishonesty.'

Bose-da, meanwhile, had arrived at a remarkable crossroads in his life. We now waited eagerly for the bus carrying airline employees. Any moment now, Sujata Mitra would appear in her all-blue sari at our counter. Shrugging off the leather bag hanging from her shoulder, she would smile sweetly and ask, 'All well?'

'How've you been?' Bose-da would respond.

Keeping her true feelings in check, she would reply, 'Fine—no worries, no anxiety. It's great fun having breakfast in one country, lunch in another and going for a film in the evening in a third.'

Whether anyone else sensed it or not, I knew that a few exchanges along these lines had wrought a revolutionary change in Bose-da. Despite all his efforts he could not control his runaway heart. He was wracked by anxiety all the time. He probably felt reluctant to share those thoughts with me, which is why he had no option but to stay imprisoned, as it were, within himself.

It was at the counter that I got an inkling of his turmoil. One day, after being on duty all night, as he handed over charge to me, I saw he had been scribbling the same sentence over and over again on the notepad. He had been so distracted that he had even forgotten to tear off the sheet he had been scribbling on. It wasn't difficult to decipher—he had said as much to me several times: The wise receptionist always keeps the counter between him and the other side, in both letter and in spirit. Bose-da was cautioning himself repeatedly because the dam of the reception could hold the flood no longer.

I felt very happy—I cannot say why. The thought that someone like Bose-da would live an unfulfilled life at Shahjahan depressed me. That is how it is in life. The inevitable does not pay heed to individual preferences. Thus it was that Sujata had started visiting Calcutta frequently in the course of her duties. I had not noticed at what point Miss Mitra had become Sujata. She loved to chat and she could not only laugh heartily herself, but also made others laugh, which was why it didn't take long for us to become close friends.

She had come to know our duty roster, too. After a bath, she abandoned formalities and came directly up to the terrace. To me she said, 'Shut your eyes.' I shut them. 'Open your mouth,' she ordered. I did so, whereupon she unwrapped a chocolate or a lozenge and popped it into my mouth. She withdrew her fingers just as I closed my mouth and snapped, 'You nearly bit my fingers off—what a greedy boy!'

'Me greedy?' I said, feigning innocence. 'Well, since I've been damned, give me another.'

Ignoring me, she looked at Bose-da. 'Your turn now.'

He shook his head and said, 'I'm not going to eat anything without knowing what it is—I can't put such a valuable life in danger.'

'Very well then, since you don't trust me, you needn't have any.'

I said immediately, 'Since you're fighting over it give me his share too!'

'There you go, taking advantage,' said Bose-da. 'No, Sujata, give the chocolates to me.'

Our terrace would be transformed during Sujata-di's visits. She once forced her way into Bose-da's room and, after a thorough examination, remarked, 'He's so neat and organized, he'd put many women to shame.'

'Excellent,' I said. 'Since you're so pleased, you might as well pay for the tickets to the cinema tonight.'

'Gladly.' She was about to take the money out of her purse, but Bose-da said, 'Trust you to be so gullible. Since he knew you would be here tonight, this fellow bought three tickets for the night show four days ago.'

'But then, I'm the older one, shouldn't it be my treat?' she said.

'If only today's young fellows respected tradition,' sighed Bose-da.

The film ended a little after twelve. Outside Metro Cinema, we saw Chowringhee in a new light. I was about to hail a taxi when Bose-da suggested that we walk.

I had seen Calcutta by night in different guises on different occasions. Most of them were frightening, but that night it was different. We paused before the statue of Sir Ashutosh at the crossing of Chowringhee and Central Avenue. A scooter sped by; there weren't many scooters on Calcutta roads in those days. 'If only I had a scooter like that,' said Bose-da wistfully.

Whoever imagined that Sujata-di would take that casual statement seriously and buy a scooter for Bose-da?

Aware that Bose-da might create a scene, she said by way of preamble, 'There's something I've done—and I'll be really upset if you scold me.'

Not having a clue, Bose-da said, 'To err is human—why should I scold you for it?'

Whereupon she handed him the papers for the scooter, informing him that she wouldn't be in Calcutta when the scooter was delivered in a couple of days. She wouldn't be back for a week or so, so he should use the time to master the art of riding it, though she did feel rather anxious about his riding a scooter in Calcutta's traffic. Handicapped by his pledge, Bose-da seethed in anger, but said nothing. Finally he admonished, 'How impulsive can you get!'

She merely smiled. 'Be careful what you say about how you got it. It might boomerang on you. Nobody in the hotel needs to know of my hand in getting the scooter.'

'If they did, both of you would find it difficult to survive here,' I said.

We kept chatting on the terrace that night. Mesmerized by his new bride, Gurberia had been tempted to extend his leave. So another telegram had arrived, informing us of his mother's continued illness. In his absence I was working as the bearer, saluting and asking, 'Can I get ma'am anything?'

Ma'am said, 'Don't get cute—just sit down, or else you'll get your ears tweaked.'

I turned my ear towards her, saying, 'Go ahead, it'll be a world record—the first responsible hotel receptionist to have his ears tweaked by a lady guest!'

I insisted on getting some tea nevertheless, and, placing the tray before her, said, 'Now we'll sit still and let you pour.'

Bose-da sipped his tea and said, 'It was very silly of you, really—now what am I going to do with this scooter? Where shall I park it?'

'You mean there's no room for a scooter in such a big hotel, where dozens of cars are parked? I don't believe you. As for what to do with it, use it to get out of this prison occasionally and get a taste of freedom under the maidan's open skies. Don't have the hotel on your mind morning, noon and night.' Bose-da continued to look grim till finally she said, 'If I've committed a crime, how may I be pardoned for it?'

'Your punishment is to sing a song, the tune you were humming in the park the other day. This will also be a sort of record for you—the first guest to sing in a hotel instead of listening,' I said.

She wasn't unwilling, but Bose-da stopped her, saying, 'There are other people on the terrace; there'll be a scandal if anyone comes to know.'

Sujata-di glanced at her watch and rose. She had to leave, but Bose-da and I kept sitting. Bose-da said to me, 'By the way, I forgot to tell you, Byron had telephoned—he wants to meet you today, it seemed very important. I don't like it. I can sense a major change round the corner. I don't like the way Marco's behaving. He's frequently been away from the hotel spending nights at Chhatawala Lane. And Jimmy's trying to take advantage and form cliques.'

'Maybe Byron will throw some light on the matter,' I said.

'I hope so. After all, Marco is a decent chap. I'll feel bad if he suffers in any way.'

Byron came to meet me the same night. As I write, after all these years, I can't hold back my tears. Perhaps it doesn't befit a man to cry. But how can I explain how often the unsought love of a stranger has given me a fresh lease of life? I am woefully aware of my shortcomings as a writer. If only I could really express what I feel, if only I could convey some of what I really want to say, my happiness would know no bounds. If any unknown reader finds in this narrative a ray of hope at a moment of great personal crisis, I will have done justice to Byron, expressed my heartfelt gratitude to him.

He sat down in my room and said with a smile, 'I had taken an advance from Marco, and I used to feel bad that I probably wouldn't be able to help him. We did manage to find out about Susan after all, but it was of no use. She's well out of reach. But see how God showers his blessings on unworthy souls.'

I looked at him, puzzled. 'It'll be public knowledge some day,' he said, 'but you probably have the right to know beforehand.' He lit a cigarette. 'You people say the Ramayana was written even before Rama was born. It's turned out to be the same with Marco. Once upon a time he had paid Lisa to act as his lover so that he could use her as a co-respondent in his divorce case. But now, all this time later, he's in love with her. Lisa didn't believe it at first, but when she realized that he had no ulterior motive, she wept. If only you could see how Marco looks after Lisa! I saw him the other day cleaning up her vomit. What's left of her body? She has nothing to offer Marco, but who knows what he sees in her now!

'They've decided to live together. Lisa has improved a great deal after the treatment over the past few days. You'll be amazed to see her. She wanted to visit Shahjahan, but Marco wouldn't agree to that. He has no illusions about Jimmy—after all, it doesn't take long for the manager's reputation to reflect on the reputation of the hotel.'

Byron said that we'd be informed of Marco's departure in a few days. The law here did not permit him to marry Lisa—and he wasn't inclined to live with her without marrying her. So he had chosen a different path. He had got a job in the Gold Coast in Africa. A long way from enlightened Europe and civilized Asia. In an insignificant hotel in an insignificant, poor town, the ever-unfortunate Marco Polo and the lifelong sufferer Lisa would spend their remaining days as husband and wife.

Byron hesitated, and then, placing his hand on my shoulder, said, 'It's worked out well for me too. Because I'd taken money from him, I couldn't make a move all this time, but now that my responsibility has been discharged, nothing prevents me from taking my leave.'

'What do you mean?'

He said in a pained voice, 'As long as I was in the

profession, I never said it, but today I can tell you. There's no hope of our being appreciated here in Calcutta. People are willing to admire private detectives in novels and films and theatres, but no one wants them in real life. But it's not that way in Australia—private detectives have plenty of opportunities there. I can even get a salaried job at a detective agency. In fact, I've been offered one, so I'm sailing on the strength of that offer. If I ever get the chance, I'll go back to private practice.'

I took both his hands in mine and said, 'I am very happy that God has been kind to you at last. You'll be really happy now.'

'How do you know?' he asked with a sad smile.

'How do I know? To put it in legal terms, there's a precedent.'

'Precedent?' He looked at me curiously.

'Someone who desperately needed peace and happiness, someone whose suffering had caused us pain, too, had many years ago found peace in that continent.'

'Who was he?' Byron couldn't keep himself from asking.

'He wasn't a man of flesh-and-blood, but I refuse to believe that he was merely a character in Dickens's *David Copperfield*. His name was Mr Micawber.'

18

On a lazy, leisurely afternoon, in a lonely corner of your home, deprived of the company of your near and dear ones, have you ever thought of the people you loved and lost a long time ago? It is quite possible that in the comfort that we draw from our memories of loved ones, it might occur to us that it is infinitely better to have loved and lost than to have never loved at all. But often when the heart is heavy with the weight of memories, the pain of having loved and lost seems to outweigh all others. I had no idea that some day I would lose everyone I had come to know and love in the strange environs of Shahjahan.

The day I saw Byron off at Howrah station, I experienced the real pain of loss. Byron shook hands with Bose-da and me, for the last time, through the windows of the train. He wasn't a relative, I hadn't even known him for very long, but still, I felt an emptiness. How was I to know that this was just the beginning?

Looking at the clock, I told Bose-da, 'Let's go back quickly. We left the hotel a long time ago.'

But he showed no inclination to hurry, saying instead, 'William and Jimmy are there—they'll manage. I feel like having a cup of tea.' I was surprised. How could he prefer tea at Howrah Station to what we got at Shahjahan?

Even as we walked into the restaurant I had no idea of what was to come. Taking a chair, he said, 'I have something to tell you. Look at what I used to be and what I am now. All this time, I used to think of myself as made of steel, but now I realize how wrong I was. You're like a brother to me, and also my only friend in Shahjahan. I need your advice.'

I was very pleased that he had thought of me in his hour of need.

He picked up an empty plate lying on the table. 'It's time for a decision. I can't postpone it any longer. I've promised to let Sujata know today. I never thought that my heart would play tricks on me after so many years of an easy existence.'

'What's wrong with that? You're not committing a crime, are you?' I said.

Playing with the dish, Bose-da smiled. He appeared to be trying to forge a compromise with his reflection on the shiny glass tabletop. Almost to himself he said, 'I've heard Nityahari say love is like measles—natural in youth, but cause for anxiety in old age. Now I can see he isn't wrong.'

I looked closely at him.

'I know it's difficult to find someone like her,' he mused. 'She has a job, she works hard, and yet she's a child at heart. I like the sense of a wild breeze about her—haven't you noticed it?'

'It's impossible for me to see any flaw where she's concerned. She's ruined my ability for impartial judgement by making me gorge on her chocolates!' I replied.

Bose-da tried to laugh, but his anxieties had conspired to choke the laughter in his throat. 'I have to decide whether I want to have the cake or eat it—my job or Sujata.'

Despite everything, Bose-da loved Shahjahan Hotel. We all knew that. Who could have foreseen that one day he would have to consider giving it up because of a doe-eyed beauty of recent acquaintance!

'Sujata thinks I'm wasting myself at the reception desk here,' he said. 'It's still not too late to get away. The experience that I've gained will get me a good job with the airlines. I haven't spoken to Sujata about our future, nor is it time yet. But if I have to make a choice, I won't be able to work at Shahjahan.'

'Why not?'

'An air hostess can't work after marriage, the manager here won't permit the terrace rooms to be converted into family quarters, and what I earn won't get me even half a room on rent in Calcutta. You must have seen Captain Hogg—he stays with us quite often. He's well known in the airlines world and is very influential. Sujata's spoken to him. He likes me quite a bit and is willing to give me a good job at the airport or the booking office. I don't know where I'll have to go—Dum Dum, Willingdon or Santa Cruz, but Sujata thinks I'll do much better with a lot less effort than I do here!'

Bose-da paused, probably waiting for some sort of response from me. What could I say, especially when he couldn't work it out for himself. Pushing away his cup of tea, he said, 'I can't imagine myself away from Shahjahan and still alive. So what if it's not an important job, so what if I don't earn a great deal? I'm very happy. Where else would I enjoy such freedom, such excitement, the romantic thrill of meeting so many people?'

I wanted to say 'Nowhere.' My selfish heart refused to let him leave our close-knit family. But how could I keep him away from happiness and fulfilment?

'No, Bose-da,' I said, 'you must go. Opportunity doesn't knock twice—even if it has knocked late, open the door.'

He took my hands in his warm ones and said, 'You must have been my brother in my previous life. I've spent many years at Shahjahan, but I've never been as fond of anyone.'

I could say or do nothing. How could I explain to him how much of my life he had shaped? What would be left of my Shahjahan days if he weren't a part of them?

A few days later I heard from Bose-da that his job with the airline company had been finalized. He was wondering when to put in his papers.

'Don't delay things,' I said. 'Lots of changes are in the offing at Shahjahan—Marco's departure is also imminent.'

He was taken aback with the news. 'Marco's leaving? Jimmy's dream will come true at last. He will rule Shahjahan. Though it might be anarchy now.'

'Why do you say that?' I asked.

'I have no illusions about that man. He's as dishonest as he is lazy, and as envious as he is incompetent; he's a master politician. I'd better announce my decision immediately. If my resignation isn't accepted while Marco's still here, I may have trouble afterwards.'

When he went to meet Marco, I was sitting on the terrace with Sujata-di. She was to leave in a while on the night flight.

'You're feeling terrible, aren't you?' she asked. 'I've probably upset all your well-set lives.'

'Why do you say that?' I asked. 'I'll get used to it.'

'Maybe you won't even remember us a few years from now. You'll sit here on the terrace talking to others.'

'After many years, perhaps, I'll recall that an accursed man was once rescued from Shahjahan by an unknown woman. Entranced by the stupor-inducing light and dazzle of Shahjahan he had turned to stone and was brought back to life by the healing touch of a woman.'

She didn't say anything. That evening we really were in no mood to talk. All these days I had been like a hyphen between the two of them, so I probably had a duty to fulfil. I asked, 'So the job's been arranged, but have the two of you completed your mutual assessment?'

A sad smile spread across Sujata-di's face as she said, 'I don't believe in rushing things. Time will solve all problems.'

'Have you informed your family?' I asked.

Her face grew even sadder. 'I don't have what people call a family. Like Satya I don't have anyone either. Just as you've never seen him go home on vacation, I, too, can't think of taking a holiday. The last time I spent some time with you here in Calcutta was the first time I took a holiday in years and had some fun. He has his Sahibganj at least—he can go there if he wants to. I don't even have that.'

'Never mind anyone else, there's always me, Sujata-di,' I said. 'I've got so much from people that the thought of repaying them scares me; I don't know how many lives I'll have to live through to account for the interest. If I can do even the tiniest thing for anybody, my load will be lightened a little.'

'You've done a lot already,' she said. 'Whom do I have but the two of you?'

Sometime later, Bose-da joined us. Even in the dark, I could see his face stamped with gloom. Taking a stool, he started scanning the Shahjahan sky, probably for the last time.

Not having the nerve to ask anything, I looked at him in silence. But eventually, prodded by Sujata-di, I spoke: 'What happened?'

He took out a cigarette and started tapping it absently on his matchbox. Still wrapped in his thoughts, he lit the cigarette and said, 'It takes ages to build something, but just a single moment to destroy it. Everything I have gathered over the thousands of nights and days here at Shahjahan, lie scattered with a single sentence. Marco Polo said, "I'm not going to stand in your way. Burn your bridges and go ahead, young man. If you like, you can come with me to the Gold Coast, the two of us will start a new hotel there. What Mr Simpson did so many years ago in India, we will do in Africa in this century." He's signed my papers. He's very busy now, he has to hand over charge to Jimmy.'

We chose Little Shahjahan for Bose-da's farewell. The ordinary employees of the hotel said, 'We'll never get another Sata Bose in the whole world. He's done so much for us—he fought with the bosses and got us our free tea; he used his own money to get so many of us treated by good doctors. If it hadn't been for him, Rahim would never have been able to stand on his feet again. We want to give him a banquet too.'

They passed the hat around and pooled in four annas each, the most they could afford. It is unlikely that any employee in any other hotel in the world has been fortunate enough to be present at a dinner such as the one we had for Bose-da. It was an unusual banquet. Since there was no break from work at the hotel, the farewell reception began at Little Shahjahan at midnight. The bearers of Little Shahjahan weren't willing to stay back late, so Shahjahan's employees took the responsibility of serving. I'll never forget the banquet in that large, tin-roofed room, held by the light of a single, sixty-watt bulb. Nityahari wanted to place a napkin flower in every glass—but where would he get so many napkins? For us there were enamelled

plates and earthen cups, but for Bose-da there was a good
china plate and proper cutlery, besides a napkin flower.

'Have you noticed the pattern?' Nityahari asked me. 'It's
not a boar's head, it's a bishop.'

Bose-da wasn't pleased with the expensive crockery. 'This
isn't right. Why did you have to get crockery and cutlery from
Shahjahan? Suppose someone objects?'

Rahim looked at him apprehensively and said, 'No, sir, we
didn't get anything from Shahjahan—we bought these for you
from New Market.'

I noticed Bose-da's eyes brimming with tears. He turned
his head to avoid my gaze.

Though the arrangements were modest, they had all the
elegance of a banquet: that was what occurred to me as I ate
with my hands. Bose-da wanted to set aside his knife and fork
and eat with his hands too, but the others wouldn't let him.

'No, sir,' they said, 'we'd have all eaten with knives and
forks if we had them. After all, this is a banquet.'

The only thing missing was music. We hadn't expected
that gap to be filled, but just when the event was in full swing,
Gomez suddenly arrived in proper evening dress.

'What's going on? You people forgot me? Why wasn't I
invited?'

The bearers had wanted some music; only they hadn't
dared invite Gomez to the dirty surroundings of Little Shahjahan.

Standing in a corner, Gomez said, 'Gentlemen, if I had the
means I would have arranged for a violin concerto for Mr Sata
Bose's farewell. But since I haven't—I have the manpower but
not the instruments—for the past three days I've been composing
a special piece in his honour. It's called "Farewell"—farewell
to the dinner, to the dance, to the cabaret; farewell to can-can,
to hoolahoo, to rock 'n' roll. Now, gentlemen, this is P.C.
Gomez presenting to you a violin recital, composed on the
occasion of the departure of Mr Sata Bose.'

The hubbub died down instantly. All of us gazed in awe at Gomez and his amazing instrument. None of us had had the opportunity to learn the language of that instrument, but that evening none of us had any difficulty understanding it. It spoke the words in all our hearts.

19

The first letter from Bose-da came from Santa Cruz.

Dear Shankar,

I've put up in a hotel here, courtesy the airlines. The story of the dhobi's son and the prince keeps coming back to me. Tired of washing clothes, the boy prayed to God for freedom, and God gave him a boon and turned him into a prince. But the prince couldn't enjoy himself. The minister's son and the general's son came to play, but he sat there glumly. Unable to bear it any longer he said, 'Come, let's play at washing clothes.' I'm sitting here in the lounge like that prince, and I keep thinking of all of you and wanting to play at washing clothes.

Sujata was here on duty. I met her for just a day. I will of course keep you informed of what's happening. I never got the chance to think at length about a home and a family—but now the prospect is becoming increasingly attractive.

My love to all of you.

I was lying quietly on my bed one day when Sujata-di suddenly came in. 'There you are—how have you been?'

I got up quickly and said, 'So you haven't forgotten us yet.'

'Talk about ingratitude! After flying thousands of miles I come straight here without even changing my clothes—not that I have a choice—and this is the welcome I get. I have my orders from your friend; the first thing I am to do is to ask after you.'

'How is he?'

'Don't ask,' she said sadly. 'It was probably a mistake to uproot a tree and try to plant it somewhere else. He isn't the same cheerful, happy-go-lucky person any more. He broods all the time, though he won't admit it.'

'Why don't you arrange it so that he doesn't have to brood any more?' I suggested.

A trifle embarrassed, she said, 'That depends entirely on him. I can give up my job anytime.'

'Then who's stopping you? Let him complete his probation—and then, in six months' time, amidst a thousand bonds you will taste freedom! Or to say it with some literary flourish: in a few months a traveller of the skies will travel in Bose-da's dreams.'

'Don't be cheeky,' she said in mock anger.

Rosie was in a very good mood. 'I have nothing more to worry about,' she said. 'Jimmy's becoming the manager. I know the extent of his education—he can't do without me for the letters.'

I didn't answer. She told me that Marco was due to leave any day.

I still remember Marco's departure. His luggage had been loaded in a hotel car. The bearers and other employees were standing in a long line in front of the pantry. In his white shorts and shirt, Marco looked a lot like the captain of a ship. Jimmy stood next to him. One by one Marco shook hands with everybody and said, 'Keep the flag flying. If I'm ever back in Shahjahan, I want to see the hotel improved beyond recognition under Jimmy's leadership.' Then turning to Jimmy he said, 'Look after my boys.'

After he left, I felt as though I were living alone in an empty, accursed castle. When I had checked in here, it was filled with known and familiar faces. Some left after breakfast; a few disappeared after lunch; others went away after tea. Now it was time for dinner, and no one was left. With the family, wife, children and relatives having gone, I, the patriarch, seemed to have sat down at an empty dinner table.

Jimmy began to show his true colours now. The hotel would no longer be run in the old manner, he had made it clear. Everything would have to be changed—lock, stock and barrel. To begin with, he had, in the modern fashion, imported a rouge-and-lipsticked young woman in place of Bose-da.

Rosie had aspired to that post, but Jimmy told her in no uncertain terms that she couldn't be the head receptionist in a hotel looking the way she did. Jimmy used William more and more for keeping the accounts—he had to concentrate on collecting payments and encashing cheques.

One day William told me that Agarwalla had bought the controlling stock in the hotel from the English shareholders. I should have guessed as much, from Jimmy's obsequious behaviour whenever Agarwalla was mentioned.

'Good news for you,' said William. 'Phokla Chatterjee's going to be looking after things. You hit it off quite well with him, don't you?'

Phokla came soon after to inspect the hotel. Falling all over Jimmy, he said, 'We want to keep the European management on, but everything should be modern; you can't run a hotel the way Simpson did. At that time women didn't venture out of their homes, now they're out on the streets.'

'Precisely, sir,' said Jimmy ingratiatingly.

Emitting a cloud of smoke from his pipe, Phokla said, 'We won't interfere in your day-to-day work. Both Mr Agarwalla and I want you to bring attractive girls here. Let Shahjahan Hotel be a meeting ground for all races.'

The hotel gradually filled up with many unfamiliar faces. Everything was done in secret. I often thought of Bose-da, Byron and Marco Polo. I wouldn't have felt quite as helpless had they been by my side. But who could shelter you all your life? As Gomez said, 'You can't depend on anyone forever except the Almighty.'

Gomez was sitting quietly in his room with the lights switched off. 'At last I think I have realized my mistake,' he told me. 'We cannot offer our music to anyone but God; we should serve nobody but our God.' I didn't respond. 'Tonight's my last concert at Shahjahan,' he said.

In the middle of all the changes, I hadn't seen this coming.

'They don't like me here any more,' he said. 'They say my instrument can no longer produce music cheerful enough to dress the Shahjahan hall in the radiant colours of youth. Jimmy and Mr Chatterjee have told me I must give them cheerful music or quit. So quit I must. Such is my Master's will. I met a priest at Bandel Church the other day. He wants to give me the responsibility for the music in a small church on the coast of South India. I have accepted this gift from God. Tonight's the last night. I must get ready for my final concert. I don't know why, but I keep recalling Chopin's last concert on that dark night in London.'

That night Gomez dressed in the best suit he had. His boys were impeccably turned out as well. He was even grasping the small baton with the ivory tip much more assuredly than before. There was still some time to go before the cabaret. Standing before the mike, Gomez bid good evening to the audience and said, 'Ladies and gentlemen. I shall treat you to some cheerful music.'

The music began. Was this the same Prabhat Chandra Gomez I had known all these days at Shahjahan? Such provocative, titillating music had probably never been played at the historic entertainment room of the Shahjahan; it sounded like the war drums of a mountain tribe whipping up a frenzy in the breasts of the predominantly male audience. It was probably to just such a rhythm that Urvashi had danced to woo the ancient sages and break their meditations. The guests at Shahjahan simply couldn't stay still any longer. Their bodies had started swaying, their well-shod feet keeping time on the carpet. If it continued a little longer, everyone in the hall would abandon their drinks and dinner and start dancing.

Gomez wasn't bothered. Without so much as a glance at anyone, he kept upping the tempo. It seemed that countless nameless and faceless courtesans down the ages had all congregated at that moment at Mumtaz, waiting to expose all over again their much-flaunted bodies. There was Connie, there was Pamela, there was Farida; there were all the rest whom Bose-da or Nityahari might have recognized. It was a night like none before and there wouldn't be one like it again. All the guests and all the entertainers from history had assembled at Shahjahan. No one had been left out of this special banquet—Karabi was there, and so was Sutherland, the top brass of Clive Street were there, bargirls with tankards in their hands and thousands of other unknown faces were also present.

I might have listened to the music some more, but the bearer said Jimmy wanted to see me.

Rosie and our new female receptionist were standing at the counter. The new lady was busy putting finishing touches to her make-up, while Rosie was chewing her nails by herself. She started when she saw me and then stared blankly at me.

'Well?' I asked. She got even more flustered at my question.

I found Phokla Chatterjee in Jimmy's room too. Jimmy said, 'I am sorry to have sent for you at this hour, but Mr Chatterjee will be going to the cabaret in a moment. He has to examine all this carefully. Besides, today's the last day of the month, so it's convenient for you as well as for us. Starting tomorrow, we don't need your services any more.'

Taking his pipe out of his mouth, Phokla said, 'We wish you success in life. I saw in the files that Marco Polo had given you a purely temporary appointment, which means you're not entitled to a month's salary. But the new management does not believe in taking undue advantage of existing regulations, so you're being given an extra month's pay.'

Jimmy handed over an envelope filled with currency notes, and without giving me the chance to say anything, Phokla said, 'Good night.'

I felt my world crumble around me. Going to the terrace, I saw Rosie waiting there.

'I'm sorry,' she said, coming up to me. 'Believe me, I tried to stop Jimmy when I was in there typing. I pleaded with him. But Jimmy had already spelt out his plan to Mr Chatterjee. They're going to have only girls at the counter.'

There were stars in the sky. Looking at them, I said, 'What could you have done, Rosie? Thanks all the same.'

But that was only the beginning. I didn't know there was more bad news waiting for me. Gurberia hadn't heard about my dismissal. 'There's a letter for you, sir,' he said.

I couldn't finish reading Bose-da's letter. It slipped from my hands and fell to the floor. Gurberia picked it up and, holding it out to me, asked, 'What's the matter, sir?'

It was the inevitable. Those whom I love never find happiness.

Bose-da had written:

Dear Shankar,

Who else can I write to? There's nobody else left. I just got back after immersing Sujata's ashes in the Arabian Sea. Late last night I got a telephone call informing me that air hostess Sujata Mitra had been killed in a car accident on the way to the airport in Delhi. She had named me as the next of kin in the form she had signed with the airline company. Among all the people in the world, she had chosen me as her closest one. The airline authorities were very courteous. Honouring her last wishes, they arranged for her body to be sent to me by air.

All my memories now seem like a long-drawn-out dream. Thinking of myself and my career, I had postponed the wedding, but she never hesitated to acknowledge me as her own. She, who treaded the line between life and death constantly, accepted things much more easily than I. Never did she demean herself by putting her interest ahead of everyone else's.

I believe her office has been instructed to pay the compensation to me. You could call me a rich man now. But the prince has been turned back into the dhobi's son. I can't survive here alone. I would have liked to return to Shahjahan, but that's out of the question. So I've decided to join the hotel that Marco's starting in the Gold Coast in Africa.

I never told you this before, but I want to tell you now, or else I might never get the chance again. Sujata held you in very high esteem. She had said, 'Mark my words: he is an exceptional person.'

Exceptional! Yes, indeed. The rooms on the terrace burst into laughter. I had put Bose-da's letter in my pocket, but they seemed to have found out what it said and were rolling in mirth at Sujata-di's opinion of me. All the bricks in the building seemed to be telling one another: Forget not this exceptional person. Like a madman I rushed down the stairs.

It was late. The cabaret had ended and Shahjahan had fallen asleep, but the tables, the chairs, the staircase all seemed to be suppressing their smiles at the sight of me. The counter I had known for so long didn't sympathize either. It too laughed at me: Aren't you ashamed of yourself, some woman drunk on love says something to someone and you believe it, you fool!

Central Avenue, Dharmatala Street, Chowringhee Road were all asleep. Only the neon light of Shahjahan kept blinking to mock a sacked and broken employee. I had nothing left to lose any more. Whatever I had was gone. A long time ago an uneducated doorman on Clive Street had shamed me in exactly the same way, and now all of inanimate Calcutta had got the chance to mock me: There goes your exceptional person.

I didn't realize that I had crossed Central Avenue, Chowringhee and Park Street and, walking on like one demented, had arrived at the Theatre Road crossing. The lamp posts by the side of the road did not fail to laugh at me either.

At the precise spot where Birla Planetarium now stands, I established communication with the stars that night. The huge clump of trees on the way to Victoria Memorial reassured me. 'We don't know, maybe you are exceptional, who knows!' Through the gaps in their foliage, the distant stars expressed the same opinion. 'We won't laugh, we won't mock you. Who knows what lies ahead—we'll just watch in silence.'

I don't know whether in the days to come some imaginative visitor to the planetarium will receive a signal of new life from the infinite skies. But on that deserted night it was the stars in the distant sky that assured me of a new life. In that wondrous moment I was reborn. From that moment on, I looked at the world, at Shahjahan Hotel, through changed eyes. I would no longer accuse the Almighty on behalf of Sujata-di, Karabi, Connie, Gomez or Bose-da. I would only express myself. I would share my sorrows with the countless souls whose lives were stricken by as many sorrows as ours.

My mind calmed, I went back, crossing Chowringhee and stopping on Chittaranjan Avenue. In the distance the tireless eyes of the neon-encrusted Shahjahan still blinked. Gazing at the amazing kingdom that was Shahjahan for the last time, I felt strange. I was reminded of an incident I had read about.

Towards the end of the nineteenth century, the English poet Rudyard Kipling, on a visit to Calcutta, had taken shelter for the night at another ancient hotel. Having become acquainted with the dreadful nights of this dreadful city, on his way back to the hotel at the dead of night he had stopped quite near where I had. The arrogant poet had said, 'All good Calcutta has gone to bed, the last tram has passed, and the peace of the night is upon the world. Would it be wise and rational to climb the spire of that kirk and shout: O true believers, decency is a fraud and a sham. There is nothing clean or pure or wholesome under the stars, and we are all going to perdition together. Amen!'

There in Calcutta at midnight, jobless and shelterless, I too could have prayed for the same perdition. But despite all my grievances and anger, hurt and resentment, I couldn't do it.

Elated at the thought of perdition, damnation and destruction, the proud poet of the West had said, Amen—so be it. But the countless stars in the sky gave me hope, gave me strength. Generous and infinite, time stretched before me. This sin-infested city would surely be sanctified some day by the healing touch of the good.

For the last time I looked back at my dear inn—the tireless lights of Shahjahan were still blinking.

I walked on.